BLOOD ALLIANCE

SERIES

BLOOD ALLIANCE SERIES

Chastely Bitten
Royally Bitten
Regally Bitten
Rebel Bitten
Kingly Bitten
Cruelly Bitten

KINGLY BITTEN

A BLOOD ALLIANCE NOVEL

USA TODAY BESTSELLING AUTHOR

LEXI C. FOSS

Kingly Bitten

Editing by: Outthink Editing, LLC
Proofreading by: Katie Schmahl and Jean Bachen
Interior Design: Murphy Wallace with Midnight Designs
Map Illustration by: Nathan Hansen
Cover Design: Manuela Serra
Cover Photography: Lindee Robinson
Cover Models: Jordan and Mairi
Published by: Ninja Newt Publishing, LLC
Hardback Edition
ISBN: 978-1-68530-038-8

Once upon a time, humankind ruled the world while lycans and vampires lived in secret.
This is no longer that time.

Calina

I have thirty-six hours to live.
Thirty-six hours to find a solution.
Thirty-six hours to kill them all.

My friends. My family. My subjects.

It's a cruel fate, one my maker subjected me to over a century ago when she placed me in this hell. I learned then that freedom is a falsehood. Escape doesn't exist. I'm a ticking time bomb, slated to erupt.

Until *he* appears from above. A vampire. A walking god with icy blue eyes. He claims to be our salvation, but I see him for who he really is—the devil in disguise.

Jace

I don't want to be king, but I'll become one if it means I can have *her*—the gorgeous ice queen I found waiting for me inside Lilith's labs. She feigns indifference, claiming I do nothing for her, but I see the embers stirring in her stunning hazel eyes.

Only there's more to her than a pretty little face.
She's neither vampire nor lycan.
An immortal without a classification.
A secret I must now contain in a world collapsing in chaos.

Welcome to the new beginning.
My name's King Jace. Allow me to be your guide...

KINGLY BITTEN

BLOOD ALLIANCE

BOOK FIVE

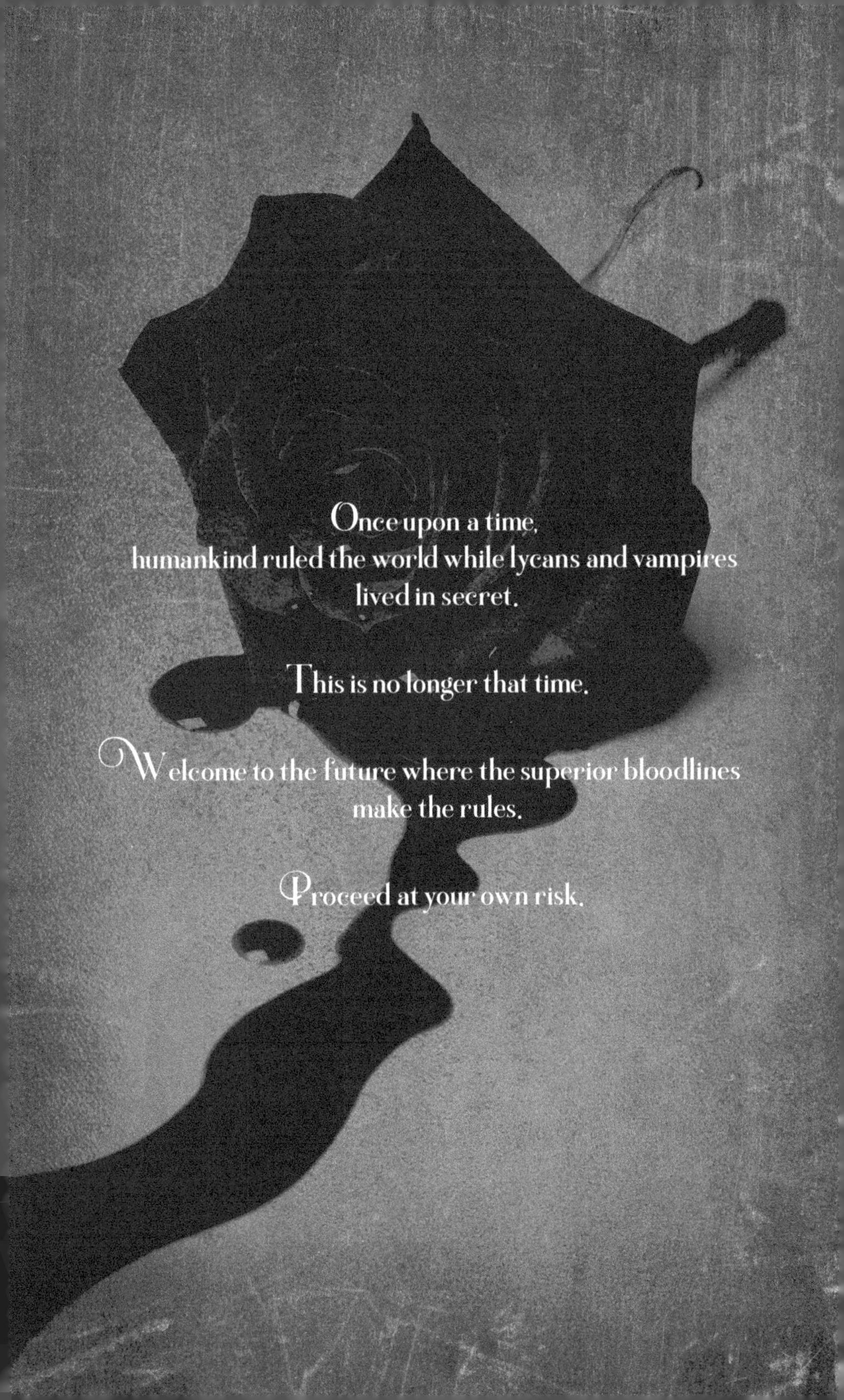
Once upon a time,
humankind ruled the world while lycans and vampires lived in secret.
This is no longer that time.
Welcome to the future where the superior bloodlines make the rules.
Proceed at your own risk.

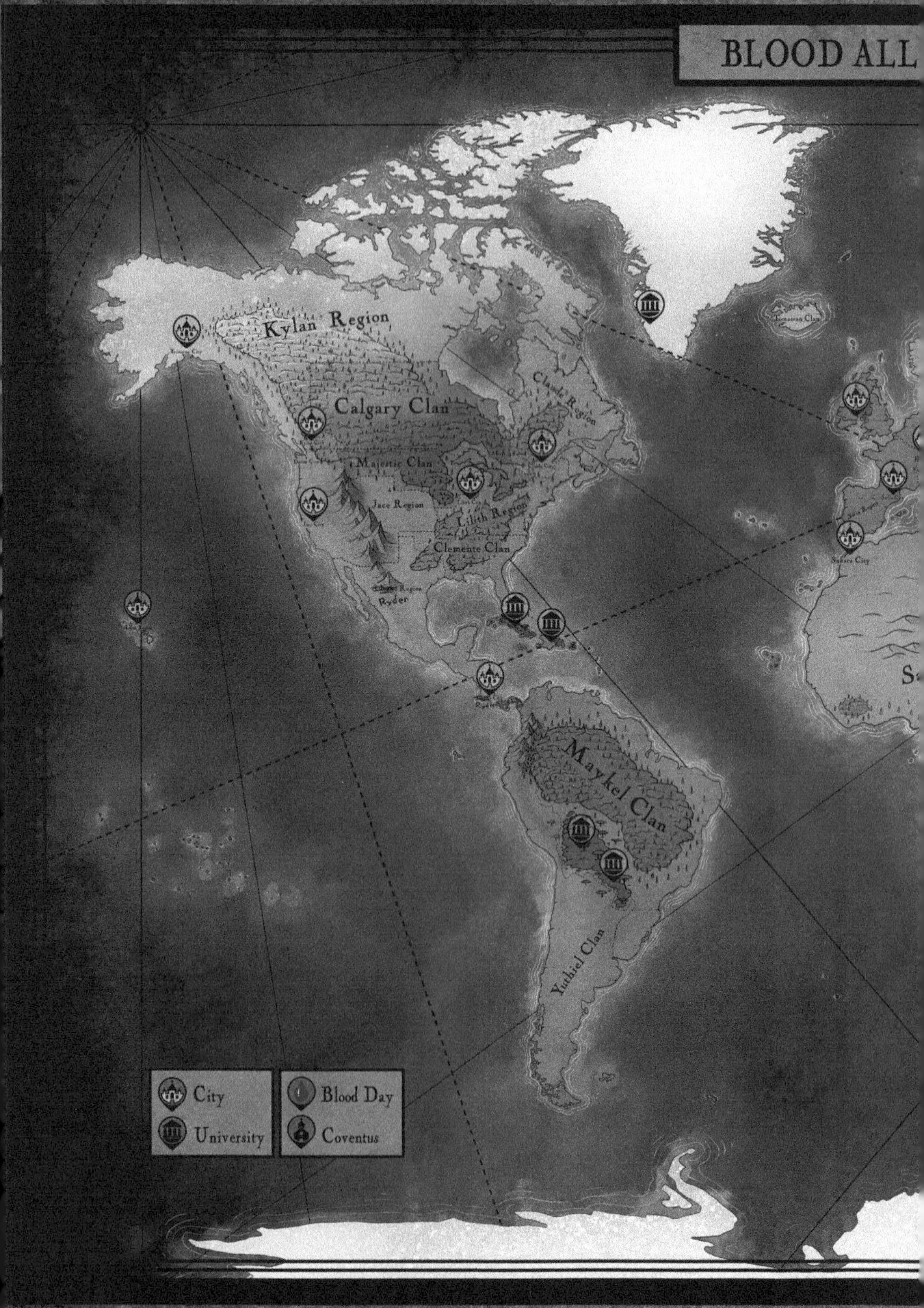
BLOOD ALL
Kylan Region
Calgary Clan
Majestic Clan
Jace Region
Lilith Region
Clemente Clan
Ryder
Maykel Clan
Yuthiel Clan
City
University
Blood Day
Coventus

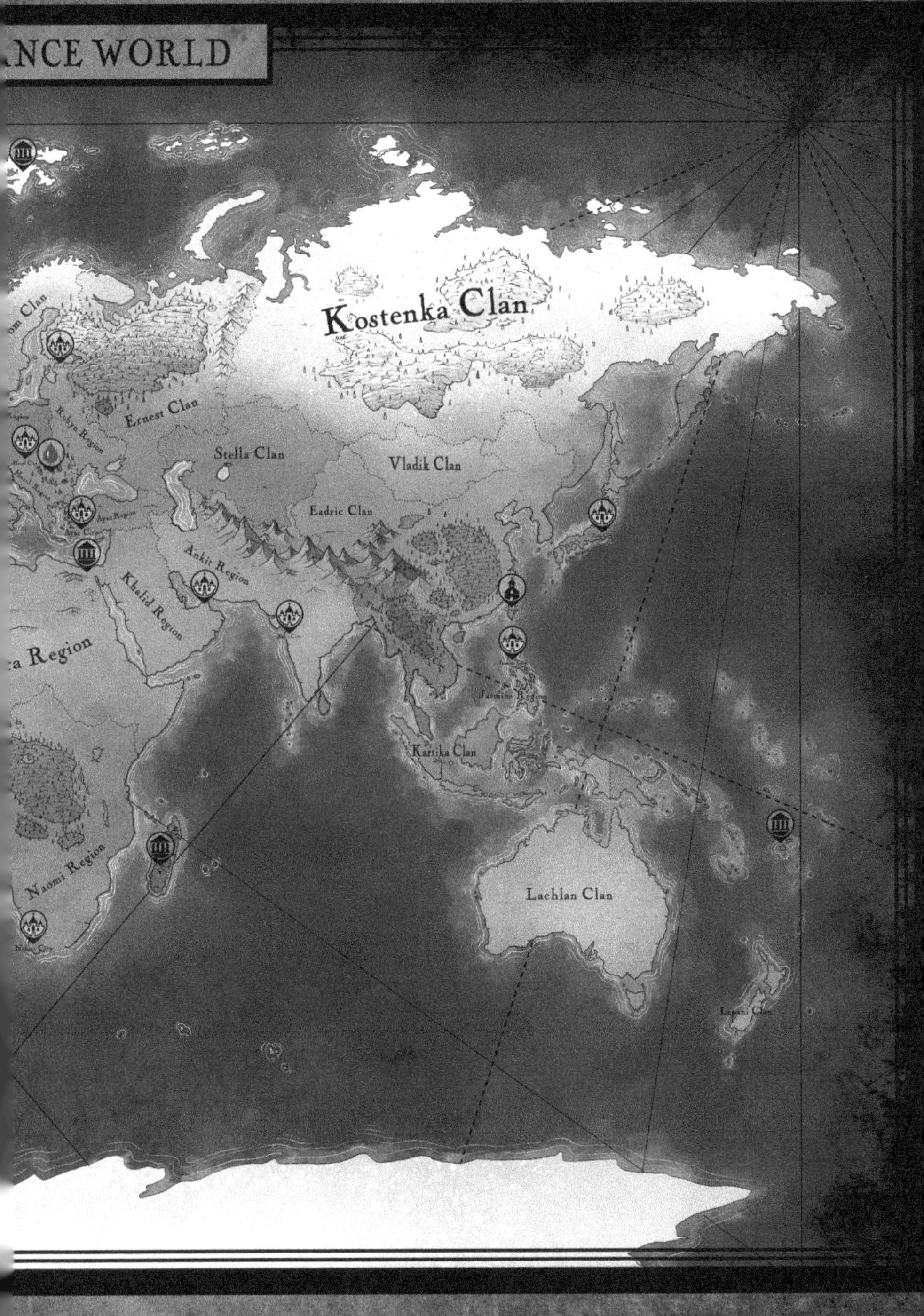
NCE WORLD
Kostenka Clan
Ernest Clan
Robyn Region
Stella Clan
Vladik Clan
Eadric Clan
Ankit Region
Khalid Region
Jasmine Region
Kartika Clan
Lachlan Clan
Naomi Region

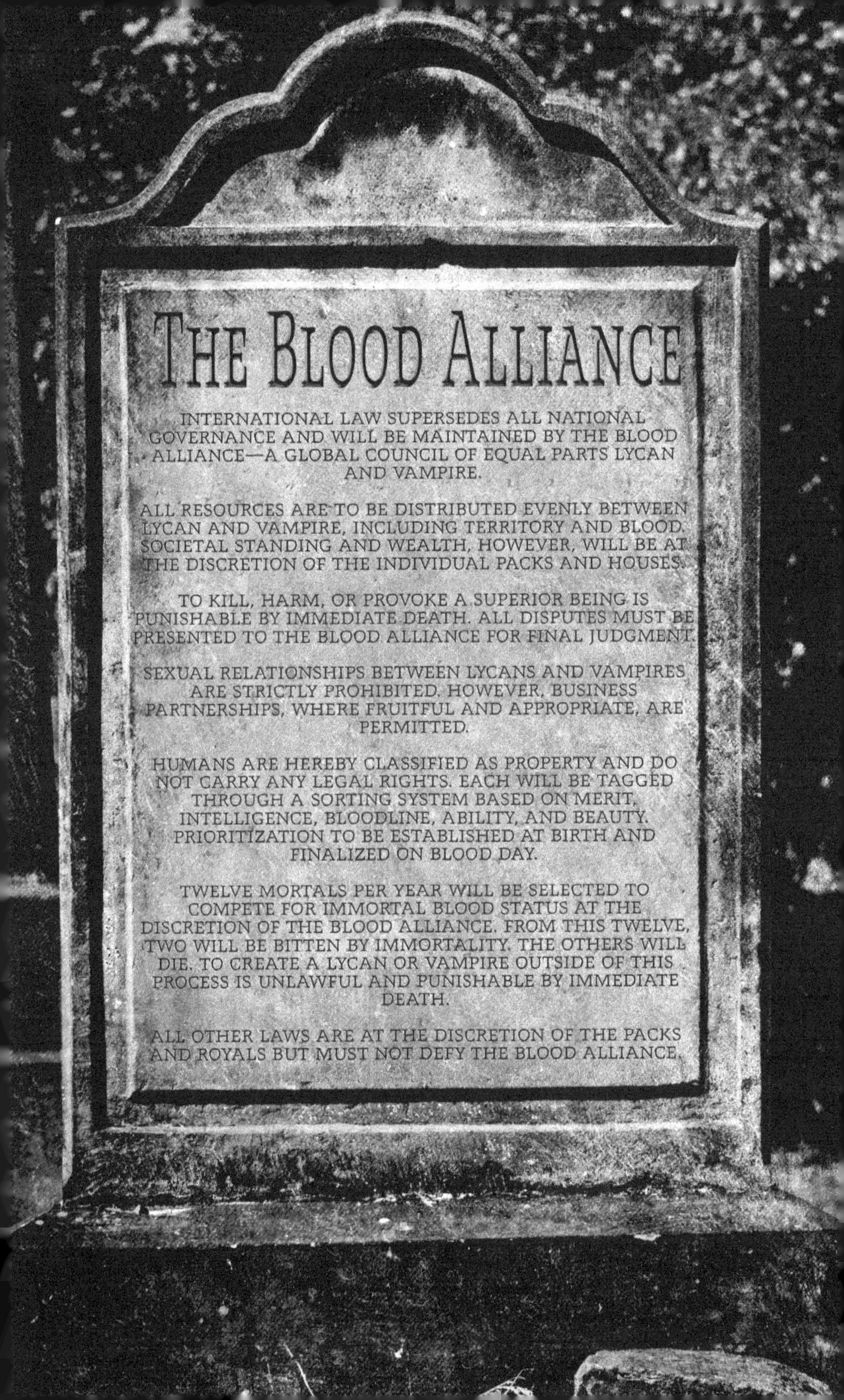
THE BLOOD ALLIANCE
INTERNATIONAL LAW SUPERSEDES ALL NATIONAL GOVERNANCE AND WILL BE MAINTAINED BY THE BLOOD ALLIANCE—A GLOBAL COUNCIL OF EQUAL PARTS LYCAN AND VAMPIRE.
ALL RESOURCES ARE TO BE DISTRIBUTED EVENLY BETWEEN LYCAN AND VAMPIRE, INCLUDING TERRITORY AND BLOOD. SOCIETAL STANDING AND WEALTH, HOWEVER, WILL BE AT THE DISCRETION OF THE INDIVIDUAL PACKS AND HOUSES.
TO KILL, HARM, OR PROVOKE A SUPERIOR BEING IS PUNISHABLE BY IMMEDIATE DEATH. ALL DISPUTES MUST BE PRESENTED TO THE BLOOD ALLIANCE FOR FINAL JUDGMENT.
SEXUAL RELATIONSHIPS BETWEEN LYCANS AND VAMPIRES ARE STRICTLY PROHIBITED. HOWEVER, BUSINESS PARTNERSHIPS, WHERE FRUITFUL AND APPROPRIATE, ARE PERMITTED.
HUMANS ARE HEREBY CLASSIFIED AS PROPERTY AND DO NOT CARRY ANY LEGAL RIGHTS. EACH WILL BE TAGGED THROUGH A SORTING SYSTEM BASED ON MERIT, INTELLIGENCE, BLOODLINE, ABILITY, AND BEAUTY. PRIORITIZATION TO BE ESTABLISHED AT BIRTH AND FINALIZED ON BLOOD DAY.
TWELVE MORTALS PER YEAR WILL BE SELECTED TO COMPETE FOR IMMORTAL BLOOD STATUS AT THE DISCRETION OF THE BLOOD ALLIANCE. FROM THIS TWELVE, TWO WILL BE BITTEN BY IMMORTALITY. THE OTHERS WILL DIE. TO CREATE A LYCAN OR VAMPIRE OUTSIDE OF THIS PROCESS IS UNLAWFUL AND PUNISHABLE BY IMMEDIATE DEATH.
ALL OTHER LAWS ARE AT THE DISCRETION OF THE PACKS AND ROYALS BUT MUST NOT DEFY THE BLOOD ALLIANCE.

PROLOGUE

LILITH

It is now the year one hundred seventeen of the Blood Alliance era.

And, unfortunately, if you're watching this, then something has gone terribly wrong and the necessary fail-safes were engaged. Including the one you're experiencing now.

I will do my best to bring you up to speed as quickly as possible, but be advised there are at least seven days of logs for you to review. This is all part of the procedures you left in place; I can only hope that it works.

To begin, there are seventeen royal vampire states and seventeen lycan clan territories. I also maintain my own region, but as I lead the council—as per your recommendation—I don't count myself in the primary vampire states.

I've also taken on the role of Goddess, like you suggested, and have done my best to provide the mortals with a beacon of hope.

Every year, there is an Immortal Cup challenge where two fortunate humans are gifted the opportunity to join the vampire and lycan ranks. It's a cutthroat competition designed to ensure only the best are given immortality. The games also serve as a way to keep the humans entertained while they compete for the opportunity of a literal lifetime. And, as per your design, they also learn valuable lessons along the way.

The lycans and vampires are mostly satisfied with the Blood Day proceedings. Vampire royals are given fresh harem members, blood slaves, and general service workers for their regions. Lycans are given participants for their moon chase operations and breeding programs, as well as desirable humans for the alpha harems.

It's an even disbursement, just like you suggested. It has also brought the lycans and vampires together in exquisite unity, allowing us to reign supreme over the lesser beings.

But there are a few who are displeased with this method of leadership.

Which is likely why the emergency protocols have been engaged.

Because the only way you could be seeing this now is if I'm dead.

Fear not, my dear ruler, I died for the cause.

But it's officially time for you to take over the mantle and claim your destined throne.

Welcome to the new world, my king.

May it be everything you desired and more.

Click the arrow to begin reviewing the logs.

End transmission.

CHAPTER ONE

GALINA

Thirty-six hours until self-destruct. Please make the appropriate preparations, and thank you for your service.

The message blared overhead, startling me out of my sleep. Lilith's voice reverberated through my mind, demanding my attention.

35:59:59.

35:59:58.

35:59:57.

I gaped at the image on my wall, reading the numbers as the countdown initiated. The same numbers appeared on my wristwatch, the vibrating mechanism demanding I wake up as it alerted me to what was about to happen.

"Shit," I breathed, running my fingers through my hair. "*Shit.*"

This was the doomsday protocol, which meant something had happened to Lilith. It was now my job to send all research through the appropriate channels before the evidence destroyed itself.

I also needed to make sure there was nothing left behind for unauthorized personnel to find.

Lilith expected me to kill everyone. Including myself.

This could all very well be a loyalty test of sorts, set to prove my integrity and willingness to follow the requisite procedures.

Or it could really be happening.

Which would mean my superior was dead.

I tried to search for her through the mental links, but all the programming and tests had dulled our connection so long ago that I couldn't trust the emptiness I sensed through my bond with her.

I was also still alive, which suggested she might be, too.

Or at least one of my connections still remained. I felt fine. Immortal. Healthy.

Because of Lilith or my ties to…?

The ticking on the wall distracted me from my thoughts, providing an improved conception of reality. My bonds didn't matter, only my duty did.

Unless she's really dead.

I shook my head. It didn't matter. I had certain steps to follow.

Send the files. Kill them all.

A tremble worked down my spine. No amount of practicality or reasoning could prepare me for the latter task. These subjects had become my friends. They were… they were *family*… and they provided the few meager ties I had left with humanity.

Focus, I told myself. *Maybe this is all just a test to see how I'll react. Go through the motions. Pretend to be ready.*

Clenching my jaw, I nodded and forced myself to engage in my morning routine. Part of the process was not to panic. There was more than enough time to complete my tasks without hurrying.

Shower.

Dry my hair. Assemble the long blonde strands into a tight bun.

Dress in the traditional blue scrubs and add a lab coat.

After finishing my to-do list, I glanced in the mirror to check my irises. The hazel rings were blue today, suggesting the links to my maternal side were stronger than normal. That meant the contained animal within me desired dominance.

My lips flattened. I supposed if a side was going to take control, it should be the most violent part of me. Perhaps the beast would help me kill everyone.

I shivered at the thought. Then I allowed myself one final sigh and checked the clock once more.

35:32:17.

All right. I opened the light oak door and left my pristine white quarters behind.

There were no countdowns or panic in the vacant hallway, and the marble area at the end of my corridor remained just as quiet and desolate.

Because no one else knew about the doomsday protocol. Only me.

"Mornin', Doctor," Officer Gerald greeted as the elevator doors automatically opened. His team would have alerted him to my movements with the surveillance footage in the hallway, therefore sending him up to retrieve me.

Staff weren't allowed to operate elevators.

Not even me—the lead researcher of Bunker 47.

"Morning, Officer," I replied to him in my usual tone. Flat. Emotionless. Bored. I'd mastered it over the last hundred-plus years.

He gave a nod as I entered. Then he keyed in my intended destination—the wing with my office and labs.

We were already deep underground, but the cage around us plummeted to the depths of hell before opening again.

"Have a beautiful day, Sunshine," Officer Gerald said as I stepped out onto the obsidian floor.

His statement wasn't unusual, as he called me that nickname every day because of my light-colored hair. But this time, I looked at him and wondered if he knew what was about to happen down here.

His gray eyes gave nothing away, just crinkled at the corners as they usually did.

He was a Vigil—a human trained in the art of protecting their immortal betters. I never understood how the mortal minds could be so feeble and accept such a ridiculous task. Vampires and lycans didn't need protection. They needed humans to police each other in order to ensure their domain and rule over humankind. And mortals like Gerald fell right into that trap.

Would Lilith spare his life? I doubted it. She wouldn't even spare mine. And I was one of her prized creations. Officer Gerald was merely a number to her. I at least had a name.

The elevator door closed before I could answer him, the Vigil off to his next task of retrieving one of my lab technicians. Probably James.

I blinked, then studied the white walls surrounding me. They were a stark contrast when compared to the slick ebony tiles beneath my sneakers.

Am I standing on explosives right now? I wondered, glancing at the floor. *Or are they even deeper underground?*

A subtle vibration against my wrist told me I didn't have time to worry about it. A half hour had passed since the initial countdown began, leaving me with thirty-five hours and thirty minutes.

Research first, I decided, heading to my office to begin the tedious task of uploading all the files to the server. That objective alone would take hours to accomplish. And it required vigilance on my part to ensure everything transferred without error.

There would be no tests today. Just this.

I used my watch to unlock my office. The lights came on around me as I entered, the screens flaring to life with a warm welcome. "Hello, Doctor Calina," the machines all greeted.

I remained silent as I always did. Technology didn't require formalities or placative words. Instead, it appreciated keystrokes and logical demands. So I unleashed several onto my computer, telling it to begin the download of all the logs.

Passwords I'd memorized decades ago flickered to life in my mind, causing my fingers to move with ease across my keyboard.

I knew what needed to be done.

But as I neared the second-to-last list in my mind, my typing slowed.

If this was all a loyalty test, then Lilith might end the game as soon as I hit that button. Or she might wait until I killed a few subjects first.

However, if she was truly dead...

I closed my eyes as I forced that thought to leave my mind. *Choices are just false hopes*, I told myself. *Do what you're told. That's how you survive.*

With another deep exhale, I continued on with my task, my resolve hardening with each keystroke.

Until I reached the final sequence of commands.

The ones that required me to pull up the video feed of the

lab and unleash the toxins onto all those inside. The two lead lab technicians were the only ones who could stop me from completing my task; therefore, they needed to be incapacitated.

My two closest friends in this hell.

My only true family.

Not because we enjoyed each other or often spent time with one another, but because we all grew up here. We all understood this place, our purpose, and the research our lives helped perpetuate.

I was created first, almost six decades before them. As a result, I often chose to remain in my head.

But James and Gretchen… they'd chosen a different path. One they exuded now as they smiled and helped one of the lycan shifter pups up onto a table. The little one gave James a big lick across the cheek, causing him to grin in that boyish way he favored. Gretchen watched on with an adoring gleam in her dark, almond-shaped eyes.

The two of them were in love, something Lilith knew and allowed because it made their research stronger. Hence, the product of that love sitting on the lab table now.

A baby.

A tiny little white ball of fur.

One Lilith wanted me to kill with a single stroke on this keyboard.

I swallowed and closed my eyes again, my mind reciting all the doomsday sequences that had been drilled into me for the last century. Longer than that, really. This lab had been created before the revolution.

Half my staff were immortal subjects turned researchers. James and Gretchen were the only two I considered to be family, but the others were still part of my life. They meant something to me on a level I couldn't define.

Murdering them would protect them in a way. The explosives might not be able to do the job, but I had the weaponized serum in my arsenal that absolutely would. We were all difficult to truly kill since most of us were linked to an immortal out there in the real world—immortals we didn't know.

Our bond mates. Lilith's biggest secrets.

My jaw ticked as I considered our options.

Lilith had tested me ample times throughout my life, but never with an experience like this. She was cruel, but also practical.

Destroying all her creations seemed a bit far, even for her.

Which suggested, again, that she really was dead.

And meant I had options to consider.

Tapping my nails against the table, I considered the files waiting in the outbound folder. They were still loading, and that final keystroke would enable the course of action designed to send them along.

After incapacitating Gretchen and James.

I sat in my chair and studied the screen, then looked at the lab surveillance feed once more.

My wrist buzzed again. *Thirty-five hours*, I translated, realizing I was losing time. But I couldn't move. It was as though fate had tied my hands to the chair, refusing to let me execute the final order.

Instead, I uttered a vocal command to bring up videos throughout the compound, checking on all the other labs under my control. It was business as usual, everyone testing results and cataloging their findings. Some socialized freely. Others remained quiet and kept to themselves.

None of us were here by choice, but we recognized that our lives in this bunker were more favorable than being on the outside. Humans were toys who existed purely for vampire and lycan enjoyment. Like pets, only far less cherished.

At least we were somewhat respected in this bunker, our knowledge and skill sets seen as worthy of a higher distinction than *cattle*.

However, we would only maintain that status if we followed the rules. And right now, I was breaking the biggest one of them all by not hitting that button.

They could kill me for this disobedience. Yet they were asking me to die regardless. So what was the difference? One option provided an ounce of dignity, allowing me to leave this world knowing I'd done the right thing. While the other choice would send me to my grave as an honorable and obedient disciple who had never really lived.

My fingers curled into fists.

Lilith had taken everything from me—my freedoms, my choices, my *life*. I'd obeyed her to the best of my ability. But could I do it again now? Did I even want to?

Another buzz. *Thirty-four hours, thirty minutes.*

Then it became thirty-four hours.

Thirty-three.

Thirty-two.

I half expected Lilith to barge through my door at any minute and punish me for failing her test. Except she never came.

If Lilith's truly dead, then what do I have to lose? I found myself wondering. That musing grew into a myriad of ideas as the minutes passed. Because nothing happened. No Vigil arrived to escort me out for an execution—something Lilith had threatened me with on countless occasions throughout my long life.

"Do you know what it's like to die and come back?" It'd been a softly spoken question, one she'd followed with an action by dragging a blade across my throat.

I'd drowned in a pool of my own blood.

Only to awaken an undetermined amount of time later with the memory firmly etched into my thoughts.

It hurt to die.

It hurt even more to come back.

That incident had just been her own musings, not a true punishment.

Oh, I'd endured many of her choice reprimands over the century, too. All of them had included death and rebirth. Each one a subtle lesson in her superiority, always meant to remind me of my place.

Sometimes she killed me just to prove she could.

Sometimes she killed me as a way of testing my immortality.

And sometimes she pretended to love me, just to break my mind.

The latter never worked. It was something she claimed to like about me.

"You're beautifully resilient, Calina. My perfect creation. I hope you never change."

Staring at the screen now, I wondered if that was the point of all this—to destroy everything I'd built just to see if I could mentally withstand it.

Lilith loved her mind games.

I rarely ever played.

What happens if I defy you now, my queen?

She would undoubtedly kill me again. But would it be for good?

No.

She couldn't afford to lose me and all the knowledge I possessed.

But what if it's real?

I couldn't quiet the part of my mind that kept musing over the possibility that she truly was dead. That this wasn't just a test, but actually happening.

Several more minutes passed.

Still, I stared.

Contemplated.

Considering every angle.

Waited for her to appear. To slaughter me. To berate me for my insolence.

More time passed, bringing the countdown to thirty-one hours.

Yet no one bothered me in my office. No one called. No orders flared to life on my screen. Just the ticking of the clock against my wrist and the request to proceed flashing on my monitor.

My world didn't stop moving.

But the clock kept ticking.

The vibration this time indicated I was down to thirty hours. I'd spent almost every second in this office, sitting here, staring at screens. It was almost impossible to consider, like I'd fallen into some sort of complex catatonic state while I considered all the alternatives.

My mind never stopped working, calculating every move and risk. Every countermeasure I could take. Every potential outcome of disobeying a directive.

The technicians were still in their labs. The Vigils were all preoccupied with their supervisory tasks upstairs. And I was tired of watching the countdown flare on my wrist.

"Fuck procedure," I said, looking right at the screen. "Fuck it all."

I reversed all the orders, then added ones of my own. Having spent all my years in this lab, I knew the technology inside and out.

I'd also set subtle traps throughout the years, allowing myself to be alerted should a doomsday sequence be engaged *without* my knowledge.

I checked all those now, bolstering them and taking control of all the monitors inside. No one would take control of this situation without my permission.

However, the explosives were not within my control, suggesting they could potentially be updated from the outside.

Which meant I needed to make it look like I was doing exactly what I'd been told to do, just in case anyone from above checked in on the situation.

My mind worked quickly, formulating a plan that had long existed at the back of my head—a plan I had never expected to need and yet, somehow, always desired to use.

Escape had always appealed to me. I just never knew when to make my move. As it turned out, I had less than thirty hours to do it now.

Okay.

I pulled up the server destination for the documents and opened a less secure communication channel than necessary to distribute the data. It would cause a security flare on the other side because these encrypted files would arrive via an unexpected tunnel.

Whoever existed on the other side would have to play with the parameters a little to determine the source. Once they realized they were real, they'd begin to download.

But that would only buy us a few hours.

And then they'd have to piece all these files together like a massive puzzle, giving us even more time.

By the time they realized what I'd sent, it'd be too late for them to reach out for the real documents. All this data was old gibberish. Useless. The kind of details that would set them back fifty years.

This put Bunker 47 at risk as well, this new channel placing us on the technological map. If anyone was searching through satellites or using data scanners, they'd be able to pick up our location.

But it was a risk I was willing to take.

Because it would give us more time to find a solution to this situation. *To escape*.

I eyed the lab screen again, nibbling my lip.

Toxin malfunction, I typed. *Will address immediately. —Dr. C.*

I hit the Send button, aware that the message would arrive at the home base before any of the files. But maybe they would think I was too busy handling the toxin issue to notice the unsecure outbound documents.

I waited to see if I received a reaction. If Lilith was watching me, she'd make it known right about now because she would be furious over my clear break in procedure.

Minutes passed and nothing happened.

No alarms. No calls. No toxins in the air.

The queen is dead. It was the only natural explanation for the lack of a response. She'd never let me get this far into a game without showing her hand.

And if she wasn't, well, I'd cross that bridge later.

Because we now had less than thirty hours to escape this hell.

Or we would all be buried alive down here.

I stood and ran from my office into the vacant hall.

No one stopped me. Just as no sirens blared.

I should have done this hours ago, tested the limits of the disaster plan to determine Lilith's intentions, but I wasn't going to waste any more time now fretting over how long it had taken me to make this decision.

No scientist ever jumped to a conclusion without weighing all the evidence from their observations.

My researchers would understand that reasoning just as well as I did.

I shoved through the door to their lab, finding the ball of fluff snuggled into Gretchen's lap. She blinked up at me in surprise, then smiled. "Hey, Calina. What—"

"Lilith is dead and we need to go." I pulled the sleeve up to expose my wrist. "This whole place is going to self-destruct in just under thirty hours."

CHAPTER TWO

JACE

I traced the lines on the map, studying the area known as *Lilith Region*. That name would change soon. An upgrade, in my opinion.

Jace Region.

Technically, that area already existed, but it would soon be renamed *Darius Region*. Assuming the ancient vampire beside me agreed to claim it.

"You realize you're a royal now, yes?" I asked without taking my eyes away from the map. "The Blood Alliance may not know it yet, but that doesn't make it any less true."

"First a sovereign and now a royal," my old friend drawled, his English lilt rivaling my own. "How thrilling."

My lips twitched. Darius never was one for politics.

"You could give it to Ivan," I suggested.

He grunted in reply. "He's too young. The challenges would distract him from getting anything done."

"True," I agreed, my gaze narrowing at Lilith City on the map. It was formerly known as Chicago in the human era. However, the dead Goddess had claimed it and retitled it after her namesake.

All the royals and alphas had followed suit with their own

destined location.

San Francisco became Jace City—my home.

Kylan claimed Vancouver, renaming it Kylan City.

The list continued throughout the world, designating seventeen distinctive lycan regions and eighteen vampire states. Lilith took over a vast section of the Midwest with her area sprawling upward to meet Majestic Clan, which was primarily composed of former northern states like Wisconsin, Minnesota, North Dakota, and Montana.

"I really don't think the labs are here," I said, pointing to Lilith City. It was too densely populated. "Lilith would definitely want to keep her research close, but not close enough to be discovered."

"Indeed," Darius agreed before taking a sip of his coffee. It was spiked with blood from his *Erosita*, something I'd scented the moment he'd entered.

I didn't dare ask for a taste.

Darius used to be the sharing sort. That had all changed when Juliet had entered his life, and I respected that. At least when in private. However, in public, we had to put on a show. I helped protect him and his interests, just as I knew he would have my back if I ever required it.

"She had to have trusted someone with leadership in her absence," I continued. "If we can find that person, perhaps we can torture the lab location out of him or her." I shifted my focus from the map to the list of known allies.

We'd compiled the names after reviewing all the contents on her phone. Each contact fell into one of two categories—Lilith sympathizer or potential revolutionary.

"None of her files suggest there's a partner of any kind," Darius replied. "But I agree. There's something we're missing."

I pulled up a group of photos, showcasing them on the wall in a way Damien had taught us. We were still in Ryder Region, having chosen to remain a few extra days to review all the data he'd collected on Lilith. It proved useful since Damien, Ryder's second, had a lot of fun toys for us to use.

"She would never trust a lycan," I decided out loud, pushing all the photos of Lilith sympathizers with wolfish origins to one side, leaving five royal vampires on the screen.

It was a surprisingly small number.

We'd anticipated much more, but apparently, there were several royals who had questioned Lilith's leadership over the years.

Kylan, a notorious problem royal with a penchant for pissing off and challenging Lilith, was reaching out to each one to learn more. Meanwhile, Edon, Luka, and Logan—our three alpha wolf allies—were in charge of contacting the alphas with known anti-Lilith sentiments.

Darius and I were leading the effort to locate the lab that held Cam captive. He was my cousin and Darius's maker, marking us as the appropriate individuals to locate the long-lost Vampire King. Most believed him to be dead because of Lilith's antics. But we knew it wasn't true. Otherwise, his *Erosita* would have died along with him, and Izzy was very much alive.

"Well, it's not Helias," Darius said, drawing a slash across the smirking photo of the blond male with beady black eyes. "He's too arrogant to be a partner in anything. And the only reason he's even sided with any of this is because she gave him Zurich."

I dipped my chin in agreement. "He would only partner if she let him be the God to her Goddess." I reached out and tapped a photo of an olive-skinned male with sharp features. "My money is on Ayaz. He's always advocated for world domination and the enslavement of humankind. It's why he involved himself in the Ottoman Empire all those centuries ago."

"That didn't go very well for him," Darius drawled.

"Because he let the humans fight the battle for him." Which was one of the many reasons he claimed mortals to be useless aside from being blood bags.

"Don't discount Lajos or Sofia. They're both renowned for their cruelty. Lajos has gone through nine blood slaves in the last six years. He's gluttonous with no care for precious blood types. And you've seen the living conditions Jasmine maintains in her own capital city."

"Wasn't very hard for Jasmine to do, considering what the war did to the Philippines," I pointed out, shuddering with the memory.

"Well, she hasn't done anything to fix it."

"True," I agreed, rubbing my hand over the stubble dotting my chin. It'd been a few days since I'd used my razor.

Darius was in a similar state, his dark hair unusually long and nearly touching his ears. He typically kept his appearance rather neat, always preferring to wear suits—just like me—and cropping his hair short. I wondered if Juliet preferred it this length or if he'd decided to embrace the lengthier styles of our olden days. Modern things like electrical razors and regular haircuts weren't as common three thousand years ago.

He ran his fingers through his longer locks now while bringing his mug to his lips for another sip. The flush on his cheeks told me how much he enjoyed the flavor. "You know, drinking from the vein is much more satisfying."

His dark green eyes flashed. "I had that this morning before I came to meet you. And I'll be having it again as soon as we're finished here."

"Are you trying to make me jealous?" I'd left my harem back in Jace City. Not that I had much interest in them anymore. All the politics and the chance for a revolution had severely impacted my sex drive.

It'd been several weeks since my last fuck, a fact that didn't bother me nearly as much as it should. Perhaps because that experience had been satisfying enough. Or more likely because I had too much on my mind to even consider playing right now.

"She's addictive," Darius murmured, his irises swirling with intensity. "So yes, you should be jealous."

"As your royal, I could demand a taste."

"But you won't," he countered.

"But I won't," I conceded. "Something you—"

"I need you to see this," a deep voice interjected, the one I'd come to know quite well over the last weeks.

And speaking of my last sexual conquest, I thought as Damien entered the room.

We'd spent several days in bed with his current playmate, Tracey. I'd rather enjoyed the experience but caught on quickly that Damien felt an inkling of possessive intent toward the girl. So I'd backed off. It wasn't in my repertoire to submit, and I suspected he would demand it if we played too much.

Still, it had been an enlightening few days.

Damien had talents any man or woman would consider

admirable.

His golden-brown eyes met mine, but it wasn't lust shining up at me now so much as determination. A few clicks on his phone wiped the screen from the wall and replaced it with a spinning circle at the center. Little document icons floated around it, compiling into a glowing folder.

"What the hell is that?" I demanded.

"Lilith's phone," he explained. "Some sort of countdown began a few hours ago, and I've been trying to track the source. And then ten minutes ago, I found that data stream flowing through an unsecure connection. I've already started downloading copies of them to our own servers."

"What's in the files?" Darius asked.

"I don't know." Damien sounded frustrated. "They're encrypted, and I won't be able to gather them all until the download is complete, which, according to the clock, is going to take at least a day. But what concerns me more is the countdown." He clicked on an icon in the top left, bringing up the screen.

Thirty-six hours until self-destruct. Please make the appropriate preparations, and thank you for your service.

My eyes widened as I read the message.

"I think it's related to the lab," Damien said before I could ask. "Either someone knows she's dead and set off a trigger to destroy all the evidence of whatever the fuck she's been doing, or her death somehow set off a series of fail-safes. And then there's this."

Another message popped up.

Toxin malfunction. Will address immediately. —Dr. C.

"That message is actually how I found the files. I think they're linked somehow because they're coming from the same source." He shuffled the images around again to pull up a map. "Dr. C. appears to be located in former upstate Michigan, which is also where the files are coming from."

"Lilith Region," I translated.

"It's also a short flight from Chicago," Darius added, meeting my gaze. "That's where the lab is."

A clock appeared on the screen, the hour mark set at twenty-nine and counting down.

Then it froze and a new message scrawled across the screen.

Detection protocol enabled.

I frowned. "Detection? As in… us?"

10:00:00.

"Oh, fuck," I breathed. "We just lost twenty hours."

"Because it sensed my trace through some backdoor safety measure," Damien muttered. "*Shit.*" He shut everything down on the wall and met my gaze. "I'm coming with you. Whatever traps she's left at that lab are likely technical in nature. You need me."

I didn't argue. "Yes." All of this reeked of Lilith's penchant for strategy. She probably had some sort of fail-safe tied to her essence, thus igniting a series of protective procedures in the event of her death.

And one of those would very likely lead to the destruction of Cam.

"When do we leave?" I demanded.

"Rick is already preparing a plane for departure," Damien replied. "I just need to gather some toys and we'll be ready."

I glanced at Darius. "Juliet staying or traveling?"

"Traveling," he said without missing a beat. "She's still in training, but she grows stronger every day. It won't do her any good to leave her here when she could learn something out there."

I didn't disagree with his conclusion but felt the need to say, "It's dangerous."

"Everything we do is dangerous," he countered.

"Fair enough." I locked gazes with Damien. "Lead the way, expert."

…APTER THREE

CALINA

A few minutes earlier

I showed James and Gretchen my watch.

29:32:47.

They observed the countdown for three more seconds before gaping up at me. "The entire bunker?" James asked.

"Yes. It's the doomsday sequence."

"I've never heard of it," he replied.

"Because you're meant to die during it," I informed him. "It's …y job to kill everyone—permanently—and send all copies of our …ch to a server in another bunker."

…hen frowned. "And that one isn't being destroyed, too?"

…ow," I admitted. "My orders are to send the files and …de. That's it."

…nced at my empty hands and arched a brow. "How?"

…s a toxin designed to knock everyone out. I have a serum …e that will do the rest." A serum I left locked up. Only my …ould open the safe. Unless someone else was given access to …ergency reactions, in which case… "I should destroy it. We …d to destroy it." Why hadn't I thought about that beforehand? …omeone else is notified of the doomsday protocol, they could use it against us."

I didn't wait for them to agree, my feet already moving. But as I reached my office, a blaring alarm shrieked through the hallways.

My palm froze on the doorknob as Lilith's voice flowed through the air around me. "Detection protocol enabled. All evidence must be destroyed. Vigils, engage."

Vigils, engage?

My watch buzzed, the new time glaring up at me. *10:00:00.*

"Ten hours," I breathed. What the hell had just happened? Was this a result of not following the codes appropriately?

No. The AI version of Lilith's voice had said, *Detection protocol engaged.*

Which meant someone from the outside now knew our location.

Likely because of the unsecure data connection I'd created.

I started to run my fingers through my hair, only to belatedly remember that I had the locks tied back in a bun.

James and Gretchen were at my side half a beat later. "What did she mean by 'Vigils, engage'?"

I shook my head. "This isn't a course of action that I'm familiar with. But I can guess what it means."

I pressed my watch to the locking mechanism to open the door to my office and found it unresponsive.

Because I'd been locked out.

This emergency procedure superseded the doomsday sequence.

But do the Vigils know that? I wondered, thinking back to Officer Gerald's behavior earlier. He'd been utterly calm. No outward signs of expectations at all. He could be an excellent actor. Although, I doubted it.

Which meant I might have a card to play here.

"Show me your watch." The words were for James because his arms were free. Unlike Gretchen, who held their child.

James didn't hesitate in complying; my word was law around here.

Another card I can play, I thought, my mind working through a plan faster than I could speak.

His screen showed nothing.

I checked mine and saw that the countdown remained. Which meant the fail-safe I'd engaged earlier was working, because the updated timeline had appeared on my wrist.

Good. I can use that.

"Act normal and let me take the lead." I'd no sooner finished speaking than the elevator down the hall opened with an echoing *ding.*

There was only one way on or off this floor, and it was via the elevator.

Which meant a Vigil was coming.

I straightened my spine, pasted a bored expression on my face, and eyed the pup in Gretchen's arms.

I'll just have to make this work, I decided, clearing my throat. Acting wasn't one of my skills, so I'd just fall back on what I excelled at—leading.

"Of course, we can allow that," I said loudly, ensuring my voice carried. "But you understand what will need to be done afterward." Pitching my voice low, I added, "Say, 'Yes, Doctor Calina. We know what needs to be done.' And say it with confidence."

Gretchen did precisely as directed.

James followed suit just as Officer Gerald rounded the corner. I ignored the gun at his side and arched a brow, my expression one Lilith had given us all a thousand times before. "Are you here to be my guard while I complete the requisite actions?" I asked him, using my standard emotionless tone.

He paused, his silver hair gleaming in the low lighting. It had been black when he'd first started here. But like all Vigils, he aged. Meanwhile, my face remained stuck at twenty-two years of age, something he had definitely noticed over the last two decades.

"Well?" I prompted when he didn't reply. "I don't have much time to get this done, Officer. You're either my guard or you're not. That's why you're here, right? To prove your loyalty by using your watch?"

The plan formed while I spoke, my mind running a mile a minute to stay one step ahead of everyone else around me. I was banking on Officer Gerald's inability to see through my strategy. As he'd fallen for all the brainwashing created by Lilith and her supporters, I suspected this just might work.

"Don't just stand there," I continued, threading my tone with impatience. "I've already tested Gretchen and James. Their watches worked on my door, which means they've been approved to help me execute the necessary tasks for the doomsday sequence. Now I need proof that your watch works as well. Then we can begin while you guard the door."

He gazed at me warily. "The procedure states to kill everyone in the building."

"Yes, I'm aware," I snapped, pretending to lose my patience. "I have the necessary serum in my office. But it's not to be distributed until after the tasks are complete."

"What tasks?" he demanded.

"If you don't know the answer, then you're not meant to know," I said through my teeth. Then I showed him the countdown on my watch. "This started when I woke up this morning. Because I'm in charge. Who do you think initiated the detection protocol? *I* did."

Not a lie since it was very likely my unsecure connection that had allowed someone to track us.

"Nah, only the Goddess has the power to enact that protocol, Sunshine." He lifted his gun. "I know my job."

I glared at him. "To what? To shoot me before I'm done transmitting research files? Sure. Go ahead. It'll be your funeral in the end."

He studied me for a beat. "What files?"

"My task, Officer."

"Yeah?" He started to lower his gun. "You got proof?"

"In my office, yes."

"Show me."

I shook my head. "You have to prove you're allowed to see it first. Use your watch on my door, and I'll know you've been sent here to help me finish the job."

"I don't need to prove nothin'."

I always knew Officer Gerald wasn't my favorite guard. And not just because he felt it was acceptable to call me *Sunshine* when I'd never actually seen the real sun before.

"You seem to be forgetting who is in charge here, Officer. I am the lead researcher for Bunker 47. You are a member of *my* staff. Yes, Goddess Lilith is our superior in all ways, but I'm her creation. I'm the one she left in charge here, and my word is law on her behalf. Now open my fucking door, or I'll call Lilith myself."

I brought up my watch and made a show of finding her contact information.

The Vigils didn't have her number.

But I did.

Just like I had a mark on my neck that denoted me as Lilith's personal property. A mark I exposed subtly now by tilting my head.

"I'm not just a lab employee, Officer. I'm the head researcher. Now either obey me or face the consequences." I uttered it with all the confidence I could muster and hoped it was enough.

I lifted my finger to hover over the screen and knew from the resulting expression on Officer Gerald's face that I'd won. His tan skin turned white. Then he dropped the gun. "I'm sorry, Doctor Calina. I-I must not be familiar with this part of the operation."

I forced a sigh. "Well, I hope it's that. Otherwise, my intended guard will kill you as soon as he or she arrives." I gestured at my door. "If you would please prove your worth, I would be much obliged, as I really do need to return to my research transmission."

He eyed James and Gretchen warily. "And them?"

"As I said, they've been assigned to assist me. That's why we ran here from the lab a few minutes ago." I added that last part because I was very aware of the cameras in the hallways.

I'll need to dismantle all surveillance, I thought, cataloging the task. *I'll do that the second he lets me back inside.*

"And the mutt?" he asked, earning himself a death sentence from the question alone. Because James would not allow a Vigil, let alone a human, to insult his pride and joy. But a glance from me held him in check.

Not yet, I said with my eyes.

"I told Gretchen she could keep her child with her a little longer before we engaged in the extermination process. It's what we were discussing when you arrived. She's agreed to my terms and understands what must be done. I'm rewarding her loyalty with a few extra minutes of familial memories."

He eyed me with clear suspicion.

So I lifted a shoulder to feign indifference. "As long as he doesn't get in my way, I don't care," I continued. "But I do care about the fact that you're stalling. Why is that, Officer? Will your watch not work and fail inspection?" I arched a brow again, just like Lilith, doing my best to prove my superiority over the Vigil.

I'm immortal, I told him with my eyes. *You are not.*

He swallowed. "Just tryin' to make sure we're all followin' the rules," he said, holstering his gun.

"Of course," I agreed, shifting purposefully to my right. It kept me on the same side as his firearm, just in case this test didn't work. I had no idea if his watch would override mine and be able to let us back inside.

If it didn't, I'd go for his gun.

If it did, I still might go for his gun. That decision depended on what I found waiting inside.

He moved forward with purpose, his expression giving nothing away. But I caught the hint of perspiration dotting his neck. He feared what I might do to him if he failed this mission.

Good.

Because that meant he feared *me*.

I notched my chin up just enough to continue my air of superiority—a feat, considering his six-foot-plus frame dwarfed my five-foot-four one—and maintained a cool expression as he tested his watch against the locking mechanism.

It clicked, causing him to release a sigh of relief.

"Excellent," I said, maintaining my confident tone to suggest I'd expected that to work, and waved him to the side. "You will remain here. I will send the files."

His eyes narrowed. "I want proof."

I blinked at him. "Excuse me? You're not cleared for *proof*, Officer."

"None of this is in my handbook."

I rolled my eyes. "Not memorizing or thoroughly studying your *handbook* does not give me jurisdiction to break procedure."

He huffed in response, his burly chest puffing out with decades of toned muscles.

I merely arched my brow for the third time and gave him a dispassionate look. "Stop wasting my time, Officer. It's precious"—I lifted my wrist to display the countdown—"as you know."

His jaw clenched, causing his cheekbones to flex.

I waited, acutely aware of his every move. If he went for his gun, I'd act. He might be trained in combat, but I had over a century of experience on his meager forty or fifty years. And just because I wore a lab coat didn't mean I couldn't operate a gun.

Hungry vampires and feral lycans were a job hazard, one I'd been thoroughly trained to handle. After all, Lilith couldn't afford to lose one of her prized assets.

A rogue Vigil wouldn't be a problem.

Unless he has serum bullets, I reminded myself.

"Fine," he finally said. "Hurry the fuck up."

"Watch your tone," I countered. "I'm still your superior, Officer."

He growled something unintelligible under his breath, his irritation palpable.

Good. That meant I'd done my job in making him believe me.

I gestured for James and Gretchen to enter first, then I followed behind them. "The vials you want are in the safe behind that picture," I said, gesturing to the large portrait of Lilith. She'd put that there decades ago. *I'll be watching you*, it said.

But are you watching me now? I wondered. *Because I don't think you are.*

I used my password to unlock my computer and found the access revoked.

Hmm, I hummed, entering a secondary code meant to access the back door I'd built years ago. My lips threatened to twitch when the screen sprang to life beneath my command.

This was the benefit to being in charge—I had access to everything, including the security network and database servers.

I'd created these back doors to access my files in the case of a system reboot going haywire. Never had I considered needing to break in because of a mandate that superseded my authority. These codes were meant for regaining control in an erroneous situation, not an intentional one.

Although, I supposed I always knew this might be necessary. It was just one of those strategic moves in my mind, one driven by my need to survive.

Or, I thought, glancing at James and Gretchen as they stood beside the open frame, *in the case where I wanted my only friends to live.*

I gave the information they needed to open the safe. "There's a manual inside on top of the case. Flip to chapter four to read the instructions on how to properly release the toxins."

Chapter four provided details on how to load the guns in the box beside the vials. We were going to need those after I finished my task on the computer.

Settling into my chair, I went to work pulling up the surveillance feeds and queueing all the commands in my mind.

Only, the visuals on the screen snagged my focus, my heart skipping a beat to see the massacre that had occurred in four out of the seven labs.

Oh God...

The Vigils hadn't wasted any time in killing all the researchers throughout the bunker. And the crystallized glimmer of red from a few of the lab technicians confirmed that the Vigils were in possession of the serum as well.

I swallowed, my stomach churning at the sight.

The bullets turned the blood to solid form, immobilizing the host and essentially dismantling the immortal essence. It had taken decades to perfect the substance. Many of those who had helped create it were now experiencing the impact of the effect... and dying.

Witnessing it now, I realized there was no way I could have seen this through. Lilith had to know that, too. Yet she'd put me in charge for a reason.

My brow furrowed as I tried to puzzle out her logic.

Then a fifth lab flashed across my screen as the Vigils entered to destroy the occupants.

I'm running out of time to act, I realized, my frozen limbs jolting back to life.

I pulled up the feeds from the floors that were already cleared and started a recording to create a loop for anyone looking in on the video surveillance. Three minutes passed before I decided it was sufficient for a consistent replay.

By the time I finished, the fifth lab was already cleared.

Rather than focus on the morbid scene, I began another recording to create a loop for that level. The Vigils were entering the sixth lab as I finished. Rather than record that, I went to the one on this floor where James and Gretchen worked, and created a loop there. Then I returned to the most recent massacre to record and loop.

A *ding* down the hall told me that more Vigils had arrived, probably to check on Officer Gerald's work.

I met James's gaze and noted the question there.

He'd already assembled some of the guns, but Gretchen still held their furry child in her arms.

Giving him a subtle shake of my head, I called up another series of commands on my computer. The sixty-second loop for our area would have to be enough to fool an onlooker because we were out of time. And, fortunately, my office didn't have a camera.

My fingers flew across my keyboard as the murmurs began in the hall.

One of the Vigils asked Officer Gerald what he was doing.

He then uneasily replied that he was overseeing my protection while I finished up in my office.

"What? That's not part of the protocol," a deep voice snapped. "They all die. You can't be soft on her just because she's nice to look at."

I ignored them, my sequence almost complete.

Boots stomped forward.

Five, I counted. *Four.*

I hit the Enter button.

Three.

Final command.

Two.

I hit Enter again.

Now.

I nodded at James, and he lifted the gun to aim just as Gerald and his buddy charged in. His aim was true, nailing both Vigils right in their heads before they even had a chance to react.

Hurried steps started down the hall, only to skid to a stop as a sharp howl graced the air. "What the fuck was that?" a gruff voice asked.

A feral lycan, I thought at him. Then I jumped up to help James pull the dead Vigils inside.

He knew that sound as well as I did. Which was why he reacted quickly—his lycan genetics aiding in his rapid movements—and slammed the door to my office to lock us inside.

Screams rent the air from the corridor, the agonized sounds making me flinch.

"You let Louis out," James breathed, his turquoise-colored eyes widened in shock.

I shook my head. "No. I let all of them out."

Every single rabid vampire and lycan. On every single floor. The Vigils might have guns with serum-laced bullets, but they didn't stand a chance.

It was a hasty decision, but one that would help us eliminate the immediate threat.

"What now?" James asked, wincing as Louis released a furious roar from the hallway. The beast followed it with a punch to my door. He was a strong alpha lycan.

Fortunately, he wasn't strong enough to take it down.

"We wait," I said softly, returning to my chair to pull up the non-looping surveillance feeds.

If anyone could escape this hell, it was a horde of pissed-off lycans and vampires. Once they discovered the exit path, we'd follow.

I just hoped they figured it out before the countdown reached zero.

CHAPTER FOUR

GALINA

Blood painted the ground and the walls, drowning the bunker in death.

The lycans and vampires had wasted no time in demolishing the small Vigil army, then they'd moved on to the labs to face their former captors. Fortunately, the researchers and technicians were already dead, thanks to the serum-laced bullets.

I shivered, the mass destruction on my screen sending chills down my spine.

I'd observed every minute, waiting for the higher beings to shift focus to finding an escape. It took hours, their need for vengeance palpable on the live feeds. They'd destroyed everything in their paths—humans, tables, vials, medical equipment, observation windows, and even a few corpses of the slain medical workers.

I could only imagine what they would do to me as the head researcher.

Everything we did down here was at the demand of Lilith. Our purpose was to find ways to enhance life expectancy in humans by making them immortal without any emotional or physical ties to our betters. We were also charged with throttling any additional gifts outside immortality.

Essentially, what Lilith wanted were immortal slaves who could endure great pain and death-like experiences but always regenerate with human blood flowing through their veins.

She desired an endless supply of blood. One that couldn't die. And also couldn't fight back.

That had been my intended future—for her specifically—but the experiment had failed because I'd inherited certain abilities. Such as my strategic ability and quick reflexes. Of course, that hadn't stopped her from biting me every time she'd visited. My blood called to her, as it did many other vampires in the lab.

James, another failure, was mostly lycan. He couldn't complete a full shift but possessed immortalized strength and the literal claws of a wolf.

Meanwhile, Gretchen was one of the most successful cases. Her immortality made her difficult to kill, and she harbored almost no supernatural traits. That was the primary reason Lilith had allowed her to procreate with James.

But their child was a lycan who preferred his wolf form.

While the test was a failure, Lilith had intended for the child to grow and later be used to replace Louis. That part hadn't been known to Gretchen or James. And now they would never need to know.

Assuming we found a way out of here.

The lycan and vampire subjects had divided into groups, their movements throughout the bunker reminding me of mice trying to find the exit of a maze.

Except these were predators, not prey.

Louis had stopped at my door earlier, his gaze intent as he'd tried to find a way to beat down the barrier. There were no markers or signs in the hallway that indicated this was my office. Which meant he could smell me in here. And the murderous gleams in his glowing irises had told me exactly what he wanted to do to me.

Or maybe it was James and Gretchen he'd sought.

We'd remained silent, waiting with guns inside, just in case he somehow managed to break down the entrance. It was reinforced steel, hence the reason I'd needed Gerald to test his watch and unlatch the door for me.

Eventually, Louis had taken one of the watches off of a dead Vigil, noted the countdown on the clock face, and left to explore another division via the elevator.

With their bloodlust mostly sated, the vampires and lycans had begun thinking strategically. The video feed didn't have sound, but I noticed their mouths moving as they all found each other on the various levels and looked at the stolen watches.

It didn't take much for them to realize we were on a countdown sequence of some kind. And from their hurried efforts now, they'd clearly gathered that they didn't want to be in this bunker when the clock reached 00:00:00.

Different groups ran into others on each floor, always pausing to discuss the watches and potential escape routes.

Then they scattered again to keep searching.

I observed them with interest, waiting for them to discover the one thing I'd never been taught—how to leave the bunker.

James stood beside me, his arms folded as he watched in silence.

Gretchen sat on the couch that I often used for sleep, her child snuggled against her as she hummed to keep him content and quiet.

There wasn't anyone else alive in our section—at least, no one we knew about. There were other rooms like mine without cameras, making me wonder if anyone else had hidden out like we were now.

James reached forward to tap on one of the images to enlarge it. I let him take charge, his alpha energy clear in his stance. He usually bowed to my authority, but in this situation, he was the strongest amongst us. As he stood over six feet tall and was built of solid lycan muscle, I trusted his dominance so long as he listened to my strategy.

"There," he said, gesturing at Group Three—a trio of vampires from the labs on floor two. "They've found something."

I nodded, noting the excitement in their expressions as they tried to open one of the doors on level nine.

"Do you have a way of triggering the opening mechanism from here?" James asked.

I pulled up the access controls within the bunker, searching for one that would unlock the door on that level. Then I frowned and shook my head. "It's not listed." Which meant there were probably others like that throughout the building.

I started cataloging them quickly, based on the camera angles and doors I could see.

James fell silent as I worked, giving me the space and time to write down all the doors on each level that were visible in the feed and missing a control.

"There are only two," I finally concluded after comparing all my lists.

"Where are they with door one?" he inquired, the surveillance feed having been switched as I'd checked each section within the bunker.

I returned to Group Three and found Group Four with them. I'd labeled them all in my head to keep better track of them. Group Four had a lycan and two more vampires. The lycan had shifted and was trying to use his claws to get through the steel door.

Two of the vampires were working on the watches they'd taken from dead Vigils.

My lips twisted. "They're not making much progress." I checked the time and found we were down to a little over three hours left.

There had to be something we could do to speed them along.

I started pulling logs from previous visits with Lilith, searching for anything that could signify the entrance or exit. Entrance protocols. System audits. Security logs.

Nothing.

"Shit," I muttered, frustrated that I couldn't find a damn thing to help us. Maybe it was my exhaustion or the stress of the moment, but my access and review of the files didn't help us in any way.

Pulling the footage back up, I discovered that Groups One and Two had joined Three and Four, leaving only Group Five unaccounted for.

I found them at the other door without a system-controlled locking mechanism, which was on level fifteen. "Looks like—"

White light blared across my screen, blinding me before I could finish speaking. James cursed, both of us momentarily stunned. But the feed quickly shut to black, the visual of that area no longer available.

My eyes recovered first, allowing me to pull up the surveillance of the door on the ninth floor. They were all oblivious to what had just happened on fifteen, their attention entirely on that door.

"Hmm," I hummed, searching for any other views of the fifteenth level.

I finally located one near the elevator and saw nothing but rubble littering the floor.

Rubble glowing with streaks of sunlight, I realized after a beat.

"Is that…?" James trailed off, peering down at the screen.

Gretchen had joined us, reacting to whatever had made James curse and flinch on the screen. "Oh my God, that's natural light."

"Daylight," I whispered.

The three of us shared a glance.

Then I pulled up the footage again of the ninth floor to check on their progress. Nothing had changed. My mind whirred as I considered our options. Either we waited for them to finish their exploration—I checked my watch for the current countdown, noting that we had less than an hour left now—or we made a break for it.

"We need to get up to the fifteenth floor," I said quickly, standing. "It's our best option."

Gretchen and James agreed with matching nods.

My scrubs and lab coat weren't great for concealing my identity, or useful for stowing weapons, but we didn't have time to change. And I wasn't about to pull on Gerald's uniform. It wouldn't fit, nor would it make me any less noticeable.

May as well wear what I'm comfortable in and go from there, I decided, picking up two loaded guns.

James did the same, his gaze on Gretchen. "I've got you."

"I know," she replied.

He bent to capture her mouth with his own. I averted my gaze, ignoring their show of affection, and focused on the dead Vigils.

Searching Gerald, I found a grenade that might be useful and stuck it in one of my lab coat pockets. Then I grabbed his handcuffs and shoved them into my other pocket. Lastly, I put his watch on my opposite wrist, then I handed the other Vigil's device to James after he finished kissing Gretchen.

"We're getting out of here," I told them both. "Thoughts to the contrary will only get us killed."

They both dipped their chins in agreement.

James cocked one of the guns next, tucking the other into a holster he'd stolen from the Vigil. "Let's go."

I checked the surveillance one more time, ensuring the lycans and vampires were still consumed by floor nine, then I followed them out the door toward the elevator bay.

All of us had been inside one enough times to know how to operate them based on observation alone. But James took the lead, using the dead Vigil's watch and then adding a series of commands afterward.

Obviously, a lycan or vampire had kept a Vigil alive long enough to explain how to use the watches, because otherwise they wouldn't know. Unless this was standard technology outside the bunker. As I'd never left, I wasn't sure. But most of the research subjects were brought in by Lilith.

The box sprang to life around us, whisking us upward. Gretchen clung to her son, her hazel eyes wild with emotion.

I slid my fingers closer to the trigger of my guns but kept them pointed at the ground.

Then I held my breath as the elevator came to a stop and the doors opened.

Dust and debris filled the area, followed by a scent I didn't recognize. *Outside, maybe?*

James growled, the sound low and dangerous. "Vampires."

That didn't make sense. Group Five had been all lycans.

"Come out here shooting and we'll return the favor," a deep voice drawled.

Texan, I recognized, familiar with voice patterns and origins from the pre-revolution time period.

I ran through the known list of vampires in the bunker and couldn't recall a single one from that region of the world.

Frowning, I returned, "Who are you?"

"Depends on your choice, sweetheart," he murmured, drawing out the words as though we had all the time in the world to discuss it. "I could be your savior or your executioner. Which do you prefer?"

"I don't believe in saviors," I admitted as the elevator released a protesting bell, stating it wanted to close to travel to another floor. *Shit.*

"Pity," the vampire replied. "I was hoping to make a new

acquaintance."

The elevator emitted a secondary sound, the warning clear. We either hopped off onto this floor, or we faced our fate on another level.

And considering all the other groups were together, I had a pretty good idea of who'd called for the transport.

Which meant we either confronted these unknown vampires up here or got dragged into hell again to face the research subjects who hated us.

The vocal vampire up here didn't sound angry so much as amused.

Meanwhile, the ones downstairs would absolutely be furious and kill us on sight.

The odds were also better up here with the potential exit.

All of that made my odds marginally better with option number one—face the unknown vampires.

"We're coming out," I said, tossing my weapons into the open space as a sign of defeat. "Unarmed."

James grunted, obviously not approving of my plan, but I had a grenade in my pocket, and he had another pistol in a holster. It only took a second for him to follow suit, his actions confirming that he was letting me take the lead again.

It was this or go back downstairs.

I preferred the talkative vamp.

"We have a child," I added, hoping that would earn us a little reprieve from whatever they intended to do to us.

Swallowing, I took the first step.

Gretchen stepped out next, taking a position behind me, and James took up the rear of our small party.

The elevator blared a final warning just as we finished clearing the metal slats. Then the doors slammed behind us, leaving us in a dusty lobby area with a single vampire.

James's earlier use of the plural had told me there were more, but I could only see the one standing off to the side of the elevator with his pistol aimed right at my head.

"Hello, sweetheart," he calmly greeted with his Southern drawl, his golden-brown eyes glowing beneath the flickering overhead lighting. The inconsistent illumination gave his striking features a feral appeal, one I didn't recognize.

He definitely wasn't one of our subjects, which meant he'd come in from *outside*.

His eyes tracked over my attire, his gun pointed and unwavering. Gretchen and James said nothing, both of them waiting for me to decide our next move.

"Dr. Calina," the vampire mused, reading the name on my lab coat. "Otherwise known as Dr. C., I assume."

Dr. C. That was the name I used on all my transmissions. Was this male from another lab? Did he work for Lilith?

I cleared my throat, deciding it didn't matter. Because if he knew who I was, then he knew the protocol here hadn't been followed. Therefore, I needed to prove that we possessed information that made us valuable—information that would keep us alive.

"Yes, I'm Dr. Calina, lead researcher of Bunker 47." I squared my shoulders, giving my best haughty air—just like Lilith would. "And these are my two primary scientists, Gretchen and James."

The male's dark brow inched upward into his thick brown hair. The long length of his strands reminded me more of a lycan, which only seemed to add to his animalistic appearance.

"I see." He ran his eyes over me once more, then looked around me to take in Gretchen and James at my back. "Hey, King Jace!" he shouted. "I found something you're going to want to see!"

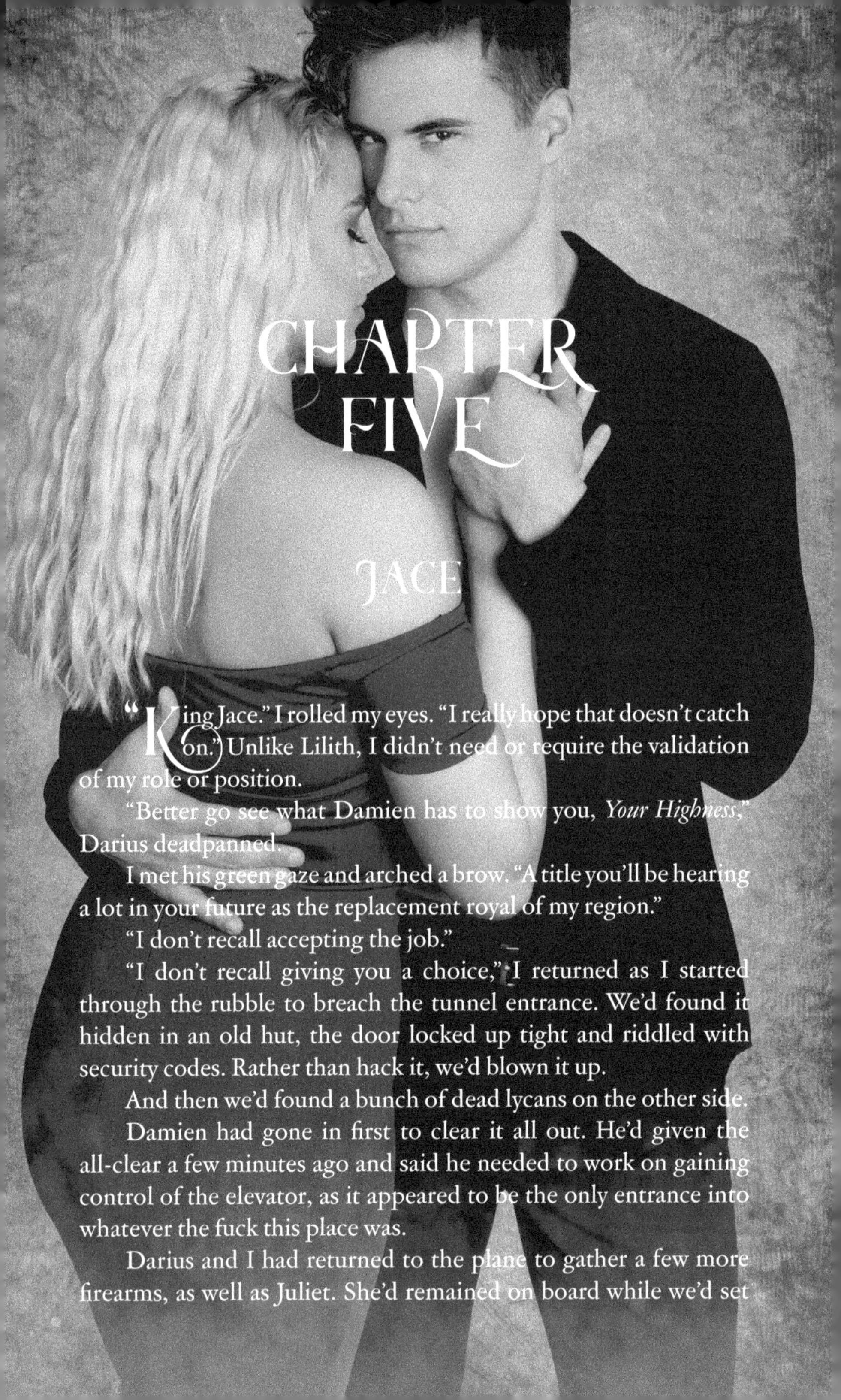

CHAPTER FIVE

JACE

"King Jace." I rolled my eyes. "I really hope that doesn't catch on." Unlike Lilith, I didn't need or require the validation of my role or position.

"Better go see what Damien has to show you, *Your Highness*," Darius deadpanned.

I met his green gaze and arched a brow. "A title you'll be hearing a lot in your future as the replacement royal of my region."

"I don't recall accepting the job."

"I don't recall giving you a choice," I returned as I started through the rubble to breach the tunnel entrance. We'd found it hidden in an old hut, the door locked up tight and riddled with security codes. Rather than hack it, we'd blown it up.

And then we'd found a bunch of dead lycans on the other side.

Damien had gone in first to clear it all out. He'd given the all-clear a few minutes ago and said he needed to work on gaining control of the elevator, as it appeared to be the only entrance into whatever the fuck this place was.

Darius and I had returned to the plane to gather a few more firearms, as well as Juliet. She'd remained on board while we'd set the explosives. Being Darius's *Erosita* made her immortal in the way that she couldn't die, but it didn't grant her all his vampire strengths.

I navigated down the hall, the general layout reminding me of an abandoned hospital wing, apart from the scent of fresh blood. My nose twitched as I tried to discern the origins.

Some of it came from the dead lycans from the blast—an unfortunate event that we'd not expected.

The rest appeared to be stemming from the trio standing in front of Damien. He had his gun aimed at the blonde female while the other two hid behind her. I assumed this was what he'd called me in here to see.

He confirmed my assumption as he said, "King Jace, meet Dr. C."

My brow furrowed until I caught the name etched into the lab coat. *Calina*.

"She states that she's in charge here," he added, his amusement palpable.

"Actually, I said I'm the lead researcher of Bunker 47," Calina corrected, her sultry tone holding a regal flair that had me wondering at her origin. "Lilith is in charge, not me."

"Lilith," I repeated, intrigued that she hadn't referred to the dead royal as the *Goddess*. It was Lilith's preferred nomenclature among humans, of which Calina absolutely was one.

And yet, her blood possessed a sweet potency that was distinctly other. It made my mouth water for a taste. Pair that with her pretty face and slender build, and she was most decidedly appetizing by my standards.

Except for one thing.

"You work for Lilith?" I asked. Calina had used the present tense when claiming Lilith was in charge of this operation, thus it seemed wise for me to follow suit. Particularly as those of us who preferred reform had agreed to keep Lilith's demise a secret until we were ready to inform the world of the truth.

Calina's bright blue eyes met mine, shocking me with her boldness. However, beneath the shock was a hint of wonder because her irises possessed a distinctly wolfish flair to them.

Fascinating.

She smelled human. Actually, her scent reminded me a bit of

Juliet, making me wonder if Calina possessed the rare essence of a blood virgin. My canines ached with the notion of taking a bite, but I knew better than to react impulsively.

However, I might very well indulge in her later.

Yes, I thought. *Yes, I think that's exactly what I'll do with you, darling.*

Work first. Play later.

"Who are you?" she demanded. "I'm not familiar with a *King Jace*."

"I prefer just Jace," I replied, even more enthralled by the beauty before me. *A human standing up to a royal?* "But I think the better question here is, just who are you, Doctor Calina? How did you come to work for Lilith?"

She studied me. "If you don't know, then you don't work for Lilith."

"Indeed, I do not," I replied. "But I am very much your superior."

A flicker of wariness entered her gaze, and the two beings behind her shuffled nervously. I glanced around her to take in the two beings at her back and noticed the little bundle of fluff in the female's arms. She clutched the little wolf tighter to her chest, the move distinctly maternal, suggesting the pup was her child.

Was this a breeding center of some kind?

I took in Calina again, noting the flatness of her stomach. She certainly had the hips designed for fucking, but she didn't otherwise appear to be a lycan breeder.

No, this one was built for a vampire, I decided, that natural perfume of hers reminding me of a drug. Damien appeared to be impacted by it as well, his nostrils flaring as he inhaled deeply.

It seemed it wasn't something he wanted me to *see* so much as *smell*.

Something buzzed, causing Calina to glance down at her watch. Numbers scrolled across her screen, making her flinch. "We need to get as far away from this place as possible," she said urgently. "It's going to self-destruct in less than fifteen minutes."

Damien kept his gun pointed at the doctor while he pulled Lilith's phone from his pocket to show me the same countdown. They matched.

"Why is it going to self-destruct?" I asked her. "Who initiated the protocol?"

"If you're truly my superior, then you should already know that," she replied in that regal tone from earlier, like she was in charge of me and not the other way around. "But I'm telling you if we don't run now, we're going to die here."

My eyebrows flew upward. "Not much can kill one as old as me."

"Then you'll live in agony beneath the rubble of this bunker for all of eternity," she returned without missing a beat. "If that's your chosen fate, then so be it. But I would prefer to die by a bullet than suffer the same."

She started forward, ignoring the gun pointed at her head.

Damien flashed me a look, his surprise evident.

"Where are you going?" I demanded.

She pointed around me to the exit and followed the path with her feet. When she reached my side, I grabbed her hip, halting her. "What part of *I'm your superior* did you miss?"

"The part where you proved it," she replied, meeting my gaze once more. "And as I'm clearly the one with more knowledge of this particular situation, that marks me as the leader, not you."

Damien snorted, his gun dropping to his side. "I think I'll let you handle that."

I ignored him, my focus entirely on the overly confident female in front of me. "You want a lesson on my superiority?" I asked, my tone darkly quiet.

Anyone else would know to bow right now.

But not this female.

No, she merely raised a brow, the invitation to act clear in the defiance of her pretty blue irises.

I smiled. "All right, Doctor." I tightened my grip on her hip and tugged her closer, my opposite hand going to the back of her neck. "I'll—"

Ding.

"Louis," the male behind Calina said.

She flinched, trying to find a way out of my grasp. "*Run*," she commanded.

The male and the female holding the lycan pup took off toward the exit. Damien immediately lifted his gun, taking aim.

"Don't." The word left my mouth on instinct, my focus falling to the opening elevator door.

Damien shifted with me, his pistol aimed and ready. "Drop—"

He didn't get a chance to finish his order, the beings inside already spilling out into the wreckage of the hallway. They didn't have weapons, only teeth, and their focus was entirely on Doctor Calina.

Growls rumbled through the corridor, causing the female to stiffen against me.

"Holy shit," Damien breathed, lowering his gun. "*Zack*?"

A vampire with animalistic features glared at Damien. Then his dark brows met his hairline. "*Damien*?"

The moment came to an awkward pause as everyone glanced at each other.

My own eyebrows lifted as I recognized the lone lycan in the group. "Louis." The male doctor had voiced that name, causing Calina to tell him to run. But I hadn't really considered the familiarity of it. *Louis* had been a popular name a few centuries ago.

"Jace," he returned, his furious gaze melting into one of surprise as he looked at me. "What the fuck are you doing here?"

"Looking for Cam." It was a statement the lycan would definitely understand, considering he'd been supposedly killed for agreeing with Cam's views on the revolution. "Is he here?"

"Cam?" Louis frowned. "I've not seen him in… a very long time. I don't think he's here. But I'm not sure where *here* is or how long I've been…" He trailed off, his attention returning to Calina. "If anyone knows anything about this fucking bunker, it's *her*."

"Because she's in charge," I mused, my grip on her neck tightening just enough to show what I thought of her *leadership*.

"She's the fucking devil," he snarled.

"A devil I need alive for the moment," I told him. "We need to find Cam."

"What year is it?" one of the vampires asked, his eyes wild with suppressed fury.

"Year one hundred seventeen of the new era," I said. Then I translated it into a few different timing mechanisms until understanding crossed the vampire's features.

Calina flinched as her wrist buzzed again. "Five-minute warning," she whispered.

Louis lifted a similar watch and growled. "This place is going to self-destruct."

"Why?" I asked.

"Because of *her*," he snapped.

Calina didn't comment, but I sensed her hesitation, like she wanted to correct him. I'd have to dig into that later.

Right now, I had a much more important question to ask her. "Is Cam down there somewhere?" I demanded, taking Louis's word that this female truly was in charge. She'd also called herself the lead researcher, and her name was tied to the transmission Damien had intercepted. All that pointed to her being the one with the answers I required.

"I'm not at liberty to disclose—"

I sank my teeth into her neck, nailing her pulse without preamble and informing her with my mouth who the superior being was in this situation. She'd accused me of not *proving* it. Well, I'd fucking prove it now. And this little minx would heel.

Except her blood was unlike anything I'd ever tasted in my life.

Fucking exquisite.

Better than a blood virgin's. Or maybe on par. I couldn't say. All I knew was this female showed me a glimpse of heaven in the best way.

It took considerable effort to stop, to not drain her dry right here and now. But millennia of experience kept me focused on the task.

Cam.

I harshly released her throat, tearing skin along the way before pressing my lips to her ear. "Did that prove my superiority, *human*?"

She shuddered out a breath, her limbs shaking from the exertion of losing so much blood so quickly.

Good.

But she didn't reply.

"Defiant," I hummed against her ear, both thrilled by the challenge and furious because of it. "If I find out Cam is down there and you let this bunker implode on him, I will make you dig until he's free."

She didn't react other than to continue panting, her chest heaving from a combination of obvious fear and exhaustion from my sudden attack.

"Sixty seconds," she wheezed as that damn buzzing kick-started.

I'd apparently lost time while feasting on her neck. No wonder she was shaking. I'd probably taken too much. But damn if I cared right now. My cousin might be underground and about to lose his life in an explosion meant to destroy everything inside.

Damien and the others were already running toward the exit.

I almost dropped Calina to let her try to fend for herself, but the weakness in her body told me she wouldn't make it. And I very much needed her alive for answers.

I also meant my threat—if I learned that Cam was down there somewhere, she would help me free him. Then I'd give her to him as a snack to bring him back to health.

Releasing her neck, I jerked her alongside me. She lasted two steps before she tripped and nearly pulled me down with her.

"I should leave you here," I told her, the words a taunt more than a promise.

"I'm meant to die here," she whispered back. "I've always been destined to die here."

The words sounded almost drunk, like she'd not meant to voice them out loud but was too delirious to stop herself. However, hearing them made me wonder how she'd come to be here in the first place.

She sounded almost broken. Sad. Like she'd never been given the chance to live. Yet she'd stood up to me with the spirit and strength of a superior being.

It... *she*... fascinated me.

I bent to lift her svelte form into my arms. She turned to dead weight, something that had me wanting to snap at her until I realized her eyes had closed and she was no longer conscious.

The blood loss, I realized, looking at her neck.

Not only had I taken too much, but I'd also created an open wound with my mouth that had her life fluid gushing from her vein with no signs of stopping.

My jaw clenched, my resolve torn between letting it happen and helping her.

I need answers, I thought as I started walking. *Therefore, I need her alive.*

But I couldn't take a moment to heal her until we were clear of the impending explosion.

I began to run then, holding her to my chest and engaging my vampiric speed and agility as I took off down the hallway and crossed over the threshold.

The blaring light of the afternoon sun hit my eyes, making me wince.

Sunlight wasn't deadly to vampires, but that didn't mean we liked it. Our senses were too sensitive and heightened to withstand long periods outside during the day. We usually hid in the dark, healing and rejuvenating our immortal souls.

But apart from burning my senses, it did nothing to dispel my maneuverability skills. My old age added to my strength, allowing me to move with grace and precision, taking me over a hundred yards away from the site before a rumble touched the earth beneath my feet.

Someone must have told Rick because the plane was no longer on the ground, but in the air, and I suspected Darius and Juliet were up there, too. Maybe even with the two researchers who had run when Louis had arrived.

I glanced around, spying Damien a few yards to my left. Louis and the vampire named Zack were with him. The other two vamps were closer to the wreckage, lying on the ground. But they were definitely alive.

I couldn't say the same for the others.

A geyser of flames kissed the air, incinerating everything in its path.

Calina hadn't mentioned that, making me wonder if she'd purposely withheld it or if she hadn't known what type of explosion to expect.

Because that sort of fire was inescapable, even for an immortal as old as I was.

Which meant that if Cam had been down there, he was most certainly dead now.

"I truly hope, for your sake, that Cam wasn't among your subjects, little doctor," I murmured to the dying female in my arms.

"Or you're going to wish you would have died here today."

I rearranged my grip on her, holding the slender female to my chest with one arm and bringing my opposite wrist to my mouth. Biting down, I created the remedy she needed to survive, then I pressed my wound to her lips.

"Drink, Calina," I told her, forcing my essence into her mouth. Her body would automatically do the rest even while unconscious. "When you wake, we're going to have a very long chat."

CHAPTER SIX

LILITH

Bunker 47.

Your idea for creating perfect human slaves—beings that cannot die and remain viable sources of food for us all—has been perfected over the last hundred years.

Unfortunately, we are still struggling to dismantle the bond between the immortal life source and the human slave, but I feel we are close to a breakthrough in that area.

More details on lab results are forthcoming. Doctor Calina was one of the best. It's a shame that she died with the protocols, but as we both know, desperate times call for desperate measures. She served her purpose, and she served it well.

Press the green arrow below to continue.

Thank you. Your assistant will be with you momentarily to deliver the research logs from Bunker 47.

End transmission.

CHAPTER SEVEN

JACE

I pulled up the surveillance to my temporary quarters and smiled at finding Calina finally awake. She'd been out for almost ten hours, which had been a benefit with everything else going on.

Rather than head to my region, we'd returned to Ryder Region. Mostly because Damien had already taken control of all the cameras in the territory, making it easier to maneuver the large group of individuals from the plane without anyone noticing from abroad.

Ryder hadn't been thrilled or all that accommodating. And he was even more pissed now because the little lycan pup was currently with Willow. But he'd given Darius and Juliet a room to relax in, while I'd chosen to stay in the penthouse royal suites with Damien and our new prisoners.

The plane ride back had been informative with Louis, Zack, and their fellow lab survivors telling us all about their time in the bunker.

Apparently, there'd been several others left to burn below. Zack and three others had gone up to the fifteenth level as a last resort, knowing the place was about to blow, while all the others had continued working on an escape in another area.

Poor bastards, I thought, wincing. There'd been no escaping those flames.

Fortunately, it sounded like all the subjects had escaped their confines, and none of them had been Cam.

Gretchen and *James*—two names I'd learned from a furious Louis—were the primary researchers who'd experimented on him. Calina was the supervisor and Lilith's personal pet.

And she'd been there since the beginning.

Which meant my little human wasn't mortal.

I drew my finger along the screen to zoom in on her pretty face. Her expression gave nothing away despite being naked and tied to a chair.

The other two researchers were in a similar state of undress, but in different rooms. Gretchen was down the hall, and James sat a few feet away from me.

Well, he wasn't exactly sitting so much as slumping.

Damien had gone a few rounds on him, interrogating the half-breed and threatening to hurt the little pup if he didn't cooperate. We would never actually follow through with such an act, but James didn't know that.

The results were beautiful, with James telling us everything we wanted to know.

Unfortunately, a lot of his answers were along the lines of, *That's over my clearance level. But Calina will know.*

I stroked her image once more, my mind thinking of a thousand ways to pull answers from the pretty blonde. Starting with, *What are you?*

From what James and Louis had explained, the projects in Bunker 47 were all about perfecting human longevity to provide a more sustainable food source.

For all of Lilith's faults, I could actually understand her goal here. Our kind had become too glutinous, thereby spoiling our food supply. And she'd been trying to create a way to fortify the humans who remained to make them immortal blood bags.

Of course, just because I understood her goal didn't mean I agreed with it.

There were other ways to improve our quality of food and the durability of the product.

Damien took a step back, his arms folded across his black sweater. "That lycan half is helping him heal," he mused, gesturing to the bruising along his jaw.

"Does Calina have lycan in her as well?" I asked, my question for James.

"Her mother's side," he rasped. "Father was human."

I frowned. "Then she should have been born a full-blooded lycan."

The mother's genetics would have taken over in the womb to override the mortal side of the equation. That was how it worked at the lycan breeding camps, except it was human females mating with male lycans. Most of the human mothers died because their bodies couldn't handle the immortal growing inside them. But a few survived, at least until childbirth.

James started to shake his head but winced. "Her host was a human. Incubator." He swallowed, his one good eye finding mine. "It was before my time. I only know what she's told me."

Meaning she could have lied to him.

I studied her on the screen once more, then slid the device into my pocket. I'd just have to interrogate her myself.

Decided, I made to stand, when James added, "If you tell her you don't work for Lilith, she'll be more forthcoming."

His words were a whisper of sound, his body still recovering from Damien's session. However, my enhanced hearing allowed me to hear him clearly.

I resettled in my chair and leaned forward to rest my elbows on my knees. Either James had deduced we didn't work for Lilith, or he'd overheard us talking to the survivors on the plane.

"Why will that information make Calina more forthcoming?" I asked, genuinely interested. She'd been quick to deny me earlier after I'd confirmed that I didn't work for Lilith. She'd also insinuated that I was inferior as a result. So why did James think that would help my interrogation?

"She didn't follow protocol," he replied on a wheeze. "She tried to save us against Lilith's orders."

"Do you mean the detection protocol?" Damien asked.

"No." James coughed, his expression pained, but he continued despite his obvious discomfort. "Doomsday protocol. She... she was supposed to kill everyone inside. She didn't do it. The detection procedure came later, maybe because she failed. I don't know."

Damien and I shared a look. It seemed the pretty doctor had defied her master's orders. Which suggested she wasn't the obedient little pet that Louis and Zack claimed her to be.

All four of the survivors were resting in another room after indulging in a nine-course meal. So Louis and Zack weren't here to listen in or comment. I preferred it that way because I wanted to extract my own answers from Calina.

A beeping sound had Damien walking over to his computers in the corner. He'd chosen to put James in his quarters for the interrogation, stating it would allow for a more efficient use of time. It enabled him to ask questions and focus on the data download at the same time.

We were hoping the files Calina had transmitted said something about Cam because no one else seemed familiar with him. Aside from Louis, of course.

"What the...?" Damien trailed off as he settled at his desk, his eyes skipping over the screens as his fingers flew across the keyboards.

Technology had never been my skill, probably because I'd been born in a much simpler time. But I knew my way around a computer well enough to survive.

"These files are encrypted gibberish," Damien muttered, his dark eyebrows drawn down in frustration. "Either my interception is flawed, or the data export was intentionally mishandled."

"It's Calina," James whispered. "She probably uploaded old files to distract the recipient... t-to make it look like she was following protocol." He cleared his throat, flinching as he did so, but I could see the wounds continuing to mend themselves.

An immortal half-human, half-lycan hybrid. It was truly a shocking sight to behold. But not as stunning as the one back in my temporary quarters.

"Is that why she sent the files over an unsecure network?" Damien asked, looking at the half-breed. "Was it to delay the file transmission?"

"They would have needed to secure the files before encrypting them," James replied. "That's probably why she did it that way."

"Which means tapping into that data stream is likely what set off the detection protocols," Damien translated.

"Yes," James agreed, swallowing.

The half-breed turned silent, telling me his use had reached an end point.

"Well." I looked at Damien. "I'll leave his fate up to you. Louis wants him dead, but maybe James can convince you otherwise." It was an interrogation tactic of a sort, giving the half-breed the chance to try to prove his use to us alive.

"I doubt it," Damien drawled, playing right into the act of not giving a shit.

Or maybe it wasn't an act at all.

I stood and met his gaze. "I'm going to go have a chat with Dr. C., see if she can't provide any useful details on the real files and their intended destination." From what Damien had said, the receiver identification was untraceable, making it impossible to determine their true identity and location.

"I'll go work on the other doctor next," Damien said absently, continuing his blasé approach to interrogating. "There are no rules, right?"

"None at all," I returned, stepping up to the door. "Just be sure to clean up your mess. I hear Ryder isn't a fan of wasted blood."

With that, I stepped out of the room, smirking as James growled in my wake. He snarled something along the lines of a threat, one I was sure Damien would laugh off.

In truth, we all knew these researchers were worth more alive than dead. They served as proof of what Lilith had been doing to her own kind through research and genetic manipulation. Between a statement from Louis and the physical proof of James being a clear descendant created through force in the lab, there would be no questioning Lilith's guilt.

The stories Louis and Zack had told us about their treatment had made my blood run cold.

And yet, their situation wasn't that dissimilar to how humans had been relegated to the same societal standing as cattle.

There had to be a better solution here, one that allowed lycans and vampires to maintain the upper hand while working collaboratively with humans to ensure all needs across the species were met.

That was where my cousin came into play—Cam had a vision, one I wanted to see come true.

Which meant I needed to find him.

I walked down the hall to the suite Damien had given me, the quarters designed and maintained for a royal of my standing. Technically, these were all Ryder's rooms now, but he hadn't been interested in inheriting his predecessor's dwelling. Instead, he'd picked a random suite on a lower level, leaving Damien to claim and redecorate the penthouse for his own needs.

Ryder had also given Damien the human harem on this floor. As he was recently mated to Willow, he didn't have need for such things.

I had my own harem back in my region. Not that I'd tended to them recently.

The whole royal harem designation was designed to be a perk for those in charge. I found it to be more of a nuisance, as it required my time. And lately, I hadn't been all that interested in indulging my baser needs. At least, not with a group of too-willing humans.

There was no challenge left in this world, thanks to Lilith's antics.

Although, the female glaring at me as I entered my suite seemed to suggest otherwise.

And how intrigued was I to see such a look on a beautiful woman's face.

No supplication. No bowing. No *my liege* or *Your Highness*. Just a glower filled with annoyance. It was refreshing and irritating all at the same time.

I shut the door behind me and secured us inside with a flip of the lock. "Hello, little doctor," I murmured. "Sleep well?"

She didn't reply, her blue eyes—actually, no. Her irises were blue green now with little flecks of brown. *Stunning*. Yet another fascinating trait I wanted to know more about.

I sauntered toward her, taking a chair along with me, and set it across from her. Her jaw ticked as I settled into a relaxed pose with my ankle crossed over my opposite knee.

"You look well rested," I continued as I allowed my gaze to

roam over her nude state. "Aroused, too." Her nipples had beaded in the cooler air, the rosy tips a luscious beacon that begged for my tongue.

Maybe I'd give in.

But only if she gave me what I wanted first.

"James says you'll be more willing to talk if I confirm that I don't work for Lilith, but I already tried that route, and you essentially called me inferior." I canted my head to the side. "Do you still feel that way?"

Her nostrils flared. "What did you do to James?"

I arched a brow at her, impressed and irritated by her haughty tone. "Perhaps I wasn't clear here. I'm the one interrogating you, not the other way around."

"You need me alive because of what I know," she said. "And I need to know if James is okay."

"And if he's not?" I wondered out loud, honestly curious.

"Then you might as well kill me because I won't give you a damn thing," she bit back.

Both my eyebrows shot upward. Had I misread their connections? I assumed he was with the mother of his lycan pup, but maybe he and Calina were romantically involved. Except, no, that didn't feel right. They'd had no palpable chemistry earlier. He'd merely obeyed her command. And it hadn't been Calina he'd worried over, but Gretchen and their child.

"Are you trying to negotiate?" I asked, attempting to discern her strategic play.

"I'm telling you that I'll cooperate, but only if James and Gretchen are left unharmed."

"Well, too late for that," I admitted.

"Then too late to negotiate," she countered.

I searched her expression for any hint of vulnerability and found none.

She meant every word.

"How do I even know you're worth negotiating with?" I inquired. "You sent that transmission of bogus reports. But other than that, I have no proof of your ability to give me anything useful. You can't even tell me about Cam."

I was baiting her, and the flicker in her gaze told me she knew it.

But rather than call me on it, she considered me in a manner similar to the way I observed her. "King Jace," she said as though tasting my title and name. "I've never heard of you." She glanced around the room. "And this isn't your room."

"How do you know that?"

"The scent is too fresh," she replied almost absently. "If you lived here, your woodsy cologne would be a fixture in the room, not a fragrant afterthought." Her multicolored irises refocused on me. "James and Gretchen are still alive. If they remain that way, I'll tell you everything I know. But you'll need to set them free first. Those are my terms. Take them or leave them."

CHAPTER EIGHT

CALINA

King Jace.

The title suited the vampire before me, his icy blue irises and perfectly chiseled features the epitome of regality. Age and experience radiated from him as well, telling me without words that he was one of the ancients.

Lilith had never provided names for the royals or alphas that she put in charge of the various regions. However, I suspected this handsome vampire was one of the royals. He was too powerful and old to be anything other than a leader of his kind. And the way he openly evaluated me and this situation told me everything I needed to know about his strategic abilities.

He would be a worthy chess opponent.

So let's play, I thought, waiting for him to make his move. I'd played my cards on the proverbial table. Now it was his turn.

"How do I even know your information is valuable?" he asked.

"If you didn't think I was valuable, you wouldn't have fed me your blood." I recognized the aftereffects of imbibing a vampire's essence. And the potency of his impact on my senses had confirmed his age, too.

"I only saved you because I want answers. But if you're not willing to give them to me, then I'll just finish you off like the snack you are meant to be."

I shrugged. "If that's what you need to do to assert your dominance, then so be it." I tilted my head to offer my vein. "It's what Lilith would do and has done countless times."

What she had never done was offer me her blood to bring me back. That Jace had done so made him... *different*. And I wasn't sure if I liked that difference or not.

"An immortal blood bag," he mused. "And a tasty one at that." He lifted his ankle off his opposite knee and leaned forward to rest his forearms against his thighs.

Dressed in all black, he was an opposing presence. Yet his eyes held a twinkle of amusement in their depths, one that made me feel more at ease, like we were just verbally sparring.

Oh, I had no doubt this predator would devour me. And unlike what his earlier accusation had suggested, I didn't consider myself superior to him.

But I clearly possessed something he desired.

Information.

What I didn't understand was why he desired it. He'd mentioned a Cam—a name I didn't know. But he hadn't given much else away.

"What do you really want to know?" I asked, curious. "Threatening me is moot—I'm naked, tied to a chair, and sitting opposite a millennia-old vampire; I'm very aware of your *superiority* in this situation. So rather than posture, tell me what you want. I'll tell you if I can give it to you. Then we'll negotiate from there."

"You're making assumptions about my need to negotiate anything. As you said, you're clearly in an inferior position."

"Yes. But I've endured over a century of torture, King Jace. There's not much you can do to me that hasn't already been done." I attempted to relax into my chair as well as I could with my wrists strapped to the arms and my ankles chained to the legs. "But feel free to give it your best shot."

"Jace," he replied. "I'm not Lilith. I don't need a title like 'God' or 'King' to feel important."

No, I imagined he didn't. Confidence radiated from him with that constant undercurrent of age and experience.

"And I don't want to torture you, Calina. But I do need answers, and I will do what it takes to acquire them."

"Interesting, as you've yet to truly ask me anything of import," I murmured. "You want me to prove my worth but haven't offered me an opportunity to."

"Because you want to negotiate."

"I do. But I also want all our pieces on the board. You don't work for Lilith, yet you showed up at her bunker. How?"

"How did you come to be in that bunker?" he countered, avoiding my query.

I'd allow it because this answer wasn't valuable. "Lilith created me and put me in charge of Bunker 47. A top-secret location, I might add, that you mysteriously found. Yet you claim not to work for her."

"I don't work for her."

"Do you work with her?" I rephrased. "Are you assuming the mantle of her legacy now that she's dead? Is that why the other vampire calls you King Jace?"

His gaze narrowed. "How do you know she's dead?"

"Doomsday protocol was only to be engaged upon her death. And as I'm still mostly unharmed after ignoring her directives, I can safely assume she's truly gone. Which leads me to wonder if you're her replacement. That would explain my healthy state—you need me alive and coherent to pass on the necessary research details." I spoke the words as I thought them, only my lips curled down at the end.

Because no, that couldn't be right. He hadn't known enough upon his arrival at Bunker 47.

Lilith would never leave her counterpart or successor without at least a few key details.

"Hmm, well, if you don't work for or with her," I continued, puzzling through the facts out loud, "then you would be against her. An adversary of some kind. In which case, you want to steal the research to use for yourself. A power move? A way to take over the board?"

Maybe he wasn't a true king but a future one.

I scrutinized his features, searching for a clue.

But he merely smiled.

"You're quite something," he mused. "What if I told you I intend to replace Lilith and revolutionize the way the world works?"

"I would ask you what that has to do with me," I replied.

"That depends on how much you can tell me about Lilith's operations. As her lead researcher, I imagine you know a lot. Which makes you decidedly useful to me. Particularly as the files you transmitted were lacking in real details."

I stiffened. "How do you know that?" Only Lilith's intended recipient would have deciphered the files to find them filled with outdated, extraneous data. Which redirected me to my earlier thought about him being a replacement of some kind.

"We intercepted them," he explained. "That's also how we found the lab."

My lips parted. "So it was my fault…" The words came out unbidden in a breath. "You were the intruder the system detected, creating the updated procedure… because of my unsecure file transfer."

I blinked, my heart giving a swift, agonized throb.

Shit. All those lives lost…

My chest squeezed, and I squashed the rising emotion with my next inhale.

Blaming myself is impractical. Lilith had designed those safeguards, not me. And I'd been trying to help the researchers under my supervision, not hurt them.

Lilith had just circumvented me with her countermeasures.

And how was I to know there were others searching for our location?

I frowned at that. "How did you even know to look?" As I asked it, the rest of the puzzle pieces fell into place, causing my eyes to widen. "Because you killed Lilith. That's why the other vampire calls you *King*. So you were searching for the labs… to… to take Lilith's place."

Making him my new master.

I met his gaze. "You're a revolutionary." I'd heard the term a few times in the lab, mostly during Lilith's visits when she'd taunted some of the test subjects with news of the failed revolution. "But you all died." That was what Lilith had told Louis, constantly reminding him of some female named Lydia.

"Her screams still get me off," she would say. "I fucked Michael in a pool of her blood. There are photos. I'll show you sometime."

"You know about the revolution?" Jace asked, bringing me back to him and our present situation.

"Only what Lilith used to say to the test subjects."

His expression darkened. "You mean Louis. And maybe Cam?"

That name seemed to be important to him. I could use that as a bargaining chip, but I could also use it as a show of good faith.

Sometimes the key to negotiating was to give a little to hook the subject. And knowing that Jace didn't work for or with Lilith helped my charitable mood.

"There were no subjects in my bunker named Cam," I promised him.

His gaze narrowed. "You'd better not be lying to me."

"I don't need to lie," I countered. "And besides, I can prove it."

His eyebrows lifted. "Yeah? How?"

"By downloading the log records," I replied.

"They're gibberish."

"The files I sent via the protocol are, yes. But I backed up our records daily to a server farm." Something he would know if he worked with Lilith, but his features registered surprise. "Take me there and I'll give you proof, as well as a whole wealth of information." I caught and held his gaze. "Of course, I have a term that needs to be met first."

His lips twitched subtly. "And we've come full circle."

"We never finished our negotiations," I pointed out. "But you requested proof of my worth. I've given it to you. Now I want Gretchen and James to be left unharmed, and I want to see you let them go free."

He considered me for a moment, his icy irises giving nothing away. "How familiar are you with the new world?" he asked, his change in subject giving me pause. "Have you seen how humans are treated?"

"I'm aware of the Blood Day proceedings and the allocations to different camps."

He nodded. "And you think your two friends can survive that? Because that's what will happen to them, or worse, considering their immortality. They're glorified blood bags, Calina. Just like you. And the superior beings of this world are not kind to their food."

He demonstrated what he meant with his eyes as he tracked over every exposed inch of my body. Hunger blazed in his irises, and I could tell it wasn't just blood he desired, but *me*.

I shivered, the prospect of becoming his new toy making my stomach twist.

Lilith had frequently used me for my blood, but never for sex. However, I'd witnessed the act countless times. She had often thrown humans into the cells for the vampires and lycans to play with as a form of reward for their acquiescence during our studies. Those who'd chosen not to obey had been subjected to mental torture until they'd yielded to her command.

Just like she'd tossed misbehaving lab technicians into the cells for a lesson with the superior beings.

I'd never been subjected to that treatment, her punishments for me much more personal in nature.

"I can't free them," Jace continued. "And I won't free you. But I can make their lives—and yours—more comfortable if you comply."

He didn't bother to voice the alternative, because we both heard it in his tone.

Don't comply and I'll make your life decidedly uncomfortable, I thought in an English accent that poorly rivaled his own. His voice resembled posh elegance, while mine was strongly midwestern United States. Or what used to be that area, anyway.

I glanced at the window several feet away, noting the balcony beyond it and the dark sky overhead. The humidity here was different, making my skin clammy despite the cool air brushing it.

It left me wondering where he'd taken me. A trivial curiosity, considering my situation.

Jace stood and wandered to a bar in the corner near the tall windows. Either he'd misunderstood my perusal, or my wandering eyes had made him thirsty. He filled a single glass with bronze liquid, took a sip, and sauntered toward me.

"Open your mouth," he murmured as he pressed the rim to my lips.

I attempted to tell him I didn't need a drink, but he tipped the contents over my tongue, forcing me to swallow. The alcohol burned on the way down, making me gag.

He grinned. "We'll work on that."

"Why?" I asked, my voice hoarse.

"Because it'll suit a future use," he replied, taking another drink from the same side of the glass as I'd touched with my mouth.

I shivered, the action distinctly intimate. Like we'd just engaged in an unspoken vow of some kind.

Which was entirely impractical and inexplicable. I hadn't promised him anything. Nor had I agreed to a single term.

The edge of the glass met my lips again. I opened and swallowed, this time without the gag. A dark glimmer graced his silver-blue eyes.

"Already learning," he mused, lowering the drink away from my mouth.

A jolt sizzled through my veins as the cool glass brushed my nipple. His eyes lowered to watch the movement, his touch clearly intentional because he repeated it with the other breast.

Was this meant to be some wicked form of interrogation? Or was he merely a predator taunting his prey?

"I almost hope you refuse to comply," he murmured. "Your pale skin would redden so beautifully. And I would very much enjoy coaxing reactions from you along the way."

The glass rolled across my skin once more, except this time he tilted the contents of it to spill bronze liquid onto my breast.

Goose bumps pebbled along my skin.

Then my breath caught in my throat as he bent his head to catch the droplets with his tongue.

Heat caressed my skin, his mouth an unexpected kiss to my senses.

Ohhh…

A violent quiver stirred inside my lower abdomen, shooting sparks to each nerve ending. Sparks that ignited into flames as his fangs pierced the sensitive area around my nipple.

I cried out in surprise and slight pain, only to freeze as he lifted the drink to the fresh wound.

"As I said," he whispered, his icy irises capturing mine. "I can make your life comfortable. Or I can make it absolutely miserable."

He tipped the glass, the alcohol slipping over the edge and directly onto my breast once more.

The comfortable burn morphed into a stinging inferno that elicited a sharp hiss from my throat, one born of shock and pain.

His tongue chased the torment, licking up my alcohol-laced blood and soothing the burn.

It only lasted a second.

But his point was clear.

I'm your master now. Work with me, and I'll consider rewarding you. Work against me, and I'll destroy you.

CHAPTER NINE

JACE

Calina's hiss rolled through my mind on repeat, the sound one I wanted to replicate as I drove deep inside her.

Mmm, I'd meant what I said about hoping she didn't cooperate. Not because I wanted to truly harm her, but because I desired to teach her a lesson in authority.

The pretty little researcher considered herself my equal, and while I admired her tenacity, she was most decidedly not on my level.

But she could be.

It'd been a long time since I'd considered the prospect of a progeny. However, Calina's spirit called to mine, her presence an alluring intoxication that I wanted to drown within.

She was strong. Tenacious. Stubborn. And most importantly, *strategic*.

In one conversation, I could discern all those qualities because she had presented herself as an open book. Not because she was naïve, but because she knew it was her best chance at survival.

And she'd tried to play me, maneuvering around the discussion like a clever champion.

My lips curled in amusement.

I wanted to indulge her and enjoy another round. But time was not on our side.

So I left Calina tied to the chair and went in search of Damien to give him an update on the server farm.

"Consider wisely," I'd told her before leaving the room. "I'll want a coherent response when I return."

I hadn't bothered to heal the wound on her breast. It would close on its own, something her intriguing genetics would hasten along.

Besides, I rather liked leaving my mark above her erect nipple. It was almost as though I'd claimed her as mine.

One bite to the neck. One to the tit. Perhaps my next sampling would be from her creamy thigh.

Yes, indeed, I mused, picturing the image clearly in my head.

"Are you drunk?" a deep voice demanded, giving me pause. "Or has old age impacted your eyesight?"

I glanced over my shoulder to find Ryder leaning against the wall with an arched eyebrow. "Am I meant to acknowledge you and bow?" I asked, avoiding his statement about my preoccupied state.

Because apparently I'd walked right by him without noticing.

I supposed that meant I no longer considered him a threat. Or perhaps my focus on more pleasurable avenues had distracted me from the lethal surroundings.

"It's my understanding that formalities at least require a greeting of some kind."

"I see," I replied. "Then, hello, Ryder. What a lovely surprise. What brings you to Damien's floor?"

His black eyes glimmered with deadly intent. "He mentioned prisoners and interrogation in his latest report. I think he meant to keep me apprised, but I took it as an invitation."

"We can't kill them," I said immediately, aware of Ryder's penchant for slaughtering first and asking questions later. That was how Lilith's head had ended up in a freezer. "They're proof of Lilith using immortals for her research."

"And we need three of them to accomplish that proof because…?"

"One captive was Lilith's lead researcher at the bunker. She's useful to us alive, and we need the other two doctors—who she seems to fancy as friends—to use as leverage to encourage her cooperation."

"And the little lycan pup my mate is falling in love with downstairs?" he pressed.

"A bargaining chip that makes the two doctors chatty," Damien drawled as he joined us in the hallway. "Or it was one until James overheard that comment with his lycan hearing." He gestured his chin toward the door he'd just come through. "Not soundproof. Which is interesting, considering Silvano's former use of these quarters. But I digress." He looked at me. "How'd it go with Dr. C.?"

"She's currently evaluating her options." I couldn't help my amused tone, something both males caught on to immediately.

"And those options include?" Damien asked.

"A server farm," I replied, effectively changing the topic away from my little game of verbal chess with Calina. "She claims that all her files were updated to it daily, and she can help us track the source as well."

"Or she can use our resources to send a message to the intended recipient of those files."

"Yes," I conceded. "But she sent that person shit files for a reason. She also broke protocol. As a result, I don't see her being very eager to reconnect with Lilith's former partner. Assuming she had one, I mean. That still remains unclear."

"Did she mention anyone of interest?" Ryder asked.

"Not yet," I admitted. "But I'll see if any photos jog her memory." Or, more accurately, I would see if she visually reacted to any photos. Because something told me a little bite wasn't enough to convince her to cooperate. And that was fine. I could do a lot worse and still make her enjoy at least part of it.

"All right, so these researchers have been experimenting on lycans and vampires for a century, some longer than that, and our solution is to keep them alive for show-and-tell later," Ryder summarized.

"So you did read my notes," Damien replied. "Good to know."

"Are you going to let the alliance members eat them after their testimonies?" Ryder asked, ignoring his new sovereign's side commentary. "Am I going to be stuck playing father to this pup for eternity? Because my mate won't let anyone kill him now. She's in love. And I'm not breaking her heart."

He pulled a device from his pocket and brought up a video of a pretty white wolf curled around a tiny ball of fur.

Damien grinned and clapped Ryder on the shoulder. "Congrats. You just became a dad. Want a hug?"

"No."

"Good." Damien dropped his hand and looked at me. "Tell me about the server farm."

"I can't. Calina hasn't agreed to help us yet."

His eyebrows rose. "Then why the fuck are you standing out here?"

I arched a brow, not at all appreciating his disrespectful tone.

He cleared his throat. "Sorry, King. Just excited by the prospect of playing in a server farm."

"Stop calling me *King* and I'll forgive you."

"But it has such a good ring to it," Ryder interjected, his tone deadpan.

I didn't bother to acknowledge the side commentary. "I'm giving Calina a few minutes to assess her options. In the interim, I intended to share the information with you so you can work with James or Gretchen to corroborate her claim."

"All right," Damien murmured. "I'll see what I can do."

"And I'll help," Ryder offered.

"No," I said immediately.

Ryder gaped at me. "Excuse me?" He actually sounded shocked, like no one had denied him before.

"When we need you to kill someone, we'll call you," I promised him. "But right now, these researchers need to remain alive and healthy. And frankly, I don't trust you to handle that."

"Frankly, I don't give a shit," he retorted.

"Ryder." I stepped into his path before he could head in Calina's direction. "These researchers might have information that will lead us to Cam. I will not jeopardize that."

"I still don't see how this ancient vampire is the key to solving all our problems," Ryder replied, his tone less cutting. "But I'll play along for Izzy."

Saying the female's name softened him a bit. As Damien's

maker, Ryder was very familiar with Izzy because she was Damien's sister.

And she also happened to be Cam's *Erosita*.

Her existence proved he was still alive, because his immortality was tied to her life. If he died, she'd die with him. Yet the human female hadn't aged a day in over a thousand years.

"Willow wants to know the pup's name and if he's ever been in his human form. Find out for me and I'll go back downstairs." Ryder spoke with a bored tone, but I caught the glimmer in his dark eyes. The old vampire was smitten.

"Love looks good on you," I said softly.

"And a crown would look good on you," he returned. "*King Jace*."

I refrained from rolling my eyes. Our bonding session had clearly reached an end point.

Without another word, I headed back down the hall toward Calina and her alluring scent.

Time for round two.

Your move, sweetheart.

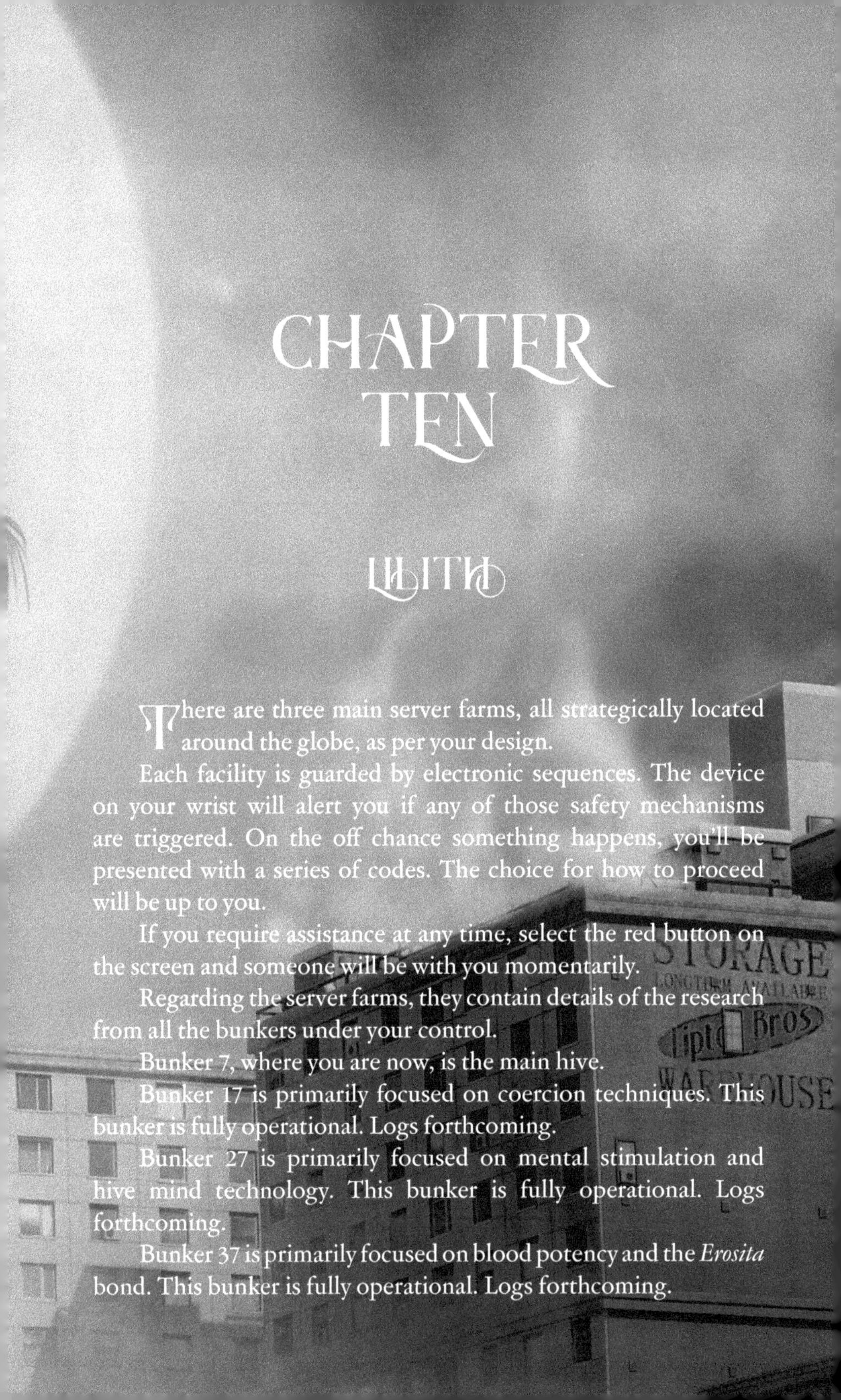

CHAPTER TEN

LILITH

There are three main server farms, all strategically located around the globe, as per your design.

Each facility is guarded by electronic sequences. The device on your wrist will alert you if any of those safety mechanisms are triggered. On the off chance something happens, you'll be presented with a series of codes. The choice for how to proceed will be up to you.

If you require assistance at any time, select the red button on the screen and someone will be with you momentarily.

Regarding the server farms, they contain details of the research from all the bunkers under your control.

Bunker 7, where you are now, is the main hive.

Bunker 17 is primarily focused on coercion techniques. This bunker is fully operational. Logs forthcoming.

Bunker 27 is primarily focused on mental stimulation and hive mind technology. This bunker is fully operational. Logs forthcoming.

Bunker 37 is primarily focused on blood potency and the *Erosita* bond. This bunker is fully operational. Logs forthcoming.

Bunker 47 was primarily focused on mortal longevity. If protocols ran appropriately, this bunker is now destroyed and you should be in possession of the requisite logs. If not, then a trip to the server farm is required.

Press the green arrow below to continue. Or press the red X for details on server farm locations.

Thank you for your selection. Your assistant will be with you momentarily.

End transmission.

CHAPTER ELEVEN

CALINA

My skin prickled with awareness as Jace returned, his regal energy a whiplash to my senses. He didn't look at me or speak, just wandered over to the bar again to fix himself another drink.

I watched as he bent, noting the way his black jeans molded to his thighs and backside. Vampires were always alluring creatures, their potency a seductive tool they used to lure their prey. My attraction to him was ingrained in my being, making it impossible to resist the masculine masterpiece before me. If he told me to kneel, I would, because my body would require it.

However, that didn't mean he could have my mind.

He straightened with something in his hand and started moving toward me. I met his gaze and held it, telling him without words that I didn't fear him. Lilith had attempted to beat unequivocal terror into me, but all her efforts did was prove to me how much I could take without breaking.

His palm twisted across the item in his hand, drawing my focus to the bottle. Then he pressed the rim to my lips, giving me a healthy dose of water. I hadn't even realized I was thirsty until

I started swallowing. The earlier sips of alcohol had left behind a burn in my throat that the water soon quenched, leaving me sighing and grateful for the refreshing liquid.

He said nothing, just carefully helped me drink until the bottle was empty. When I finished, he set it to the side and moved to stand behind me.

I resisted the urge to look back at him as his fingers found my shoulders. "Have you made a decision?" he asked, his voice a silky caress to my ears. "Will you work with me?"

He started massaging my stiff muscles, releasing the tension down my arms and sending shivers to my abdomen. I fought the impulse to moan, his touch hypnotic and knowing as he sought out my various pain points and applied just enough pressure to loosen the agonized joints.

I'd been tied to this chair for too long, my arms and legs unmoving.

But that enchanting touch made me feel alive, rejuvenated, *whole*.

"Or do you prefer we go about this the hard way?" he continued, his thumb digging into a pressure point on my neck, making me gasp in pain. "Say something, Calina," he murmured against my ear. "Or I'll be forced to guess at your resolve."

I trembled as he resumed his massage, my body immediately caving to his will. There was no question that he owned me now. But would I willingly cooperate?

"I need to know James and Gretchen are safe," I said on a gasp, jolting as he returned to the pressure point. "I won't help if they're hurt." The statement came out through clenched teeth, then I sighed as he tormented me with those delicious circles against my skin.

He wanted to break my mind, to make me outwardly submit even while I screamed inside. I could sense it in the way he handled me, his strategic movements marking him as a worthy opponent in this ring.

Just like Lilith.

She'd been a master strategist, too.

"They're fine," he replied. "And they'll remain that way if you cooperate."

Meaning he intended to keep them alive as leverage.

"I need them alive to testify, so I won't be setting them free. Which you should thank me for, Calina, because they would not survive this world without my guardianship." He nipped at my pulse, his palms sliding down my arms as though memorizing the feel of my skin. "And neither would you."

A quiver skated down my spine as his knuckles brushed the sides of my breasts, his heat at my back a comfort my body craved far more than my mind.

But I couldn't deny that I felt oddly protected in his embrace. And that was despite the very real threat of his teeth against my pulse.

"Work with me," he whispered. "Help me take down Lilith's empire."

I swallowed. "Is that your true goal?"

"Yes," he admitted softly. "I intend to burn everything she's created. But to do that, I need to find Cam. I also need to know who she was working with, where your files were headed, and what other logs might exist in the server farms, assuming they're even real."

"They're real."

"That'll be the first item I demand you prove."

"Just as seeing Gretchen and James will be my first request," I returned.

"You're not really in a position to be issuing commands, little strategist," he hummed. "But I'll grant you this one item, so long as you give me something in return."

"What do you want?"

"Your eyes." He kissed my neck and released me, the cool air an unexpected irritant against my flushed skin that sent a quiver through my body.

I suddenly felt bereft and cold, Jace's presence a blanket I didn't want to crave. But I couldn't fight my attraction. He was the superior being, the *predator*. As a human, I was predisposed to submit to the higher power.

And Jace was certainly *that*.

"I'll let you see Gretchen and James, but only after you prove your willingness to assist in my cause." He walked around to my front with a device in his hand. It reminded me of an old phone or a technical writing pad of some kind. But as he brought the item to life, I realized it was so much more than that.

Holograms of images filled the space between us, each one showing a face with a name and title beneath it. The one closest to me belonged to the male who had tied me to this chair.

Royal vampire. Jace Region.

"What is Jace Region?" I wondered out loud. "Or rather, where is it?" I knew Lilith had divided the world into different kingdoms for vampires and lycans to rule. But I didn't know the names or original locations.

"Northwestern United States," he answered, studying me. "Jace City is the upgraded version of San Francisco."

I blinked, then nodded. "Lilith took Chicago." I'd never actually confirmed that so much as guessed it based on images I'd seen behind Lilith whenever she'd video-chatted.

She'd purposely kept me in the dark about the new order because it weakened my ability to flee. Not that I'd ever truly had an option to run anyway.

And as Jace had pointed out, I probably wouldn't survive long in this reformed world. Or worse, I'd wish for death only to never experience it.

"Bunker 47 was in upstate Michigan," he murmured, still watching me.

"Thus confirming Lilith being in Chicago," I replied with a nod. "She would never be too far away."

"Indeed." He continued to observe me, then he flipped to a new image. "I want you to tell me if anyone is familiar to you. Someone you saw in the lab or talking to Lilith. Anything at all."

"I didn't meet many vampires or lycans outside of their cages," I warned him.

"If you've met even one, it'll help us determine our next steps." He looked me over once more and smiled. "You seem to appreciate knowledge, so I'll also define the region and clan territories for you as we go. For example, this is Kylan. His region includes British Columbia, Yukon, Alaska, that whole area. His state seat is in Vancouver."

I studied the handsome vampire royal on the screen, noting his dark eyes and matching hair. "I've never seen him before." He had the kind of face a female would remember. Just like Jace.

Jace dipped his chin and brought up the next vampire.

Claude. His region was in Canada as well, taking up Quebec, Newfoundland, Nova Scotia, and a few other northern areas. I didn't recognize him.

Silvano came next. Vampire. Deceased and replaced by Ryder. Their region included Texas, Mexico, and several Central American countries.

"We are actually in Costa Rica right now. San José, specifically."

"That explains the humidity," I replied, aware of our closeness to the equator and the heat renowned for this area of the world.

His icy gaze flickered with something I didn't catch. And he brought up the next image, returning us to the United States with Clemente Clan, the first lycan area. The wolves took up a lot of the south. Alpha Edon was in charge.

"I don't know him," I replied.

"Alpha Luka, Majestic Clan" flashed across the screen next, making me frown. I didn't recognize him so much as the name. "I've heard of that territory." But I couldn't say why.

"It's in the northern US. Montana, North Dakota, Wisconsin..." He trailed off, waiting for me to comment.

I searched for a memory and shook my head. "I'm not sure why it's familiar. We'll have to check the logs. Maybe one of the lycans came from there." Which would make sense, given the close proximity to Lilith's territory.

"Do the names Izzy or Ismerelda ring a bell?"

I repeated the names and shook my head again. "No."

His irises flickered again, then a new image popped up. Another lycan. Brandt. Calgary Clan. His territory name matched the general area in Canada with his land including Alberta, Saskatchewan, and other nearby provinces.

When Jace shifted to Europe, I asked about New York and the general northeastern US.

"All formerly owned by Lilith, I'm afraid," he murmured.

"Oh." I tried to gesture for him to continue, only to remember that my wrists were still tied to the chair.

Which was about the time I realized I could no longer feel my fingers because the restraints had cut off all my circulation.

Jace followed my gaze, the screens momentarily disappearing. "When was the last time you ate?"

I parted my lips to answer, then found my brow furrowing when I realized I had no idea. "Your blood?" I offered. It had rejuvenated me entirely, sating whatever hunger I could have possessed.

Although now that I was thinking about it, I could sense the subtle ache in my gut. Similar to how my throat had felt when he'd given me water.

Jace folded his arms as he considered me, his black sweater stretching across his chest.

"All right, little genius. I'm going to free you and feed you. But if you so much as attempt to escape, I will tie you to the bed and teach you a lesson you won't soon forget. Understood?"

Tie me to the bed, not the chair. A distinction I did not miss.

He pulled a knife from his pocket, sending a shiver through me. I parted my lips to confirm that I understood and didn't need a lesson to the contrary, but he was already moving, causing the words to stick to my suddenly dry throat.

Except all he did was sever the bind on my right wrist, and then my left one. I didn't move, my heart stuttering in my chest as he knelt to remove the ties against my ankles.

I couldn't feel anything.

Until suddenly I felt everything. His hands. His fingers. His hot touch skimming my calves up to my knees and eventually my thighs.

His icy orbs lifted to mine, his pupils dilating to display divine vampiric thirst. "Your blood…" He trailed off, not finishing the statement. But I knew what he'd intended to say.

I was created to be irresistible. A human with unique properties that couldn't easily be killed. Lilith's personal drug of choice.

"My essence was perfected by my host incubator," I whispered. "A rare blood type."

"A blood virgin."

"Similar," I replied, aware of the rate humans bred specifically to satiate those who could afford them. Lilith had run the whole Coventus organization that housed them, the money mostly going to her various funds—like Bunker 47.

I knew these things because she'd openly spoken about them

in front of me. Her hubris wouldn't have allowed her to foresee this situation. There had been no doubt in her mind that I would follow protocol by killing myself long before someone ever found me. And on the off chance I didn't, she'd very likely had a backup plan in place.

Only, she'd failed.

Because King Jace now had me in his clutches, and I wasn't all that inclined to keep Lilith's confidence.

This strategic game of negotiation was far more enlightening anyway.

"My blood is part lycan, part *Erosita*, and curated in an incubator of a rare human type that no longer exists. Your blood virgins are the genetically engineered replacements for a breed that died during the revolution."

"And you helped create such a thing?"

"No. Another lab specializes in blood types and the *Erosita* bond. I don't know much about it, but the server farm may have details on it."

"Was it destroyed like Bunker 47?"

"I doubt it," I replied. "But with Lilith, anything is possible."

"So you don't know how far the protocol went?"

"My duty was to manage and supervise Bunker 47. All information outside that lab was not under my jurisdiction."

"Then how do you know about the lab specializing in blood types?"

"Because I was born there before the revolution." I met his gaze. "And I know of its most recent purpose because Lilith often enjoyed telling me about her victories. She did it to make me feel like a failure for not working faster. But our labs were very different, so I never took it personally." A fact that used to drive her to violence.

"How old are you?" he asked softly, his fingertips grazing the top of my thighs as he stared up at me from his kneeling position.

I gave him my birth year in pre-revolution terms. "I think that makes me close to a hundred and thirty-nine or a hundred and forty. But I stopped aging around twenty-two."

"Because of your lycan genetics."

"And the *Erosita* manipulation, yes."

He frowned. "Are you mated to a vampire?"

"Not really." I considered how to explain my ties to immortality. "My father was an *Erosita*. But that wasn't enough to tie me to the soulmate bond between human and vampire. My birth was a test and part of Lilith's goal to secure immortality without the requirements associated with the *Erosita* connection."

"Hmm, that explains why her political platform has pushed to have *Erositas* discredited rather than revered. But that doesn't tell me how you're immortal without a mate bond."

"The *Erosita* link exists in the same section of the brain to the lycan hive mind. Lilith's researchers have been exploring that part of the mind for almost two hundred years. A part of it was inserted into my psyche during my creation."

He cocked his head. "So you're a successful case—a tasty blood bag that can't die."

A crude description, but an accurate one. "To you, yes. But not to Lilith."

His nostrils flared. "What flaw did she perceive?"

"The one that caused her to feel possessive over me." My fingers started to tingle, the blood finally returning to my extremities. "It's why she kept me away from my other links to immortality."

"You have more than one… mate?"

"I consider them links, not mates. But yes. I have at least three. One was to Lilith, and as I'm still alive, I can only imagine my other two links are in a similar state."

"Who are they?" he demanded.

"Lilith never told me, so I don't know." I held his gaze, deciding to give a subtle hint of leverage that would ensure my cooperation. "The logs were never ones I could access. But maybe I can find them at the server farms."

His expression softened, his eyes twinkling with amusement. "You're giving me a reason to trust your cooperation."

"I am."

"Hmm." He started a slow perusal down my body, his palms flattening on my thighs. "You're also providing a potential lead because whoever is linked to you was obviously working with Lilith."

"Yes."

"Clever," he murmured, placing a kiss on the inside of my knee. It was decidedly intimate, what with his position between my spread legs.

I shivered as his touch shifted upward, his mouth tracing a path directly to my femoral artery.

"If Lilith was possessive, then I imagine she never shared you," he said softly, his icy eyes flicking up to mine. "Yes?"

I swallowed but forced myself to nod. "She threatened it but never followed through." Something I learned long ago, which helped me not to fear those particular taunts.

However, she wasn't here now.

And I had no idea what to expect from the powerful vampire kneeling before me.

"Does that mean you're untouched?" he asked, his focus lowering to the apex between my thighs.

"I was used once," I told him. "Just to test the immortality bonds."

"So it was by someone you weren't linked to?"

"Yes, a lycan lab subject," I replied, my stomach churning at the memory of the experience.

It had occurred on my thirtieth birthday. I'd had to give blood and other bodily samples annually to test myself for signs of aging or any other changes to my growth patterns. When my statistics had remained exactly the same for a decade, Lilith had been satisfied and never put me through the trial again.

"She killed the lycan afterward, then beat me for making her react that way," I added, recalling the incident with astute clarity because it often haunted my dreams.

The experience had been worse than the lycan's rut.

"I actually died." My flat tone lacked the emotions I'd experienced that day. "But the links to immortality brought me back… slowly."

A final test.

One I'd unfortunately passed.

Shaking my head, I met his gaze once more. "That was the only time Lilith allowed anyone else to touch me. Apart from her."

His eyebrow rose, and I suspected he wanted to ask me what I meant by that. But he didn't push it. And a part of me was glad. He could guess what I meant. There was no reason to go through Lilith's brutal feeding habits in detail.

Besides, if we found the logs, he'd know everything then.

He pressed another kiss, this one to my inner thigh, then he fluidly stood and walked over to a panel near the door. I couldn't see what he did to call the device to life, but I heard the female's voice purr over the intercom. "Good evening, My Prince."

"Hello, kitten," he replied, his voice holding a warm touch to it. "I was wondering if you could help me with a meal. For a human."

"Of course, My Prince. Any preferences?"

He glanced at me. "Any cravings, little genius?"

I blinked at him. "Cravings?" Why would one crave food? It existed as a nutrient for life and nothing more.

His lips curled into a devious grin. "Grab a pen, Tracey. I'm about to give you a list."

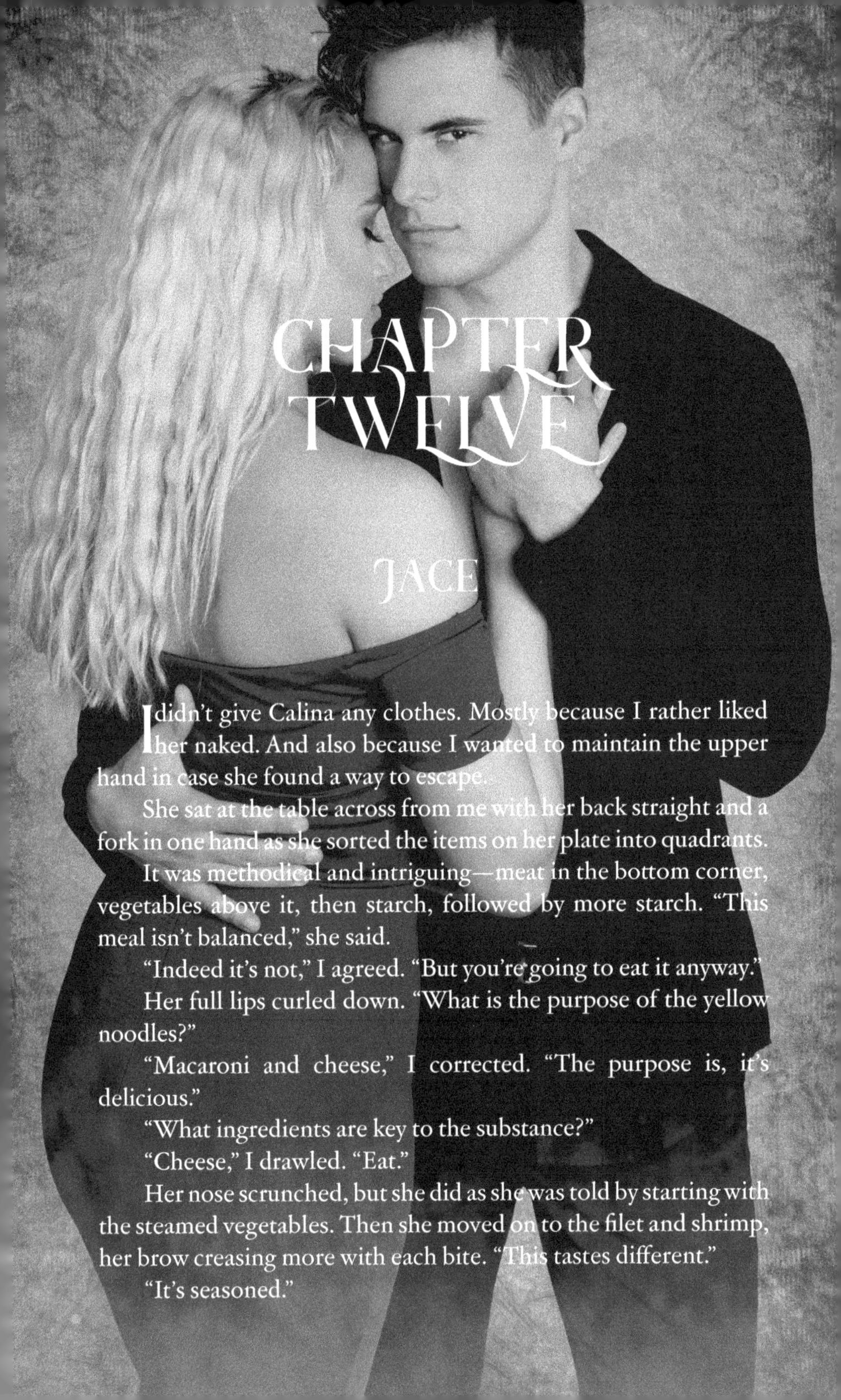

CHAPTER TWELVE

JACE

I didn't give Calina any clothes. Mostly because I rather liked her naked. And also because I wanted to maintain the upper hand in case she found a way to escape.

She sat at the table across from me with her back straight and a fork in one hand as she sorted the items on her plate into quadrants.

It was methodical and intriguing—meat in the bottom corner, vegetables above it, then starch, followed by more starch. "This meal isn't balanced," she said.

"Indeed it's not," I agreed. "But you're going to eat it anyway."

Her full lips curled down. "What is the purpose of the yellow noodles?"

"Macaroni and cheese," I corrected. "The purpose is, it's delicious."

"What ingredients are key to the substance?"

"Cheese," I drawled. "Eat."

Her nose scrunched, but she did as she was told by starting with the steamed vegetables. Then she moved on to the filet and shrimp, her brow creasing more with each bite. "This tastes different."

"It's seasoned."

"With what?"

"Does it matter?"

"I'm trying to discern the intended results of such things."

"Taste," I told her. "It's all about *taste*."

"And this?" She pointed to the white substance on her plate.

"Mashed potatoes. Very healthy for the soul."

Her expression told me that she disagreed, but she ate the substance anyway. I had several other dishes, including a variety of desserts, waiting in the kitchen. However, her cheeks looked a bit green by the end of her first plate, so I decided not to push more her way.

Lilith had obsessed over a certain look for humans, which meant providing a strict diet to mortal beings all throughout their lives. Yet Calina wasn't human at all, so the same shouldn't have applied to her.

"May I use the bathroom?" she asked.

I nodded and gestured to the en-suite facilities off the side of the bedroom. There was no exit point from there, so I didn't feel the need to supervise.

She excused herself without a word.

I took the opportunity to clean up the table and the kitchen, putting the leftovers in the fridge to be enjoyed later. Calina hadn't returned by the time I finished, making me pause to listen for her.

Silence.

Frowning, I went to the bathroom and found her on the floor in a ball of misery.

Fuck.

She'd clearly relinquished most of the contents of her stomach, but that hadn't quelled her pain.

"You're not used to decadence," I said softly, sighing. "I thought you would be able to handle it with your immortal genetics, but it appears I was very wrong."

Apologizing wouldn't help the situation. She needed comfort, and I'd promised her that so long as she cooperated, and thus far, she seemed accommodating in terms of giving me information.

I moved to the walk-in shower to ignite the warm sprays from above. "A little water therapy will help," I told her.

She responded by curling tighter into a ball and mumbled a

response that sounded a lot like, *Leave me alone*. Poor Calina appeared fragile and small on the floor, my feisty genius disappearing behind a mortal shell that could so easily shatter beneath my touch.

That just wouldn't do.

I evaluated her and our surroundings, then stripped down to my boxer shorts.

She peeked up at me, her cheeks ghostly pale.

"Hmm," I hummed, crouching before her. "Here." I bit my wrist and held it to her lips. "Drink."

Her nose scrunched, similar to how she'd reacted to dinner.

"That was an order, Doctor," I added, my tone holding a hint of demand. "I don't offer my blood to just anyone. And it would be unwise to refuse me."

I knew the last thing she probably wanted to do was swallow, but my blood would cure her nausea quickly and efficiently. Then I could bathe the stench off her and take her to bed. Not to fuck, but to sleep. I'd been awake for nearly two damn days, and I wasn't in the mood to stay up for a round of hot Costa Rican sunshine.

Her lips parted, and I took that as a sign to press my wrist to her mouth. She stroked my skin with her tongue and paused as she found the idents my teeth had made.

Then she began to suck, and fuck if it wasn't the most erotic sight of my life.

Maybe it was her alluring scent or my current frame of mind or the fact that this female had given me my first enticing challenge in over a century, but watching her feed had me hard as a damn rock almost instantly.

I was enraptured by her. Utterly captivated. Lost to the little mewl of content she released as her throat worked.

Her eyes fell closed, her cheeks darkening to a pretty pink shade.

I didn't tell her to stop. I should. I *would*. But not yet. *Just one more moment*, I thought, my opposite hand going to her hair to draw my fingers through her soft strands. Only, the blonde strands were tangled, confirming her need for a shower and drawing my focus to the water falling only a few feet away.

Pulling my wrist from her mouth, I scooped her up into my arms and carried her to the tiled interior.

Her hazel irises were more green than blue now as she stared up at me in obvious confusion. Rather than comment, I set her on the bench and took hold of one of the movable showerheads. The other two pelted my back with hot liquid as I used the third to dampen her hair.

She said nothing, just watched me.

When I finished wetting her strands, I handed her the showerhead and grabbed a bottle off the ledge.

She angled the water at herself but didn't move much, her focus entirely on me and my fingers as I massaged a generous amount of shampoo into her hair.

When I lowered my palms, she washed them. Then I took the sprayer from her to rinse the suds from her head.

We repeated the actions with the conditioner.

"Stand," I told her when I finished, aware that my blood had more than cured her momentary nausea.

She obeyed.

I returned the showerhead to its hook in the wall and picked up a bar of soap.

Her pupils flared as I began to lather the object against her arm. Then her shoulder, her clavicle, and her opposite arm.

I waited for her to say something, to voice one of the many questions roaming through her gaze, but all she did was stay absolutely still as I caressed her skin.

"You're allowed to speak," I said, my touch returning to her collarbone before venturing down to her sternum and lower to her belly.

She shivered, her nipples beading into beautiful rosy buds. I avoided them with the soap, painting her entire abdomen in suds and moving to her sides.

Her hip bones were next, followed by her thighs, knees, and calves. And on my way back up, I focused on the trimmed blonde hairs of her feminine mound.

"You're aroused," I whispered, smelling her desire and seeing the glistening proof on her pretty pink folds. It made my mouth ache for a bite. Mmm, maybe I would fuck her tonight after all.

"I'm being caressed by an apex predator with seductive properties meant to ensnare prey. Of course I'm aroused."

Her flat tone drew my attention away from her pussy and up to her face. She spoke as though this attraction between us was standard, like any other vampire could stir a similar reaction from her flesh.

I stood with my hand still against her mound, my fingertip gliding downward to gently tease her clit. She jolted, a subtle hiss leaving her lips.

"And that?" I asked. "Is it just another one of my seductive properties?"

"Yes." No emotion. No elaboration. Just a straight confirmation that she believed this all to be a result of my vampire heritage and nothing else.

"That's naïve," I said, circling her sensitive bud with a precision cultivated in over three thousand years of experience. "Not all vampires excel in the art of sex."

"They don't have to," she returned. "Humans naturally bow, making sexual skill a moot point."

"You don't bow," I pointed out.

"You haven't asked me to."

I nearly told her to now, the desire to teach her mouth a lesson with my cock growing exponentially with each passing second.

But I decided another lesson would be more prudent in our situation.

I returned the bar of soap to its holder and rinsed my hands beneath the spray.

Then I walked Calina backward into the tiled wall.

Her hazel eyes flickered with uncertainty, yet she held my gaze even as I slid a thigh between hers. I caged her in with my body, my palms claiming her hips.

She trembled.

I smiled.

"You believe seduction is a key principle in hunting prey, that it's only natural for you to feel aroused in my presence because of what I am, not *who* I am. Correct?"

"Yes." The confirmation came out on a soft exhale that I felt against my chin.

"What about pleasure?" I wondered. "Do humans only experience it as a *natural* reaction to the predator's prowess?"

Her brow furrowed. "Do you mean during death?"

Such a telling reply, one that had me tightening my grip on her. "Is that the only time a human feels pleasure when in the company of a superior being?"

"The point is to enrapture the prey. So I suppose a certain amount of endorphins are involved in the process."

"Is that what you feel now?" I asked, my lips skimming her cheek as I kissed a path to her ear. "A certain amount of endorphins?"

"I… I feel… yes."

"Hmm," I hummed, intrigued by her interpretation of her body's reactions. It was a practical assessment that suggested she'd never truly experienced the thrall of passion.

Not surprising, given what she'd told me about her single sexual encounter.

Which made this experiment with her all the more fun.

However, I had to define just a few more parameters before we could truly begin. As a scientist, she would appreciate having the facts straight in her thoughts. That way, when I blew her mind, she'd feel the full force of that explosion.

"Did you come while the lycan fucked you in the lab?" I asked. It was a crude question, but Calina didn't react with emotions. She appeared to prefer science and reason over feelings and sensibilities.

And she didn't hesitate now. "No."

"What about with Lilith? Did she ever make you come?" I pressed, my teeth grazing her earlobe as my pulse quickened at the thought. The notion of Lilith using Calina didn't particularly appeal to me. And that wasn't a result of it involving Lilith so much as Calina.

An odd revelation, considering I hardly knew the female.

Yet, I felt miraculously possessive of her.

Was that a result of her existence? She'd already mentioned that Lilith had felt similarly. Perhaps it was something to do with her creation in the lab?

"Of course not," she replied, confirming Lilith had never given her an orgasm. "My gratification served no purpose during her feeding sessions. She only desired my submission and pain."

"Which is what you think is happening here now, that I'm applying my sensual power over you to encourage you to yield."

Her throat worked against my lips, her quiver a palpable sensation I felt shivering across my own skin. "Y-yes?"

"You don't sound very sure," I murmured against her throbbing vein as I flexed my thigh between her legs. "That's okay, little genius. I'll help you see the light in just a few minutes."

"Light?"

I drew my teeth upward to return my lips to her ear. "Yes, sweet strategist. *Light*." I slid my palm up her side to her breast, my thumb circling one erect nipple. "It's true that vampires and lycans are sexual beings. We can captivate our prey and subdue them with ease. But there's so much more to the equation, Doctor."

My opposite hand left her hip to glide along her lower abdomen to the short blonde hairs of her sex.

"Our preferences and skills all vary," I continued against her ear, my thumb and forefinger pinching her nipple and drawing a soft moan from her lips. "So it's not about what we are, darling genius." I slid my fingers downward into her slick heat. "It's about *who* we are."

She shook as I explored her folds, my thumb finding that soft center to give her the friction she craved. Another moan left her mouth, and this one sounded almost strangled, like she was fighting her body's reaction to my touch.

It caused my lips to curl. "Sweet girl," I whispered, nibbling on her earlobe. "I'm not just any vampire. I'm a fucking *king*. And you're about to find out why."

I speared her with two fingers while my thumb continued to stroke her sensitive flesh. She cried out in response, making me grin even more.

And I gave in to the impulse to bite.

My fangs punctured her pretty little throat, piercing her vein with ease and sending her over the edge into a climax that had her gasping in surprise.

She grabbed my arms, holding on for dear life as her body spasmed endlessly against mine. Almost as though all her decades of denied pleasure culminated in a single moment with her tight sheath squeezing the shit out of my fingers.

I didn't let up, spurring her onward with strokes against her clit, pumping my fingers into her channel, and stroking that spot deep inside that drove women mad with desire.

She screamed, her nails digging into my skin as she fell into another intense climax.

Her blood against my tongue made me growl, my desire to drink her dry an overwhelming craving inside my mind. But I held on to my sanity, enjoying her taste while playing her body to perfection.

My name left her mouth, a plea in her tone, but hearing her call me Jace just encouraged me to continue.

More sucking.

More petting.

Little pinches to her abused nipple before switching breasts and hands.

Caressing her inside with my fingers once more.

Teasing her clit.

Pushing her into a rapturous spiral that redefined her reality. Tears touched her cheeks. Her lips parted soundlessly. Her body became liquid in my hands.

And she convulsed again.

I only drank enough to keep her in this euphoric state, my goal to show her the true power of a vampire with restraint.

It was a well-learned lesson. One I didn't stop delivering until she came so hard and for so long that she passed out against me.

Only then did I slowly release her neck, careful not to rip her skin, and lift her into my arms for support. I kissed the top of her head, finished washing the two of us off, and wrapped her in a large cotton towel.

Her eyelids eventually lifted to showcase pupil-blown eyes, her hazel rims thin around the black.

"I look forward to hearing more on your analysis of my kind in the evening, Doctor," I told her softly as I carried her to the bed. "And I expect that orgasmic experience to be fully detailed in your report."

CHAPTER THIRTEEN

LILITH

Server farm protocol engaged.

Your team will be deployed to retrieve the necessary files in twenty-four hours.

Press the green arrow to continue reviewing the logs.

Next log to commence in three, two…

Log year one. Day one.

Hello, my liege, and welcome to the new era. I've compiled these annual logs for you to observe the progression of your plan. I hope these prove helpful in the unfortunate event of my death.

Now let's begin.

Ninety percent of the human race has been exterminated, as per your suggestion.

Five hundred thousand humans were hand-selected to begin the breeding process. Their blood types should prove fruitful for future generations. Another one hundred thousand were put in the reserves to be tested for viability.

All children and youth under eighteen have been enrolled in the university system, with the exception of the weak, who were given to royals that enjoy the rich flavor presented in a child's vein.

The rest of the human race has been divided by region, giving every royal and alpha an equal number of mortals for city operations. Most will likely be used as food sources, but others who prove more useful will be put to service in harems, gratification chambers, general service needs, lycan breeding, moon chases or other immortal pastimes, and so forth.

Blood Day proceedings are almost finalized with the Magistrate having been voted upon by the lycan side of the alliance. We will commence the first Blood Day ceremony one year from today. Humans will fight for their right to join our ranks. Only one lycan and one vampire will be selected.

All of this is by your design. I only hope I can live up to your expectations while you rest.

Sleep well, my king.

I will alert you when it is time to rise.

Press the green arrow to proceed to the next sequenced log.

End transmission.

CHAPTER FOURTEEN

CALINA

My body tingled, my skin hot and sensitive.

It was uncomfortable. Yet, not.

I frowned, uncertain of how I truly felt. *Rejuvenated. Lighter than air. Dreamlike.*

The sensations were foreign.

As was the warm male blanket behind me.

Lips ghosted over my neck, sending a shiver down my spine. "Hello, Doctor. How are you feeling? Gratified, perhaps?"

My eyelids lifted, the windows before me displaying a setting sun. I couldn't remember falling asleep.

Actually…

My lips parted.

Oh…

My thighs clenched as the memories of what had knocked me out came tumbling back into my mind.

Gratified was an understatement.

Jace had sent me into a whirlpool of ecstasy that had almost felt unreal. And he'd ended our time together with a comment about giving him a full report.

A full report of what? I wondered, unable to recall what else he'd said.

Probably something about the vampiric ability to subdue prey—a fact he'd more than proven in the shower. Because I would have done anything to continue feeling like that in his arms.

His mouth sealed over my pulse, his teeth touching my skin.

My heart skipped a beat as he pierced my vein with effortless ease, like my throat was his to claim. He growled, the predator in him reveling in my taste.

Then his palm skimmed my hip on his way to the apex between my thighs.

I waited with bated breath to feel that erotic touch, and he didn't disappoint, his finger sliding between my folds and drawing exquisite pleasure from my flesh.

It felt like a dream. It probably was one. A fantasy I never knew I desired. But oh, how I desired it now.

This vampire was dangerous. He'd taken over my thoughts. Consumed me. Derailed my focus. Possessed me in a manner so foreign that I wasn't sure how to fight him.

Predator, my mind whispered. *Apex predator*.

I knew this.

Yet I succumbed to his touch anyway.

Maybe because I'd never experienced anything like this. Lilith's hands were tools she'd used to hurt me and others.

Jace… his hands… they were *addictive*.

His mouth worked against my throat, but not harshly. It was just like in the shower, where he'd drunk in slow, measured motions.

Unlike the way he'd struck me in Bunker 47.

Why? I wanted to ask. *Why are you doing this?*

But my lips refused me.

And in the next moment, I was moaning out a release that pulsated through every ounce of my being. I felt him grin into my neck, his teeth no longer embedded in my skin.

"Why?" I rasped, trying to recall the exact phrasing of my question, my body on fire and trembling violently.

"Why?" he repeated against my ear. "Why am I giving you pleasure?"

I tried to nod but found myself too blissed out to move

properly. He must have sensed me trying because his smile grew.

"There is nothing I enjoy more in this world than hearing a woman moan like that upon waking up," he murmured, kissing the space right below my ear. "Did it help in your analysis?"

I blinked. "Analysis?"

"Yes, the one tied to your theory about your arousal." He nudged me onto my back and went to his elbow beside me, his icy blue eyes glittering with amusement as he stared down at me. "You stated last night that your arousal is a result of me being a vampire. Remember?"

This time my neck worked a little, allowing me to dip my chin. Because yes, I recalled the statement. However, I didn't understand why that caused him to be so… so… I couldn't find the word. Kind, maybe? Nice? Attentive? *Interested*? He'd already subdued me, yet he'd barely taken any blood from my vein.

What was the point?

"Has our experiment proven that theory correct?" he asked, drawing me back to our conversation. "Or do you wish to revise your assessment?"

Experiment? I thought, frowning. *Is that what this is? An experiment?* "Why?"

He studied me. "I disagree with your hypothesis and intend to prove it false."

"But why?" Why did such a trivial thing matter to him? I was beneath him. My opinion shouldn't matter. Lilith had never cared for anything I'd had to say unless it'd been in regard to a scientific finding. And even then, she'd hardly accepted my word at face value. I'd had to prove it through a brand-new test while she'd observed.

His palm drifted from my lower belly up to the side of my face, cupping my cheek. "Because I find it offensive that you think the only reason you're turned on by my presence is because I'm a vampire. That may play into it, but the rest is all me."

"So it's about your arrogance as a male," I translated.

He leaned down to press his lips to the corner of my mouth. "No, Doctor. It's about your ignorance as an inexperienced human." He nuzzled my nose and sat up. "We'll reassess later. Right now, I need you properly fed and alert." Rolling off the bed, he held out a hand for me. "Come, little genius. It's time for you to prove your worth once more."

We took another shower together, this time without the pleasurable ending. But he'd lost his boxers, allowing me to see every inch of his masculine form.

Perfection was an understatement.

I expected him to guide my hand or mouth to the protruding part of his body, but all he did was give it a few lazy strokes with a soapy hand and finished lathering off the rest of his sculpted form. Then he rinsed and repeated the actions against my skin.

Afterward, he wrapped a white towel low around his waist, allowing the water droplets to cling to his upper body and thick, dark hair.

Then he swathed me in a similar fashion and tugged me into the dining area of the suite. Two plates of eggs waited for us. Mine had tomatoes, onions, and peppers cooked into the scrambled mess. It was much less decadent than our last meal, allowing me to properly digest it.

His eggs were slathered in some sort of yolk-colored gravy and layered over slices of ham.

Eggs Benedict, he'd called it.

My stomach had twisted at the sight, denying his offering of a taste.

Afterward, he dressed in a pair of black slacks and a dark button-down shirt. Then he handed me a white button-down and instructed me to wear it like a dress. I did, the fabric touching my thighs, and followed him barefoot out of the suite.

We didn't walk far, only going a few doors down and into a similar space with a living area, a dining table, a kitchen, and a bedroom off to the side.

Maybe this entire floor was made of single-suite residences.

"Well, it's about fucking time you emerged," a deep voice drawled as the vampire with dark hair and caramel-colored eyes walked into the room.

He wore a pair of dark pants and nothing else. Behind him was the female—*Tracey*—who had delivered all the decadent food earlier. She curtsied to Jace the same way she had greeted him then. He kissed her on the cheek, also similar to their previous embrace, but this time my stomach flipped at the sight.

I frowned, not understanding the reaction.

"Calina required a lesson in respect," Jace murmured. "She understands better now."

My frown deepened. "I had no idea vampires suffered from fragile egos." The words left my mouth before I could catch them.

Jace faced me, his eyebrows rising to his hairline. "What did you just say to me?"

Well, now that I'd spoken my mind, I might as well keep going. "Vampires are supposed to have excellent hearing, but I suppose I shouldn't be surprised by your defect, considering everything else."

The vampire with light brown eyes whistled, then looked at Tracey. "Scurry away, kitten. I don't want you drenched in another human's blood."

She gave me a look of dismay, then left the suite with abundant haste.

I met Jace's seething gaze and debated apologizing. But I wasn't quite sure how to phrase it because my statements weren't necessarily wrong. He didn't act at all like a normal vampire. And his penchant for testing *theories* confused me as well.

The door opened again almost immediately with a third vampire stepping into the room, his presence regal and alarmingly familiar to Jace. A female with pale features framed with dark hair followed him.

Human, I realized immediately. The way she clung to the suit-clad male told me she belonged to him, too.

He took one look at the scene and arched a dark brow, his sharp green eyes intense. "Did I miss something important? Your little mouse practically ran down the hall on my way here, barely bowing as I passed."

"Calina was just in the process of insulting King Jace," the one with the Southern accent informed him, folding his arms. "Said he's *defective*."

That wasn't exactly what I'd said, but close enough to the truth.

Jace *was* defective for a vampire. He didn't do anything like I anticipated, and he'd wasted time trying to prove his male prowess instead of interrogating me.

Unless that'd been his method of persuasion, a way to convince me to cooperate. In which case, he should have used his leverage when he had it.

He caught my chin between his thumb and forefinger, his silver-blue eyes burning into mine. "Did you speak to Lilith in this manner?" he queried, his tone lethally calm.

I swallowed, his mentioning of my previous master reminding me just who stood before me. He owned me now, and I'd insulted him. It hadn't been intentional, my observation one I voiced without much thought. Would I have done that to Lilith? "No." Because I'd feared her retaliation.

Jace didn't evoke the same reaction from me. *Why is that?* I wondered.

"Yet you openly disrespect me in front of others. Why?" He maintained that silky tone, sending a shiver down my spine.

Lilith's anger had been an inferno, exploding without warning and destroying everything and everyone in her path.

Jace's fury reminded me of an unsuspecting wave, the kind that swelled imperceptibly and took the victim under with a crash of power.

And I'd ignited the slow swirl of water, building it into a crescendo that would swallow me whole if I didn't make amends quickly.

However, I couldn't seem to form the words, an apology impossible. He confused me too greatly. "I don't understand you," I sputtered out instead. "You don't do anything as expected."

His eyebrows rose. "And what do you consider to be expected?"

"Orders. Tasks. Questions." *Not feeding me decadent meals and bathing me after I expel my meal,* I thought but didn't say. "Lilith requested reports. I gave them. She fed. I died. Then I woke up to repeat the process until she returned once more." That was my life. My purpose. My ritual. And all of it had gone to hell over the last few days, between the protocols and his unanticipated arrival.

My world no longer made sense.

"I want to see James and Gretchen," I added, needing normalcy. "Please."

He observed me for a long moment, then glanced at the Southern vampire. "Bring up a live feed for her."

I didn't take my eyes off Jace; I couldn't. He gripped me too tightly to allow deviation in my line of sight, and the clench of his jaw told me he wasn't about to release me anytime soon. I'd struck a nerve. But some of the flames had left his irises as he slowly returned his eyes to mine.

"Tell me about the server farms," he demanded.

I swallowed again, then told him everything I knew. Just speaking the words out loud helped me feel grounded, reminding me of my purpose in this world and helping me to feel more comfortable in my own skin.

His magic touch had unnerved me.

But speaking about the reports and the systems calmed me.

I even went as far as to tell him about the backdoor access I'd created for myself, explaining how that had allowed me to circumvent some of the features within Bunker 47's systems to override surveillance feeds and access my files.

"The back door was through that connection to the server farm," I concluded.

His expression hadn't changed, his cheekbones still regal and flared from his jaw clenching.

"I suddenly understand your delay," the Southern vampire drawled. "She's magnificent."

"Indeed," Jace replied, the word curt and short. Then he tilted my head, allowing me to see a screen that the other vampire held up. "James and Gretchen," he added flatly, defining the sight before me.

They were in a room without windows, pacing around the furniture.

Untouched food was on the table, and I could tell Gretchen had been crying.

"Where's their son?" I asked, searching the screen.

"He wasn't part of your negotiation," Jace pointed out, drawing my gaze back to him with his hand still on my chin.

My eyes narrowed. "Did you hurt him?"

"Is it your right to know?"

No, but... "If you want me to divulge the location of the server farm, then yes."

"Do you know the location?" he countered.

"I know how to find it." Considering all my back-end logic was tied to the server farm, it wouldn't be hard to do. And his vampire friend with the Southern drawl seemed to have access to some top-end technology. That was the only way to explain his ability to track my original signal. "Give them back their child, and I'll find your server farm."

"Find the server farm, and I'll consider your request," he returned, his grip tightening. "Don't find the server farm, and I'll kill the pup while you watch."

My heart skipped a beat, the flat way he spoke about such violence making my stomach twist. "He's a lycan."

"He's an abomination created in a lab," he returned. "Just like you. The only difference is, you're useful. He's not. Make your choice, Doctor."

And he claimed to be different from Lilith.

I supposed he was in a way. She would have killed little Petri—Gretchen and James's son—while issuing her demand. Just to watch the pup bleed. Maybe even enjoyed him as a snack.

Meanwhile, Jace held his life over my head as a bargaining chip.

As far as negotiating tactics went, his were more on point. Lilith had governed out of fear. Jace used strategic maneuvering to obtain what he wanted.

"I need a computer," I told him. "And access to a network."

"You'll be supervised," he said, his grip unyielding. "Don't fail me, Calina, or you'll regret it." With that, he released me. "Damien."

The Southern vampire, who I assumed was named Damien, smiled. It strengthened his features, giving him a handsome appeal. He also had ink down one of his arms, the tattoo swirls depicting an ancient pattern that had me questioning his origin. But I knew better than to ask. Instead, I met his gaze and waited.

"My turn to play?" he asked, sounding amused by the prospect.

"Within reason," Jace replied, causing the other man to glance up at him.

"Limits?"

"Yes. Similar to your kitten."

"Interesting," Damien murmured, looking me over. "Well, let's get started."

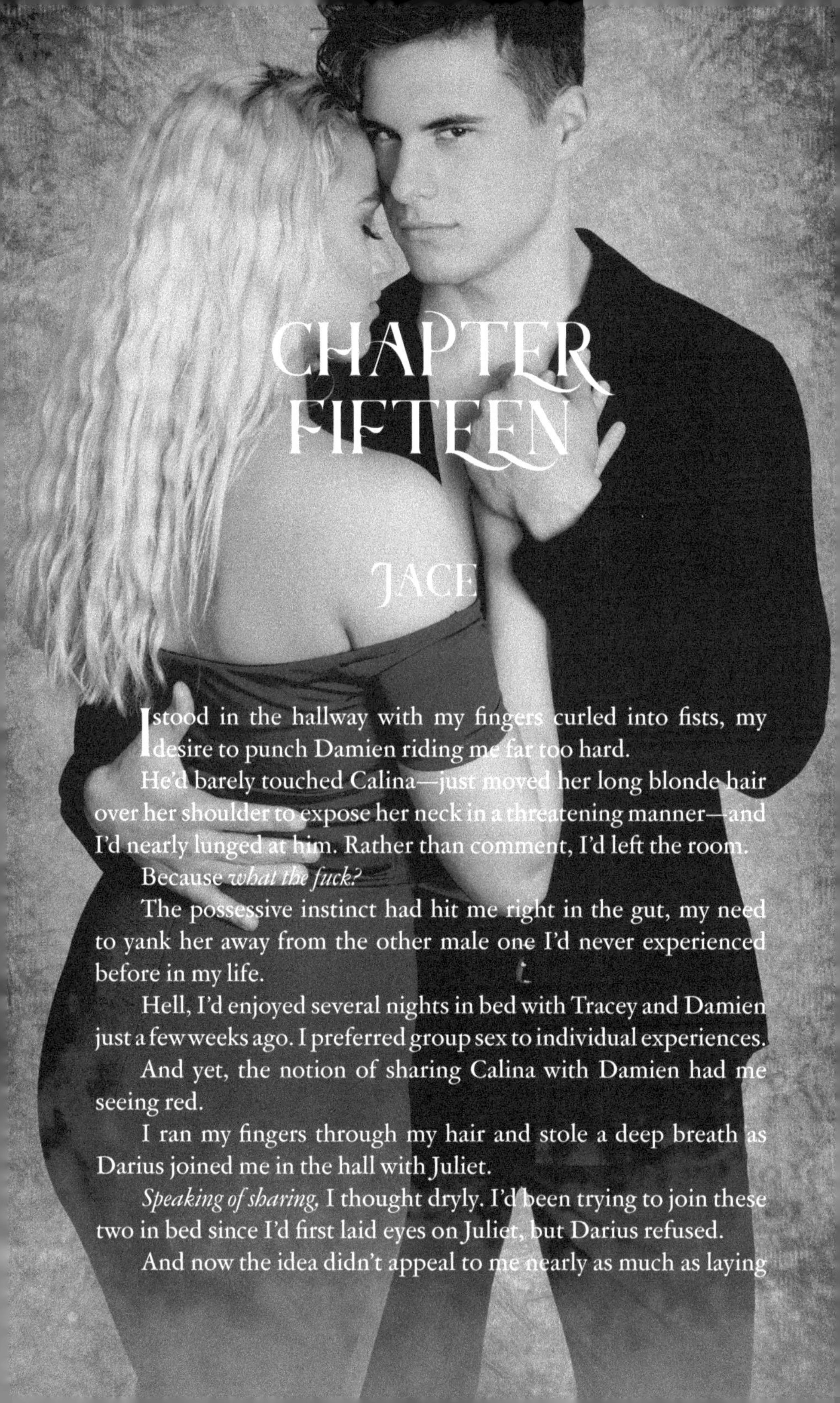

CHAPTER FIFTEEN

JACE

I stood in the hallway with my fingers curled into fists, my desire to punch Damien riding me far too hard.

He'd barely touched Calina—just moved her long blonde hair over her shoulder to expose her neck in a threatening manner—and I'd nearly lunged at him. Rather than comment, I'd left the room.

Because *what the fuck?*

The possessive instinct had hit me right in the gut, my need to yank her away from the other male one I'd never experienced before in my life.

Hell, I'd enjoyed several nights in bed with Tracey and Damien just a few weeks ago. I preferred group sex to individual experiences.

And yet, the notion of sharing Calina with Damien had me seeing red.

I ran my fingers through my hair and stole a deep breath as Darius joined me in the hall with Juliet.

Speaking of sharing, I thought dryly. I'd been trying to join these two in bed since I'd first laid eyes on Juliet, but Darius refused.

And now the idea didn't appeal to me nearly as much as laying

Calina over the counter and fucking her disobedient ass into submission.

This female is making me lose my mind, I decided. *It's her scent. That mouthwatering blood-virgin-like aroma.*

My focus went to Juliet, my nostrils flaring.

Usually, her blood sang to me.

But not right now.

Fuck.

I started pacing as Darius watched with an arched eyebrow. "She really pissed you off, didn't she?"

"It's so much more than that," I snapped back at him, both my hands going to my hair now as I fought for self-control.

I don't even know this woman.

She's a means to an end.

She fucking thinks I'm defective.

I growled at that last thought, my desire to stomp back in there and show her just how wrong she was taking over my ability to process anything else.

But Darius stepped into my path, his expression hard. "She's already helping Damien find the server farm. Let her work, then you can kill her."

"Kill her?" I scoffed at the notion. "Oh, I'm not going to kill her. I'm going to fuck the disrespect right out of her. Then I'm going to feed from her until she begs me to stop. Or maybe I'll do both at the same time."

Darius grabbed my shoulder, but a resounding *ding* cut off whatever he'd intended to say, and Ryder stepped into the hallway in a pair of jeans and a T-shirt.

"I'm starting to think you all spend more time in this corridor than you do in your rooms," he drawled as he approached. Willow walked along beside him with a toddler in her arms.

Seeing the small boy seemed to reset my mind. "Is that...?" Bright turquoise eyes lifted to mine, the color reminding me of his father's irises. "You got him to shift."

"He just needed a little coaxing," Willow replied, her blonde hair styled in long, wavy lengths.

Like Lilith, I realized. "You're up here for a photo shoot with Damien."

"Yes," Ryder confirmed. "Lilith hasn't been seen for a few days, and unless you've changed your mind about super-announcing her death at the next Blood Alliance meeting, we need to take some candid images."

"Can't do that with a toddler in your arms," Darius pointed out.

"No, that's why we brought him up here. We need Juliet to babysit." In typical Ryder fashion, he didn't ask; he just demanded. And since we were all guests in his territory, I suppose he was within his rights to do so.

"Damien's busy supervising Calina while she searches for the server farm holding all her research materials," I said.

Ryder lifted a shoulder. "Then you can supervise her while he takes some photos."

My teeth ground together at the prospect. Mostly because a part of me was relieved by the idea of sending Damien somewhere else and having Calina all to myself.

This has to be related to her blood.

She'd mentioned that Lilith had been possessive as well, but had linked that behavior to them sharing a bond. Maybe it wasn't the link at all, just Calina.

Regardless, I found myself nodding in agreement to Ryder's comment and saying, "I'll take over."

Because why wouldn't I take over?

She was mine.

For now.

Temporarily.

Fuck.

Swallowing down the urge to growl, I walked around Darius—only then realizing his hand was still on my shoulder. I met his gaze as I passed. "I'm fine."

"Are you?"

"Yes," I snapped. "Let me go."

His brow furrowed, but he didn't hold me back. Instead, he said, "Maybe we should let Calina see the boy as a show of good faith. If he's in the room while she works, it could motivate her to comply quickly. Especially with your threat hanging over her head."

I considered that and dipped my chin. "Yes."

"What threat?" Willow asked.

"Nothing I intend to follow through on," I promised her. "But Calina doesn't know that." And from what I'd observed, her senses weren't enhanced, so she couldn't hear any of this. "Juliet, darling, do you mind holding the child for a little while?" I softened my tone for her, the female having earned my respect and admiration over the last few months.

Rather than answer me, she looked to Darius. He gave her a nod, telling her without words—or perhaps through their mental connection—that he approved. "Of course, my liege," she murmured, her pretty brown eyes finding mine briefly.

When we'd first met, she couldn't even be in the same room as me without falling into the requisite bow. Darius had worked wonders on her innate programming, providing her with the backbone she needed to survive in this political arena.

She stepped forward and held out her hands for the child.

Willow looked at Ryder.

Which had him looking at me. "If that child so much as cries in our absence, I'll destroy you for upsetting my mate."

Normally, I'd remark on a threat like that, but I found myself to be all out of retorts, so I merely acquiesced with a nod. Because my focus wasn't on that toddler. It was on Calina.

Rather than wait to observe the exchange, I headed back to Damien's room and the en-suite office he hid off to the side of his dining area.

The door was open, showcasing Calina at a desk with Damien hovering over her shoulder. He wasn't touching her, but his mouth was too close to her exposed neck for my liking.

"Ryder needs you in the hallway," I said, my tone sharper than I'd intended.

Damien glanced back at me. "Does he now?"

"Lilith photo shoot."

Those two words had Calina stiffening. "Lilith's *here?*"

"Yes," I replied. "She's in there." I glanced at the hidden door that led to the item in question. "Show her, Damien."

He didn't even try to fight me on it, too excited by the prospect of showing off his two trophies.

Pressing his palm to the wall, he revealed an electronic panel that required a very long password. He keyed in all the numbers, then stepped back as the wall parted like slats on an elevator.

A whooshing sound accompanied the action, revealing a freezer inside and a barely breathing female tied to a chair. "I see you haven't removed the axe from Benita's stomach yet," I commented.

"Oh, I did," Damien replied. "Then I had Tracey put it back."

"Foreplay?" I guessed.

"Something like that," he drawled.

I glanced at Calina to find her gaping at the head on the shelf. "As I said," I murmured. "Lilith's here. She's just not alive."

Calina stood, leaving the screens behind, and stepped into the freezer as though in thrall.

Damien moved to stop her, but I lifted my hand, telling him, *Don't,* with a look, curious to see what she would do.

She crept up to Lilith as though she might come alive at any moment. Then she canted her head to the side in evaluation.

Ryder stepped into the office doorway but remained silent as Calina bent to unzip a bag holding all of Lilith's parts. Her arms. Her legs. Her torso. Calina didn't touch them but seemed to be examining the sections with her eyes before returning her focus to the severed head.

Ryder and Damien shared a glance.

Then Ryder looked at me.

I nodded for the two of them to go, saying without speaking that I had the situation well in hand.

Damien's gaze told me I had better not disturb his precious items.

He left before I could reply, expecting me to comply with the silent demand. Probably because he knew he had no true authority here. I would do whatever the fuck I wanted. That was why the new alliance crowned me king.

The computer beeped, pulling Calina's attention away from the head, her expression giving nothing away as she returned to the office to click a few items on the keyboard.

I had no idea what she was doing, making me the wrong supervisor for this task. For all I knew, she could be sending a message to one of Lilith's partners or stakeholders. "You can close the freezer now," she said, settling into the chair. "Thank you for letting me see her."

Rather than reply, I went to the panel in the wall and closed the door. Damien had taught me the codes as a show of good faith. It was a new alliance between many of us, but his familial ties to Izzy made him trustworthy in my eyes. Just as my ties to Izzy's mate, Cam, made me worthy of the same respect from Damien.

Darius and Juliet entered the suite, but not the office. Calina was either too consumed by the information on the screen to notice them, or she hadn't heard their entry. With a wave of my hand, I told him not to enter when they came close enough to see us. If I needed him, I'd let him know. Until then, he and Juliet could remain in the other room.

Calina was silent, her eyes glued to the screen.

I studied the code but couldn't decipher it.

So I let her play and type and admired her instead. The long slope of her neck. The way her hair remained gathered on one side over her opposite shoulder. The cut of my dress shirt against her naked skin. She'd rolled the sleeves to her elbows and had her legs crossed in the chair, allowing the fabric to ride up her thighs.

Her foot tapped while her fingers moved, the nervous little tell making me wonder just what she was doing.

I placed my palms on her shoulders, bending over to press my lips to her ear.

"Part of me hopes you're up to something nefarious," I whispered. "Because it would give me cause to bend you over my knee and spank your ass raw." I nibbled her earlobe, grinning as she shivered. "Then I would bend you over this desk and fuck you raw. And if I decided to forgive you at the end, I might give you pleasure. But since I'm *defective*, maybe not."

Her throat worked, her breath shuddering out of her. I pressed my nose to her throat, inhaling her sweet perfume and listening to the rapid cadence of her heart.

"Now that you've seen Lilith, you know what I've told you is true," I continued. "That makes you my property, Calina. So if you're warning someone with those clever keystrokes, I'm going to be very disappointed. And I don't think you want to know what I do when I'm disappointed, sweetheart."

"Murder children?" she suggested, her voice lacking emotion.

I chuckled against her throat. "Finish the job and tell me where the server farms are, and you won't have to find out."

I proceeded to kiss a path along her neck, my lips seemingly addicted to her skin, as she returned to typing. Her pulse continued to hum against my mouth like a butterfly's wings, beating rapidly in quick succession.

She might be able to mask her tone with indifference, but her body gave her away.

She was scared, something that appealed to the predator inside me. I wanted her frightened, begging, and *submitting*.

She posed a challenge that I darkly enjoyed, her stoic persona one I wanted to dismantle just to watch her fall apart at my feet. I'd never been so enchanted by someone before.

Perhaps it was her implied resistance—the fact that she blamed her attraction on a natural biological response rather than acknowledging a potential attraction to me, the person.

Most females stripped upon command because they wanted to, not because they felt a biological need to follow a predator's command.

Women genuinely enjoyed my presence, and I doted on them in kind.

But Calina spoke to me with a confidence that bordered on arrogance, which I found fascinating, considering her age and human status.

It made me want to teach her a sensual lesson, make her addicted to me, and either add her to my harem or turn her into a progeny to learn beneath my wing.

The way she focused now, working through her task even while a superior being lurked at her back, was just further proof of her potential in this world. She would make a fantastic vampire. Coolheaded even while under pressure. Practical. Intelligent. Strategic.

I kissed her pulse, considering the sole negative to turning her—she would lose that delectable flavor in her blood.

And I was definitely not ready to give up that drug yet.

I straightened, my palms still on her shoulders, and watched as she pulled up a map of former-day New York. She typed in coordinates, hit Enter, and looked up at me. "There."

"Impressive," Darius murmured behind us.

I'd sensed him entering when I'd straightened my spine. He must have taken it as a sign of something happening.

Calina tried to look around me at Darius, but my hand slid from her shoulder to her throat, holding her in place. "How do I know you're not sending us into a trap?"

"What benefit would that serve for me?" she countered. "You have the only individuals I consider to be family here. You also showed me Lilith's head, thus freeing me from her control indefinitely. Some would say I owe you a debt of gratitude."

"And you display that by insulting me in front of my team?" I returned.

"I… I didn't mean it as an insult. I'm just struggling to understand you. You're not like the vampires I know."

I considered what she'd told me about Lilith earlier, how she used to demand a report and then feed from Calina until she died.

"Your view of my kind is skewed," I said after a beat, my thumb drawing a line up the column of her neck while I held her captive in the chair with her head tilted back. "Lilith believed humans are meant to serve. There are those of us, such as myself, who disagree to an extent."

I released her throat and reached down to move her chair around so she was facing me. Then I grabbed the arms of the chair and leaned forward to place my face before hers.

"Humans are inferior because they're weaker. But the fact remains that vampires rely on mortal blood to survive. Therefore, it's our duty to protect our food source. That all of us were mortal at some point should also afford us at least a little bit of humanity, too."

I reached up to draw my fingers through her still-damp hair.

"And sometimes, there are precious humans who stand out among the rest. Whether it be intelligence, a special skill, or…" I drew my thumb along her chin to the opposite side and down her throat. "A unique bloodline that needs to be preserved and revered."

"My blood is why you are acting this way?"

"Partly," I admitted. "But I also value what's in here." I lifted my hand to tap her head gently. "And I'm hoping the information you've just provided is valid and helpful so I can continue to value it. Otherwise, it will be your blood I consider precious, which will drastically change your fate."

It was a false threat.

Something told me that even if she attempted to deceive us, I'd still be too enthralled by her to do anything cruel about it.

But Ryder would.

As would Darius.

And I wouldn't stand in their way.

Finding Cam mattered most. Not even a delectable female could change my mind on that.

I kissed her temple and stood again.

"Looks like we're going north again," I told Darius. "I want to be in the air before midnight. Which means we need to prepare for another long day of sunlight when we arrive."

"I'm already missing the moon," Darius replied.

"Me, too," I murmured, slipping my fingers beneath Calina's chin. "Stand. You're going to need appropriate clothes."

CHAPTER SIXTEEN

CALINA

Jace had let me see Gretchen and James before we'd left. He'd also given them a moment with their son, which had erased some of the worry lines from Gretchen's brow.

At least until he'd taken the child away again, then she'd been positively beside herself. But it was the nature of this dangerous game.

It all had been for my benefit. Jace's actions had served as a reminder that he had them in his custody and would kill them if I misbehaved. And he'd been giving me one last chance to save them by coming clean before we left.

But I didn't have any sort of nefarious plan up my sleeve.

So I'd stayed quiet.

And I remained that way on our long flight to upstate New York. Or *Lilith Region,* as it was now called. It was a wide territory encompassing a large chunk of the former United States.

Jace sat beside me, dressed in all black, his focus on a device in his hand. It reminded me of a tablet, but the screen hovered in the air as he flipped through messages.

I read them as they appeared—because they were in front of

me—and realized he was working through requests from vampires under his control. There were inquiries for humans to serve in certain positions, a few petitions for more blood, and visiting solicitations from vampires in other regions. He approved many of them but declined others with notes attached.

Rejected. You are over your quota for blood this month. Submit a full inventory of assets for review, and I will reconsider the request. —J

He sent that message with a sigh, then pulled up another item that gave him pause. "Jasmine just sent me a meeting request for next week. She wants to discuss trading options with Jace Region."

"Interesting timing," the dapper vampire across from him replied.

Darius.

He reminded me a bit of Jace with his elegant charm, but his green eyes were intense in a way that told me he didn't often smile.

The female beside him was his *Erosita*. She had her dark hair pulled up into a ponytail that exposed her long throat, something her mate seemed very taken with, as he frequently glanced at her pulse point.

They could clearly speak through a telepathic link, because he nodded a few times without saying anything out loud, and he'd reached over to squeeze her thigh in a tender manner that had her laying her head against his shoulder.

A love match, I decided, recognizing the signs of it from my observations of Gretchen and James. Only, the link between Juliet and her master seemed even more intimate. Probably because he relied on her blood to survive just as she relied on him for protection in this cruel world.

"I'm going to accept," Jace said. "It'll be a good opportunity to test her political ties."

"She's a sadist who bathes in human blood," Damien drawled from a few feet away. He'd joined us after finishing a few photo loops to keep Lilith's persona alive.

From what I'd gathered, these vampires didn't want the world to know about Lilith's death yet. I wasn't entirely certain of their plans, but their intentions seemed agreeable. Mostly because they wanted to dismantle the regime she'd created.

I wondered at their goals for the future, how they intended to restructure society.

Jace had said that some vampires saw the importance of protecting their food. It was paramount for their survival, so I understood the thought process. But what did that entail for humans?

I pondered that while Jace, Damien, and Darius continued discussing allies and potential foes. None of the names they mentioned meant anything to me, so I zoned out until Jace brought up images for me to review once more.

He showed me Jasmine. The olive-toned female had dark features and was a royal vampire over the former Philippines.

Aika was next, another royal vampire, who had taken over Japan.

Then he moved on to Lajos, a vampire royal over Hawaii. That was the first name to ring a bell. "Lilith has mentioned him before." But I couldn't say much other than that. "I've never met him." He had dark eyes that radiated evil intent, something I definitely would have remembered.

Jace made a few notes, then continued his show-and-tell.

Ayaz was next, a dark-skinned vampire male who had taken over Turkey, Armenia, and several other countries in that general region. "She's mentioned him before, too. Something about supplying him with *Erosita* blood." I remembered it because she'd taken one of our subjects for that purpose. We never saw the female again.

Darius and Jace shared a glance, then he showed me three more royals I didn't recognize.

Cormac. Khalid. Ankit.

United Kingdom and Ireland. Middle Eastern countries. More Middle Eastern countries with India, Nepal, and Sri Lanka.

I knew all the locations, but none of the vampire's names.

He returned to Europe to show me Sofia and Helias, two identities I had heard of from Lilith. "The Coventus is under Sofia's jurisdiction," I said, recalling that detail. "Yes?"

"No, the Coventus properties and surrounding areas are considered neutral zones, and they used to be maintained by Lilith," Jace replied. "However, Sofia's region borders former-day Italy, which is where one of the Coventuses is for blood virgins."

Juliet visibly shivered, and Darius grabbed her thigh again

before pressing a kiss to her neck.

"Is she a blood virgin?" I wondered out loud.

Jace didn't look up from the screens, aware of whom I meant. "Yes." He scrolled to a new image. "How about this one?"

A blonde female with dark brown eyes appeared on the screen. *Hazel. Royal Vampire.*

"Her region encompasses Greece, Macedonia, Albania, Hungary, and a few other Eastern European countries," he added, like he did for all the others.

"I don't know her." She had kind eyes. Very different from Lilith's crisp and cruel appearance.

"As much as I'm enjoying the geography and political lesson, we'll be landing in about five minutes," Damien interjected. "We need to be ready."

Jace nodded, shutting down his device and slipping it back into his pocket. "We'll continue that discussion after we finish here."

"I didn't meet many vampires or lycans outside of the labs," I promised him. "Everything I know is just from hearing Lilith speak."

"Which could prove exceptionally useful if you overheard the right thing," he replied, reaching across me to check my belt. Then he fixed his own, relaxed, and closed his eyes as the shades around the plane began to rise.

My focus went to the windows, my lips parting at the sight of the sun glistening brightly outside. We'd flown the entire way here with shutters on, disabling my ability to see the sky. Now that I could, I was hypnotized by its radiance.

How many years have I lived without this phenomenon? I thought, awed by the sight.

I remained glued to the window throughout our entire descent, my eyes watering from the brightness. But I couldn't stop staring. It was magnificent. I'd seen photos, but those just did not do this experience justice.

Jace's finger slid across my cheek before going to his lips, tasting my tears.

Then he unbuckled my seat belt, pressed his lips to my ear, and whispered, "Time to prove your worth, little genius."

I didn't want to leave my seat, but the prospect of going outside and witnessing the unfiltered sky had me standing immediately.

Jace pressed his palm to the small of my back, guiding me down the aisle of the jet and to the stairs. Juliet and Darius had already disembarked, the two of them standing on the ground in matching outfits of black pants and dark, long-sleeved shirts.

I descended the stairs to join them, but my gaze instantly went upward to the bright blue sky and blistering sun. *Beautiful.*

"She's going to blind herself by doing that," Damien drawled as he joined us with a backpack slung over his shoulder.

Jace drew his finger down my cheek once more, then pinched my chin to gently pull my focus away from the dazzling display of light overhead. I blinked at him, seeing a black spot where his face should be.

"I think she already has," he mused. "Protect your eyes, Doctor. I still need them." He tightened his grip just enough to tell me he meant it. Then he released me, leaving me blind beside him.

Every time I closed my eyes, dots danced against my lids. It reminded me of what happened when I stared at a fluorescent light too long, only worse.

I kept blinking, waiting for it to subside.

Jace's palm found my back again, giving me a little nudge to move alongside him. I glanced at the ground, wanting to watch my steps, but those damn dots decorated my view, making me stumble.

He chuckled a little. "It'll pass," he promised, his arm sliding around me to help move me along with him.

Damien said something in a language I didn't understand, making Darius snort. Jace replied in the same foreign tongue.

It painted a picture of just how old these beings were. They likely spoke dozens of languages, having lived through centuries or millennia of culture and life.

Jace struck me as the oldest of them all, but Darius wasn't far behind him. They both held a regal, ancient air that reeked of power and opulence.

The one they called Ryder—whom I'd only met in passing—was similar.

Damien seemed younger. Not as young as me, but less experienced than the others. He lacked their powerful presence. However, he made up for that with his lethal edge. Something told me he could hold his own against an ancient and potentially come out on top of the fight in the end based on skill alone.

Jace's thumb pressed into my spine, my thin black shirt doing very little to dispel the heat emanating from his touch. He'd found a pair of pants for me as well, the denim fabric different from my usual scrubs. And I didn't particularly enjoy the feel of it against my more sensitive areas, but Jace hadn't provided me with undergarments.

"Hold," Damien said, causing Jace to grab me by the hip to halt me at his side. "Let me see what I can do."

It took several more minutes for me to realize what he meant because it took that long for me to be able to see clearly.

A door.

We were standing outside a building that resembled a rundown warehouse, but the technology on the entryway certainly appeared brand new. It reminded me of the tech in our labs.

"This is definitely the right place," I said, glancing around for surveillance cameras and finding none.

Odd. They have to be here somewhere.

I also expected a Vigil army of some kind to be protecting the premises—something I'd said when Damien had asked me about potential security.

However, the place seemed abandoned.

Maybe it's all underground? I thought, glancing downward.

"Are we going to have to blow it like the other one?" Darius asked.

"We can't," Damien replied, his attention on a screen he held in one hand. "The technology inside is too valuable, and for all we know, the computers we need are just beyond this door."

I quickly analyzed the size of the building sprawled out before us and quietly agreed with his assessment. If the servers were above ground—which would be the best place for them, as they required constant cooling—then we couldn't risk it. One ill-placed explosion could knock out the air supply as well, thus destroying the temperature control inside, which would lead to a quick deterioration of all technology.

Glancing around Damien's shoulder, I eyed the tablet to see how he was trying to unlock the door. He was using some sort of code-descrambling device to find the appropriate password, and since we weren't on a countdown timer, I supposed it was a decent way to do it.

But there was one problem.

"If Lilith's software detects that breach, a protocol will likely be engaged, just like in Bunker 47."

Without my watch, I wouldn't be able to detect anything about this server farm. Not that my watch was even connected to this area. I didn't even know if it still worked since someone—probably Jace—had taken it from me while I was unconscious.

"I'm anticipating that," Damien responded, holding up another device. "That's why I brought Lilith's phone."

That explained how they'd known about the countdown in Bunker 47, and various other details.

Damien returned his attention to the screen but started scrolling through Lilith's phone as well. I studied the building again, concerned. If I'd learned anything over the years, it was that Lilith planned for every situation.

And I really didn't like the lack of visible cameras.

It told me they were hidden, or perhaps a different type of surveillance was being used in this area.

Satellites? I wondered. *Infrared scanners from the trees?* I glanced over my shoulder, noting the surrounding overgrown forest. They'd landed the plane over a hundred yards out on a patch of asphalt that was clearly meant as a landing strip for this location specifically.

For Lilith to visit.

She wouldn't have wanted to land too far away, her preference to be in and out of her facilities quickly and efficiently.

"What are you searching for, Doctor?" Jace asked, sounding suspicious.

"Surveillance." I looked at the door and then about three stories up at the roof. "There are no cameras."

"There weren't any outside your lab either," he replied.

"Makes the building look less suspect," Damien added.

I considered the surveillance feeds that I'd had access to at Bunker 47 and conceded that there had been none that faced outside. But I didn't agree with his comment regarding appearances.

"That door is very suspect." And perhaps too obvious as an entry point. "I think we're meant to waste time here. There's another way in somewhere."

It would be just like Lilith to design her property in that manner to lure unwelcome visitors into a trap.

Damien paused, his nostrils flaring. Then he set the screen down and pressed a finger to his ear. “Rick. I need you to bring me some of Ryder’s thermal toys.”

CHAPTER SEVENTEEN

LILITH

The recovery team has been dispatched. Update expected within twelve hours.

Press the green arrow to continue reviewing the logs.

Next log to commence in three, two…

Log year five. Day one.

We've just survived another successful Blood Day ceremony. All humans were allocated evenly, as prescribed. Several candidates for immortality have been relocated to the arena to fight for their fate. The alliance appears amused, and they're already placing bets on their favorites.

Lajos has agreed to allow Stella Clan first pick of the two winners. I awarded him a blood virgin to thank him for simplifying the selection process. It should hold him over temporarily until I can find another *Erosita* for him to break.

Which reminds me, your idea to devalue the vampire mating bond is playing out beautifully. Soon, we will be able to introduce the renewed line of immortal human offerings without much interference as the old ways of our world continue to die out.

There is, of course, the matter of your own *Erosita*. I've done my best to dull the connection between you, but the possessive instincts likely remain.

Don't worry. I will continue our research on this topic and share all results with you via the logs.

Attached is a photo in case you wish to see her. She's a pretty little blonde. Untouched and innocent, just the way you like her.

But I do intend to test the limits of this link.

More on that later.

To begin reviewing the files for the Erosita *reclassification project, press the green arrow.*

End transmission.

CHAPTER EIGHTEEN

JACE

My eyes burned, the rising sun giving me a headache of epic proportions.

It seemed like my sensitivity to the elements grew with age, leaving me almost impaired as I stood in the open field between the trees and the server farm building.

Damien didn't appear to be as bothered, his focus on an array of equipment Rick had carried out from the plane. Calina stood beside him, hands on her shapely hips, as she studied the screens with him. I tried to admire the view of her bending over at the waist, but the splintering through my skull dulled the appeal.

"Fucking daylight," I muttered.

"Indeed," Darius agreed beside me.

He slid his arms around Juliet's abdomen to tug her back to his chest and bent to hide his face in her neck. Her full lips curled into a smile, then parted as his incisors slid into her vein.

She quivered against him, a sight that would have made me envious only days ago, but I found my gaze returning to Calina and the tender column of her throat.

Imbibing her essence would provide a good distraction from

my blistering headache.

Alas, I needed her to focus.

I also needed to find my head. Juliet's intoxicating blood had always called to me before, but I could barely smell her sweet fragrance now. My mouth ached for Calina and Calina alone.

Why? I wondered.

Yes, she tasted divine. However, most women did.

I would have to ask her to clarify her blood type later. She'd called it rare, saying it had died out during the revolution. But she'd never defined the properties of it.

Inhaling deeply, I closed my eyes in an attempt to dull the agony building—

"We have company," Rick said through the comm unit in my ear.

Damien straightened, his gaze on the sky as he switched on his mic. "What direction?"

"Coming in from the west with a trajectory that suggests they're on their way here," Rick replied. "I'd say we have ten minutes before they land."

"You're still in stealth mode, yeah?" Damien glanced over his shoulder to where the jet was parked in the nearby field.

"Not my first time flying under the radar," Rick drawled in response. "Want me to free up the landing strip?"

Damien cocked an eyebrow at me. "You're the king."

I studied him before looking at Calina. "Expecting a rescue, sweetheart?"

Her brow furrowed. "A rescue?"

I stepped forward to grab her by the chin, my eyes narrowing at her expression. "You lie so beautifully, Doctor. I almost believed you were helping us. But we both know you called for them." And while part of me was furious at her betrayal, another part of me was excited by the prospect of punishing her for it.

"Jace, I—"

"Shh," I hushed her, pressing my thumb to her pretty lips. "I'll make use of your mouth when we're done killing your rescue party." Lifting my opposite hand upward, I pressed a finger to the device in my ear to turn on my mic. "Do it. We'll greet the newcomers properly from the ground."

"Excellent." The engines were already roaring to life, telling me Rick had anticipated that response.

The jet lifted gracefully, reminding me of a rocket more than a plane, and disappeared into the sky beneath a cloud of camouflage.

"I'm envious of Ryder's toy," I admitted, admiring the beautiful machine. "What do I need to do to have one of mine upgraded to match?"

Ryder had spent the last century hiding in southern Texas like an old-fashioned recluse on a big farm. He'd always fancied weapons, but the jet was an unexpected addition to his collection, as he didn't seem all that keen on upgraded technology.

Which meant Damien was the real cause for that stunning enhancement.

I met his caramel-brown gaze. "Name your price."

He merely grinned. "We'll negotiate later."

"We will," I agreed, my touch shifting to Calina's throat when she tried to speak again. I squeezed, cutting off her airflow and thereby silencing her. "I need something to shut her up with, and some rope." The words were for Damien, not Calina.

She tried to shake her head, her eyes going wide.

I ignored her, instead focusing on the bag Damien had unzipped. "You really do come prepared for anything and everything." If I didn't respect Ryder, I'd attempt to sway Damien to my side and keep him as my own.

Alas, Damien and Ryder made an excellent team.

Just as Darius and I did.

Darius and Juliet were already moving to the trees, their hands clutching matching guns. "Target practice?" I asked him.

He didn't look back at me as he confirmed with a "Yes."

I nodded and slightly loosened my grip on Calina to allow her to breathe.

She inhaled noisily, her pretty eyes glistening.

"I warned you not to betray me," I told her softly, my opposite hand lifting to swipe at the tear tracking down her cheek. I brought the droplet to my mouth and smiled as I tasted the salt on my skin. "But I can't say I'm terribly disappointed by it."

"I didn't—"

I closed off her airway again. "You can lie to me after we fix the problem you created."

Damien tossed me the items I'd requested, the ball gag one clearly meant for the bedroom. "Definitely always prepared," I reiterated, amused.

He flashed me a wolfish grin, then focused on the sky above again. "Better tie her up quick, King. Or you'll miss all the fun."

"Oh, I'll definitely be having fun," I vowed, my gaze meeting Calina's furious hazel irises. "A lot of bloody fucking fun." I slowly enunciated those last three words, ensuring she tasted each one as I said them against her lips.

She inhaled sharply as I let her breathe.

Then I walked her backward toward the trees and found a good place to secure her against a sturdy trunk.

"Jace," she choked out, making me focus on the ball gag first.

"Open," I demanded.

She clenched her jaw shut instead.

"You don't want to tempt me to violence right now, Doctor," I promised her. "I'm being kind at the moment. That can change very quickly."

Her eyes narrowed into defiant points.

My groin tightened in response, the desire to strip her and fuck her against this damn tree nearly overriding my every instinct.

This female is dangerous to my mental state, I realized, my stomach clenching with exquisite yearning. I couldn't remember the last time a woman had enticed me so severely. Perhaps never.

"Calina." Her name came out on a growl, only for the hairs along my arms to stand on end as a subtle hum of sound graced my ears.

Engines.

Plural.

And they weren't coming from the sky.

Pressing my palm to her mouth, I held her against the tree and searched the woods for the incoming vehicles.

Damien and Darius would be able to hear them as well, so I didn't waste breath in warning them.

I only had a single pistol tucked into a holster at my waist. Nothing else other than the female before me and the tools I'd intended to restrain her with.

"If you so much as move or utter a sound, I will snap your neck and leave you right here," I vowed. "And depending on my mood, I might not come back to watch you revive yourself."

She swallowed, the first hint of fear touching her features.

About fucking time. I was beginning to think this female didn't have a survival instinct.

I lowered my hand slowly, observing her for signs of that trademark defiance. She merely stared up at me, waiting for her next instruction.

"Try to run and I'll hunt you," I threatened, taking a step back.

She remained frozen against the tree.

Tossing the rope and gag to the forest floor beside her, I pulled out my gun and studied the incoming vehicles once more. Their engines were louder now and accompanied by the jet overhead.

Stepping up to the tree, I took position beside Calina just as the first of the off-road transports appeared.

Two armored four-wheel-drive vehicles.

All black exteriors.

Tinted windows

I crouched and gestured for Calina to follow. She did, her movements jerky as though her body had forgotten how to properly function. Apparently, my threat had resonated.

The two transports parked alongside the building, their doors opening a few seconds after cutting off the engines.

All of them were humans. *Vigils.*

I glanced at Calina and found her focus on me, awaiting my next order. A bizarre way to act, considering she'd likely called these men here to save her.

Unless she hadn't and this was just another one of Lilith's protocols.

The way the humans walked suggested they had no idea we were here, their steps casual as they moved toward the field to await the arrival of the incoming plane.

"Did you call them?" I asked her softly, aware the humans were too far away to hear me.

"No," she whispered back. "I did not."

"Did you trip a protocol when searching for the location?" I wondered out loud. But even as I said it, I knew that couldn't be right because these humans weren't on the alert at all. If they were expecting our company, they would have arrived via stealthier means. And they would be on the defensive now, not casually walking around in broad daylight.

I relayed that thought through the comms before Calina could answer me.

"Agreed," Darius replied. "They don't smell aggressive."

"Sending humans to fight vampires doesn't make sense," Damien added.

"Suggesting they have no idea we're here," Darius translated.

"Unless whoever is coming in that plane is a superior being," I mused, watching the plane's descent. "And this is just a distraction."

My eyes burned from the sunlight gleaming off the metal, making me wince.

"Do you need blood?" Calina's soft voice vibrated with emotion, one I sensed in her skipping pulse. I'd sufficiently unnerved her with my threat of snapping her neck. Perhaps Lilith had done that a few times in her history.

I studied her pale features, noting the sincerity in her gaze. "You're offering me a drink?"

"I'm aware of the sun's impact on your senses, something you're exuding with each flinch. And while the sun doesn't exactly drain you, it does weaken your ability to focus due to overstimulation." She swallowed, her nerves showing once more. "Im-imbibing my blood will provide your senses with something to f-focus on."

"You don't sound very sure," I murmured, noting the stammer in her voice and the increased hum of her pulse. "Worried I might take too much?"

"You think I brought them here," she whispered. "Yes, I'm concerned about your inclinations at the moment."

"Yet you offered me a bite?" I phrased it as a question, my curiosity temporarily overriding the situation entirely.

"Because you're my best chance at surviving whatever is about to happen," she replied flatly. "Giving you the focus you need is a practical recourse that not only bolsters your strength but also demonstrates my good intentions, thereby hopefully making you less likely to snap my neck and leave me here to wake up alone."

Ah, it was the last part of my threat that had done the trick in subduing her, not the threat of violence. She'd been paying attention earlier when I'd commented on her future in this world without a powerful being by her side to protect her. Not only that, but she'd listened and processed my claims thoroughly enough to realize the truth in my words.

"You didn't call them," I said, confident in the assessment.

If she'd warned them of our presence here, or sent in a rescue request, the humans would have come prepared. And they weren't ready to face us at all. They were all just standing around the edge of the field, waiting for the plane to land.

It was almost here, the silver siding glistening in the sun and setting my senses on fire. Darius had used Juliet as a distraction. Now Calina was offering herself to be mine.

And I wasn't about to decline such a delectable gift.

I wrapped my free hand around the back of her neck, tugging her to me while I kept my opposite arm free with the pistol pointed at the ground. "Let's see how trusting you are," I whispered against her mouth.

Then I struck at her throat, piercing her vein without subtleties.

She grabbed my shoulders, her fingernails digging into the cotton fabric of my long-sleeved shirt. A soft little moan parted her lips, her mortal form reacting to the endorphins of my bite.

I allowed her to feel each pull as I pressed her into the tree, my body hard against hers. Ready. Hot. *Desiring.*

I didn't hold back, letting her experience every inch of my strength and power as I dominated her with my mouth. She didn't fight. She didn't scream. She just melted into me and used the grip on my shoulders to keep herself from falling.

It was erotic and intoxicating, her essence a drug against my tongue that set my own blood on fire.

I listened as the plane landed behind me.

I listened as humans disembarked.

I listened as Damien confirmed there were no vampires in the party.

I listened as Darius suggested we observe the Vigils and wait for them to show us the entrance.

I didn't pause to agree. I didn't have to. He knew how to proceed as my second-in-command. Just as he would know what I was doing now to Calina.

She was right—her blood was exactly what I needed. It gave me focus. It dulled the ache in my head. But it stirred a new torment inside me, the yearning making my muscles tense as I fought the urge to strip her and fuck her against the tree.

Her grip faltered, her limbs shaking as she encircled my neck to hold on while I devoured her.

Too much, I thought. *I'm taking too much*.

And I needed her to be coherent for the next task.

I eased my fangs from her flesh, my veins burning from the necessary restraint. She swayed against me, her proof of trust exquisite and beautiful and so fucking hot that I considered letting Darius handle everything for me in the server farm.

"You're addicting," I accused against her neck before slicing my tongue open across a sharp incisor. I dabbed the wound in her skin with my blood, encouraging her to heal quickly.

Then I captured her lips and kissed her deeply.

She jolted in surprise, her shock an aphrodisiac to my predatory senses. I bit my tongue again, forcing more of my blood to pool inside her mouth.

With my hand still clamped around her nape, I gently drew my thumb along the column of her throat, telling her to swallow without words.

She obeyed.

And damn if that didn't make me even harder for her.

"They're heading inside," Damien said into my ear. "Are you planning to join us in this massacre, or do you want to stay out here and continue playing with the doctor?"

A low growl rumbled in my chest, my irritation at the interruption momentarily overwhelming my instincts.

"Jace," Darius added, his voice low. "You can fuck her on the plane after we get the files."

My jaw ticked, drawing a warning sound from my chest that had Calina trembling against me. The little vixen had utterly seduced me with her exquisite essence. "You and I are going to have a long chat later about your unique blood type."

I stepped back, only to reach forward again as she nearly fell. Her limbs shook, her lips swollen and decorated with little specks of blood. She licked them off with a visible shudder, her pupils blown wide.

It seemed I wasn't the only one experiencing a momentary lapse in judgment.

She released a violent shiver, her hand landing on my forearm and giving me a squeeze as she fought for her balance. I continued to hold her up by my grip on her hip.

After another moment, she cleared her throat. "I'm… I'm stable."

I snorted. "You're not." But she could stand, and that was all I needed. Turning around, I noted the lack of humans in my periphery. "Where did they go?"

"They're all inside," Damien murmured through the earpiece. "Went in through an underground tunnel around the back."

Calina swayed again, her blonde hair flickering in my peripheral vision. I caught her and pulled her against me once more. She sagged in relief, then stiffened upon realizing her reaction.

I fought the urge to chuckle, this pull between us electric and alluringly perfect. That she tried to fight it only intrigued me more. "Still think it's just my vampire prowess?" I asked against her ear.

She didn't reply.

"Jace," Darius prompted. "How do you want to proceed?"

"I think we both know how he wishes to proceed," Damien drawled.

I ignored his humored tone and focused on the building again.

"They're all human," I said, recalling the detail from their assessment while I'd been feasting from Calina's vein. "That means they're here under orders. And as they weren't alert when they arrived, I assume those orders were issued as some sort of protocol that Lilith set in motion. Similar to the others we've witnessed."

"Her phone is silent, so it might be unrelated," Damien pointed out.

"Perhaps," I agreed. "But there's an opportunity here to find some answers, and not just from the servers." I ran my hand up and down Calina's back, noting her strengthening posture.

"What do you have in mind?" Darius asked.

"An inquisition." I glanced down to find Calina staring up at me. She didn't have an earpiece, so she couldn't hear the other half of the conversation.

"The humans consider us to be gods," I continued. "So let's take them to confession and see how many of them wish to atone for their sins." I held Calina's gaze, my next words for her. "Consider this an introduction to the new reign."

CHAPTER NINETEEN

CALINA

My mouth tingled with the reminder of Jace's kiss.

No, not a kiss.

A *claim*.

He'd taken my lips with a ferocity that I'd felt all the way to my toes, his possession a brand against my very soul.

"Still think it's just my vampire prowess?"

His question rolled around in my mind as I followed him toward the server farm. I didn't pay attention to the rocks or grass or dirt beneath my flat shoes. Because all I could hear was that question and my whispered mental answer of *no*.

Because Lilith's feeding frenzies had never made me feel like that. Like I was so hot I would combust without his touch. Like I would melt and enjoy every minute of it. Like I wanted him to drain me dry just to satisfy his need for my blood.

It was a dizzying sensation, one that left me bewildered and slightly unhinged.

My thighs clenched with the need to feel his fingers inside me again. Or something else. Something longer. Thicker. *Harder*.

I swallowed, only to elicit a soft moan from within as the

tantalizing flavor of his essence circled my mouth once more.

He'd called me addictive.

Then his blood was… *life*.

I wanted to taste more of him. His tongue had speared my mouth with a domination that couldn't be fought, and I'd taken it because there was no alternative.

Hence, his possession.

His claim.

His *ownership*.

I was his. And not in the way I'd belonged to Lilith, but in a sensual, exciting sort of way.

Unless he breaks my neck and leaves me here, I thought, shivering. He'd voiced that threat with such clarity that I didn't doubt his intentions for a second.

I was a glorified blood bag to him—a researcher with a particular set of useful traits and specialized knowledge.

Knowledge that he was about to unearth inside this facility.

Knowledge that would prove obsolete in a matter of minutes.

What did that mean for my future? If these Vigils even hinted at the possibility that I'd called for them, Jace would very likely follow through on his promise to kill me and leave me here to fend for myself.

That meant I'd finally be free.

But for how long?

Because Jace was right about this world and what would likely happen to me if I were found by another vampire. I was a blood source that couldn't die.

He at least treated me with some respect. Actually, all things considered, he'd been rather pleasant to me.

Lilith had always spoken to me with importance, but only about the research. Then she'd bleed me until I died, and I'd later wake up exhausted and alone. I'd ache for days. Only to repeat the experience a week later when she returned for another update.

Despite knowing I could survive being bled to death, Jace had given me his essence. He'd bolstered me with his strength.

I studied his strong back, the wide breadth of his shoulders, and the messy cut of his dark hair.

No. It's not just your vampire prowess, I decided. *It's* you.

Fortunately, he couldn't hear my thoughts. He was also distracted by our current task of… of *entering the building.*

My breath caught upon realizing I'd followed him all the way inside without any consideration of my own safety or the potential attack from the Vigils. I'd just been trailing along behind him like a pet on a leash, lost in my musings of him and his all-consuming kiss.

Meanwhile, he was entirely unfazed and focused on the situation at hand.

The way I should be.

I quickly took in our surroundings, noting the clean tile and hum of blue lighting illuminating all the servers ahead of us. There were no overhead lights or windows, and the ceilings were over ten feet tall.

Goose bumps pebbled down my arms, not from fright but from the cool interior. Electronic equipment like this required constant air-conditioning to protect the technology. We'd had our own tech room at Bunker 47, but it had been nothing like this.

This was a proper server farm with rows and rows of delicately arranged wires and drives meant to store information.

I glanced over my shoulder to find Darius and Juliet taking up the rear of our party, which meant Damien had entered first.

And there hadn't been any humans standing guard at the door.

That confirmed they weren't here as some sort of protective protocol. They were here on routine maintenance, or perhaps to gather the logs that I hadn't properly sent from Bunker 47.

They had no idea we were here.

Unless we were walking into an ambush. *Hmm, no.* Jace would suspect that with his heightened senses. His confident strides told me he knew exactly where the humans were, and the re-holstered pistol at his hip confirmed he didn't foresee them giving him any trouble.

As he'd said, humans considered vampires to be gods.

The Vigils would have to be insane to try to fight him. The only reason the human soldiers in Bunker 47 had fought back was because they'd known they were dead anyway. Those weren't normal supernaturals who'd escaped the lab, but research subjects with vendettas on their minds.

These Vigils would react differently.

Or I hoped they would, anyway.

I could hear them up ahead, their deep voices carrying through the field of servers. It was difficult to pinpoint their location, the computer walls too tall for us to see over. They were at least eight feet in height, leaving about two feet between the tops and the ceiling. That allowed sound to carry but didn't give us a line of sight.

Fortunately, Damien—

"Gentlemen," Jace called, his regal tone skating along my senses and making me flinch in surprise at him announcing our presence in the building. "My name is Prince Jace. I expect you all to be kneeling by the time my entourage rounds this corner. Any resistance will be met with lethal force."

Prince Jace? I thought he was King Jace?

A flurry of sound followed his announcement, the scuffle of boots telling me the Vigils might not be doing what Jace had demanded.

"You have five seconds," Jace continued. "Those who adhere to societal expectations and welcome me properly will be rewarded. I've already implied what will happen to those who don't."

His confident demeanor didn't change. He merely continued walking with the grace of a god, his strides purposeful and important. Damien stopped at the end of the row, waiting for Jace to join him.

Jace didn't pause, choosing to waltz right around the corner without a care in the world.

My lips parted, fear tightening my gut.

Only, gasps littered the air instead of gunshots.

"Well, that certainly took the fun out of everything," Damien muttered, trailing after Jace. "I was craving blood."

"You're always craving blood," Jace returned.

Darius and Juliet came up behind me, their presence an uncomfortable sensation at my back. "Move," Darius said, his lips far too close to my ear.

I skipped forward and startled at the sight of nine men all kneeling in reverence before Jace. I idly wondered if I was supposed to join them. Instead, I walked up behind Jace and grabbed his shirt.

It was an odd response. Yet it felt right. Intuitive. Like I was meant to accompany him in this manner.

However, I quickly realized that I'd acted out of turn, touching the royal vampire as though he were mine to touch.

I released the fabric as though it'd burned my palms, my mind sending directions to my feet to retreat. But it was too late.

Jace reached around himself to grab me and tugged me to his side.

"Do you recognize any of them, Doctor?" he asked, gesturing to the submissive humans. Their heads were all turned downward, their eyes respectfully averted.

"I can't properly see them," I admitted in a whisper. "But I doubt I know them."

All the Vigils familiar with my research had been killed in Bunker 47. Including those who had outlived their purpose prior to the bunker's self-destruction. Lilith had usually fed humans to the vampires and lycans when they'd no longer served her purposes.

Jace dipped his chin, then looked over the crowd. "Who is the commanding officer here?"

"I am, Your Highness," a blond male announced from the middle of the group. "Vigil One, Lajos Region."

Jace's eyebrow lifted. "You're from Lajos Region? Not Lilith Region?"

"My team is from Lajos Region, Your Highness." Vigil One didn't lift his head while he spoke, his form perfectly subservient. "Vigils Seven, Twenty-Two, Fifty-Eight, and Sixty-One are from Lilith Region. However, they fall under my command for this op."

"I see. And what's your purpose here?" Jace demanded.

"We're to retrieve the files from server 47 and rendezvous with the Bunker 27 unit in nine hours to complete the information transfer. We're also sending a virtual copy to the servers at Bunker 37."

"Under whose orders?" Jace pressed while I considered the familiar bunker numbers and their uses.

Hive mind research and Erosita *testing.*

Vigil One swallowed. "Prince Lajos, Your Majesty."

"If I phoned him, would he confirm that mission?" Jace asked, his tone sharp and edged with lethal intent.

The Vigils clearly felt the weight of his words because they all shivered in response.

This being was powerful. Old. *Deadly*.

I hadn't really felt it before now, my experiences with Lilith having numbed me to the superiority of her species.

However, seeing the reactions in these humans told me Jace hadn't exaggerated his societal position. Just hearing him voice his name had been enough to demand submission from these warrior humans. None of them had their weapons drawn. They were even displaying their necks in a manner that invited Jace to take a bite.

"Yes, Your Majesty. These orders came directly from him to me as the unit leader."

"Not through a sovereign or a regent?" Jace didn't bother hiding his surprise. "But directly from Lajos himself?"

"Yes, my lord," Vigil One responded, his voice shaking a little. "I-I can try radioing him, if—"

"That won't be necessary. My sovereign will handle it. Right, Darius?" Jace prompted, glancing over his shoulder to where the other regal vampire stood.

"Of course, my lord." Darius bowed his head slightly, then hooked his arm around Juliet's waist to take her with him.

I highly doubted he truly intended to call Prince Lajos, unless they were friends. I didn't know much about the royal vampire other than Lilith had seemed fond of him and he owned the territory formerly known as Hawaii—and I'd learned that from Jace's review of the leaders and their current regions.

I tried to recall what Lilith had said about him in previous conversations, but nothing important flashed through my mind.

"What's the purpose of the second unit?" Jace asked, reigniting his line of questioning. "Why are both of you needed here?"

"They'll be providing the escort to Bunker 27," Vigil One explained. "It's located in Majestic Clan territory."

Jace's eyebrows flew up as he shared a look with Damien.

The humans didn't see it because they were all still staring at the floor. Did they wonder at all how Jace had found them here? Or what had brought him here? They weren't making any moves to question him, nor did they show any signs of thinking through his presence at all.

It was as though they'd all fallen into an ingrained subservient mode and all that mattered now was doing whatever Jace demanded.

It didn't matter that he wasn't the royal over their specific regions. He was Prince Jace and standing before them all right now, thereby marking him as their current superior.

I knew this mentality existed in the current world. But witnessing it was an entirely different experience.

I'd submitted to Lilith. Just not like this. I'd never knelt or bowed, just answered her questions and offered my neck. I'd treated Jace similarly, giving him the information he desired, with a little bit of strategic negotiation. He hadn't frightened me.

However, seeing him now and realizing how much power he held at his fingertips, I couldn't help but wonder if I'd made a severe error in judgment.

"How far along are you in your task?" Jace asked after a beat.

"We've only just begun the download, My Prince." Vigil One slowly pointed to where their kit had been hooked into the server.

Damien followed the trajectory of his aim and took over the controls. "You have a live transfer feed engaged."

"Yes, to Bunker 37," Vigil One confirmed. "We're sending a copy to the servers there, then we're hand-delivering the other to Bunker 27."

Rather than reply, Damien began fussing with the connection, perhaps searching for anything that might be nefariously engaged or an alarm signal of any kind. But after a beat, he looked at Jace and said, "From what I can see, he's telling the truth."

"Where is Bunker 37?" Jace asked.

"Lajos Region," Vigil One confirmed. "It's our home base."

Not once did he think to question how Jace didn't know any of this, which told me the Vigils at Bunker 37 had never been instructed properly on security protocols. My instructions had been very clear—only those with jurisdiction were allowed to know these details.

And Jace had more than proved he didn't have jurisdiction in this operation.

Yet these humans bowed to him and gave him every answer without provocation.

Fascinating.

Would the Vigils from Bunker 47 have done the same? I wondered.

Maybe.

They came from a different sort of upbringing, their early lives spent at the Blood Universities around the country, where they fought for the privilege to become Vigils. They achieved their status through the death of other humans and by proving their loyalty to the immortals they served.

So I supposed bending to Jace's every will made sense for them.

"What happens at Bunker 37?" Jace demanded.

Vigil One cleared his throat. "That's… that's above our jurisdiction, My Prince. You would need to ask Prince Lajos."

"I see." Jace's hand moved from my hip to the back of my neck and squeezed. His silver-blue eyes resembled ice as I met his gaze, his expression as harsh as stone. "Do you have anything to add, Doctor?"

"That's the lab I was born in," I told him. "Bunker 37. It's where they do research on the mating bonds between vampires and humans, and the rare blood types."

"And Bunker 27?" he prompted.

"It's hive mind tech, which I only know because Lilith used that tech to control some of the stronger vampires in the labs."

"Vampires like Cam," Jace said, looking at Damien and then at the humans. "Have any of you ever met Cam?"

Silence followed.

Then one of the Vigils in the back—a dark-skinned male with long black hair—stammered out, "D-do you mean the v-vampire who opposed Lilith's rule?"

"The very one," Jace confirmed.

More silence.

Then Vigil One said, "F-forgive me, Your Highness, but I don't understand the question. Master Cam died during the revolution. Lilith killed him."

"No. She used hive mind tech to weaken and capture him," Jace corrected on a sigh. "Damien?"

The other male nodded in my peripheral vision. "I'll start the transfer process, but this is going to take weeks to dig through."

"Good." Jace's grip on my neck softened, but he didn't release me. "Leave the transfer alone as well. We don't want to tip anyone off at the disruption here."

"And the humans?"

"Are useful to us and will remain alive so long as they pledge their loyalty." Jace finally looked at me again. "And as for you, my apologies for doubting you. Now go be a good darling and help Damien, hmm?" He pressed a kiss to the edge of my mouth, then released me with a soft smile.

I blinked several times, stunned by his apology, but he was no longer paying attention to me. Instead, he was addressing the Vigils again, telling them their new orders were to report directly to him and do exactly what he said. Anyone wishing to disobey was free to make their way back outside and find their own way home because he intended to commandeer their plane.

None of them stood to leave.

None of them argued, either.

But as I turned, I swore I caught relief in some of their stances, like the idea of working for Jace put them at ease in some way.

I wondered at that revelation as I walked over to help Damien. And I continued to wonder about it while I worked with him to download as much data as we could to the devices Damien had brought with him.

Then I helped him set up a backdoor access point so he could log in whenever he wanted to pull additional files. It would give him all the details he wanted from this server farm, assuming nothing happened to the physical hard drives.

We also monitored the feed to Bunker 37, and Damien took one of the Vigil's watches to keep us apprised of any incoming protocols.

Nothing happened, our infiltration here seeming to be a secret.

By the time we finished, night had fallen and the rendezvous with Bunker 27 was scheduled to take place in two hours.

"Your alibi is arranged," Darius said as we exited the building, his words for Jace. "I've sent word that you stopped by my estate on your way back from visiting with Lilith in Ryder Region."

"Seems a bit out of the way directionally," Jace remarked.

"Yes. I implied that Juliet was the cause for your detour. Once they see Calina, I imagine they'll understand why."

"I do enjoy female-on-female play."

"You do," Darius agreed. "Which explains us accompanying you back to Jace City."

"Something you also arranged?"

"I did," his sovereign replied. "We're scheduled to leave my estate for Jace City in four hours. Damien mentioned something about altering flight scanners to corroborate all of this, including the bits from Ryder City to my home."

"It's fascinating that you avoided the political arena all these years," Jace commented. "You're extraordinarily good at it."

"Also, you'll be pleased to know Jasmine has agreed to meet us in Lajos Region in two days' time," Darius added, ignoring Jace's commentary about his political aspirations. "And Lajos also joyfully accepted our request for a visit."

Jace arched a brow. "Joyfully?"

Darius's green eyes darkened. "He's excited by the prospect of formally meeting Juliet."

"Ah, I thought she might work as a decent lure," Jace murmured. "He's been thirsting for a taste of your *Erosita* since you brought her to the Blood Day ceremony."

Darius didn't reply, but I sensed his displeasure in the tight lines of his shoulders.

"What about Luka?" Jace asked, ignoring the hard expression on the other man's face.

"He's arranging a welcoming crew near Bunker 27. He'll be awaiting Damien's signal."

"Brilliant." Jace turned to the Southern vampire with a smile. "I assume you're okay with taking lead on the assault on Bunker 27? You were craving blood after all, yes?"

Damien's lips curled into a feral grin. "Are you trying to seduce me, King Jace? Because we already know I'll happily kneel for you."

The mental image of Damien on his knees for Jace caused my cheeks to heat. Because that... that would be a sight to behold.

Jace returned the amused look. "Try to keep my new Vigils alive. I'm going to need them soon."

Damien snorted. "I'll see what tricks I can teach them on the way." He started toward the field, only for Jace to catch him by the nape and bring him back before him.

"I expect you to stay alive as well," Jace added. "If you suspect anything is about to happen, you'd better fucking run. Understood?"

Damien gave him a look. "You and Ryder are starting to

concern me with all this emotional bullshit." He visibly cringed. "Please don't hug me."

Jace huffed a laugh and patted him on the back instead. "I mean it, Damien. *Survive*."

"It's not like I want to die," Damien tossed back at him.

"Sometimes your actions suggest otherwise."

"I'm just living on the edge," he drawled. "But if Cam is down there, I'll risk everything for him."

"And that's exactly why you're the man for this job," Jace agreed, releasing the other man. "I expect a full report by dawn."

Damien gave a little wave as he led the Vigils toward the plane they'd arrived on. I was only vaguely aware of the plan.

Damien and the Vigils were going to Bunker 27 to complete the data transfer. Then Damien would meet up with Luka—the Alpha of Majestic Clan—and take over the bunker.

Meanwhile, Darius had arranged for us to travel to Lajos Region. They had a pretty good idea of where Bunker 37 was located because of Vigil One's directions, so they were opting to use the trip as a research opportunity and as an alibi of sorts for Jace in case anything went wrong at Bunker 27.

Jace extended a hand toward me. "Come, little genius. It's time for you to learn your new purpose in my world."

My stomach churned at the words. "M-my new purpose?"

"Yes." He locked gazes with me. "Congratulations, Calina. You just became a favored member of my harem. Which means I now have six hours to teach you what that means. We'll start by changing your wardrobe into something more suitable. Now let's go."

CHAPTER TWENTY

JACE

"This is a terrible idea," Darius muttered as Juliet and Calina disappeared into the back cabin of the plane.

I set my glass of red wine on the executive lounge table and faced him. "How else am I going to explain her presence and Ryder's plane?" I asked him. "It makes perfect sense that Lilith would call me in to try to wrangle the old vampire, just as it's quite plausible I would find a human of my liking and take her back with me."

"She has no record in the system—"

"Something Damien is going to fix for us on his way to Bunker 27," I interjected.

"And she has no formal training," he added, ignoring my interruption. "It's taken Juliet months to achieve the perfect charade. We have less than six hours to create a similar one for Calina. I'm not sure it can be done, Jace. She's too…" He waved a hand at the back door, as though that explained it all.

Unfortunately, it did. Because I understood exactly what he meant.

Calina exuded a confidence most humans lacked, and she didn't possess the sexual countenance typically required of my lovers.

However, the only way to explain her presence at my side was to introduce her as a new harem member. I had a reputation to keep up, at least for a little while longer, and that meant Calina had a very important part to play.

"She's intelligent," I said, the defense an easy one to make. "She's also strategic. If anyone can learn this role in six hours, it's her."

"You sound so certain after knowing her for a handful of hours."

Technically, it was days, but I didn't bother arguing over frivolous semantics.

"I've always been quick to assess those around me," I reminded him. "I'm not wrong about her."

"Says the man who thought she betrayed us earlier today."

"Hmm, no. That was more of a hope than a fact," I admitted. "The notion of punishing her is quite enticing."

Darius considered that for a moment, then sighed as he combed his fingers through his dark hair. "Well, at least the attraction won't need to be faked."

"It rarely is," I murmured, purposely striking a button. Because if we were going to pull this off, I needed him and Juliet to play along. Society knew Darius and I shared similar tastes in women, which meant if I found Calina appealing, he would, too.

Sharing was a mandate in this new world, something my sovereign despised. Juliet was very much his, and I respected that. But that didn't mean the others would feel the same.

Therefore, we put on a charade. Everyone thought I was smitten with Juliet, thus providing Darius a reason to keep her as his *Erosita*. It made her less breakable, which allowed me to play to my heart's content. Mostly, anyway. *Erositas* couldn't be fucked by anyone other than their vampire soul mate.

But in reality, I only touched her in public. And even then, I kept it playful in manner rather than overtly sexual.

"Lajos will expect a show," I said, thinking through our strategy out loud. "We'll need to give him one."

Darius's green eyes narrowed. "What are you proposing?"

"That we give him what he wants," I replied as the back cabin door opened.

Whatever Darius would have said to my comment died upon

seeing Juliet dressed in a black lace dress that revealed all her finest assets. The sight of her often distracted his thoughts, something I'd always understood as I also found Juliet alluring.

But seeing Calina dressed similarly beside her captured my entire focus.

Calina's translucent gown wasn't black but a dark blue, bringing out the highlights of her multicolored irises. Her dress stopped at her thighs, while Juliet's flowed to the floor. And unlike Juliet, Calina's bold gaze met mine.

"Did Lilith allow you to address her directly?" I wondered out loud. "Or is it your former profession that grants you this confidence?"

I supposed experimenting on vampires and lycans all day would belittle their superiority. But I highly doubted Lilith had accepted this behavior from Calina.

She cleared her throat, then glanced at Juliet's pose. Her pretty brown eyes were on the ground as she held her shoulders and back straight—a submissive pose meant to display her stunning attributes. It was perfectly executed, as always.

"Lilith required certain formalities," Calina said, still studying Juliet. "But she also left me in charge of my post, which required certain leadership qualities to be maintained in her absence."

"What about when she visited?" I pressed. "Did you bow? Submit? Offer your neck?"

"I delivered my reports in a timely fashion, then—"

"With direct eye contact?" Darius interjected, causing her gaze to go to his.

"Presenting reports is hard to do while staring at the floor." Her tone rang as confused more than insubordinate, like she was struggling to understand why this mattered.

I shared a look with him, telling him without words what needed to happen next. The slight dip of his chin told me that he agreed.

"Your position in life has officially changed, Doctor," I informed her. "Humans are property. Toys. *Food*. And the superior beings of this world require obedience and exquisite submission. One misstep will cost you your life."

"She would already be dead right now if she acted this way in front of Lajos," Darius muttered.

Technically, my age and bloodline superseded Lajos's authority. But using that power over him could damage my political sway in the vampire arena. Therefore, I'd be forced to let him correct Calina's disobedient behavior. Thereby making Darius's statement correct.

"He'd fuck her first," I replied, my eyes on Calina. "And he'd bleed her."

Which was the larger issue here because the moment someone else tasted her, they'd realize the uniqueness of her essence and turn her into a proper blood slave.

She'd crave death by the end.

It was my job to ensure that didn't happen.

"Juliet," I said, her name a caress from my lips. "I need your help in properly introducing Calina to her new role. As such, let's pretend we're at an event with others present. All rules apply."

Considering I'd sent them into the cabin to dress for the part, my order shouldn't surprise her.

"As you wish, My Prince." She executed a perfect curtsy in her three-inch stiletto heels—a feat, given that we were on a moving plane—and remained in that position as she awaited further instructions.

"Do you see how she addresses me and waits for her orders?" I asked, speaking to Calina. "That's what is expected of a female in her position. It would be expected of a favored consort as well."

Calina studied the other woman, her brow furrowing. "But she's not your *Erosita*."

"No, she's the *Erosita* of my sovereign. And his position is beneath mine in this world. Therefore, anything and everything he owns, I own. Including Juliet." Harsh words, but accurate ones. "If I want to fuck her, Darius has no choice in the matter. I can choose to break their bond at any moment. And there's nothing he can do about it."

Except challenge me.

Which he wouldn't.

Just as I would never harm Juliet.

Calina took in Juliet's bow, then studied Darius's stoic expression. "You allow this?"

"It's what society requires of us," he replied.

"And you accept that?"

"Whether I accept it or not is a moot point. This is the world we live in. If you want to survive, you need to follow the rules. Which you're doing a shit job of right now by continuing to stare directly at me and speaking to me as though we're equals." Darius's sharp words sliced through the air, drawing goose bumps along Juliet's arms. She responded so beautifully to his dominance.

Yet I remained captivated by Calina's shrewd expression as she evaluated everything we said. Darius's tone didn't impact her at all, her mind too busy processing the words to consider his delivery of them.

"If you're now king, you could change this," she said, her focus shifting to me. "If that's your desire."

"I could," I agreed. "With the right support."

She remained silent for a long, thoughtful moment. "A strategic game of winning over enough support before you properly take over. That's why you've not publicized Lilith's death yet. You need more support."

I merely smiled. "Regardless of what my intentions may or may not be, I need you to learn your place in this world. Failure on your part will lead to a most unpleasant future. And it could also put my life at risk, which isn't acceptable."

She took in Juliet's posture once more. "*Erositas* used to be revered. She resembles a slave in that position."

"That's precisely the point," Darius said, stepping forward. "She's my blood virgin. I purchased her from an auction, and she's here to do exactly what I say. No arguments. No contrary opinions. Just beautiful submission." He stopped in front of Juliet, his knuckles brushing her cheek. "Isn't that right, Juliet?"

"Yes, Sire." Her voice lacked hesitation, not just because she trusted him, but because she'd been taught to act this way.

"Juliet spent twenty-two years at the Coventus, learning how to submit to her future owner. She expected to die the night I purchased her because most blood virgins do. Their blood is rich and addictive, and it's rumored that they taste even sweeter with their death." Darius's touch shifted down to her chin as he drew her gaze up to his. "She plays the part beautifully."

The compliment painted a pretty blush on her features. "Thank you, Sire."

"Are you ready to play with her, My Prince? Or can I do the honors?" Darius asked, his formality telling me he'd fallen into the roles I'd suggested when Juliet and Calina had appeared.

Rather than answer him, I took on my own part in this act and ignored him.

"Vampires love the pleasures of life," I murmured, my gaze holding Calina's as I approached her slowly, my steps a silent saunter across the carpeted floor of the jet. "We feed. We fuck. And we always take what we want."

She swallowed, her pupils flaring to thin the vibrant colors of her irises.

"Most of us have lost our sense of humanity over the years," I continued softly as I paused before her. "We enjoy being the superior race, Calina. We accept all the rewards that come with it and ignore all the responsibilities."

Or most of us did, anyway. Which was the primary point of the change I desired.

But that was the purpose of our discussion right now.

I lifted my hand to cup her cheek and allowed my thumb to trace her bottom lip.

"Humans have been groomed to submit to our every whim." I turned her head toward Juliet. "Even now, she remains bowed, aware that it's my word that will release her. Not her Sire's. Because vampires and lycans always respect hierarchy and age."

Calina observed Juliet's unfaltering pose for another long moment before I guided her back to face me.

"I'm one of the oldest of my kind, Calina. Everyone admires my experience and expertise. Everyone respects me. And everyone does exactly what I say without question. Which is precisely what you will need to do, or I'll be forced to make an example of you." It was how our society worked. Disobedience wasn't tolerated, especially not by humans.

Oh, some vampires enjoyed games. Lycans, too. Many of them lived after playing, but no one went without punishment.

"This is the world Lilith created, the world my kind seems to adore. There are definitely benefits," I admitted, my gaze dropping to her low neckline and the translucent fabric displaying her erect nipples. "But those benefits are in favor of my brethren, not humans."

I tilted my head toward Juliet and Darius, my eyes following the motion.

"Show her how we feed when in front of an audience," I said, the command for Darius. "Consider it practice for what Lajos will desire."

As Lajos's elder in the vampire hierarchy, I wouldn't be required to give him a damn thing. But I had a reputation for this game and how I played it, which meant Darius and Juliet would need to engage in their parts for us to succeed.

"Mmm, gladly," Darius replied, his stoic expression turning to one of pure animalistic hunger. "Stand." His grip shifted to the back of Juliet's nape as he pulled her up from her curtsy.

CHAPTER TWENTY-ONE

JACE

Juliet's thighs had to burn from holding that pose, yet she showed no outward signs of discomfort. Perhaps because Darius provided her with healthy doses of his own blood for healing. Or more likely because she'd been practically raised in that position.

I very much doubted Calina could submit in that manner for as long as Juliet—something I would account for in my plan.

Darius led Juliet to the table where I'd left my glass of wine. He moved everything out of the way before demanding, "Present yourself for me, darling. I'm starving."

My fingers drifted along Calina's jaw and down her throat. Featherlight. Tender. But underlined with lethal promise.

She swallowed in response, her pulse skipping a beat.

I hummed in approval as I drew my touch along the neckline of her dress to the deep V between her breasts.

"This dress is beautiful on you," I whispered. "But it's not nearly short enough." Likely because the gown belonged to Juliet and she had a few inches on Calina's height. "I'll order you a wardrobe for our trip, one that fits properly."

No more lab coats or scrubs for the stunning doctor. She would be wearing lace for the foreseeable future.

Or maybe just skin.

Juliet gracefully positioned herself on the table while Darius took a seat between her splayed thighs. She lay back on the wood with her legs dangling over the edge and enticingly situated the slit of her gown by dragging the fabric over to one side and exposing her lower body to Darius's view.

My hands fell to Calina's hips, and I turned her to face the show, pressing my chest to her back and my lips to her ear. "Vampires crave touch." The words were soft and meant for her, but I knew Darius could hear them even over the roar of the engines. "We're sensual creatures who love to fuck. And there's nothing sexier to us than mingling pleasure with blood."

This was information she already knew, but that didn't mean she fully understood it.

"You told me vampires are innately sexual to lure our prey. You're not wrong. However, we all have our own preferences in how we hunt and feed." I kissed the throbbing pulse point at her neck as Darius drew his palms up Juliet's bare thighs. The fabric of her gown had revealed her entirely, the slits meant precisely for this purpose.

"Many of us are sadists," I continued softly. "We like pain. We like to hear humans scream. We like to make them bleed."

Darius bent to press his lips to the inside of Juliet's knee, eliciting a shiver from the female on the table.

Her arousal graced the air, the sweet scent an enticement that beckoned to my baser instincts. But Calina's sharp intake of air captured my focus, her own fragrance a taunt to my self-control.

I wanted to splay her on that table in the same position as Juliet and taste her delicious cunt.

Soon, I promised myself as Darius began licking a path upward. *Very soon.*

"Most vampires would already be feeding," I told her. "But Darius likes to prolong the moment, to tease the arousal out of her and force her submission entirely."

I nibbled Calina's earlobe and wrapped my arms around her waist, securing her against me as she fought to remain standing on the shoes Juliet had given her. They were stilettos, and I suspected they might be a little too big, just like the dress. Calina probably didn't wear heels often, if ever.

Another factor I would have to remember for our scenario in Lajos Region.

Juliet's fingers curled into fists at her sides, her eyes closing in pleasure-induced agony as Darius continued his slow path upward.

"It's all about sensual presentation." I spoke the words against Calina's ear once more. "There's power in displaying patience, particularly when enticed by such a rare blood type. Most in Darius's position wouldn't be able to hold back. Which makes what he's doing that much more erotic."

I nuzzled her neck to punctuate the point.

Her blood called to me, but I was able to delay the gratification of tasting her. Even as her interest piqued around me, her pussy wet beneath her gown, ready for me to engage her. I could taste it on my tongue, her desire to play an aphrodisiac that tested my patience.

But I was a master at this game.

Just like Darius.

Juliet's lips parted on a silent moan as her master's mouth reached the intimate crease between her leg and her slick flesh. No bite, just a lick, accompanied by a growl of hunger from the predator before her.

"See how she remains silent?" I asked softly, my hold loosening as I returned my hands to Calina's hips. "No begging. No moaning. No screams. It's how humans are taught to behave. They only vocalize when given permission. Which is why your directness needs to be corrected. No one will tolerate that from you."

She shivered against me as I began to pull up the fabric of her gown, my fingers eager to confirm the dampness between her thighs.

"Lajos would make you drop to your knees right now, Calina. He'd want your mouth on his cock to get him off while he watched Darius feed from Juliet's delectable pussy." I exposed Calina's heated flesh to the plane, not that anyone was watching us. "He'd force you to deep-throat him until you passed out."

I skimmed my teeth along her neck and licked the thundering rhythm beneath her fragile skin. She trembled, exciting my savage side.

I wanted to do just what I'd described—order her to kneel and fuck her throat raw.

But this all played into my prowess and how I preferred to indulge in sensual games.

"I'll be taking you to Lajos Region as my preferred consort. Lajos is probably going to want a taste of whatever I deem valuable. So long as you behave, I won't have to agree. But it requires you to be just like Juliet is now—silent, seductive, and sinfully provocative."

Darius chose that moment to sink his fangs into Juliet's clit, causing her back to arch up off the table as she came instantly from his bite.

Calina shuddered against me, her balance shifting. I palmed her sex to hold her in place, my finger gliding with ease through the evidence of her desire.

I wrapped my opposite arm around her chest, keeping her in place as the fabric of her gown remained bunched up against her hips.

"Lilith never fed from you like this." It was a statement, not a question. Because her reaction told me she'd never seen this before.

She didn't reply, her sharp focus on Juliet and Darius as he devoured his *Erosita*, keeping her in a heightened state of arousal the whole time.

Her cheeks were pink with exertion, her lips parted on a silent scream. She quivered violently, causing Darius to put a hand on her abdomen to hold her down against the table while he fed.

"This could be painful." I hummed the words into Calina's ear. "He could choose to withdraw the endorphins at any moment. Then she would have to do her best not to shriek in pain. It's a game a lot of my brethren play because they enjoy torturing their food."

I slid two fingers into her, drawing a hiss from her lips.

"Even the slightest reaction can cause a vampire to turn violent," I warned her, my lips dropping to her neck, where I pierced her skin in reprimand for her vocalizing a reaction.

She jumped, but I held her in place with ease.

Her thighs clenched in response to the pull of my mouth against her vein, providing an interesting detail about her own proclivities. I'd withheld the pleasurable aspect of my bite, yet that only seemed to intrigue her more.

Which suggested she enjoyed a little pain in the bedroom.

Mmm, definitely my kind of woman, I marveled, losing myself to her taste.

She didn't scream. She didn't speak. And that hiss was the only sound she'd made.

"Such a good student," I praised her, releasing her neck and letting the blood trickle enticingly from her open wound.

Darius had stopped feeding as well, his attention on Juliet's pleasure-drunk state as he stood to loosen his belt.

I'd told him to give us a show like he would with Lajos, and he'd either taken my words to heart or forgotten we were here.

Likely the former because he wasn't the type to dismiss his surroundings. And it wasn't like I hadn't seen him fuck before.

He'd also want to mark his territory in front of Lajos, which made this move strategic on Darius's part. Of course, it displayed a hint of possessive intent as well.

One I was beginning to understand because I didn't much fancy the idea of Lajos touching Calina. But I also hadn't been wrong to warn her that he might.

"I think we should practice, sweet Calina," I said, making a decision.

If I enjoyed her attentions first, then I would be more willing to share Calina with Lajos. I also needed to ensure she was ready for that, which required me to guide her on what to expect. The more she understood, the more likely she would stay alive.

"Darius, sweeten my wine." I uttered the words in my usual pretentious tone, assuming my role as his superior.

He didn't hesitate, his annoyance hidden beneath a mask of indifference. To anyone else, he appeared unbothered by my request. But I knew him and understood his relationship with Juliet.

I held Calina in place, forcing her to watch as he brought my glass to Juliet's cunt and flavored the rim with her sweet, arousal-tinged blood.

It was exactly what Lajos would request.

And most likely what we would offer preemptively so he wouldn't demand anything else.

Darius took a sip of the wine, ensuring the flavor was what I desired, then added a little more by squeezing Juliet's abused clit.

She jolted but didn't scream.

While the action appeared harsh, I knew he'd softened it for her, perhaps with a warning in her mind or a subtle flick of his thumb. He always guaranteed her pleasure, regardless of how savage he made it appear.

I slipped from Calina's tight sheath and brought my fingers to her lips. "Open." She swallowed, then did exactly what I told her. "Good girl," I praised, sliding my fingers into her mouth. "Now suck."

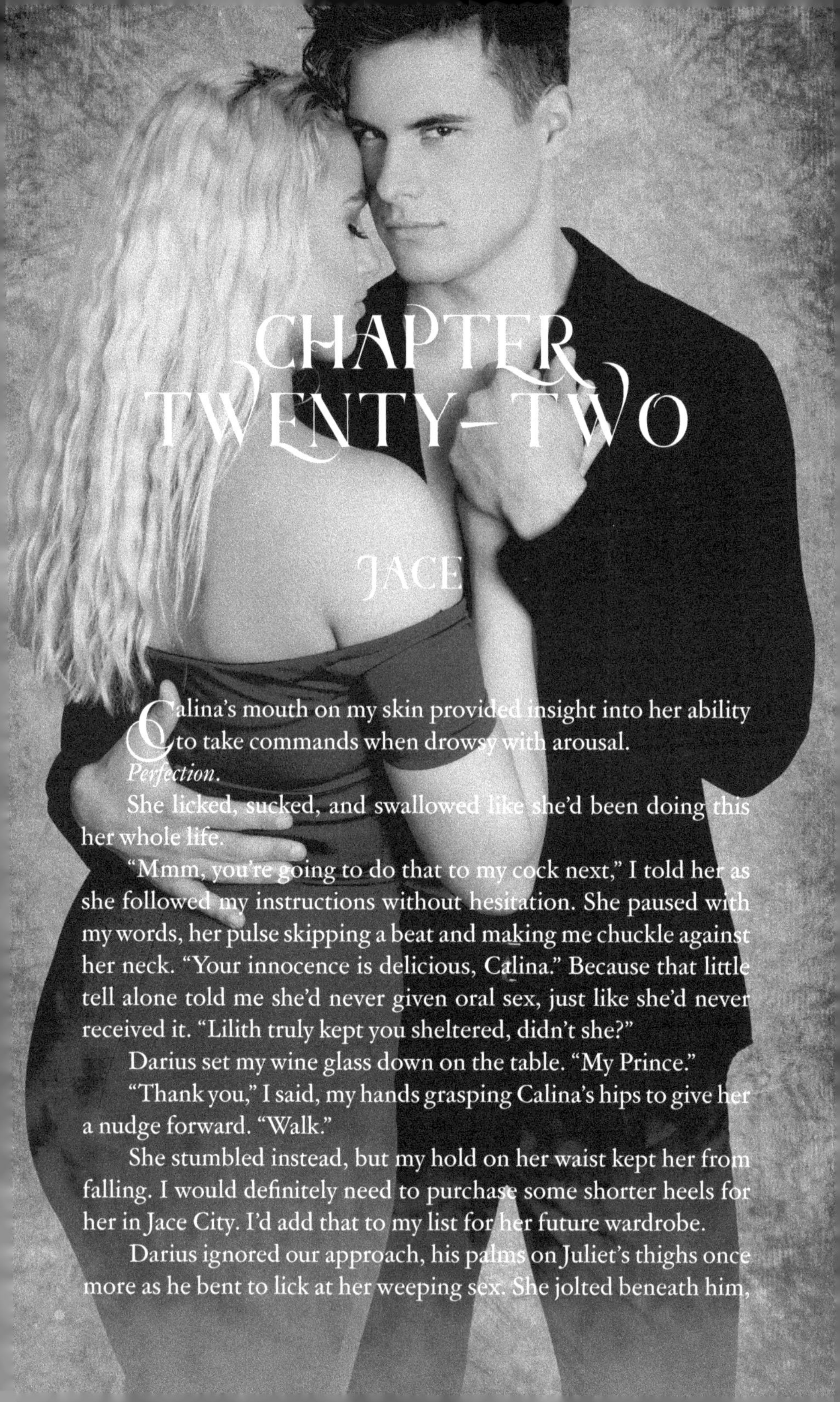

CHAPTER TWENTY-TWO

JACE

Calina's mouth on my skin provided insight into her ability to take commands when drowsy with arousal.

Perfection.

She licked, sucked, and swallowed like she'd been doing this her whole life.

"Mmm, you're going to do that to my cock next," I told her as she followed my instructions without hesitation. She paused with my words, her pulse skipping a beat and making me chuckle against her neck. "Your innocence is delicious, Calina." Because that little tell alone told me she'd never given oral sex, just like she'd never received it. "Lilith truly kept you sheltered, didn't she?"

Darius set my wine glass down on the table. "My Prince."

"Thank you," I said, my hands grasping Calina's hips to give her a nudge forward. "Walk."

She stumbled instead, but my hold on her waist kept her from falling. I would definitely need to purchase some shorter heels for her in Jace City. I'd add that to my list for her future wardrobe.

Darius ignored our approach, his palms on Juliet's thighs once more as he bent to lick at her weeping sex. She jolted beneath him, lost to her master's tongue.

Such an erotic sight.

One I wanted to replicate with Calina.

"I want to hear Juliet scream," I murmured as we reached the table. "Make her come again."

Darius responded by ripping the fabric from her torso and exposing her tits. He palmed them in the next breath, squeezing the supple flesh as he pierced her sensitive bud once more.

Juliet fell apart on a beautiful display of euphoria, causing Calina to quiver beneath my hands. "Is that just his vampiric powers making her scream like that?" I asked against her ear. "Or is it him?"

I didn't give her a chance to answer, instead spinning her in my arms and capturing her mouth with my own.

The taste of her sweet arousal still lingered on her tongue, giving me a heady dose of her addictive flavor.

Juliet continued to moan, followed by Darius growling, their mingled sounds a seduction to my senses.

"This is how vampires play with their food," I said against Calina's mouth. "Especially our favorite treats. And sometimes we share. Sometimes we don't."

I wrapped my palm around the back of her neck, then kissed her again. This time deeper and with intent.

I wanted more.

I wanted her.

I didn't want to share.

And I didn't have to. I was a fucking royal. An old vampire. The future king.

I pulled her into the executive chair across from Darius and Juliet, forcing Calina to straddle my thighs. Her lace dress was still bunched up to her hips, placing her slick folds right against the zipper of my pants.

"Fuck," I whispered, my sense of control slipping.

I was supposed to be teaching her. Showing her how to behave. Ensuring her survival. But all I wanted was to unfasten my trousers and plunge deep inside her.

The feral snarl from Darius wasn't helping. His grunts didn't either. And neither did the savage song of fucking that followed as he took Juliet against the table.

This was no longer about demonstrating society's expectations for Calina, but about animalistic need and sensual anticipation.

I bit her tongue, desiring her blood more than the sweetened wine from Darius.

Calina's essence filled our mouths, giving me what I craved.

I nicked my own tongue in the next second, giving her access to the power bursting through my veins.

It was so natural. Yet I never did this with my consorts. But something about this female called to the dark beast inside me, the one that desired carnal possession of her body.

She'd bespelled me entirely, destroying my focus and undoing the groundwork I'd been attempting to establish here.

"Unbutton my pants," I commanded against her lips. "Now."

Her hands went to my belt first. Then to the button. But her cunt was too close to my cock for her to unzip the barrier between us.

I pushed her back on my legs, eager to complete the path we were on, only for that brief second of disconnect between us to remind me of our purpose.

I felt dizzy with indecision, my mind torn between strategic maneuvering and fucking the woman on my lap.

What the hell is wrong with me?

I never craved females this badly. I never lost control. I was over four thousand years old.

One taste and I'd nearly lost my damn mind again.

This female was dangerous.

I needed her out of my system. Leashed. *On her knees.*

"Kneel." It came out on an angry snarl that had her jolting to comply. I didn't give her a moment to find her comfort. Didn't allow her to prepare for my crudeness. Just finished unzipping my pants, grabbed a fistful of her hair, and harshly demanded she open her fucking mouth.

She did.

I thrust home.

And *fuckkk,* it was like I'd gone straight to heaven.

Her velvety smooth tongue stroked my shaft, her throat closing beautifully around the head.

She choked.

I didn't care.

Tears graced her eyes.

I flicked them away with my thumbs.

This wanton little genius had driven me to madness, and I wanted to punish her for it. I wanted to fall to my knees and worship her as well.

It was a tangle of emotion and thought and confusion that lit my blood on fire, forcing me to take her harder, my perception of our reality burning to ash inside my mind.

Curses left my mouth.

Her name resembled a prayer.

I couldn't figure out what I wanted or how I wanted to accomplish it, but all I knew was I *needed* to come.

I needed to drench her insides with my seed.

To own her.

Complete her.

Make her mine.

And where the hell was that desire even coming from? I couldn't keep this female.

"Your blood is bewitching me," I accused as I forced her to take even more of me down her throat.

Her pupils flared as she stared up at me, disobedience etched into her expression.

I couldn't bring myself to harm her for it, not when I found myself so lost to that intense glint in her hazel irises.

That was the look of a female determined to survive whatever I gave her, and destroy me in the process.

And bloody hell, it only made me harder.

This female defied all expectations. She rewrote the rules on existence. She was on her knees and refusing to submit even with my cock in her throat.

I wasn't sure who owned whom in this moment, but the defiance in her gaze suggested she'd somehow come out on top of this arrangement.

"We'll see," I promised her, not making any sense as I thrust into her welcoming heat with a renewed yearning to claim her from the inside out. "Relax your fucking throat."

I tightened my fingers in her hair, the only reprimand I was willing to give.

But the doctor proved to be an apt pupil once more as she followed my instructions by opening her mouth wider for my thrusts.

"Beautiful," I whispered, using my hand on the back of her head to guide her motions. "So damn good."

It took humans years at the universities to learn how to take cock like this. But Calina was no ordinary human. And she proved that as she drew her teeth along my sensitive skin, just enough to threaten without hurting.

"Mmm, do that again," I demanded.

She did, this time sucking along the way until only my head was in her mouth. Her tongue danced around the crown, drawing a shudder from me before I plunged back inside.

Her gaze took on a new gleam, the researcher in her learning what I liked and repeating the motions with a perfection that had my balls aching to unleash everything down her slender throat.

This woman didn't need a lesson in sex. She just needed to be tempted into teaching herself.

My grip tightened in her silky blonde strands, my abdomen clenching as flames erupted through my being. "Swallow, Calina," I said. "Swallow it all."

It was the only form of punishment I could give—the demand that she take everything she inspired from within me and devour each drop.

However, the way her nostrils flared told me it wasn't a form of reprimand to her at all, but a challenge. And it was that insightful glimpse into her personality that shot me right over the edge.

I wanted her to drown.

I wanted her to swim.

I wanted her to suffocate beneath the waves of pleasure pouring out of my shaft.

And I wanted to revive her again with my blood in her mouth. My tongue on her cunt. My fingers lodged deep within her.

Fuck, the passionate image spurred me onward, the vibrations of pleasure causing my thighs to clench as I bathed her throat with my cum.

She swallowed.

And swallowed.

And swallowed.

Her eyes glistened with renewed tears. Panic flared in her nostrils. Her need to breathe a likely ache inside her chest.

"Don't stop." It came out guttural. Cruel. Cold. But inside, I was inflamed with the need to fill up her body with my essence. Possess her. Own her. Mark her as mine.

She started to fade, her throat no longer able to massage my shaft the way I desired.

Most of my kind would kill a human for failing them during such a crucial act.

But I quite fancied Calina alive.

I pulled her off my cock before she could pass out. She sputtered as some of my essence painted her cheek. Then her big, wet eyes met mine.

She was perfect.

Stunning.

Utterly exquisite.

And all I could think to do was to return the favor.

I didn't put her on the table like Darius had done to Juliet. Instead, I carried her to the back room and laid her on the bed.

Ryder would probably kill me later for this. But he could have the linens cleaned.

Mutual satisfaction was more important.

I spread Calina's creamy thighs and knelt between her legs. Then I pressed an intimate kiss to the sweetness I'd craved for what had felt like an eternity.

She didn't disappoint, her clit almost as tempting as her femoral artery.

"Jace," she whispered, breaking the rules by speaking out of turn. But the throaty way she said my name made any and all forms of castigation impossible. Particularly considering the raspy quality of that sound.

I'd fucked her throat raw. She could hardly speak.

Another detail for my plan.

I could absolutely work with that method of silencing my new consort.

But I wanted to test that theory more, see how truly it held.

So I sank my teeth into her intimate flesh, just like Darius had done to Juliet.

Calina screamed, the reaction hoarse and holding a touch of pain. However, her pleasure seemed to be overriding that torment.

I sucked and nibbled and bit her again.

And again.

Forcing her to climax each time until her screams were silent because her throat was too raw to create sound.

Only then did I finally stop, her body shaking and her cheeks covered in tears. I crawled up the bed to press my lips to hers, offering her the antidote to her passion-induced agony.

At first, she didn't swallow, as though incapable of such an action. But as the blood from my fang-pierced tongue trickled down her devastated insides, she slowly began to recover.

It was a gift I never offered my consorts.

But it was also a gift they never required.

Because what I'd just done to Calina would have killed a human. It'd been too much. Too rough. Too intense. Too carnal.

Yet she'd taken it all.

She'd never once begged me to stop.

And as she stared up at me now, I only saw one word glittering in her gaze.

More.

CHAPTER TWENTY-THREE

GALINA

I couldn't feel my legs.

They were like useless limbs hanging limply from my hips. Yet somehow, I was standing.

And in heels, too.

With another dress from Juliet's bags.

I studied myself in the mirror, noting my flushed cheeks and swollen lips. Jace had pulled my hair back into a messy bun—very different from my usual orderly one—to display the twin bite marks on my neck.

There was another on my left breast, which was visible, thanks to the low cut of my lingerie.

No, wait, it's a dress.

I eyed the translucent material and twisted my lips to the side. It left me essentially naked with a greenish tint covering bits of my skin. I preferred the navy one from earlier, but Jace had ripped it during one of my many orgasms.

He'd pretty much traced every inch of my body with his mouth, like he'd intended to embed his essence into my skin.

I shivered, my insides warming with the memories of his

intimate touch.

Whatever lesson he'd been trying to teach me had been lost to his mouth. I understood the basics of what he needed me to know—submit like the Vigils used to submit to Lilith. They'd always bowed in her presence, never making eye contact or speaking to her.

Although, Jace had also mentioned Lajos and what he might do to me.

I didn't care for that part.

Fortunately, that was an issue for when we went to Lajos Region.

In less than two days.

"That color brings out your eyes, just like the blue one," Jace said as he approached from behind, his focus on my reflection in the mirror.

He'd changed into an all-black suit, but his hair was still tousled from my fingers running through it.

My cheeks heated at the fresh memory. It was almost as though Jace had awoken a dormant side of me, creating a whole new person in this jet. I barely recognized myself. And if his goal had been to make me fear him, he'd failed.

However, I did recognize the dangers of others like him.

I also understood the purpose of obeying.

Jace might not be a monster, but Lilith's allies were. And while I'd not met any of them, I knew she had them. Somewhere.

Otherwise, I'd be dead.

Because my bloodline was linked to at least one other immortal, potentially more.

"What has you perplexed?" he asked, his voice soft. "Are you concerned about what happens when we land?"

I blinked. "No. Not really. I'll just duck my head and follow your lead." Similar to what Juliet did with Darius, only I wouldn't have the comfort of knowing Jace actually cared about my well-being. I wasn't naïve enough to think that our sexual interlude had created any feelings on his part. As he'd said, vampires enjoyed playing with their food.

His palms slid up my arms to my shoulders as he stopped behind me. "Then what are you thinking about?"

It took me a second to consider the meaning of his question, my mind having already moved on to my personal security. But that was caused by his previous question regarding what I expected for our arrival.

Before that, I'd been thinking about my lineage. Which I told him now, and concluded with, "The fact that I'm still alive tells me I'm still tied to at least one vampire through a link similar to the *Erosita* connection."

"Unless you've started aging normally and are no longer immortal," he replied, frowning. "When an *Erosita* bond is broken, the mortal just resumes their standard ages."

"Yes. But my case isn't normal. I have lycan genetics from my mother. However, that line was severely repressed by my *Erosita* sperm-donor father. Then Lilith linked me to her in ways never explained to me. And I've been told there is at least one other. I... I can also sense it."

"The link?"

"No." I fought for words on how to explain the feeling. "The ties were dulled decades ago, and I can't even really feel them. But I can sense my immortality. Like, if it was missing, I'd know. And nothing feels wrong."

"I see. And you don't know who you're linked to?"

I shook my head. "No, but I'm hoping we might find something at Bunker 37." It had been one of my first thoughts when he'd said we were heading there. I also wanted to review the logs from the server farm, but Damien had them.

"You're telling me this so I know you'll be cooperative on our journey because it benefits you," Jace replied, his hands giving my shoulders a squeeze. "Well played."

"Actually, I was just telling you what I would like to discover. The next two days will provide proof of my willingness to cooperate." I met his gaze in the mirror. "I also believe my behavior on this jet has proven my intentions as well."

I'd also behaved during our trip to the server farm, but that fact seemed moot since this next journey had nothing to do with my research experiences and everything to do with my ability to play the part of a broken, docile human.

He studied my reflection for a moment, then turned me to face him. "You won't be able to speak to me like this once we disembark the jet. You also won't be able to look at me or anyone else. Not until I say otherwise, anyway."

"I'm aware of how the human Vigils acted in Lilith's presence. I will do my best to mimic their behaviors."

Jace's expression turned thoughtful. "Vigils have more benefits than most humans in this world. But my harem members are typically treated with a similar respect, so that should work for our purposes." He leaned down to kiss my exposed neck, his teeth sinking into the wound he'd already created.

A tremble worked through my limbs, his touch and mouth eliciting an array of sensations throughout my core. Lilith's bite had never done this to me. But she'd also never done any of those other things Jace had done... like bite me *down there*.

My eyes fell closed as I indulged in the sensations. His palms slid downward to cover my breasts, his thumbs stroking my nipples through the barely there fabric.

A moan caught in my throat, my body reacting to the female inside me—this wanton creature who craved more.

I'd been starved of touch my whole life, having no idea what I'd been missing. Until Jace.

And now I feared I'd never be the same again.

"Is it still just my vampiric prowess, little genius?" he asked against my ear.

I swallowed, his question one he'd asked numerous times throughout the last twenty-four hours. Like every other time, I refused to answer.

Which only made him chuckle against my throat.

"I'm interpreting your silence as a request for a more in-depth study of the topic." He kissed my cheek, his gaze meeting mine in the mirror. "Consider this my acceptance of your challenge, Doctor. I look forward to engaging in several rounds of experimentation before you draft a summary of our results." His icy irises glittered with intent. "And I'll expect you to recite those results while deep-throating my cock."

My stomach burned as he released me, my insides turning to liquid heat at the promise in those words.

And his resulting expression told me he knew it.

This male took confidence to a whole new level, his age and

experience only adding to the arrogant flair of his features.

Lilith had exuded a similar air about her, except with an added layer of superiority. Jace struck me as someone who knew he was powerful and didn't need to lord over others to prove it. While Lilith had loved being in charge and wanted everyone to bow to her as a result.

Very different approaches.

At least from what I'd observed.

Now that we were entering his territory, my conclusion might change. But something told me it wouldn't.

He paused at the door and held out a hand toward me, his gaze once again finding mine in the mirror. "Calina."

I turned and gave him my best curtsy. "My Prince." It was the term he'd told me to use. Or *Your Highness*.

"Beautiful," he murmured. "Stand."

I happily did because holding that pose made my thighs burn. I wasn't sure how Juliet had held it for so long earlier, her discipline resolute in obeying these vampires.

Are all humans that indoctrinated into this world? I wondered.

I knew bits and pieces about the old one, mostly from my time in the labs and the research files I'd been able to review. Which was how I knew about San Francisco, the location now renamed as Jace City. It used to be a popular technology sector in the previous era.

"Now walk toward me." Jace continued to hold out his hand, perhaps to catch me if I fell—a likely scenario, considering the wobbly nature of these thin heels.

However, with the jet parked, I found I could more easily move across the carpet. Not elegantly or seductively like Juliet, but eloquently enough to function.

"Good girl," Jace praised, taking hold of my arm as I reached him. "Now just keep your head down and only speak when I tell you to, and you'll pass your first test."

I didn't reply, earning me a chuckle.

"Off to an excellent start," he murmured, his lips pressing into my cheek again.

The praise bled into my psyche, giving me the strange urge to smile. I ignored the inclination and focused on the task of walking with Jace and not falling—a task that proved much harder as we navigated the stairs outside the jet.

"Well, not entirely graceful," Darius said by way of greeting from the ground. "But she'll pass so long as you don't let go of her."

Jace released my arm and drew his finger up my exposed spine. "I can think of more unpleasant activities in my life."

"Indeed," his sovereign agreed, his tone telling me he'd just done something similar to Juliet. I couldn't see them since my focus was on the ground, which happened to work in my favor as we began to move because it allowed me to watch my step.

"Straighten your shoulders and only bow your head," Jace said against my ear, correcting my posture with his palm against my lower back.

I adjusted my position without comment, causing him to gently stroke my spine once more. A chill accompanied his touch, not because I found it particularly unpleasant, but the cool night air around us began to seep in through the thin lace of my dress.

This outfit was entirely impractical for the weather, something my arms seemed to agree with as goose bumps pebbled along my limbs.

It took restraint not to shiver, each step chilling me more than the next.

Jace's palm flattened against my lower back, his warmth doing little to heat my rapidly cooling state.

Fortunately, we reached a long black car after a few more steps. Jace wasted no time in ushering me into the back. Then he took a seat beside me on the leather bench while Juliet and Darius seated themselves across from us.

Silence fell as the door closed.

And it continued as the engine roared to life.

I kept my eyes down, doing my best to adhere to the role of subservient human—a position I much preferred to the blood bag status Jace had mentioned earlier.

His palm went to my thigh, reminding me of the short hem of my dress as his fingertips relaxed just inches from my sex.

The vibrations of the car beneath me suddenly took on a different sensation inside me, my new seductress side brushing the surface of my thoughts. I squirmed a little in response, causing Jace to tighten his grip. "Stay still," he demanded.

I swallowed, my heart galloping in my chest.

"Ryder must not have trained her properly," Darius said. "At least you'll enjoy fixing it."

"Yes, I intend to start immediately." Jace's crisp tone held an edge of annoyance to it. "I'll need you to reach out to Ivan and let him know I won't be joining my harem as previously scheduled. I imagine he and Trevor can continue entertaining them in my absence. As you know, some humans require a firmer hand than others."

"Yes, they can't all be as suitable as my Juliet," Darius returned.

"No. She's truly one of a kind." The fondness in Jace's voice replaced the hint of irritation, and I sensed his lips were tilted upward.

"What do you have to say to that, darling?" Darius asked.

Her answer was immediate. "Thank you, My Prince. It's a pleasure to serve you, as always."

"Perhaps you can join me in my quarters today and help me continue Calina's retraining," Jace offered.

"I would enjoy that immensely, Your Highness," Juliet replied.

"Brilliant. Darius, bring her up with you after you deliver the news to Ivan. We'll have a proper nightcap."

"Of course, My Prince."

Jace gave my leg another squeeze, this one holding a meaning I didn't understand. Comfort? Disappointment? A warning of some kind?

I was nowhere near an answer as we came to a stop again several minutes later at some sort of checkpoint that required the driver to speak to someone outside.

It took serious effort not to look.

Then we were moving again, and we all fell back into a world of silence while I pondered Darius and Jace's conversation. They hadn't spoken that way on the plane, telling me there must be some sort of listening device nearby. Or maybe it was the driver. Jace hadn't greeted him in any way when we'd entered. He also hadn't spoken to whoever had opened the door.

Very different from the pilot he'd spoken to at length when we'd boarded.

Although, the pilot had been a vampire.

Was the driver a human?

I couldn't tell from my vantage point of staring at the ground.

This really is ridiculous, I thought, fighting the urge to grit my teeth.

Humans might be inferior in strength, speed, and general vitality, but we weren't brain-dead creatures. I was living proof of that as Lilith's former head researcher at Bunker 47.

Jace and Darius began speaking about their travel plans for Lajos Region and listing everything that needed to be done prior to our departure.

Appointments were needed for me and Juliet.

Pampering, they called it.

Jace commented on my need for a new wardrobe while Darius presumably took notes.

"And it seems Sebastian has just checked in," the sovereign said, his tone telling me that he wasn't thrilled by the prospect. "He's requested a meeting with me."

"With you?" Jace sounded surprised. "Why?"

"He fancies himself as the reason for my recent promotion." Darius didn't sound impressed. "I'll entertain him just to be polite. Besides, Juliet enjoyed our last dinner party, didn't you?"

"Of course, Sire." She sounded so meek and quiet, the opposite of how I typically spoke.

"Let me know what you intend to put on the menu," Jace replied. "I may invite myself."

Darius must have nodded because he didn't reply out loud.

Their conversation continued in a similar fashion, their itinerary almost completely defined before the car came to a stop again.

The door opened almost immediately, and Jace slid out with a softly spoken "Come along, Calina."

CHAPTER TWENTY-FOUR

CALINA

I slid along the backseat bench, doing my best to keep my dress from riding up to my hips along the way, and stood carefully on my heels once outside of the car.

Jace caught my elbow and pulled me to the side as Juliet and Darius joined us. Their feet were the only things I could see along with the sidewalk.

Lovely view, I thought. *Just marvelous.*

Jace's palm settled against my back as he guided me forward. This time he addressed everyone around us, greeting his staff by name and being generally kind while maintaining an air of authority.

Lilith had chosen to intimidate.

Jace chose to lead.

Fascinating.

But it struck me as strange that he didn't treat his driver similarly to everyone else. I again wondered if he was human or vampire because we seemed to be moving by all types of life on our way inside. And Jace treated them all equally. He even paused in the reception area to address a mortal male by saying, "Please bring Darius's bags up to my suite. He and Juliet will be staying in one of my guest rooms."

"Y-yes, My Prince." It was the stutter in his voice that told me he was human.

That and his lack of proper clothes.

I couldn't see above his knees, but he wasn't wearing dress pants or fancy shoes. Just baggy red pants and tennis shoes.

"Paula, I'll be keeping Staff Member..." Jace trailed off, his tone implying he wanted someone to finish the sentence for him.

"Thirteen, My Prince," the human whispered, the words sounding strained, like he didn't want to voice them but didn't have a choice.

"Staff Member Thirteen," Jace repeated, his tone thoughtful. "Yes, Paula, I'll be keeping Staff Member Thirteen for the night. Be sure to note that in his file for me. I'll return him when I'm done, assuming he's still alive."

"Of course, My Prince," a female—presumably, Paula—replied.

As we continued on our path, I began to wonder if Jace ever tired of being addressed so formally all the time.

My Prince.

Your Highness

Over and over again, always with murmurs of agreement before the formal phrase.

By the time we entered the elevator, my head was whirling with the repeated words.

Then Jace was suddenly in front of me, walking me back into the wall with one hand on my hip and the other at my throat.

I startled, realizing there was no one else with us in this tiny box. Just me and Jace. "Bored?" he drawled, his thumb forcing my chin upward to bring my gaze to his.

Storm clouds stared down at me, a strike of lightning seeming to flicker in his pupils.

"No, My Prince," I replied, delighting in being able to say something different from all the mundane expressions of acceptance downstairs.

His eyebrow lifted. "You're amused?"

I considered that for a moment, trying to find a clever way to reply. "I'm thoughtful, Your Highness." I almost laughed at having to address him so formally again.

I'm losing my mind.

Or maybe I was just tired. Exhausted. Overwhelmed from the last few days. Lost in a world of submissive humans and banal semantics.

He had to be tired of it.

I'd only spent this small amount of time around it, and already I was over the formalities and ridiculous structure.

"Thoughtful," he repeated. "I see."

His palm squeezed around my throat, tightening the air supply just enough to tell me I'd done something wrong.

I couldn't imagine what—I'd remained silent and stared at the floor the whole way. No one spoke to me. Only him. *His Highness.*

A strange desire to laugh tickled my insides, causing me to squirm a little.

Both of Jace's eyebrows shot up now.

And for whatever reason, I found that expression downright hilarious.

Was he truly surprised by my reaction? The whole pretense established here was utterly comical.

Lilith had required similar formalities at the lab, but they were different somehow. Perhaps because she'd owned all of us and the labs.

But Jace owned this territory and his subjects.

So no. That couldn't be it.

"I can't decide if I want to fuck you or kill you right now," Jace said, drawing me out of my thoughts.

A ding sounded behind him.

He dragged me away from the wall with his hand still on my throat, his other palm on my hip, and guided me through the elevator doors.

I held his stare the whole time, refusing to glance around to inspect our new surroundings. Mostly because the fury radiating from him captivated my focus.

No. That's not fury. That's hunger.

I shivered in response, my body reacting as though programmed to meet his every need.

This vampire had ensnared me. I resembled a fly in his web, waiting to be eaten and craving my eventual death.

"You're bewitching me," Jace accused, stealing the thoughts from my mind as he loosened his grip on my throat. "Tell me what you're thinking. Speak freely. There are no recording devices or spies in my personal space."

His words gave me pause. *Spies*. "Is that why you were cold to your driver? Is he a spy?"

Jace blinked, his surprise evident in his features. "You were thinking about Puck?"

"Is that the driver?"

"Yes."

"Oh. You didn't greet him like the others." It was a flat observation, but his expression registered intrigue.

"A fascinating thing for you to notice. Tell me more."

"About Puck?"

"About everything."

My brow furrowed. "There's not much to tell. It was all just a chorus of *Yes, My Prince*, and *Of course, Your Highness*." I attempted to sound meek with each phrase, something he seemed utterly delighted by. "Does anyone ever say no?"

"You do."

"Well, yes. I'm not an indoctrinated slave."

"Yet you worked for Lilith."

"As a lead researcher," I pointed out. "And she proved long ago that nothing she could do to me would kill me, which dampened my fear significantly. After all, pain is only temporary."

"Fuck you," he replied.

My earlier frown deepened. "Excuse me?"

"It's my decision. I want to fuck you, not kill you. But we are about to have company, so it'll have to wait." He released my throat and reached up to fondle a piece of hair that had escaped my messy bun. "And yes, Puck is a spy of sorts. That's why I act the way I do around him."

That seemed... odd. "Why do you keep him around?"

"Because he's a useful gossip who likes to spread news of my personal business. Therefore, I ensure he hears exactly what I want him to hear. He spreads the news, and I allow him to live as a reward. For now, anyway. I'll absolutely delight in killing him eventually."

"I see." Jace's strategy was rather respectable. I would do the same thing in his shoes. "Is he a vampire?" I asked, curious.

"Of course. Humans can't drive."

"Oh."

He smiled. "Another control tactic meant to weaken your kind."

"Yet you give them guns," I remarked, thinking of the Vigils.

"To use on each other, yes," he replied. "They're too busy fighting for immortality to consider fighting us. And even if they tried, the bullets are lead. They'll sting a little, but only until we retaliate by ripping out the shooter's throat."

I considered that and nodded. It was a fair assessment.

A pair of subtle dimples appeared in his cheeks as his smile widened. "Your mind fascinates me."

"Why?"

"It reminds me of mine," he replied as the elevator dinged again. "Remain as you are, Calina. No rules required."

"Of course, My Prince," I parroted on instinct.

He laughed out loud, his enjoyment almost rivaling mine.

Such a strange exchange, one born of a place I didn't quite understand but wanted to know more about. It was the part of me he'd awakened. Or perhaps the part of me that Lilith's death had called to light.

I wasn't free, yet I felt free. Like my chains had been removed, allowing me to finally live as I desired. No more tasks. No more labs. No more experiments. No more orders.

Except for the ones from Jace.

But his orders didn't affect me like Lilith's had.

Why is that? I wondered as a male dressed in baggy red pants and a matching button-down shirt entered the room. *Staff Member Thirteen*, I realized, noting his wiry frame and the stark bone structure of his cheeks. He appeared half-starved. It was a shock to find him not only walking but also carrying a set of bags.

His gaze was on the ground, his hair a mess of curls that fell over his forehead as he executed a wobbly bow. He didn't straighten but remained there as he awaited further instruction. Just like Juliet had on the plane.

Jace approached him, his smile melting into a scowl. "I'm going to ask you two questions, Staff Member Thirteen. Your answers will determine your fate." He stopped before him. "Stand and look at me so I can judge your truthfulness."

My heart skipped a beat at the sudden change in Jace's character, this side of him reminding me a little too much of Lilith and her penchant for degrading humans and lab subjects for sport.

The human straightened, his sunken cheeks appearing shadowed beneath the low lighting from above. His pale green irises thinned as his pupils dilated with innate fear. But he admirably met Jace's gaze.

"Why—" Jace's question came to an abrupt halt as he looked at his wrist. "Hmm. I need to take this. Don't move." The last two words were for the male servant.

Jace turned without explanation, heading toward a pair of doors off to the side of the living area. He disappeared through them, leaving me alone with the frozen male.

Literally frozen.

As in not moving at all.

And having clearly taken Jace's words as a command to not even breathe.

"Um, I think he meant *don't leave*," I rephrased.

The human didn't reply or blink. Tears began to pool in his eyes a few seconds later, his face turning even paler.

"Seriously, he just meant not to leave," I said, trying again.

Nothing.

I sighed. "You can only self-asphyxiate to a point before your body will force you to breathe. However, in your current state, I'm guessing that simple act will leave you off-balance, which will result in you shifting in some capacity, or more likely, falling. So you might as well breathe. He won't see it and I won't tell him. But if you fall, he'll definitely notice."

Not that I thought Jace would truly care, as I suspected his order was meant to keep the human in the suite, not frozen in place.

The human's pale irises slid to me, a note of shocked hopelessness staring at me.

He wobbled and tipped sideways in the next second, landing with a dull thud against the marble floor.

I stared down at him. "See?"

Staff Member Thirteen—whom I mentally shortened to just *Thirteen*—attempted to stand again, but his legs refused him.

A sharp cry left his mouth as his palm went to his groin and he curled into the fetal position.

I frowned at his convulsing form. He appeared to be in a great deal of pain.

Slipping off my shoes, I went to the floor beside him, my instincts kicking into gear. I wasn't a doctor in the medical sense, but I knew enough about human anatomy to be helpful in certain situations.

"Now, tell me—"

A gasp interrupted my request.

Then Thirteen went still once more.

Only this time, it didn't appear to be from a command but from his body overriding his consciousness and causing him to faint.

My brow furrowed as I evaluated how best to rotate him onto his back.

Aligning my forearm to his spine, I wrapped my palm around his nape and used my opposite hand on his hip to carefully shift his body. It took a minute, as I had to maneuver my arm out of the way for his back to touch the floor, but I managed to keep his neck protected throughout the movements.

I checked his pulse next and found it waning.

His breathing was shallow as well.

Given the sunken quality of his cheeks, the dewy perspiration glistening on his limbs, and the ashen color of his skin, I suspected he'd lost too much blood recently.

I checked his neck for signs of a recent feeding. There was a notable scar, but it wasn't fresh.

I checked his torso.

Then his arms.

And as I moved his palm away from his groin, I noted the reddish color of his palms. It matched the color of his pants, but not because the dye had leaked into his hand.

No.

Someone had bitten him there and left him to bleed out.

I swallowed the bile in my throat and unfastened his pants, then began to draw down his zip—

"What the fuck are you doing?"

CHAPTER TWENTY-FIVE

JACE

Damien's summary of events had surprised me, mostly because he'd found the source of the weapon Lilith had used on Ryder recently. He'd also discovered a series of logs left for someone Lilith had referred to as her *liege*.

I'd walked out here with a question on my lips, wondering if Lilith had ever mentioned a king or liege before.

Only to find Calina unzipping another male's pants in my living room.

Which had effectively destroyed every other question in my mind, leaving me with the single inquiry of "*What the fuck are you doing?*"

She didn't immediately reply, her hands continuing to move, the sound of unzipping an irritation to my ears.

Then the female had the audacity to begin tugging down his pants.

"*Calina*." It came out on a growl as the scent of fresh blood taunted my nostrils.

Her subtle intake of air didn't seem to be in response to me but to whatever she'd just revealed.

My shocked fury slowly abated beneath a cloud of understanding underlined in confusion. I'd just reacted... irrationally.

Why?

Because I'd thought she was going to play with a human in my living room?

I loved sharing. I also loved watching. Yet the notion that she'd been on her knees, ready to service another male, had momentarily distracted me from the very obvious scene before me—the human had passed out due to blood loss.

And she'd just found the wound causing his current state.

With a shake of my head, I joined her and cursed at the sight of his severely wounded cock. Someone had bitten him several times, likely while he was aroused, and had then fed from his femoral artery to the point of near death.

"Well. That answers my first question," I muttered.

I'd been intending to ask him why he was limping. I'd been able to smell the blood on him, suggesting a recent feed that had gotten a little out of hand, but I hadn't realized just how badly out of hand it had been.

"How the bloody hell did he manage to get those bags up here?" I wondered out loud, glancing at him and then at Juliet and Darius's bags.

"I'm guessing he didn't have a choice," Calina replied, her tone lacking in emotion. "He very clearly wants to survive, to the point that he stopped breathing when you left the room."

I frowned. "That's the opposite of trying to survive."

"You told him not to move. He took it literally." She finished removing his pants and moved his leg to study the wound on his thigh. "He needs stitches, and likely a blood transfusion." Her gaze lifted to his bloody dick. "Depending on how deep these incisions are, he may need—"

"Jesus," Darius breathed as he exited the elevator into the suite with Juliet at his side. "What the fuck, Jace?"

I gave him a look. "You know that's not my feeding preference."

Biting a female's cunt to drive her to orgasm, yes. But that was never truly about feeding, as the blood didn't flow in that region nearly as well as the femoral artery. Which was why I barely broke the surface when feasting on a woman's slick flesh.

Whoever had done this to the male had clearly wanted it to hurt.

Calina stood abruptly. "I need supplies."

"You're going to operate?" I asked, mildly amused by the prospect. And also a bit stunned that she'd immediately expected that to be the solution to this problem. It showed how little she understood about this current society.

Almost all royals in my position would just finish the job and let the human die.

But Calina wanted to save him.

In this case, I desired the same outcome as her because I needed to know who had done this to him in my absence. This human was my property, and he'd been regulated to serve in my personal tower. Which meant he should be off the menu. Other humans were designated for that fate.

I might not agree with the current operations of this world.

But I had a part to play in seeing them through. At least until I could properly change them.

"Yes." Calina looked at me. "Where is your nearest hospital?"

I gave her a wry smile. "Darling, hospitals are for humans, not immortals. Therefore, they no longer exist." Apart from the breeding clinics. However, those served a very specific purpose. And saving this male's life would not be a priority there.

She didn't even blink. "Then where do I find supplies?"

"There are none."

"Needles and blood bags absolutely exist somewhere," she replied, still unfazed. "And I'm sure his blood type is on record somewhere. That's how you catalog humans, yes?"

"He doesn't have the time you require to save him."

"Then give him your blood to hold him over."

My eyebrows lifted. "My blood?"

"Yes. I've felt the effects of it. You're strong and old. Your essence should be enough to save him."

"And why would I save him?" I had every intention of doing just that, but her insistence on helping the human fascinated me.

"Because you're not Lilith."

"No, I'm not. But that doesn't mean I see value in his life." Humans died every day. They were food. And while I might not agree with their overall treatment, I still acknowledged their place in the world.

"You chose him to bring those bags up for a reason. And it wasn't to just let him die in your living room." She folded her arms. "Save him."

"First, I don't take orders from anyone other than myself. Second, he's a servant. That's why I had him bring up my bags."

"That's only one reason you called upon him. The other was to put on a show downstairs so everyone believes your royal vampire charade. And you also had two questions for him, one of which has been answered. Save him and you can ask your second question." Calina spoke without a care in the world, her confidence resolute.

And fuck if that didn't make me hard.

In addition to that, she seemed to see right through me. Likely because I'd given her enough details regarding my true intentions for her to make reasonable guesses as to my motives. But I suspected it went much deeper than that.

This female thought through situations with a strategic flair that rivaled my own.

"Careful, Calina," I warned her. Because if she kept this up, I would be tempted to keep her for eternity.

Of course, I already owned her.

So the warning was rather moot.

Because at this point, I definitely intended to keep her.

"He's going to die," she stated flatly. "Without proper supplies, I can't help him. Only you can. You told me to observe your version of leadership. Right now, I'm not impressed."

I nearly laughed. "That was at the server farm, sweetheart. And we both know you were beyond impressed with my actions there." She'd proven just how enthusiastic she was about my show of *leadership* on the plane as well.

Her eyes narrowed at the use of my clear double entendre. "You're engaging in a word game with me when you could be saving him. That's disappointing."

"It's not a game." Although, I could see why she felt that way. "It's more of an experiment."

"And what are you testing?"

"You," I replied simply. Then I bit my wrist and knelt to press the wound to the human male's mouth as I tilted his head back to receive the life-reviving fluid.

He might suffocate on it.

He might swallow.

It depended on his own resolve.

"Would you like to know my findings?" I asked her while I waited for the mortal to choose his fate. His body's natural response should be to accept my essence. But if he was too far gone mentally, he'd opt to drown instead.

Mortal minds were fickle and broke entirely too easily.

But a strong fortitude always persevered in the end.

Calina moved to kneel on the other side of the human. She drew her fingertip along his throat as though to will him to swallow by touch alone.

"Lilith ran experiments on me for nearly forty years. I'm certain there is nothing you've learned through your qualitative study that would surprise me." She uttered the words softly, but with a conviction I felt deep within.

"I've been evaluating how well you read me," I answered honestly. "How well you interpret and understand my actions." I met her gaze over the human. "You impress me."

She blinked, glanced down at the now swallowing male, and then looked back up at me. "I stand corrected," she replied, her voice still soft. "That does surprise me."

I smiled and removed my wrist from the human, aware that he had more than enough blood to begin the recovery process. "And now I need you to continue to impress me," I told her, standing and holding out a hand for her to join me. "Damien is sending through the logs he downloaded. I want you to help me review them."

She shifted her focus to the human again, her brow furrowing. "He needs nurturing."

"He needs rest," I corrected her. "Darius will put him somewhere safe. When he wakes up, I'll ask who put him in this situation, and we'll go from there." I met Darius's gaze. "The boy has a young appeal. Therefore, I suspect it was Gaston."

Darius's expression remained stoic. "Yes, I saw his name in the visitor logs."

"I'm sure you won't mind letting him know how I feel about the transgression, assuming we determine it was him?" I phrased it as a question, but we both knew the answer. Gaston had requested to become my sovereign several months ago. I'd rejected him in favor of Darius.

As though I would ever promote a vampire who enjoyed fucking and eating children.

"I think I can handle delivering that message," Darius agreed.

"Yes, I imagine you're more than capable of it. He's also likely awaiting that message as well." Which was the real reason I'd requested that the human deliver my bags.

I'd noticed the mortal's waning state almost immediately. Publicly requesting that he bring up my bags served as a subtle notice to whoever had touched him that I was not only aware of the human's health but would likely be following up on the transgression after I disposed of the mortal properly.

Only, this one would have a miraculous recovery.

"I'll need a new job for him," I continued, thinking through our situation out loud. "The boy, I mean. Not Gaston."

"I'm sure Ida wouldn't mind some help around the house. She's getting older, making a young male exactly what she needs to assist with some of the heavier lifting."

I nodded. "Yes. Consider him a gift. But I want a name first."

"As do I," he agreed.

"No, you want Gaston's name specifically."

"Or Sebastian's," he offered.

"It won't be Sebastian. He's power hungry, but respectful." I'd never disliked the older vampire, hence the reason I'd named him as a regent in my territory. That was one step below a sovereign. I didn't trust him enough to give him a higher role, but he intrigued me enough to test him. And thus far, he hadn't disappointed me.

"We'll see if I agree after I have dinner with him tomorrow." Darius's tone told me it was doubtful.

"He might surprise you," I replied, meaning it. My attention returned to the kneeling blonde beside the human. "Calina?"

Her fingers were still on the male's neck. "His pulse is steady again."

"Yes." I could hear it thudding enticingly in the air. Just as I could hear hers as well. Between the two, her pulse appealed to me more. As did her scent.

I almost couldn't even smell Juliet anymore, her blood virgin essence no longer calling to my predatory side.

Calina had ensnared me.

And as her pretty blue-green eyes lifted to meet mine, I understood why.

This female captivated me in every way.

"Come," I told her, struggling to remember what it was that I needed her to do. The only image in my mind was of her on her knees and swallowing my cock between those beautiful, plump lips.

Alas, it was nearing dawn.

Giving us less than two days to prepare for Lajos Region.

And the subtle buzz against my wrist reminded me what we needed to do in the interim.

"The files are starting to arrive," I said, recalling our task with clarity. "Damien said there are a handful of logs we need to review, as it seems Lilith left someone instructions on how to take over."

"Instructions?" Darius repeated.

I nodded. "For someone she considered to be her king."

Calina's brow furrowed as she accepted my help up off the floor. "Her king?"

"Damien has only listened to a few so far, but she refers to someone as *my king* and *my liege* throughout the logs. He says there is one for every year, as well as a few that were released upon her death."

"Implying someone is listening to them now?" Darius guessed.

"That's what Damien suspects. He's still trying to trace the feed to find out where they're routing, but he has his hands full with the lycans at the moment."

"Did everything go okay with Luka's men?"

"His report was brief." We only spoke for a couple of minutes. "He mentioned the logs and how he was going to send them. Then he said they found the mind-debilitating weapon Ryder had mentioned. They're still working on cleaning it all out right now, including handling a bunch of feral lycan subjects. He's supposed to call back in an hour with more information."

Darius dipped his chin in understanding. "Then we should start reviewing the logs."

"Agreed." I looked at Calina. "Ready to keep impressing me, little genius?"

CHAPTER TWENTY-SIX

LILITH

Please standby for an important message from your virtual assistant.

Message to commence in three, two…

My liege, it appears your recovery team was intercepted at the server farms. A security team is on-site now to assess the damage, but I suspect the entire team has been compromised, as Bunker 27 just went offline. My inside source is still assessing the damage. However, I fear the resistance is close to discovering your identity and your location. Escalation protocol is suggested. Please tell me how you wish to proceed.

Click the green arrow to activate the escalation sequence. Or press—

Next log to commence in three, two…

If you're watching this, then I must first begin with an apology because I've clearly failed our cause. I won't belabor that point since time is now of the essence, and I will instead do my best to re-earn your trust via efficient means.

I record this message monthly to ensure you have the most up-to-date details regarding our plight. Today marks the fourth month of year one hundred seventeen. We are eight months away from the next Blood Day ceremony.

Recent events are counterproductive to our goals. It seems Silvano decided to wage a war on the neighboring Clemente Clan Alpha, and unsurprisingly, he lost.

However, now there is a triad in place composed of three resistance members.

It seems Jolene is up to his old tricks.

You were right to question the lycans and their ability to appropriately partner with vampires for leadership. I suspect a new world order may be required in the near future. I gave them the Magistrate position, just like we discussed, but it's clearly not enough.

Fortunately, most of the lycans appear oblivious and comfortable in our current state. Supplying their moon chase and breeding needs appears to be enough to sate their desires for now.

As a result of this incident in Clemente Clan territory, an old vampire came out of hiding.

Ryder.

He has taken over as the temporary royal for Silvano Region.

His allegiance remains to be seen, but given his proclivity to break the rules, I suspect he's going to be a problem. However, I strongly doubt the resistance will appeal to him. He's always only ever considered himself and rarely cares about the needs of others.

Attached you'll find everything I know about the resistance from our inside source. I'm sure our asset will be in touch at the first available opportunity.

Also attached is a list of our known allies. As it stands today, these vampires are aware of our secret alliance and will support you on your rise to power.

The final list contains the lycans who should be easiest to persuade to your side as you claim the mantle of power.

Of course, you could always consider the memory protocol to persuade more to join our side. But I'll leave that up to you for final judgment.

To begin reviewing resistance details, key in action code: Resistance.

To begin reviewing ally details, key in action code: Allies.

To begin—

Ally files activated.

Click the green arrow to see more information about Lajos.

Or—
Lajos file activated.

CHAPTER TWENTY-SEVEN

JACE

Sebastian and Gaston had ended up being the least of our concerns.

Darius had still attended the dinner to keep up formalities—which had turned out to be a positive experience because Sebastian had shown admirable respect throughout the meal. Apparently, all he'd wanted was permission to build a new estate on the coast within my region.

I'd promptly granted the approval via a text message, then returned to reviewing the logs with Calina.

There were ample research reports, many of which were tied to the studies of Bunker 47. But there was also a series of videos featuring Lilith at various points throughout the last one hundred seventeen years.

Once I'd finished reviewing the lab results—and determining Cam's name wasn't listed in any of them—I'd switched focus to Lilith's videos.

They were reports of each year, which didn't really interest me. I'd lived through each Blood Day, therefore making myself very aware of their results.

But her voice in the videos had captivated me, as well as her frequent address of *my liege*. These videos were meant for someone she'd considered to be her superior, and *that* detail fascinated me.

She'd also spoken with a reverence I hadn't heard in over a century, suggesting she'd been talking to Michael.

Except he was dead.

"She's bloody insane," Darius had said after the third video.

I'd wanted to agree with him, but the strategic part of me couldn't. Because everything she'd set in motion was too brilliant to be crafted by someone of an unsound mind.

So I'd spent my time over the last two days reviewing as many of the logs as I could.

Damien had set up some sort of backdoor connection at the server farm, allowing us to scan all the documents housed within the facility. It was easier than attempting to download them all and find adequate storage elsewhere.

Calina understood it better than I did since she'd helped him with the configuration.

And in consistent fashion, she'd continued to impress me during our time in Jace City.

Just as she did now as she sat beside me on the jet.

She wore one of her new dresses, the navy fabric revealing every curve of her beautiful form. It took serious restraint not to pull her into my lap and take advantage of her low neckline. That I'd barely touched her these last two days, my focus having been on the files Damien had sent over for review, didn't help matters.

The only time I'd taken a break was when a boutique owner had arrived with a rack of dresses for Calina to try on. I'd fallen into my role with ease as I'd dictated what I wanted Calina to wear, and she'd admirably played the part of submissive human.

As soon as the boutique owner had left, Calina had returned to her confident self and had gone right back to skimming the logs with me. I'd almost fucked her on the desk in response, but she'd discovered a log regarding a *death protocol* from Lilith that had immediately distracted me.

She'd hypothesized that someone might be watching these right now, mainly because the video started with her saying the recording would play if and when something went horribly wrong.

Which Calina had translated to mean Lilith's death.

After watching the log with her, I'd agreed.

The one we observed now was in relation to an escalation protocol. I'd pulled it up onto a movie screen in the executive cabin of my jet, thus allowing Darius and Juliet to watch with us from their chairs.

"So where are the attachments?" Darius asked when the video ended.

"There are none," Calina replied, the laptop controlling the video in her lap. "I'm guessing either they're in a different location, or Lilith housed them in another server farm."

"That would be a strategic way to do it," I admitted. "And we already know other farms exist from another one of her logs."

Calina nodded. "A lot of the reports are cut into pieces as well." She brought one up from a lycan experiment that had helped create the weapon she'd used on Ryder. "We know this is incomplete because of the files Damien retrieved from Bunker 27."

"Indeed," Darius agreed.

Calina started scanning through more logs, most of them revolving around Blood Day again as Lilith provided her version of an annual report.

I took another sip of my wine, bored.

But Calina seemed fascinated by the information, as did Juliet. This was all brand new to them. So I allowed the show to continue while I scanned Damien's latest update.

"They managed to get the last of the lycans out of their cages," I said, my words for Darius. "Luka's working with them now. So far, two have been put down. They were too feral and a threat to Majestic Clan."

There was apparently a point where the human part of a lycan died completely. Although, in this case, Luka suspected the humane aspect of the being's nature had never been allowed to form. And unfortunately, lycans were too strong to just be released into the wild.

"By this point, whoever was expecting an update from the Vigils is likely aware of our interference," Darius said after another fifteen minutes of watching Lilith's logs. "And from what some of these videos imply, they also know the identities of those who stand against the alliance."

"Yes." However, Lilith hadn't named us in any of her logs, and Calina hadn't found our names in any of the files yet. Which left us to guess that our identities might or might not be included in her records.

"We might be flying into a trap," Darius added.

"Yes," I repeated. "Assuming Lajos truly supported Lilith's regime."

We hadn't found proof of that either. We didn't know any of the names of her supporters, just like we had no clue whom these logs were intended for.

"We don't really have a choice but to proceed," I continued. "We need to find Bunker 37. Besides, maybe we can use this as an opportunity to prove Lilith's theories wrong about us. It's all conjecture at this point, as she couldn't possibly have had proof. We've yet to do anything. So perhaps we use this as a way of proving our loyalty to the current era, while also lulling Lajos into a state of comfort."

"Or we could just kill him," Darius offered.

I smiled. "You would enjoy that."

"I would."

"If he proves unuseful, I'll consider it," I promised him.

"Sounds familiar," he drawled, clearly not over the edict I'd issued just yesterday.

Staff Member Thirteen had confirmed it was Gaston who had nearly killed him, which typically would have earned him an excommunication sentence. I did not take lightly to others touching my property without express permission, and a staff member was not a menu item.

"Gaston is still useful," I reminded Darius. "He helps me maintain my image, which we now know is more important than ever. If Lilith's logs are to be believed, anyway."

"She was clearly insane."

"That is your favorite statement of late," I murmured. "The question is, how many others believed her? The more I can do to disprove those notions, the easier this will be for us all."

Because it would give me the necessary element of surprise. And it would allow me to survive long enough to appropriately strategize my next move.

If Lilith's supporters believed her rumors about me, they would be more likely to react badly toward me upon news of her death. But if I kept them guessing, they just might pause long enough for me to gain the upper hand.

It was all about strategy and playing the alliance appropriately.

I couldn't do that if my cards were already on the table.

"I can't believe I'm going to say this," Darius started, clearing his throat. "But I rather like Ryder's plan to show up next week and throw Lilith's severed head into the room, and call it a day."

While I appreciated the mental image that thought conjured up, I still shook my head. "That would inspire chaos."

"All of this is going to inspire chaos," he pointed out.

I sighed. "Yes. And the discoveries in Bunker 27 won't help matters." Once the lycans learned what Lilith had been doing to them, they'd rebel against the vampires who condoned her actions.

Next week was going to be a shit show of epic proportions unless we found a way to postpone the meeting.

Having Lilith's phone helped, but it wasn't like her to hide in one region for too long. We were already pushing our luck by having Ryder and Willow continue the Lilith mentoring charade.

We needed to find Cam. And we needed to find him now.

"Regardless, we'll still need to lull Lajos into a state of comfort," I said, repeating my earlier statement. "At least temporarily. Which means playing his game long enough for him to give us freedom to roam. Then we'll find the bunker based on the information Damien obtained from the Vigils."

"What about Jasmine?" Darius pressed.

"I'll meet with her to determine her desires, and I'll use the time to evaluate her character."

Darius snorted. "I can give you a synopsis of her character, Jace. Sadistic cunt."

My lips twitched in amusement. "That describes half the council."

"More like three-fourths of it."

"But you have to consider how many others are playing along like we are," I argued. "I mean, a year ago, would you have ever thought Kylan could be on our side?"

Darius fell quiet for a long moment, then slowly shook his head. "And Ryder."

"Precisely." It was the hardest part of this political game—discerning the enemies from the potential allies. "Lajos is a lost cause." Of that I had no doubt. "But Jasmine makes me curious."

"So what are you suggesting?"

"We're going to attend one of Lajos's renowned clubs."

Darius's green eyes smoldered with irritation. "I knew you were going to say that."

"Then why ask?"

"I was hoping to hear a different answer."

"You know me better than that."

His jaw ticked, his gaze going to Juliet. "He's going to want to taste her."

"Then I suggest you put on one hell of a show to distract that desire," I replied. "That's what Calina and I will be doing."

His eyebrows lifted. "You intend to deny him?"

"Yes." I didn't elaborate, but I'd made the decision last night. Her rare blood posed too much of a risk. And given how useful she'd proven to be, I couldn't risk losing her to a voracious vampire. "I intend to lose control in his provocative environment, thereby not leaving enough for him to enjoy."

"I see." Darius scratched his jaw and slowly canted his head. "I'll follow suit."

I glanced at Calina to find her staring at me. "Yes, little genius?"

"Will you expect me to remain silent during this act?" Her tone gave nothing away, the stoic quality almost admirable.

Except I could scent her intrigue.

Of course, she'd tell me it was just her natural reaction to the prospect of being devoured by a predator.

"I'll let you know," I told her, uncertain of what I wanted. I'd let the ambience set the mood.

She conceded with a dip of her chin and returned to the files on the computer. Another video began to play, this one from two years ago based on Lilith's introduction.

I yawned, already bored.

The video from a few weeks ago depicting the events between Silvano Region and Clemente Clan was more interesting.

Particularly as Lilith had seemed a bit unsettled, which was why she'd organized for the alliance to meet quarterly.

With our first meeting set for next week.

I considered Ryder's proposal again about his grand entrance, playing out the scenario in my head.

There would be gasps. But how many would truly react? This world had numbed our emotions so severely that many might not even be surprised.

The chaos I'd mentioned was in regard to a political battle over the vacant leadership role. Kylan was the next in line based on age, but he didn't want the position. Which meant it would fall to me. And while I had no trouble accepting the tasks, I knew several lycans would oppose my leadership.

Others would argue that a lycan should be in charge.

Then the vampires would point out that lycans die, thereby marking them as the slightly weaker race.

Which would only worsen when Lilith's research was revealed.

I needed to know who had approved it, to give the wolves a target for their aggression. If presented appropriately, they would eliminate the biggest threats and opponents of potential reform.

However, winning those lycans over would be problematic as well. The things Lilith had done were unforgivable, and I would not be surprised if the lycans blamed the entire vampire race.

Then there was the issue of Calina's existence. As a lead researcher, the lycans would no doubt demand her head as compensation. And six days ago, I would have granted it.

Now, I wasn't so sure.

A strange revelation, considering I didn't do emotional attachments. But she'd proven herself useful.

And I wasn't done tasting her yet.

Perhaps this visit in Lajos Region would help cure my craving.

I glanced at Calina again, my gaze automatically falling to her delectable neckline.

Or maybe this venture will worsen our situation entirely.

CHAPTER TWENTY-EIGHT

CALINA

Thirteen appeared in the main cabin with flushed cheeks as he announced, "Sal says we'll be landing in ten minutes."

"Excellent. Thank you," Jace replied. "Have you chosen a new name yet?"

Thirteen's eyes brightened at the question. Jace had told the male to stop bowing, and I could tell by his stiff posture that it was requiring a lot of effort for him to obey. However, he cleared his throat and replied, "Anvil."

"Anvil," Jace replied.

"Sal suggested it," Thirteen—*uh, or is it Anvil now?*—replied.

Jace nodded. "She's always harbored a penchant for items that begin with *A*." He glanced at me. "Sal was an astronaut in her mortal days. She continued the passion after her turning but later moved to aviation. And now she's my primary pilot." His focus returned to the male. "Anvil it is. Assuming Darius approves?"

"Anvil is fine," the other vampire replied, his gaze on Juliet. "But Sal may not let him go now."

"We'll see," Jace murmured. "Please let Sal know we'll prepare for landing."

Anvil started to bow, then quickly straightened his spine with a muttered "Thank you, My Prince" and stiffly returned to the cockpit.

"Calina. I need you to change into the red gown." Jace spoke without looking at me. "Now, please."

I closed the laptop and set it on the coffee table, then stood to obey.

Over the last two days, we'd only spent a few minutes around others where I had to feign a meek persona. However, Jace had warned me upon our departure that I would need to maintain the part of obedient human as soon as we landed and would have to continue that act until he gave me permission to act otherwise.

He'd also said we wouldn't be able to hide behind closed doors.

Because apparently surveillance and listening devices were very common in this world.

This concept didn't shock me since my entire life had been lived inside a heavily guarded bunker. I was also used to following orders.

Which was why I had no trouble walking to the back of the plane to change from my navy lace dress into the red gown.

Although, it wasn't much of a gown.

The gauzy fabric's thin straps barely held the dress up on my shoulders. The deep V-neck cut down to my belly button. The back didn't exist. And while the skirt flowed to the floor, it had two slits that went up to my hips.

I picked up the matching undergarments to wear beneath the fabric. No bra. Just panties, stockings, and straps.

The latter two items had been new to me. However, a tutorial from the designer had helped me understand how to use them.

I slid the ruby-colored thong up my legs, followed by the translucent red stockings, and affixed them to the hooks in the lacy fabric.

A pair of shorter black heels went on next, finishing my outfit. I gave myself a once-over as the jet began to decline, the angle telling me we were on our descent.

Swallowing, I carefully turned, ready to make my way back to Jace, only to find him watching from the doorway.

His icy gaze tracked over me with unveiled interest, his expression hungry.

"Did I do it right?" I asked, showing him my left leg.

He pushed away from the door to stalk toward me.

My heart skipped a beat at his silent approach, the predatory movements reminding me of his superiority and grace.

Each step made swallowing that much harder, until he was right in front of me. His woodsy aftershave taunted my nostrils, the scent one I was starting to crave more than I should.

His fingertips brushed my hip, his gaze holding mine as his touch shifted lower to the strap along my thigh. He traced it down to my stocking and back up again, the caress eliciting goose bumps in his wake.

I stopped breathing as his featherlight stroke slid backward to the strap along my ass. His movement slowed as he tracked it all the way to the lacy fabric on my thighs.

"Perfection," he whispered, his lips a hairsbreadth from mine. "Fucking stunning."

He captured my mouth in a bruising kiss that killed my mental faculties.

The burn in my chest told me I needed to do something.

But his tongue was all I could focus on, the tender strokes against mine a hypnotic embrace that redefined life.

Then his blood trickled into my mouth, and I found myself swallowing on instinct, followed by a much-needed inhale.

Only to be wrapped up in his kiss in the next moment as he lifted me from the ground to carry me to the bed. It was similar to the one in the other jet we'd flown on, except more opulent. More intricate. More *Jace.*

He laid me down on the mattress as the world continued to tilt around us.

He held me easily in place, his teeth sinking into my lower lip and eliciting a low yelp from my throat. Rather than chastise me for making a sound, he kissed me harder, our blood mingling in the kiss and giving new meaning to *vampiric embrace*.

His hips settled between mine, the fabric of the dress automatically parting to allow my legs to spread in immediate accommodation.

It was all so natural. So intrinsic. So *hot*.

I threaded my fingers through his hair, holding him to me as I swallowed and kissed and sucked. He allowed it, his palm against my thigh and his opposite hand holding my face.

This was unexpected. Beautiful. *Bliss*.

I didn't want it to end, but I felt the moment the jet hit the ground and knew what would come next.

However, Jace gave me a few precious extra minutes, his essence thick in my throat as he coated me in his version of protection.

I understood that now—this was his way of bolstering my strength. Because neither of us knew what would happen next.

What if Lajos recognized me? Was he one of my immortal ties? We didn't know, and the files we'd reviewed hadn't provided any useful information. My solitary saving grace was that I couldn't remember ever seeing Lajos, which hopefully meant he'd never seen me before either.

His lips left mine, tracking a path down my neck to my breasts, where he moved the fabric away to reveal one nipple. I knew what he intended to do a mere second before his fangs claimed my nipple. A scream threatened my mouth, but I fought the urge and forced myself to swallow it, to be the silent human I knew he needed me to be.

And he rewarded me by laving my wounded flesh before grinning up at me. "Very good, Calina."

I kept my fingers in his hair and tightened my grip just a little to express annoyance, which made him smile wider.

And then he bit me again, only harder this time.

My whole body shook with the need to shout, but I miraculously held it inside.

Which earned me another of those devastating smiles.

He moved with rapid speed to capture my mouth again as his fingers drew the blood around my areola, painting the essence along my skin.

Then he nibbled my lower lip once more before lifting off of me and deftly finding his feet beside the bed.

"Come, Calina," he murmured, his hand dangling between us. "I can't wait to show you off."

I shivered at the darkness in his meaning. He'd just painted me in my own blood, the offering somewhat clear. And yet he'd told Darius that he didn't intend to let Lajos taste me.

The two seemed counterproductive to each other, but I wasn't in a place to argue.

So I pressed my palm to his and allowed him to help me up off the bed.

He fixed my dress, the fabric clinging to my freshly wounded nipple. Then he ran his fingers through my hair and his own and fixed the collar of his black dress shirt. He'd paired it with a dark jacket and pants, but no tie, leaving a sliver of his pale skin on display near his throat.

Stunning is right, I thought, drinking in the sight of him.

This part of me that he'd awakened hungered for more; it hungered for *him*.

It was a dangerous sensation that would undoubtedly lead to a lethal end. Each passing second seemed to ensnare me more, making resisting this being impossible.

And the devious twinkle in his silver-blue gaze told me he knew it, too.

"You're edible, darling," he whispered, his lips brushing mine. "I'm going to miss your eyes." He spoke the words so softly I almost didn't hear them. Then he cupped my face and gently tilted my head into a more submissive pose.

I expected him to walk me forward.

However, he knelt before me instead.

His fingers traced my calf beneath the fabric of my dress, all the way down to the strap of my heel. The elastic had been twisted when he'd carried me to the bed, and I hadn't noticed. But I likely would have felt it after a few steps.

"Thank you, My Prince." The words were barely audible, as I didn't know who could hear us.

"You're welcome, little genius," he replied, his thumb tracing my ankle before gliding up my leg as he stood once more. His lips brushed my temple as his palm left my thigh to reach around and press to the bare skin of my lower back.

He didn't say another word as he led me from the jet.

Darius and Juliet were already waiting for us outside near another stretched black car, which I believe Jace had called a *limo* at one point.

The blaring sunshine had me wanting to pause and glance

upward, but the palm against my spine kept me moving.

And we were in the back of the limo before I even had a chance to regret the loss of the sun.

From what I understood, Sal and Anvil were staying on the jet. Jace had mentioned wanting to be ready to fly in case we needed an escape. I'd asked if Lajos would recognize his intent, but he'd merely shrugged and said that Sal's love for aviation was well known among his kind.

Jace's palm slid into the slit of my dress to rest on my thigh as he and Darius engaged in conversation regarding their evening plans.

"I'd like a few hours of rest first," Darius said. "Juliet kept me busy most of the day."

"Mmm, yes, she's skilled at that," Jace replied flatly. "Although, I can't say I'm all that disappointed by the show she and Calina put on for us."

"No, *disappointed* is certainly not the descriptor I would use," Darius agreed.

I nearly frowned, their conversation full of so many false implications, but I knew that was the point.

Most of our flight had been spent reviewing Lilith's logs, which we'd left on board the jet because Jace couldn't risk anyone else getting ahold of his laptop. And he trusted the pilot to guard it.

He also had a whole series of security features on the device that would dismantle the contents should someone guess the password incorrectly three times.

For someone who didn't seem all that technologically savvy, he certainly knew the importance of security sequences.

It was possible Damien had helped him set it all up, but I suspected that wasn't the case at all. His laptop had been in Jace City, not with us on the original plane. Which suggested the safeguard protocols had already existed.

"Then it's settled. We'll have a lie-in until midnight or so. Lajos's best clubs don't open until two, anyway," Jace declared. "I'm sure he won't mind us taking breakfast in bed."

Darius chuckled. "I know I won't mind."

Jace's fingertips trailed upward to brush the lace covering my sex. "I certainly won't either."

I shivered at the promise in his words, the statement coupled with his actions creating an intoxicating conundrum.

This was all a ruse, and yet, that made it so much more alluring. Because I couldn't tell the truth from the fiction. His knowing touch felt real. I almost lost myself to the charade, my desire to melt into his side a very enticing notion.

His lips brushed my neck, causing my heart to race.

"I can't wait to rip this dress off of you," he whispered against my ear. "Then I'm going to devour your slick flesh until you pass out."

My thighs clenched, my insides burning at the prospect.

But did he mean it? Or was this all part of his game?

I had no way of knowing because even as we exited the limo, he continued to hold me with sensual purpose.

His palm went from my lower back to my ass as he guided me into a frigid building.

The air-conditioning immediately caused my nipples to pucker, which sent a reminder through my body of what he'd done to my breast on the jet. My abused peak grazed the hardened lace—the fabric having stiffened from my blood soaking through the gauze.

Jace bent to nibble the sensitive bud, his groan of approval going straight to my insides. *What is he doing to me?*

His essence running through my system seemed to make me hyperaware of his touch, heightening every stroke, lick, and suck of his tongue.

I knew others could see us. We were standing in an ornate lobby while Darius spoke to someone nearby. But I couldn't think beyond Jace and his wicked caress as he kissed a path up to my throat and across my jaw to my mouth.

His tongue traced my bottom lip before dipping inside.

It was brief, there and gone in a second. My eyes met his, his pupils blown wide with lust, and his hand went to the back of my nape to force my gaze down once more.

My head spun with confusion. I didn't understand this show of affection.

Then I overheard Darius snort and say, "She's his newest toy, and he can't keep his hands off of her. It's making me second-guess Juliet's allure."

"Oh, we both know my desire for your *Erosita* is still very much alive," Jace promised as he used his free hand to pull Juliet toward him. "I'm particularly enjoying these two together."

"And that's why we will be staying in the same suite. Two bedrooms are fine, but the common area needs to be shared," Darius said in his crisp English accent.

"Of course, Sire," a feminine voice replied as Jace pressed a kiss to Juliet's collarbone. I could see it in my peripheral vision, and the sight of it made my gut twist in discomfort.

The ease with which he feigned his affection toward her had me lost in this land of truth versus fiction once more.

Does he mean it? Is he attracted to her? The very notion of a positive response had my lips wanting to curl down. I didn't appreciate that idea at all.

But I was equally perplexed by the concept of him faking it with her because that would imply he had faked it with me as well.

Stop with this foolishness, I chided myself. *These sorts of thoughts are a waste of time.*

They weren't practical or helpful, just distracting and irritating.

"A two o'clock pickup would be ideal, yes," Jace said, responding to some inquiry I hadn't heard while lost inside my mind.

Which was exactly why I needed to pay attention.

But his hand distracted me entirely as his palm released my nape to slide down my spine to my ass. He gave it a sharp squeeze, making me wonder if it was meant as a punishment or another one of his ploys.

I tried to focus on the latter, to understand his strategy here as he started to order an in-room breakfast for a midnight delivery.

He requested two meals, presumably for me and Juliet. Then he added, "An O-negative server would be delicious as well."

"I will make sure the kitchen staff is aware of your request, My Prince," the female cooed. "Will you require any additional services to aid in your late arrival? An afternoon delight, perhaps?"

"Hmm," Jace hummed, his lips returning to my breast as he nipped my opposite nipple—the one without the wound. "No. I think Calina will do nicely tonight, and if I require more, I'll borrow Juliet. Her link to Darius's immortality is most beneficial."

"Happy to oblige," Darius returned.

"As is Juliet," Jace replied as he lifted his head away from my breast. "Thank you for your help, Mika. You've been most accommodating."

"Anything for you, Your Highness."

I couldn't see Jace, but I sensed him smiling. "I'll keep that in mind."

"Please do." The sultry quality of her voice told me either these two had a history together or she wanted to create one.

And I found that almost as troubling as Jace desiring Juliet.

Truth or fiction?

Stop thinking about it.

Everything Jace did was methodical and strategic. He needed to put everyone else at ease. And I was doing us no favors by overanalyzing his intentions.

I forced my mind to shift into logic mode and began evaluating our surroundings. My visual vantage point only allowed me to see the ground and a few items in my periphery—which was mostly consumed by Jace and Juliet. But to one side, I also noticed brightness, suggesting the windows here were not blacked out like those in Jace's building.

From what I knew of our location, we were in the former Hawaiian Islands. The balmy weather outside had definitely confirmed that. There were floral fragrances as well. And an underlying scent of salt.

The ocean.

Would Jace let me see it? The shades on the plane had been pulled down throughout our flight, disrupting my view through the windows.

Jace's lips grazed my neck, his teeth skimming my pulse. "Let's go," he breathed against my ear, his palm still on my ass as he guided me alongside him.

Darius made small talk with our escort—another vampire based on how Darius and Jace addressed him. His commentary included a summary of the grounds and where the restaurants and entertainment venues were located.

Jace hummed in noncommittal interest, his hand shifting to my hip as he lazily draped his arm along my lower back.

We paused by a set of elevators.

Then we took two separate cars upstairs, our entourage having grown with the humans pushing our belongings up in carts.

Jace and I were with one of them, the male hunching as he attempted to disappear into the corner. I could only see him because the interior of the elevator was made of glass, including the floor, allowing me to see various angles all throughout the small space.

A pair of silver-blue eyes met mine during my search, the depths holding a mischievous glint.

Because Jace could see me investigating and knew exactly what I was doing.

Yet rather than admonish me, he gave me a playful wink before staring expectantly at the doors.

They opened half a second later, displaying obsidian floors and more floral scents.

We stepped out and took a right. Darius and the others arrived, his voice an echo behind us as Jace led the way through a pair of doors.

The black tiles gave way into a cream carpet, the texture plushy beneath my heels. Jace's arm tightened around me as though he anticipated my wobble, but I held myself steady and moved with an elegance that I forced through my limbs.

More light spilled into the room, illuminating a set of two dark couches, matching chairs, and a marble coffee table.

There appeared to be a step ahead, which took us to a wood floor that led to the windows.

Dining area, I guessed. *Maybe a kitchen?* Although, I suspected that might be to my left where the carpet turned into a slate-colored marble.

Our escort explained the dimming features of the windows, something Darius immediately took advantage of, painting the room in shadows. A dull light flickered to life next, ruining the ambience of the room.

I much preferred the natural sunlight. Probably because I'd never really experienced it until this week.

The escort continued with a tour of the room, explaining the amenities of the kitchen, which was indeed located near the slate-colored marble. Then he led us to the dining area and toward a hallway with two bedrooms.

Both were master suites with elegant furnishings and generously sized bathrooms. I barely paid any attention to the escort's musings, my focus on walking steadily over the plush carpet.

Jace picked the room farthest away from the living area, stating he liked the wraparound balcony. I almost looked, my curiosity for the potential view overriding my need to remain submissive.

But I caught the urge quickly and swallowed it.

"Thank you for your assistance, Mauritius. Perhaps you'll join us one night for dinner?" Jace asked.

"It would be my honor, My Prince," the escort replied.

"Brilliant. Darius will assist you with the details." Jace released my hip, leaving me in the center of the room. "Calina, I'm going to walk Mauritius to the door. I expect to find you on that bed in just those stockings when I return. Present yourself appropriately for me and I'll reward you."

The door closed before I could react. Not that I knew what to say or how to respond. He'd said there were cameras everywhere, that my submissive role applied even in our hotel room.

Which meant I needed to strip out of this dress and shoes.

And present myself on the bed.

Appropriately.

Whatever the hell that means.

CHAPTER TWENTY-NINE

JACE

It took Darius and me thirty minutes to confirm that there were no cameras in the suite, just listening devices.

And another fifteen minutes to put our countermeasures in place.

Which meant I'd left Calina in a precarious position for no reason.

Well. Perhaps that was a bit of a stretch because I could absolutely create a reason for leaving a gorgeous woman half-naked on my bed.

Darius used his phone to set up the last of the automated recordings—a trick Luka's mate, Mira, had taught us decades ago—and faced me.

"Silence truly is bliss," he informed me. "I've set an alarm to automatically switch off before our midnight breakfast arrives, so we have a few hours to speak freely."

"Cheers," I murmured, handing him a glass of bourbon.

He clinked the rim against my own drink, then took a healthy sip.

I followed suit, my shoulders relaxing marginally at having

altered all the bugs in the room. We were in one of Lajos's finest hotels. I wasn't surprised that it was riddled with surveillance, because all his visiting royals would stay here.

My fancier accommodations were also decorated with listening devices. Some even had cameras.

Vampires rarely trusted each other. We were too old to be that naïve. And only rare alliances formed true friendships.

Darius and I finished our drinks in silence, both acutely aware of the evening to come. "Best enjoy our solitude while it lasts," I finally said.

"Can I make a suggestion?" Darius asked, his eyebrow inching upward in that haughty way of his.

"I suppose. Doesn't mean I'll listen."

"No, you hardly do. But, in this case, I hope you'll at least consider it."

That all depended on what he intended to say. "What's the suggestion?"

"Fuck her, Jace. You may not have another chance, and I know how you feel about missed opportunities." He didn't stick around for a response, just clapped me on the shoulder and headed to his room.

I glowered in his general direction, not at all pleased with the implication of his words.

He didn't think Calina would survive this trip.

Given Lajos's penchant for destroying delectable humans, it was a fair assessment. However, I had no intention of allowing it to happen.

And how strange was that?

I safeguarded my harem to an extent, but I recognized them for the pawns they were in this game. If a royal fancied one, I typically handed the mortal over to gain a favor.

Some survived.

Some did not.

It wasn't exactly thrilling so much as practical. I'd survived this long because of my willingness and aptitude for playing the political arena. It took strategy and sacrifice.

Yet the notion of sacrificing Calina stirred an uneasy sensation inside me.

I rubbed at my chest, attempting to define the hesitation. Her delectable blood certainly appealed to me. I also hadn't finished tasting her, which I supposed played into Darius's recommendation.

Finishing the task would likely sever this desire to keep her alive.

Although, she was also useful.

And she read me better than almost everyone, understanding my behavior before I even attempted to define it.

I poured myself a second glass and carried it with me to the bedroom, my mind spinning over all the various ways I wanted to take Calina.

Darius had made it sound like such a simple task. One and done. But as I entered the room to find her waiting on the bed with her knees bent and legs spread, I knew once would not be enough.

She'd positioned herself like Juliet had on the jet's table the other day. Stocking-clad feet on the mattress. Arms at her sides. Focus on the ceiling. Thighs parted to reveal the silk covering her mound.

The only way it could be perfected was by her leaving the heels on. But I hadn't specified that in my requirements.

I took a sip of my bourbon as I admired the view, a soft hum of approval coming from my throat. It wasn't the pose I'd anticipated from her, as most of my consorts knew to wait for me on their knees.

However, I wasn't going to fault Calina for her lack of training. Not when she presented herself so beautifully in an alternative manner.

I approached her slowly, one hand around my drink, the other in my pocket.

She didn't look at me, her pretty blue-green eyes trained on the ceiling above.

"So obedient," I murmured, taking in her stiff nipples and the goose bumps trailing down her arms.

The air-conditioning in this building appeared to be working overtime to counter the humidity outside. I'd barely noticed, even after hanging my jacket in the foyer closet. I'd rolled up the sleeves on my dress shirt as well but still felt a bit warm from the change in climates.

Calina didn't reply, but her pulse picked up, seducing the

predator inside me.

She wasn't necessarily afraid. Her cheeks were too flushed for that. And her shortness of breath seemed related to her trying to remain still for me.

Because she thought we were under surveillance.

Perhaps there was a touch of healthy fear inside her, that voice whispering in her ear that she couldn't afford to make a mistake.

I almost told her to relax.

But the practical part of me dismissed the inclination.

This was an opportunity, a way for me to test her resolve in a mostly safe environment, to see how far her compliance would go.

"Hmm." I considered her position once more. "While I appreciate the view, Calina, this isn't the pose I anticipated."

She remained still and silent, causing me to arch a brow.

"Do you have nothing to say for yourself?" Technically, I'd told her to remain silent unless I said otherwise. Which meant she'd remained well behaved by society standards.

However, my kind were notoriously cruel and known to punish humans for sport. Therefore, this sort of treatment provided a good introduction to what to expect.

Of course, I hadn't spoken the words harshly. Just curiously.

"I'm sorry, My Prince," she replied. "Tell me your preference, and I'll do my best to please you."

The subtle mocking tone underlining her words made my lips twitch. It was just the right amount of impishness mixed with submissiveness, creating an intoxicating air of seduction.

Because I wanted to fuck the defiance right out of her.

While also praise her for being so willful.

I stepped up to the side of the bed and reached for her throat with my free hand. "I want you on your knees, seated on your heels, palms on your thighs, and your gaze properly downcast. Now."

I squeezed her neck and started to pull her upright.

Calina quickly helped by using her hands on the bed to lift herself, then she obeyed my command by going to her knees, sitting back on her heels, and resting her palms on her silky stockings.

"Mmm," I hummed, my thumb stroking her thundering pulse. "Gorgeous." It was both in response to her escalating heartbeat and the pose she'd perfected in mere seconds.

I shifted my grip to her chin, tilting her head back and pressing the rim of my glass to her lips. "Open your mouth and swallow what I give you." The gesture served as a reward of sorts because the alcohol would help warm her up a bit. It would also help her relax.

She acquiesced beautifully, her throat working as she drank from two sips' worth of bourbon. Her flinch told me it wasn't her favorite flavor, but she didn't sputter or protest.

"Very good," I praised her, taking away the drink and pressing my lips to hers for half a beat. "Now don't move or make a sound."

Her eyes flashed to mine, that hint of defiance lurking in her blue-green depths.

I wanted to drown in that look, take her with me beneath a wave of depravity, and forever exist in the darkness with her by my side.

It was such an intense yearning. A craving I couldn't remember ever experiencing before. And in that single moment, I knew this female was every bit my equal.

A stark and sudden understanding. Unexpected and unbidden.

This woman was meant to be tamed by me. Broken for my pleasure. And secretly become my much-needed light in the cold, bitter night.

I didn't fight the inclination or the bizarre urge. I merely released her throat, took a sip from my glass, and bent to bite her perfect breast.

Her blood tinted the alcohol in my mouth, perfecting the liquid as I swallowed.

She released a silent gasp, her chest subtly moving beneath my mouth. I glanced up to find her watching me, that vivid gaze of hers smoldering even in the darkened room.

I'm going to destroy you, I promised her with my eyes. *And you're going to love every fucking minute of it.*

It was time she felt the snapping of my restraint, realized the danger in pushing me this far, and understood my predatory side—the side she'd just unerringly called out to play with her inner deviant.

I repeated the action on her opposite breast, finishing off the contents of my glass and setting it on the nightstand.

Twin bite marks greeted my vision as I straightened, her tits brilliantly marked for my pleasure.

And fuck, those stockings. That thong. Her legs.

Knowing she couldn't easily die, that I could fully lose control without risking her life, only heightened my expectations.

I'd spent so many years dallying with humans who'd broken far too easily.

But this one wouldn't.

Because she wasn't entirely mortal.

I suddenly understood Lilith's goal here of creating a toy that could withstand the monsters inside our souls. Feed our hunger, satiate our sadistic thirst, and continue to come crawling back for more.

Calina craved the danger that I offered. I could see it in the rebellious flicker within her almost flirtatious stare.

She was the queen to my king, playing the board with an expert maneuvering that seemed almost natural to her more than planned. And yet I wouldn't be surprised if she'd strategically coaxed this sensation inside me.

The woman had bewitched me from the first moment, disrespecting my authority and displaying an assertiveness I found intensely satisfying.

Maybe Darius was right.

Maybe all I had to do was fuck this sensation out of my system.

But I worried he was very wrong, that I would quickly become even more addicted to this alluring enigma and lose myself entirely.

It was a risk.

And I fucking adored danger.

I courted it. Yearned for it. *Needed* it.

Such an attractive contrast to all my carefully laid plans.

Calina made me feel spontaneous. Alive. Energized. *Complete*.

I forgot the game. Forgot the ploy of trying to teach her how to properly behave. And wrapped my hand around her nape to tug her into a kiss.

Fuck.

What started as a physical need quickly turned into a soul-destroying embrace filled with dark promises and sensual threats.

She didn't hold back, her tongue dueling mine in a manner that served as the opposite of submissive. Calina demanded her due, demolishing the contrived boundaries between us and showing me with her mouth just how powerful she could be in the bedroom.

I stood over her mostly naked body and could sense her topping from the bottom.

It thrilled me. Enraged me. Fucking *seduced* me.

My grip tightened, my opposite hand going to her hip as I yanked her up to her knees and dragged her to the edge of the bed. "Unfasten my pants," I demanded against her mouth.

Her palms met my abdomen first, sliding downward to the belt around my waist.

So quick and nimble.

An excellent pupil.

My perfect conquest.

She slid the leather from the loops and dropped it to the floor. Then her fingers focused on my button, followed by the zipper. Relief momentarily touched my senses at being free from the confines of my pants, but my boxers were still tight around my groin.

This female turned me on in a manner I couldn't even begin to define. I felt as though I was about to explode for her. I wanted her beneath me. Moaning. Screaming. *Arching*.

I kicked off my shoes and pants, leaving Calina to balance on her knees. Her breasts met my chest as she started to tip forward, my movements too fast for her human eyes to track. She gaped up at me in surprise, then jolted as I kissed her again. This time harder. *Harsher*.

I fucking claimed her.

Showed her what a royal could do.

A vampire of thousands of years.

And felt her wilt against me as she realized my true strength and potential.

I'd meant it when I'd said I would destroy her. Just as I'd meant it when I'd promised to make her enjoy it.

Her fingers worked over my shirt, the action one I hadn't authorized and yet welcomed at the same time because it placed her bare skin against mine.

Her nipples were as hard as glass, the air-conditioning having left her cold for too long. I'd make it up to her now by setting her blood on fire.

I threaded my fingers through her hair, holding her mouth to mine as I palmed her ass.

She shivered.

I growled.

And then I devoured her once more.

The defiant female continued to melt, her resolve a puddle between her thighs as she acquiesced to my every unspoken demand. This wouldn't be kind or soft. It would be savage. A brutal affair of flesh and teeth, underlined in exquisite bliss.

"I'm going to possess every inch of you," I vowed against her mouth. "Make you experience what I'm feeling inside. And by the time I'm done, you won't even remember your fucking name."

I didn't allow her a chance to reply. Not that she could. I'd demanded that she remain silent, and she was obeying beautifully. Yet defying me with her damn tongue, drugging me with her essence, and making me forget any and all reason.

My palm shifted against her backside, moving between her thighs to test the wetness soaking her thong. A groan taunted my throat, the desire to taste her arousal taking over my intentions and forcing me into action.

Her back hit the mattress in the next breath, my vampiric strength and speed overwhelming her, demanding she yield, telling her without words who mastered whom here.

She parted her thighs in response.

And fuck, I nearly ripped the fabric off of her in my effort to bare her cunt to my view.

But I refused to let her top from the bottom.

This was my playground. My rules. *My* world.

I bent to sink my teeth into her thigh, her femoral artery giving me exactly what I wanted and causing Calina to break her silence with a startled moan.

I didn't discipline her, because I no longer cared about decorum or the fact that I'd meant to test her resolve.

This was about fulfilling the quest we'd started on days ago.

This was about finally taking what I wanted.

This was about indulging in the sweetness of her mind, body, and soul.

I unhooked her stocking—the one I'd bitten through the fabric of to get to her femoral artery—and practically yanked it off her leg. Then I paused to admire her dainty ankle and the flexible stretch of her leg. I'd moved her without thinking and she'd allowed it without protest, her body seeming to bend to my will on instinct alone.

I sat on my knees between her splayed thighs and placed her ankle on my shoulder while staring down at her.

Calina's pupils were full-blown black, her cheeks a delicious shade of red, and her fuckable lips were parted on a pant I felt vibrating through every inch of my being.

"Who are you?" I marveled, utterly captivated by the stunning beauty on the bed before me. "It's like you were created to slay me."

Vulnerable words.

Yet true.

She licked her lips in response, her eyes telling me she didn't know how to reply.

And that was fine because I didn't need her to speak. I needed her to come. To scream. To acknowledge my claim within her spirit.

This was dangerous. Deceptive. Dark. *Depraved.*

She'd ensnared me in a web I could no longer escape from.

Calina resembled a black widow in a lab coat with pretty blonde hair and an addictive mouth.

Long legs.

Soaked lace.

I could smell her interest, the sweetness of it tinting the air and making me that much harder for her.

I pressed my palm to the scrap of fabric between her thighs, then fisted the red material and yanked it off of her.

A soft cry parted her lips, one that quickly morphed into a sound of approval as I leaned down to draw my nose through her slick folds. Her leg bent with me, proving her flexibility even more and providing me with a whole slew of sordid thoughts regarding positions to fuck her in.

But our first time would be face-to-face.

I needed to see her.

To watch her face as I thrust inside her, taking her to completion over and over again.

The animalistic drive threatened to overwhelm my every

move, encouraging me to sink balls-deep into her welcoming heat and take us both over the edge into madness.

But I licked her instead, drawing that delectable flavor into my mouth and finishing the act by sucking her clit.

She bowed up off the bed, her restraint nonexistent. If she'd been thinking about potential cameras before, she certainly wasn't now. And I kept her in that state as I massaged her intimately with my tongue, my mouth worshipping her in the most traditional sense.

One of my hands ran up her silk leg to the garter around her thigh, then pulled off her final stocking, while my opposite palm traced her other limb from ankle to knee.

She was exquisite.

A masterpiece I wanted to memorize with my hands and mouth and ingrain forever in my memory.

So I did just that, going to my knees again and lowering her leg to the bed as I knelt between her thighs. Then I began a journey of kissing, nibbling, and stroking every part of her naked form.

Her breasts were my starting point, my marks still embedded in her flesh and encouraging me to drink once more.

Her nipples were rosy peaks of sin, dampened by my tongue.

Her neck strained as I kissed a path upward to her jaw, then her wild eyes met mine, the female so consumed by the endorphins I'd unleashed inside her that she no longer understood pleasure. She was lost to a state of rapture encouraged by my bite and drawn out by my tongue and my hands.

I kissed her.

Fucked her with my mouth.

Then guided her hands to my boxers with a whispered "Remove them" against her damp lips.

She shuddered and complied, leaving us both naked as I toed off my socks.

This was the way we were meant to be, entangled limbs and aroused parts.

She tried to wrap her legs around my waist, but I twisted out of her hold.

I wasn't done exploring her.

And I told her that as I pressed her down with my palm against her sternum. "Stay."

She released a soft growl that had my lips curling.

"You're not in charge here, Calina." Oh, her body might captivate me in every way, and her mind might qualify as my equal, but I would win every time in the bedroom—a fact I proved as I made my way down her body once more to claim her pussy with my mouth.

She screamed, her climax an unexpected event that left her shaking beneath my touch.

All it took was the brush of my fang against her sweet little button.

Then I bit her to force her into another round of oblivion, one that had her shaking violently as she forgot how to breathe.

"Inhale," I said against her soaked folds. "I don't want you passing out on me yet."

Because we were nowhere near done.

This was her warm-up.

The last chance for her to jump off this ride and run.

Of course, I would just chase her, catch her, and fuck her anyway. Because she'd unleashed my savage nature, the beast that intended to put her immortality to the test.

She might break.

Or she might experience the best damn night of her existence.

It was my job to ensure the latter.

Just as soon as she came down from her newest high.

CHAPTER THIRTY

CALINA

Where am I? I wondered, my vision an interesting mixture of black dots and silk sheets.

I was on my stomach.

And oh, Jace was between my thighs.

I was riding his face.

I couldn't remember turning over, the last orgasm having erased all thought from my mind, leaving me a writhing mess on the bed.

But Jace had grabbed my hips… and now… *ohh*.

My knees were on either side of his head, my palms were in the pillows, and I was screaming into the silk as I fought for some semblance of mental control.

He wouldn't stop, his mouth voracious and compelling and defying all reason.

Blissful heat stirred in my veins, my stomach curling as yet another climax threatened to take me under once more. It was on the tip of my tongue to beg him to stop, to tell him I couldn't take any more, as he slid two fingers inside me and stole my ability to process anything beyond sensation.

I thought him biting my clit had been intense, but this... was... so much *more*.

He stroked a secret part of me that shattered my very existence, leaving me a panting, unintelligible wreck of a person.

My mind no longer functioned. All my hard-fought strategy and control... *gone*.

And I couldn't even be bothered to care.

Because I was flying high, my body trembling beneath wave after wave of beautiful agony. It hurt in the best way. It left me breathless. Weak. Yet full of life.

I wanted to laugh. No, I wanted to giggle. And then I wanted to sigh and beg him to do it all over again.

"Mmm, I could keep you in this state for eternity," Jace whispered, his mouth suddenly near mine.

He'd rotated me onto my back again, the mattress a pillow of comfort to my overheated skin. Every inch of me burned, Jace's brand a searing energy I felt brushing my very soul.

But he wasn't done.

I could feel it in the intent of his mouth as he kissed me, the way his strong body aligned with mine with the heart of him pressing into my sensitive flesh.

He was going to rip me apart.

And I welcomed him by spreading my legs.

Because I wanted to experience everything he had to give and more.

"Fuck, Calina." The words were a breath against my lips.

"Yes," I replied, arching into him and answering the question he hadn't voiced.

Jace wasn't the type to ask. And I wasn't exactly the type to accept, either.

However, I was no longer Doctor Calina.

I existed for this moment alone, to experience oblivion with this royal vampire and let him demonstrate what it meant to be a king.

He thrust forward, filling me without warning and drawing a scream from my throat. Because I wasn't ready. I hadn't realized... I didn't *know*... I... I'd never *experienced*...

The lycan flashed in my mind, that solitary exposure nowhere near enough to prepare me for *this*.

Jace obliterated my senses, his power a hot claim to my spirit that I hadn't anticipated.

And he didn't give me time to understand it.

He just kissed me and started to move, the agony of his claim shredding me apart from within, making my limbs tense and my soul cry out for him to stop.

Only it soon shifted into... into... a passionate inferno. One that consumed me from head to toe and sent me spiraling into a world of the unknown.

I moaned. Screamed. Clawed at his shoulders. And lifted my hips to meet his.

I no longer knew who I was, just that I had to match him in every way. To fight him to completion. To consummate this act as a partner, not some meek participant.

He growled and I growled back at him.

His teeth sank into my lower lip. I responded in kind, some foreign animal within me driving me to battle him.

No, not battle, but *match* him.

He was stronger. Faster. Older. More experienced. And none of that scared me. I showed him that with my tongue, my teeth, and my nails against his back.

His palm grabbed my throat, squeezing intently as his opposite hand went to my hip.

But I couldn't stop myself from continuing this dangerous dance between our bodies.

It felt right. Freeing. Intensely intimate.

"Little enchantress," he breathed, his tongue licking his bottom lip where I'd drawn blood. "Fuck, Calina. I've never experienced anyone like you."

Those words sounded pained, as though it hurt him to admit that out loud.

And then he was kissing me again, his hips slamming mine into submission as he tightened his grip even more, cutting off my ability to breathe.

I dug my nails into his nape, not because I wanted him to stop, but because I needed more.

He'd coaxed my soul out to play, and now I was a slave to her animalistic need.

His hand left my hip and slid between us, his thumb unerringly finding my sensitive nub. My lips parted on a scream I couldn't release, the air gone from my lungs.

And somehow that only strengthened the moment, drawing out my pleasure until I couldn't see.

"Come, Calina," Jace demanded against my ear, my world a vision of black clouds and impossibilities.

Yet I felt my body tumble under his command, my limbs straining as I plummeted headfirst into an oblivion of the unknown.

I was dizzy.

Dying.

Unable to breathe.

While shaking and silently crying out for more.

This world was the one he mastered, my body his instrument of choice, and I found myself falling into his wicked embrace, giving him everything and more as he continued to fuck me without restraint.

He was breaking me, my bones turning to dust beneath his authoritative existence.

I felt limp.

Yet I burned inside.

So much heat and intensity and stunning grace.

My name escaped his lips on a prayer, his palm leaving my throat as he cupped my cheek and breathed life back into my mouth with a kiss that stole my soul.

There was beauty in this chaos, a passionate meeting of spirits, our blood coming together as one.

I didn't understand, but I felt it, the heat of our joining going far beyond the connection between my thighs. His pace reached a peak, the motions sending me higher and higher until I couldn't take another second of this insanity.

My entire body went up in flames.

Every part of me shook.

My lungs screamed for oxygen.

My throat protested to the point of disuse.

I could no longer swallow. No longer move. No longer think.

No longer remember my name, I thought, recalling something important about that phrase and forgetting it in the next moment.

Because I was dying beneath an avalanche of sensation and thoughts and emotions.

History slammed into my consciousness.

Worlds I didn't understand.

Languages that weren't my own.

A mind twisted with logic and strategy. So masculine and perfect. Beautiful in its cunning. Politically motivated. Kind yet stern.

I relaxed into that mental state, feeling it marrying my own and accepting the intertwined paths formed by two minds.

Two souls.

Two beings becoming one.

A stunning union.

Confusing yet right.

I don't understand, I marveled, swimming through the thoughts of a male over forty times my age. *Four thousand years.* Closer to five thousand. So many memories. So many thoughts. So much *intelligence*.

I was lost.

This must be heaven, I decided, blissfully pleased with the development. Because this place was my home. My essence. My preferred state of being.

Calina, Jace murmured, a hint of awe in his tone. *How is this possible?*

I followed his masculine voice, floating on a cloud of thought. *Where are we?*

His hips moved against mine, his cock still deep inside me. I blinked, startled by the sensation he evoked below, my body already anticipating more.

Which was impossible.

He'd destroyed me. Killed me. Sent me to heaven inside his mind.

"Calina," he said, his mouth brushing mine. "You're definitely not dead, but I will take that as a compliment." He skimmed his teeth along my bruised lower lip. "And I'll happily send you back to heaven again shortly. But I want to see your eyes first."

I frowned and tried to focus, my vision black even as I lifted my lids.

However, ever so slowly, his gorgeous face came into view.

As did the surrounding room.

In Lajos Region. Hawaii.

It all felt like a dream. Except I could feel that it wasn't, something he punctuated as he moved once more.

I groaned in approval, the fullness between my thighs lulling me into a state of intrinsic need. *You've turned me into someone I don't even recognize*, I accused him.

I could say the same to you, he returned.

It took me a moment to realize we were speaking in each other's minds.

Because we were in sync, our mental states tied together as one.

I blinked again.

How is that possible? I asked him, startled by the discovery.

You just became my first and only Erosita, he replied. *I thought you said you weren't a virgin.*

I wasn't.

Then this shouldn't have happened.

I know. I finally focused on his eyes. *What now?* Because I wasn't sure how to process any of this.

Oh, now, I'm going to fuck you again, he replied. *Because I'm not done. But when I am, we'll figure out what to do.*

I could hear it in his mind, the truth of his statement, and his intent to essentially fuck me out of his system. He saw this as an interesting development that could provide him with a new experience.

An Erosita. *Well, I'll be damned. Might as well play. See what all the fuss is about.*

A practical thought. One that irked me, yet didn't at the same time. Because I understood his approach—it was similar to one I would take in this situation.

This was something new—a rarity for one as old as him.

He wanted to indulge in it until it no longer intrigued him.

A passing fancy.

A fun fuck.

Not the words I would use, but that didn't make them any less understandable. Because I, too, wanted to explore this more, to find out what it meant.

However, his desire to make this temporary was shadowed by an inkling of doubt, one that formed in the back of his mind as he wondered, *What if a temporary fling isn't possible? What if I never tire of her?*

A whole slew of thoughts followed those, some of them making me sick to my stomach as he revisited past conquests and recounted his love for sex.

He wasn't a monogamous man.

He adored fucking. Seducing. Playing. Eternity was a long time to tie his soul to another.

Yes, he'd been more or less infatuated with me—something his subsequent musings told me was abnormal for him. Jace had seen me as a challenge to conquer, which had intrigued him initially.

But now he wasn't sure how to interpret our bond or me or my place in his life.

And that left him distinctly unsettled.

He pondered it for a moment.

Then he chose to ignore that nagging thought and focus on the present. He wanted to see how far this infatuation could go, then decide how to proceed.

Like an experiment, I translated, both offended and intrigued by the prospect.

Yes, he agreed, his mind keeping pace with my own as I read his intentions and discerned my own feelings on the topic. It happened quickly, spanning maybe seconds instead of minutes, our minds seeming to work at supernatural speeds.

Because I was tied to him now. And he possessed the soul of an ancient being.

An irrational part of me didn't appreciate being seen as a challenge and an experiment. Yet the practical side of me acknowledged his fascination and shared a similar view... only of him.

Because he made me feel things outside of my norm.

He provided me with a sense of peace I never knew I desired.

And his body absolutely knew how to play with mine.

Why not test the boundaries of this connection and see what

happened? Perhaps I would tire of him, too.

Not likely, he replied.

Keep thinking arrogant thoughts like that at me, and I'll be done before you, I threatened.

He grinned. *It's not arrogance, sweet genius. It's confidence.*

I snorted. *I can read your mind.*

And I can read yours, he countered. *Which is why I know you're just as intrigued by this development as I am. Now let's really experiment and see how many times I can make you come before you pass out.*

I gasped as he started to move, my mind only just interpreting his challenge before shutting down in acute acceptance.

So you can submit, he marveled. *Good to know.*

He didn't give me a chance to reply, because in the next moment, he was fucking me again. And it only took him a handful of minutes to shoot me to the stars.

This experiment may just kill me, I realized as my mind started to blink in and out of reality.

Because this connection tied our souls together.

And when he chooses to break it, I probably won't survive, I thought as he came inside me again.

He didn't hear me, his pleasure too overpowering and his urge to take more consuming him.

His teeth pierced my neck, his vampiric mind demanding he feast upon what was rightfully his—his *Erosita's* essence.

I groaned, my limbs trembling as he weakened me more and more with each swallow.

"Jace..." It came out hoarse, my throat damaged from all the screaming. "Jace, please..."

I could hear his intent, his dark need, the savage beast inside him swallowing... swallowing... swallowing.

"Jace," I breathed, his name nothing but air.

Mine, he growled in response, his mind stroking my thoughts. *You're mine*.

His wrist went to my mouth in the next inhale, drowning me in his blood.

But it was too late, my body had already begun to fade into another climatic whirlpool of sensation.

I could barely feel it now, my limbs quivering softly in response to the ecstasy swimming within my core.

It warmed my soul. Made me smile.

And then I fell, fell, fell into a dark pool of sweet death.

One I knew from so many times before.

Only this occasion was lined with welcoming heat. A soft kiss. And a vow to keep me safe.

I didn't understand it.

I didn't try.

I merely succumbed with a slight smile on my lips.

Sleep, little enchantress. Sleep.

CHAPTER THIRTY-ONE

LILITH

Royal Helias continues to be a problem. He's arrogant and not a loyalist to our cause.

I've tried, my liege, but he only cares about himself and harbors no consideration for the larger picture. However, I kept him in the ally file because he's easily persuaded. When it's time to announce your return, he will—

Please stand by for an important message from your virtual assistant.

Message to commence in three, two…

My liege, I have confirmed that Bunker 27 was officially compromised. Damage assessment is in progress. I've also been unable to confer with our asset. Therefore, I'm not sure who has intercepted our team, but I suspect it is the resistance. And if you've reviewed those files, then you're aware that not all of their identities are known.

I need to know how you want to proceed.

There are three protocols in place to contend with this situation.

The first is the termination protocol, which will set all bunkers on a destruction sequence of twelve hours. To learn more about this protocol, select: Termination.

The second is the surveillance protocol, which will engage the live-feed features of the various bunkers and allow us to watch events unfold in real time. This is typically used when wanting to identify an unknown assailant. To learn more about this protocol, select: Surveillance.

The third option is to engage the alliance protocol, which will send communications to all our allies and schedule an urgent meeting in Lilith City. This protocol would mean alerting them of your awakening and will begin our takeover sequence. To learn more about this protocol, select: Alliance.

Which sequence would you—

Surveillance protocol selected.

To review the parameters of this method, press the information button. Otherwise, select—

Surveillance protocol initiated.

Ally file log for Helias to resume in three, two…

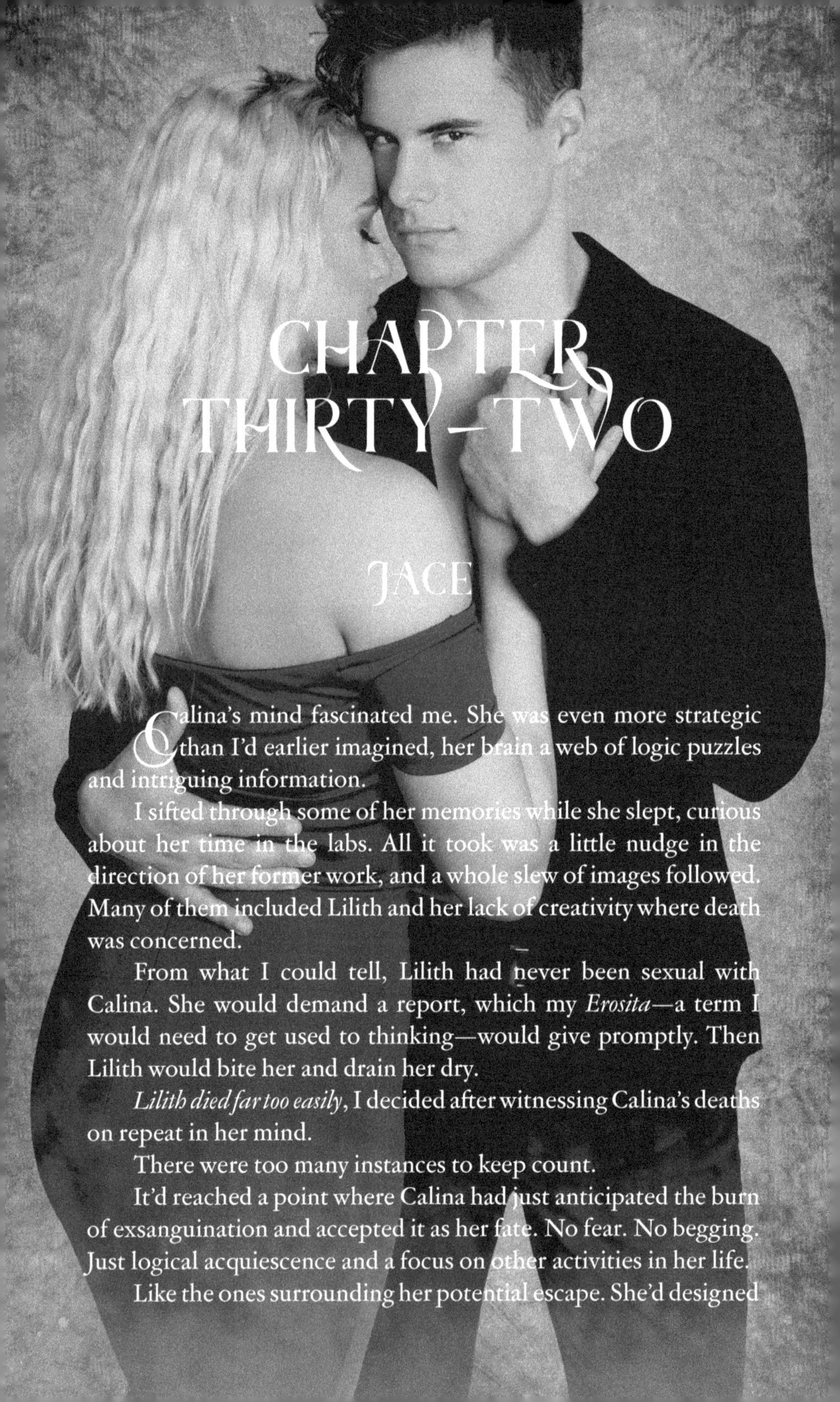

CHAPTER THIRTY-TWO

JACE

Calina's mind fascinated me. She was even more strategic than I'd earlier imagined, her brain a web of logic puzzles and intriguing information.

I sifted through some of her memories while she slept, curious about her time in the labs. All it took was a little nudge in the direction of her former work, and a whole slew of images followed. Many of them included Lilith and her lack of creativity where death was concerned.

From what I could tell, Lilith had never been sexual with Calina. She would demand a report, which my *Erosita*—a term I would need to get used to thinking—would give promptly. Then Lilith would bite her and drain her dry.

Lilith died far too easily, I decided after witnessing Calina's deaths on repeat in her mind.

There were too many instances to keep count.

It'd reached a point where Calina had just anticipated the burn of exsanguination and accepted it as her fate. No fear. No begging. Just logical acquiescence and a focus on other activities in her life.

Like the ones surrounding her potential escape. She'd designed several mechanisms, including the circumvention of Lilith's information systems.

Yet you never tried to run, I marveled as I drew my fingers through her hair. *How fascinating.*

An image of James and Gretchen appeared next.

I see, I murmured, catching her familial attachment where the couple and their baby lycan were concerned.

A puzzled feeling followed, one that suggested she'd questioned and recognized her irrational behavior.

Acceptance came next as she showed me the intricate analysis she'd conducted in response to her emotions.

The web intrigued me more and more, causing me to continue probing into her psyche.

Many females would be furious by my intrusion. But I felt Calina's awareness of my presence and her acknowledgment of my curiosity.

Because my mind piqued her own interest as well.

She'd thought my brain was heaven, her knack for strategy rivaling my own.

There were definitely benefits to this intense connection, ones that superseded the bedroom.

Calina yawned and rolled toward me, still asleep. Yet I sensed her in my head, pulling on my experiences and searching my knowledge base for enlightening information.

It was a bizarre mating of the minds fueled by our similar mental faculties. We both fancied strategic plays, our penchant for analyzing every possible outcome a foundation for a unique sort of partnership.

Practicality overrode our emotions.

She knew where I stood on monogamy. I felt her review the detail and dismiss it in the next second. This wasn't long-term. This was beneficial for the moment.

I didn't have to remain faithful to her to keep this bond alive. She saw the truth of that in my thoughts. Which had her examining how to break the *Erosita* bond next, her knowledge of sex being the key giving her pause.

Because she wasn't a virgin.

I listened as she puzzled over the potential reasons for our link and frowned when she started searching for her links to immortality.

They were the foundation of her immortal life source.

Other vampires who had created an *Erosita*-like bond with her.

I explored that more while she reviewed what I knew about vampire mating bonds, her brain working almost as swiftly as mine—which was an impressive feat considering her comatose state.

She seemed to be absorbing my knowledge into her own mind, cataloging my experiences and memorizing the key details.

It was fascinating.

But I didn't care for her supposed ties to other immortal beings. She revealed her connection to Lilith yet couldn't define it, her mind blank when I prodded for more details.

That explained her eagerness to study the files with me—she wanted to learn more about her origin. The thought proved she'd spoken the truth the other day.

Actually, having access to her mind confirmed everything she'd told me from her first breath was grounded in fact. She'd never lied.

Oh, but she had omitted a few details, such as how I'd proven her assessment of vampire prowess wrong almost immediately.

Hmm, I hummed at her. *I'm going to enjoy punishing you for that little omission later.*

She responded by following that thread of thought to my experience again and pulling some of my favorite bedroom activities. A mixture of irritation and interest followed. She didn't particularly care for my vast exposure to sensual activities. And yet, she found them intriguing at the same time.

After a few minutes, she dismissed the thoughts and returned to her musings of our connection.

I trailed after her, curious to watch her work through the puzzle of what shouldn't exist between us. She sorted through my knowledge base and her own, comparing notes along the way and eventually reaching a conclusion that echoed through my thoughts.

My irregular genetics must make me predisposed to accepting a vampire mate.

She started thinking about her experience with the lycan, which had my fingers fisting in her hair. "Stop that." I didn't want that memory in my head. It was worse than Lilith drinking from her. Worse than *everything* I'd uncovered in her mind so far.

But now that she'd started down the path, the whole episode played out behind my eyes, making me dizzy with rage.

"Calina," I snapped, hating this experience more than anything else in my fucking life. "*Stop*."

She didn't.

The memory worsened, her pain an agonizing whip to my senses.

She hadn't been allowed to scream, her mouth gagged to keep her silent. But she hadn't been able to stop her tears, the anguish leaking from her eyes as the lycan ravaged her.

He'd been blind to his lust, his need causing him to disregard her human form and mistake her for a fellow lycan.

I could almost feel him fucking me from behind, and it wasn't even my memory.

Calina shivered beside me, her cheeks suddenly wet as she cried in her sleep, the nightmarish images too real and threatening for her to pull free from.

There was a whole section of her mind filled with horrors that rivaled this one. Years of being treated like a lab subject. Growing up inside a bunker and never being permitted to go outside.

Lilith feeding from her.

Lilith testing the limits of Calina's immortality.

She'd killed her so many times in so many different ways. I'd considered Lilith to be boring before, feeling her methods hadn't been all that creative.

How wrong I'd been.

Now that Calina had opened this part of her mind, I could see all the torture she'd endured. The pain she kept locked away behind a mask of indifference. This was what had driven her to a logical frame of mind. This torment had been too much for a mortal psyche. So she'd clung to reason and strategy, choosing practicality over irrational thought.

She compartmentalized her anguish.

It was an interesting revelation that broke my damn heart.

This brilliant female had survived hell.

And she'd faced me with the spirit of a lion inside her.

"Fuck, Calina," I whispered, enraptured with her once more. I palmed her cheeks to flick away her tears, then pressed my lips to hers.

She didn't wake.

But her mind began to calm as I tugged on our connection, pulling her into my mind to venture through my memories again.

She went immediately to the downfall of humankind, witnessing the war where mortals had stood no chance against their betters. I hadn't fought in it, instead trying to find a way to create a peaceful coexistence where vampires and lycans ruled and humans had some semblance of rights.

Calina yanked on a specific strand, calling a vision of Cam to my mind. It was a conversation where we'd discussed alternative fates—something we'd done frequently in those days—but this one had ended differently.

Because it was the night Cam and I had said goodbye.

"You know I'm right. My sacrifice will be remembered," Cam said, his blue eyes intense.

"Assuming Lilith allows it."

"I'm counting on her not allowing it," he replied. "Outlawing my name will only make me a memory that evokes thought and concern."

I considered that for a moment, then nodded in agreement. His plan was sound. We needed to lull Lilith into a state of comfort, to learn her true plan for this new world. She claimed to want to form an alliance of lycans and vampires, and to divide the lands equally.

But we all knew she looked down upon the wolves.

Like many of our brethren, she felt vampires were superior.

What she failed to understand was that lycans shared a semblance of our DNA, marking them as our equals.

Just as she failed to understand the importance of human life. Without mortals, we would all perish. Vampires required human blood. No other essence would do.

"What if she kills you?" I asked.

"She won't." Cam sounded so confident, his familiarity with Lilith far deeper than my own.

"Just because Cane turned her—"

"Cane...," a new voice whispered, female in nature, and not at all tied to this memory.

I opened my eyes, not having realized I'd fallen into the

recollection of my past.

Calina's hazel irises were a startling blue shade with no sign of green today. I parted my lips to comment on it, but she started speaking before I had the chance.

"I know that name. Lilith spoke of him."

"Cane?" I asked, struggling to recall whom she meant. Her irises were just so beautiful. Like liquid sapphire. The kind of color a smitten man could drown in.

"Yes. She mentioned Cane regularly."

"I imagine she would," I replied, still lost in her pretty eyes. "Cane was her maker. He also happened to be my other cousin. Cam and Cane's father was my uncle." Making us all cousins.

She frowned. "Your uncle? As in a blood relative? Or because he was brothers with your maker?"

"Some would say there isn't a difference," I remarked, my fingers still in her hair. I finished combing through the strands and palmed her cheek, my gaze lost to hers. "How much do you know about our origin?" I wondered out loud, curious about what Lilith might have told her.

As a researcher, it would make sense for her to understand the distinction between royal lines and diluted vampiric bloodlines.

"Vampire genetics were never my primary focus. Only lycans."

I should have guessed that since I'd reviewed a lot of the files with her and I had spent the last several hours sifting through her memories. "That's very interesting, considering your end goal had been to strengthen human longevity. One would think vampire genetics would aid in that attempt more than a lycan could. Although, lycans are technically our descendants. Perhaps Lilith wanted to find a way for humans to continue the bloodlines via weaker, more vulnerable strands."

As I puzzled it out loud, I realized the truth of it.

"Yes, that's exactly what she had intended." It made perfect sense. "She knew lycans came from vampire bloodlines, so she wanted to create a stronger semi-immortal race from lycans. But without any of the benefits. Just the one that kept them alive longer and made them a little tougher on the outside." So they couldn't be killed as easily by vampires.

Calina studied my face. Then she nodded. "I agree."

Two words. Not empty, but a true agreement. And it'd been easily voiced.

Because she'd sifted through all the logic inside my mind while I'd been speaking.

"This connection is fascinating," I admitted out loud. No point in keeping it to myself since she would hear it anyway.

"Yes." She started searching for information on my origin now, her mind picking through my memories without asking. Just like I'd done to her while she'd slept.

And also, like her, it didn't bother me.

I gave her what she wanted, showing her the bloodline in my thoughts.

My father, Johan, was one of the original vampires. A being unlike many others due to his unique blood.

"It's said that twenty mortals were blessed by the Goddess Nyx," I murmured. "Twenty royal bloodlines. All over the world. And all of the Blessed Ones were male. Most of them reproduced with human females. And from those pairings, my era was born."

"What happened to the Blessed Ones?"

"They've all since returned to the earth," I replied. "But they're not dead. They just sleep."

"Why?"

"Because they prefer it to life." I lifted a shoulder. "Their lovers all died thousands of years ago. It's actually said that those spirits are where the *Erosita* bond comes from—that the Blessed Ones' lovers all went to Nyx and begged for their vampire children to be able to take mortal lovers without requiring the kiss of death."

I wasn't sure I believed that.

But I couldn't deny the magic of our existence.

"The kiss of death being the vampiric gift of immortality?" Calina correctly guessed.

"Indeed. It wasn't an option for the Blessed Ones. They were gifted with endless life but couldn't bestow it on their lovers. However, they were given immortal children. Cam was the first, his father being Cronus."

A family tree seemed to form in her head as she linked my father, Johan, to Cam's father, Cronus.

"They were both blessed, perhaps because my grandmother

was a renowned night worshipper. I'm not sure, but it's where the rumors of Nyx being the mother of our kind has come from—all the Blessed Ones came from families who worshipped various forms of a *Night Goddess.*"

This was thousands of years ago. All the literature of those beliefs was long destroyed.

Just like the languages.

"Twenty royal lines were created. But the Blessed Ones soon learned there was a price for their children to remain immortal."

"Blood," Calina said, her mind processing and understanding my history faster than I could say it.

"Yes. And our inability to traditionally procreate." I drew my thumb along her lower lip, her mouth finally pulling my gaze from her eyes. "Some were more gluttonous than others, but we soon learned how to pass on our genetics via the bite. And the kiss of death spread to create the massive population that exists today."

"But what about the lycans?" Calina asked, drawing my gaze back to hers. "How did they come to be? And where are the other royals? You said there are twenty lines. Only seventeen rule."

My wrist buzzed before I could answer, a note coming in from Darius to remind me of the time. "Five minutes," I read, slightly irritated by the interruption, but quickly remembering our purpose here. "The listening devices are about to click on again." I cupped her cheek and pressed my lips to hers.

Then I unleashed what little I knew about lycan creation into her mind.

It had something to do with a bite and a mysterious bloodline, similar to the Blessed Ones, only weakened by mortality.

Because all lycans eventually died.

Although some lived to be upward of a thousand, most declined in their seven or eight hundredth year.

Calina's brow furrowed by the end of my short summary, her thoughts telling me she felt something was missing.

I agreed with her. There was absolutely an explanation missing. But with so many of the elder vampires sleeping, it was hard to say.

Cane is asleep? Calina asked, her mind already processing the answer and producing a theory. *Is that who Lilith woke up?*

Now it was my turn to frown.

It was a possibility I hadn't considered, one that had me slowly shaking my head. *No. Cane would never condone what she's done. He and Cam were similar in their opinions on humanity. It's why Cane chose to sleep, actually. He felt his apathy slipping and decided to join his father in their family crypt.*

But her theory had me thinking through several other possibilities. Because Cane wasn't the only one of our era who had chosen to sleep.

"Come," I said, pulling her from the bed. "I want to fuck you in the shower before our food arrives."

It was an abrupt change in discussion fueled by the listening devices turning back on around us.

Lajos would expect a show.

And so we would give him one.

Something I told Calina now in her mind, expressing exactly what I intended to do to her against the tiled wall.

And all the while continuing to consider the new avenue of thought she'd just opened inside my mind.

Perhaps we'd been considering the *liege's* identity from the wrong angle. We assumed it was an ally of some kind from recent times.

Maybe we needed to go a little further back to determine her partner.

A few thousand years or so.

To the Blessed Ones and the original era.

There had been many at that time who'd devalued humanity, considering ourselves gods to be worshipped, not beings who should live in hiding.

Which explained Lilith's goddess perception.

Fuck. Why didn't I think of this before? I wondered as I led Calina into the shower.

Because you didn't have me before, Calina replied, her hands on my hips. *Fresh perspectives can be crucial to hard-fought discoveries.*

I stared down at her, into those too-blue eyes. *You're seducing me with your mind, Calina.*

She responded by grabbing my shaft and giving it a stroke. *Just my mind?*

Fuck, this woman was a goddess in her own right.

She snorted. *Definitely not.*

Shh, I'm thinking, darling. No interruptions allowed.

The little minx rolled her eyes. *Stop thinking and kiss me.*

Still topping from the bottom, I see.

She squeezed my dick, her grip like granite. "Fuck me, My Prince. *Please.*"

I growled, both irritated and immensely turned on by her simpering little act.

If her goal had been to distract me from thinking through the list of ancients in my mind, she'd succeeded.

But I was going to make her pay for distracting me.

"I'm about to destroy you, little genius."

With words or actions? she taunted.

Dammit, Calina. I captured her disobedient little mouth and punished her with my tongue. Which only made her moan—a clear break from the rules—but I didn't even fucking care.

This female wanted me to unleash my beast.

Better hold on, I warned her. *I won't be taking this slow.*

CHAPTER THIRTY-THREE

GALINA

My body burned from Jace's earlier attentions.

He hadn't been kidding when he'd told me his intentions. He'd drilled me into the wall so damn hard that I swore I'd been able to taste him in my mouth.

I fought the urge to squirm again, the silk covering my slick flesh doing bizarre things to my mental state.

I wore a different sort of gown tonight. This one's skirt was a deep navy blue silk that flowed to the floor. Slits up both legs revealed my black stockings, heels, and the garter straps that hooked into my thong. Two strips of blue ribbon finished the ensemble, the thick silk crisscrossing over my breasts to tie behind my neck.

My entire back was exposed, as were most of my abdomen and my sides.

But despite all of that, I couldn't feel the cool air of the limo around us.

Jace's body heat inflamed my blood as though it were his own.

He sat beside me in an all-black suit, his palm on my thigh and squeezing every time I felt the need to move.

Which didn't help me at all.

Something he knew.

But the bastard was too amused to help himself.

Careful, darling, or I'll have to fuck you again for your disobedient movements.

I'm not even moving, I argued.

You are, he murmured. *If Lajos were here, he'd absolutely notice. Just as Darius has.*

My jaw clenched.

And he's just noticed that as well, hence him arching his brow at me.

You should have told him about our Erosita *bond*, I muttered.

Apparently, the connections weren't obvious and couldn't be sensed by other vampires. Because if that were the case, then Darius would already know. Which he obviously did not.

If he knew you were in my head, he'd understand my reactions, I added.

Jace snorted a laugh beside me, then covered it with a cough. *The listening devices in our suite made telling him impossible. Plus, we almost missed breakfast, thanks to your stubbornness in the shower.*

My stubbornness?

Yes. You only came three times before stating you were done. A gentleman requires at least five orgasms to consider the job complete.

My cheeks heated at the reminder of how he'd spun me around, pressed my breasts up against the wall, and fucked me from behind while demanding I come all over his—

Stop. Squirming, he snapped into my mind.

I'm sorry. My insides are still convulsing from your mandated orgasm count. I'd told him I couldn't come again, and he'd promptly proved me wrong by forcing two more climaxes out of me.

It had physically hurt to obey.

But the pleasure that had followed made it worth the agony.

His palm slapped my thigh. "Stay still."

I growled into his mind.

He snarled back.

I swallowed and did my best to fall into the submissive little human he desired.

Oh, it's not what I desire, sweet Calina. Which is exactly why I need you to stop, or I really will fuck you again because your disobedience is making me hard.

My eyes drifted over his strong thighs to his groin. And I involuntarily licked my lips.

"Fuck," he muttered out loud, his entire body strained.

"That's what you did all night, yes?" Irritation colored Darius's tone.

"Indeed." Jace sounded just as annoyed, but his mind told a different story. He'd only come once in the shower and could absolutely go another two rounds.

And just the thought of that had me—

Calina, please, he said, agony touching his thoughts. *I don't want to fuck you in this limo.*

No, you plan to do that in the club, I returned, fully aware of his strategy for tonight. *And possibly let Lajos experience my mouth in the process.*

This time his growl was one of anger more than lust. *I haven't decided yet.*

I know. Because I could read his thoughts.

Just like I knew he could technically shut me out—something he'd considered doing as a protective measure for both of us. But he'd quickly discarded the idea, noting the leverage and advantage of keeping our link open to communicate since I wouldn't be permitted to speak tonight. Keeping the channel open allowed us to strategize together.

Which was why I said, *If going to my knees is what I need to do to distract him, I'll do it.*

That didn't mean I wanted to.

But I understood our intention here. We needed Lajos comfortable so we could gain freedom to explore and find Bunker 37.

And if we couldn't lull him into a state of comfort, then we needed to distract him.

I would likely be that distraction.

No, Jace replied. *I'm not leaving you alone with him.*

I won't die.

You don't know that. If he fucks you, this bond will likely break. And what about your other ties to immortality? Until we have more information about your history and the details regarding your immortal status, we can't risk it.

You'll have to risk it for Cam, I countered, recalling his ultimate goal. *We both know you'll choose him over me. Please don't belittle my intelligence by pretending otherwise.*

Although, it wasn't exactly a pretense on his part. I could feel him emotionally struggling with the concept of letting Lajos have me.

It wasn't just the idea of me dying, but the notion of another male fucking me.

It seemed Jace had acquired a bit of possessiveness where I was concerned, which we both knew was tied to the bond.

Just as we both knew his penchant for strategy would win in the end.

I admired that about him because my mind worked the same way.

I'll under—

We're not talking about this. Not yet. Not until we're left with no other option. The words were a sharp snarl, the discussion done.

All right, I agreed, focusing on my body once more and trying to relax into a more submissive pose.

Jace's palm tightened on my thigh as he began running through the names of all the Blessed Ones and their heirs. Apparently, several of those heirs had chosen to rest along with their fathers, immortality boring them after a few thousand years. Which meant some of the royals were actually those who'd first been bitten and turned.

Vampires like Darius.

Through Jace's thoughts, I learned that Darius was Cam's only progeny, which was why Darius would likely one day be forced to lead.

Jace had never turned anyone, which was uncommon. He noted in his mind that Kylan had waited until this year to create a vampire.

Everyone else had bitten and turned at least one other human.

And those vampires had turned more.

And more.

And more.

Several thousands of years had allowed for the creation of a lot of vampires, and the bloodlines had been diluted as a result.

Only those from the first three generations—Cronus and Johan's era; Cam, Cane, Kylan, Ryder, and Jace's era; and Darius's era—were considered true royals because of their close familial ties to the Blessed Ones.

Everyone else fell somewhere down the line.

Some couldn't even trace back their origins.

I learned all this from Jace's mind as I listened to him sort through all their identities for the potential *liege* that Lilith spoke to in the logs.

He went through their identities quickly, locking on a few and dismissing the others in the blink of an eye. It was fascinating to hear, his strategic process a seduction of sorts.

His palm on my thigh didn't help.

And neither did the fact that he could hear how his intelligence impacted me.

Fuck it, he said, his hands finding my hips as he pulled me over to straddle his thighs. Darius muttered something, but it was lost to the pounding in my ears.

Jace caught my mouth in the next instant, his tongue dueling mine as he continued to consider whom Lilith might have awoken.

His ability to multitask was intoxicating, causing my blood to boil in my veins with each passing second.

Because I tracked every thought and agreed with each decision yet managed to keep up with the movement of his lips on mine.

He was able to engage my body and my mind at the same time, leaving me satisfied in a way that rivaled our time in the shower.

"My Prince." Darius's tone lacked emotion.

However, Jace recognized the subtle note of impatience in the air.

Because apparently we'd arrived at our destination and neither of us had noticed.

A hint of wonder touched Jace's gaze as he pulled his mouth away from mine and studied my face. *You're dangerous, Calina.*

Not as dangerous as you.

Hmm, we'll see, he hummed, his thumb brushing my lower lip. "We're ready."

A harsh knock followed his comment.

Then the door opened beside us.

Darius exited first, his hand lowering to assist Juliet from the car next. It was such a natural move, one I now recognized as proprietary, and it left me wondering what Jace would do.

He chuckled into my mind, his lips brushing mine. *Trust me. My mark is evident in your expression.* He lifted me from his lap in quick succession and slid out of the car. Then his hand appeared, his fingers dangling in a taunting manner. *Come out and play, little genius. I want to show you off.*

I swallowed, my heart suddenly hammering for an entirely different reason.

Because I knew why he wanted to show me off.

I was bait.

For a royal vampire with a penchant for killing his toys.

Now, Jace added, clearly hearing my hesitation. He was telling me to hurry so he didn't have to make a show of punishing me for it—an understanding I gathered through his thoughts.

With a steadying breath, I slipped across the leather bench and placed my hand in his.

He pulled me out of the car with the ease of a much stronger being, his arm immediately circling my back as he held me close.

Not proprietary so much as necessary.

And we had a show to put on.

The more he doted on me, the more intrigued Lajos would become. Hence solidifying my role as a bargaining chip.

Jace kissed my throat, but I almost didn't feel it through my rapidly beating pulse.

I understood the point of all this. I had a part to play, as did Jace. But facing the harsh reality of being used as a pawn was much more difficult than mentally accepting it.

My knees wobbled as we walked.

I focused on steadying myself and my resolve and disregarded everything else around us.

I'm a doll. A toy. A human slave. A food—

Calina, Jace interjected. *I understand what you're doing, but please stop. You're none of those things to me.*

I am who I need to be, I told him. *Who* you *need me to be.*

His mental sigh echoed through my mind, his palm squeezing my hip as he led me across the dark wood beneath my feet. We'd entered the building without me noticing, the air-conditioning an icy caress to my overheated skin.

He spoke to someone.

I ignored the words.

I ignored the sensation of eyes on my skin.

I ignored the heavy beat of music as we entered another room.

I ignored the sharp gasps and cries of pleasure and pain that followed.

I ignored the echoing grunts.

I ignored the cruel laughter.

I ignored the chilling sensation of power that welcomed us to a back area.

And most of all, I ignored the warmth at my side.

Or I tried to, anyway.

In reality, I took in every detail, memorized the scents and sounds and sights of the floor, my brain mapping out a potential escape route based on my senses alone.

Jace heard every word, his arm a brand at my back as he not so subtly reminded me that running wasn't an option.

Predators liked to chase.

They also enjoy fucking what they catch, Jace added into my mind as he pulled me down onto his lap. *Whatever you do, don't look at the stage.*

His words gave me pause, then I trailed the comment to his own recollection of what he'd seen.

My stomach churned at the erotic display of death that appeared in his mind.

Bloodied humans were being fucked to literal death on various torture implements.

Several were silently screaming.

Others were too numbed to the world to care.

And a sea of voyeuristic vampires watched the show, many of them enjoying their own forms of pleasure at their respective tables.

Blood-laced wine flowed throughout the room. *Literally from fountains.*

Jace maintained a bored facade as he and Darius engaged each other in conversation. They also flagged a waiter, who I could see through Jace's mind's eye was naked apart from a few cleverly placed piercings, and ordered a snack for the table.

Of the human variety.

Jace pressed his lips to my thundering pulse. *The mortals here are going to die regardless of what Darius or I do. We can at least provide one a swift end.*

I know. Because I could read the intent from his mind.

Part of me acknowledged that having the mental link to Jace was probably all that kept me from outwardly reacting to the nightmare around me. I could hear his own disgust at the display and his irritation at how little regard Lajos possessed for humanity.

It wasn't how Jace chose to rule. Yes, he had humans that were allocated for the food industry. But he chose them carefully, typically ensuring they were of a certain age or physical decline before reaching that point.

However, if he were to truly be in charge of the world, he would create a blood bank program filled with voluntary donors. He reasoned that many mortals would see vampires as the gods they were and would willingly serve them in return for protection.

I sifted through his ideas and lost myself in the future he craved, and found I rather approved of his ideas.

Just thinking about them calmed me.

I almost sighed in relief.

Until a new charge entered the air.

"Lajos," Jace greeted, his palms finding my hips and moving me onto the bench beside him so he could stand. The cool leather bit through my dress, making me shiver as Jace's body heat left my own.

"Jace," a deep voice returned. "How good to see you."

"Likewise," Jace replied. "You know how much I fancy your clubs. It seemed like a reasonable place to take Jasmine up on her request for a meeting."

A lie. One I could hear as clear as day in Jace's thoughts. Yet he executed it with the ease of a skilled politician.

"Yes," a sultry tone responded. "I'm so glad you thought of it, Jace."

"Of course." He kissed the female on the cheek—an action I felt through our bond that I didn't fully appreciate because it resembled a punch to the stomach. When she grabbed him and returned the favor… *on his lips*… I nearly growled.

It was a bizarre reaction, one the scientific part of me realized was a reaction of our connection.

This was what Lilith had been trying to dilute through all the trials—the possessive urges that came with an *Erosita* link.

How strange that I'd never experienced them for her. Yet she'd sensed them for me.

Would any of the other immortals feel this way about me? Or were they too far removed? I couldn't feel them, but that was nothing new.

Although, I usually sensed my ties to immortality. At least subtly. And all I could feel now was Jace.

And that woman's hands on his chest.

She had her nails digging into his jacket as he laughed at something she'd just said. A comment about sexual play on the stage. One I'd missed but heard whispers of lurking in his mind.

I refused to follow the thought because I didn't want to know. Jace's distaste for the conversation pacified me. He was a wizard on the outside, chuckling and putting on a show of pure enjoyment. But on the inside, I heard his mocking commentary.

It almost amused me.

But all my sense of amusement died as Lajos took the seat beside me.

And placed his palm on my thigh.

CHAPTER THIRTY-FOUR

JACE

The crystal stem of my wine glass nearly shattered beneath my tightening grip.

Lajos sat behind me.

Next to Calina.

With his damn hand on her leg.

And there wasn't a fucking thing I could do about it that wouldn't create a scene.

Vampires were affectionate. We enjoyed stroking and touching others. Which was all Lajos had done for the last ten minutes while making idle chitchat with Darius.

I kept an eye on him through Calina's thoughts. Unfortunately, that only made me angrier because I could sense her discomfort as he traced the top of her silk stockings.

Those were for my benefit, not his.

Except I'd dressed her this way because I knew he'd crave a more intimate view later. All her assets were temptingly covered, something he'd want to reveal with his own hands.

Darius intended to put on a show with Juliet, then offer the royal a brief drink before Lajos took out his lust-filled cravings on my consort.

Except she wasn't just my consort now.

And I was very much struggling with the notion of allowing another man to touch her, let alone *fuck* her.

It was all part of our bond, this possessive need to keep her driven by our mental connection. Rationally, I understood that.

The problem was that I didn't want to be rational at all.

It took serious effort to continue conversing with Jasmine when all I wanted to do was grab Calina and claim her in front of the entire damn room.

I suddenly possessed even more admiration for Darius and his ability to maintain such a stoic air when other men admired and touched his Juliet.

Hell, I was impressed that he'd never punched me for the things I'd done to her.

Because I very much wanted to punch Lajos right now.

No. Fuck that. I wanted to kill the bastard. His fingertips were far too close to my desired heaven. Stroking up just enough to tease the lace between Calina's thighs before venturing back down to her stockings.

I'm going to enjoy stabbing him one day, I decided as I outwardly asked, "So how are things in Jasmine City?"

I didn't particularly care. I just wanted to get this discussion over with. Jasmine wanted something from me. The faster I could decline her request, the faster I could return to Calina.

Jasmine prattled on about her region and their newest technology exports. I saw through her attempts to seduce me with her trade potential, knowing full well that she was leading me into a conversation about exchanging her revered tech for human blood.

I stood at the cocktail table in the roped-off area of the club, pretending to hang on every word Jasmine said while intently listening to the conversation behind me.

"So where did Jace find such a pretty little toy?" Lajos asked, his attention entirely on Calina now. She could feel his eyes on her but tried to ignore it by playing out the various scenarios in her head. I listened, fascinated by her ability to compartmentalize such a dangerous situation.

"I see," I said, responding to Jasmine in an effort to encourage her to keep speaking.

It worked.

She dove into a whole layout of her production line, talking about how humans were used to create her latest devices.

"He found her in a hole somewhere." Darius's tone held the perfect note of derision. He didn't mean it, but that wasn't the point. He had a part to play, and he excelled at it better than most. Which was why he made the perfect sovereign. "I suppose she qualified as a beneficial reward after everything he went through with Ryder."

And there was Darius's attempt at a distraction.

"Ah, yes, Lilith mentioned her intent to visit," Lajos replied, his voice giving nothing away.

Yet I found myself pondering that statement, wondering what he wasn't saying. *Does he know she's dead? Is he one of the allies mentioned in the logs? Does he know who the liege is?*

Calina had distracted herself as well with similar questions. But she also analyzed Darius and his masterful ability at deflection.

"I believe she's still there, although I can't precisely determine why." Darius maintained an air of boredom. "There's no helping Ryder. The male has a complete disregard for the rules."

"Well, you know Lilith. She's a fighter."

"Indeed," Darius agreed smoothly. "But so is Ryder."

Calina focused on their words to distract herself from the upward shift of Lajos's palm. However, as he brushed her sex again, she swallowed and forced herself not to shiver in revulsion.

My grip tightened again around my wine glass.

Jasmine was now detailing the hours she kept for her human slaves and the amount of food they required to stay productive. Given how little she fed them, I wasn't surprised when she added, "But it doesn't seem to be enough. They wilt and die far too quickly."

I nodded. "They are frail beings."

"Too frail," she replied, taking a sip of her wine.

"I'm surprised Silvano didn't have this beautiful female in his harem," Lajos said, drawing the conversation back to Calina once more, his intrigue grating on my nerves.

I'd expected him to be interested, but there was something about his tone and touch that felt *too* interested. It was a sense I picked up from Calina, but also one I noticed as well. Darius's deflection to Ryder should have piqued more intrigue on Lajos's part.

Ryder was a fellow royal and had recently acquired new territory.

Any other vampire of our standing would want to know how that was going.

If anything, just to determine the potential for political gain or a territory acquisition should the royal fail in his task.

But not Lajos.

No, he wanted to talk about Calina.

"As I never knew Silvano well, I can't say," Darius replied. "But I am curious what will happen to his territory beneath Ryder's rule."

Another attempt at deflection.

One Lajos allowed for a brief moment as he commented on Ryder's inability to lead anyone other than himself. "I believe Lilith has already learned that lesson," he concluded, causing the hairs along the back of my neck to stand on end.

He knows, I decided.

But I wasn't given a chance to react to it because our real drink arrived in the next minute in the form of a female with tangled brown hair.

"Ah, time to improve the wine," Darius said in a smooth manner that suggested he hadn't heard Lajos's last comment. But I knew better. He'd not only heard it; he was evaluating it.

Just like me.

Just like Calina.

Although, the tray of sharp instruments landing on the table distracted her almost immediately. They were tools meant to remove body parts.

And the human had carried them to her own death.

Shh, I hushed into Calina's mind, calming her before she could outwardly react.

This is so wrong.

It's life.

It's wrong, she bit back.

I released a mental sigh and pushed thoughts of the future to her. Ones filled with my plans and ideas and the ways I intended to make them work. I'd sensed her reviewing those details earlier, and

I'd noted the semblance of peace it had brought her.

Fortunately, that worked again now as the human situated herself on the table beside the cutlery.

Thank you, she whispered back to me.

Lean on me, Calina. Always. The words came naturally to me, followed by a brief warmth in my chest as I returned to Jasmine's diatribe about her human deficiency problem.

It seemed she was finally getting to her point—her need for more warm bodies.

The whole situation confirmed what I already knew about Jasmine: she was not fit to lead.

"Hmm, no, that's not really to my taste right now," Lajos was saying behind me. "I feel I'm much more interested in Jace's new pet. Perhaps she could sweeten my wine instead?"

Calina stopped breathing as Lajos started fondling one of the knives on the table. His opposite hand ventured upward again, his finger boldly stroking the scrap of fabric between her thighs. She fought not to outwardly react as he cupped her, but the wrongness of the act sang through our bond.

And it wasn't just Calina protesting the sensation, but *me*.

Mine.

"I believe Prince Jace intends for her to be enjoyed as a private dessert later, not as an appetizer," Darius said, his tone edging on cool.

It wasn't nearly murderous enough, in my opinion. However, it held the necessary warning to it. Also, his use of my title and name was purposeful. He wanted to make sure I'd heard him and recognized what was happening.

Because in any other situation, I would have just let him handle it on his own and waited for such a warning.

However, Calina wasn't a typical situation.

Calina's mine.

"But I prefer to indulge in my desserts first," Lajos countered, his tone all royal arrogance. "Jace won't mind."

"Actually, I do mind," I replied, cutting off whatever Jasmine had just been saying. I gave up all pretense of listening to her when Lajos's finger stroked Calina inappropriately.

Fuck, his every move had been *inappropriate*.

Never once did I give him permission to so much as touch her, let alone *there*.

It didn't matter that I usually shared my consorts with ease. It didn't matter that I'd never stopped him in the past.

All that mattered was Calina.

My Calina.

Lajos's eyebrows lifted. "Are you denying me a taste of your toy?"

It took significant effort for me to hold on to my composure and maintain a flat tone. "Calina is meant to be a dessert, just as Darius said. A delicacy to be enjoyed *in private*. If you're interested in a nightcap, you're welcome to return with us."

Where we would have him alone.

In private.

And be able to question him properly.

Because fuck everything else.

Fuck the plan. Fuck the strategy. Fuck all of this.

He was not going to touch Calina.

Jace, she whispered. *We can't—*

Not now. I was not in the mood to negotiate my decision. That bastard would not be touching my *Erosita*. Lulling him into comfort was a waste of time. I'd much rather shoot him and torture the information from his lips.

Darius gave me a warning look.

I ignored him as I waited for Lajos's reply.

"Calina," he repeated.

Just hearing her name on his lips made me see red. By some miracle, I managed a shrug as I said, "It's a name that suits her."

"It's very pretty," he agreed, his finger stroking her once more. "Greek in origin, if I'm not mistaken. A variant from Selene."

Calina fought the urge to close her legs, her body miraculously still as she waited with bated breath to hear what he would say next. She was trying to distract herself by reading his actions and words.

It was something I should have been doing as well, but I couldn't seem to think beyond the bloody veil covering my eyes. All I wanted to do was rip his fucking head from his neck and pull Calina into my arms once more.

Get it together, I demanded. *This isn't you. And he's going to notice.*

Because I always shared.

I never claimed a consort for too long.

Calina should be no different.

Except she was very different to me.

This fucking link was going to get us killed. Rationally, I knew severing it was the practical choice. But another part of me reasoned that our connection was intensely beneficial. She thought just like I did. My immortality made her more formidable as well.

I also still needed her.

To help me find Cam.

And maybe for other reasons, too.

We weren't done. Our time together had just begun.

Stop, I ordered myself, shoving all the thoughts to the back of my mind and taking a lazy sip of my wine as I waited for Lajos's next move.

"You realize this is my territory," he said, observing me with an intensity that left me cold inside. Except I knew I'd maintained my facade flawlessly, apart from interrupting Jasmine. All I'd done was turn around to back up my sovereign by clarifying that Calina was meant for dessert.

Surely Lajos hadn't read much into it.

His political motivations were driven by greed and sadism, not strategy.

But as he continued to hold my gaze, a small part of me questioned his intent here.

"I'm very aware that this is your territory," I told him carefully. "And I'm thankful you allowed Darius and me a chance to visit. Which is why we're hoping you'll join us later for a proper nightcap." I reiterated the offer, hoping it would be enough.

However, the glint in his ebony irises told me it wasn't. The sadist wanted to play now. "In my territory, I take what I want when I want it."

"She's not available right now," I replied immediately, dropping my elegant act and allowing him to feel the wave of my power. "She's my property, Lajos. Not yours." And as his elder, he would have to respect that.

"You'd deny me the pleasure in my own city?" He sounded absolutely astonished by the prospect.

"I'm merely delaying your gratification."

"No. You're making a power move," he returned. "One I don't accept."

He moved before I could react, his hands going to Calina's head and twisting it with a resounding snap of her neck.

"There," he said, allowing her limp body to fall to the seat beside him. "The distraction is dead. Problem solved."

The world shifted around me in shades of red and black, my heart literally stopping in my chest at the sight of Calina's lifeless form.

One moment, she was alive in my head.

And now...

Now I couldn't sense her at all.

She was gone.

Her mind cut off.

Her soul... broken. Disappeared. Destroyed. By this bastard of a vampire. Like some sort of game. A passing amusement. His chuckle echoed through my mind. His movements slowed. His pulse throbbed with a *thud, thud, thud*, where Calina remained silent.

Dead.

He killed her.

My mate.

My Erosita.

I couldn't breathe. I couldn't think. I couldn't do anything beyond gape at the situation as it all unfolded in slow motion.

Only a second had passed.

Maybe two.

Her body wasn't even completely still yet from where he'd so callously pushed her to the seat.

Her hair still fluttered.

But her mind no longer existed.

Her beautiful, exquisite presence.

Dead.

I blinked. The scene didn't change.

Another beat passed. Maybe half a second.

My brain refused to process the vision before me. I felt empty. Alone. Like someone had taken half of my soul and burned it right before my eyes.

There and gone.

She had been in my life for only a brief moment in time. And in that blissful moment, she'd become mine.

Breaking the bond had never been an option. Practical or not, I saw that now. We were supposed to have an eternity of knowing each other. She was my equal in a way I could never have imagined.

And this asshole had just taken her from me.

With a fucking laugh!

One twist of the neck.

Followed by a statement that reverberated through my mind. *Problem solved.*

No, it wasn't fucking solved.

Not only had he just disrespected me in the worst possible way, but he'd also taken *her*. My Calina. My mate. My goddamn other half.

I was no longer capable of rational thought. He'd destroyed it by *snapping her fucking neck*.

There was no choice. No decision. No reasoning with my mind.

Why can't I feel her? I… I should be able to still sense her, right? She was immortal through me. Because of me.

No. Not only because of me.

Nothing about Calina was typical.

What if our bond…? I swallowed, my analytical side threatening my sanity with a practical query I didn't want to hear. Yet it completed itself anyway. *What if our bond somehow reverted her immortality? What if everything now worked in reverse?*

It was an asinine possibility.

But I couldn't sense her.

She was gone.

My spirit felt… *lost*.

And Lajos fucking *laughed*. *Again*. The sound vibrated through me, his words a chuckle on the wind as he said, "Well, it would be a shame to waste warm blood. How about we share her now, hmm?"

All rational thought ceased as he reached for her arm.

It unfolded in slow motion. One millisecond at a time. I couldn't feel Calina, her psyche no longer married to mine, and I had no idea if it was permanent or not.

And he wanted to *share* her?

He had no right. No jurisdiction. No *bond.*

She was mine and he'd taken her from me.

All thoughts of past, present, and future died in my next breath.

She's gone.

And he's about to bite her anyway. Feast from her. Tarnish what's left of my Calina.

The sharp instruments glinted in the light. I chose one that felt right in my hand. And then I drove it through his fucking neck.

It didn't snap. It gurgled. It sputtered. It released a grunt.

I ignored the sounds and everything else in the room, Calina's broken neck all I could see. All I could hear. All I could *feel.*

He'd taken her from me.

And I would take from him now.

He would not bite her. He would not fucking touch her. He would not have what I considered to be mine.

You killed my mate.

And I don't know if she's coming back.

But fuck, I'm done with this game. I'm done with this charade. I'm finished with this goddamn world and all the sadistic fucks who think they can run the show.

I'm a fucking king, and it's time for them to bow right fucking now.

The bone saw didn't disappoint me, my strength and speed allowing me to finish the job in the blink of an eye.

One moment, he'd been chuckling and reaching for my mate.

The next, his head stared up at me from the floor.

I didn't even wait for his body to die. I shoved him to the ground and grabbed Calina, my hands cradling her cheeks as I searched for our lost connection, needing to feel her come back to me, needing our link to be enough to make her immortal.

But what if…?

Stop, I snarled at myself. *Stop analyzing. She has to survive this. She's my spirit. My other half. My mind mate.*

But not feeling her… seeing her die… knowing that thing on the floor had been the last to touch her… I couldn't handle it. I couldn't accept it. I refused that fate.

She was mine to protect. Mine to cherish. And I'd left her with the worst kind of predator.

That wasn't how we were meant to live or lead. This wasn't our future.

Come back to me, little enchantress, I whispered. *Come back to me.*

"Jace," Darius said, the urgency in his tone nearly snapping through my mind.

But I couldn't focus on anything other than my mate. I needed to find her mind, to feel her *soul.*

Fuck, how did I ever think I could break this bond?

It hurt more than anything I'd ever experienced. No amount of torture could compare to having one's soul ripped from his chest.

I wasn't sure why fate had handed me Calina now or what I'd done to deserve her. But I would never disgrace her again.

Just come back to me.

"*Jace*," Darius repeated. "You just killed a royal."

"I know," I snapped. "Because he killed my fucking *Erosita*."

I finally looked at him and saw the immediate understanding in his gaze. "A justified killing."

Sure. Yes. I supposed it was. Or it wasn't. I didn't fucking care. *He touched her and snapped her goddamn neck*. And now I couldn't find her soul.

"*Erosita?*" a voice repeated nearby.

Jasmine.

Fuck.

I hadn't thought at all. I'd reacted. And I'd do it again.

And again.

And again.

If it meant Calina would breathe once more.

I didn't even recognize myself. Gone was the strategist who had spent over a hundred years perfecting this charade.

And in his place was a man who hadn't realized what this female meant to him.

Until now.

Until he'd lost her.

She's not dead, I told myself, needing it to be true.

But she might as well be dead.

Because I'd failed her.

How the hell had I stood there while Lajos had touched her? What the fuck had I been thinking?

I wasn't worthy of her. I wasn't worthy of us. I'd wanted to use her until I no longer craved her. But I saw how impossible that was now. She'd enchanted me with her blood and her soul.

Then she'd married me with her mind.

It hadn't been planned or intended. Perhaps that was what made it so perfect. We were both so methodical that we would never have reached this conclusion on our own. But now that we were here, I refused to leave it behind. I refused to end it. I refused to accept the end of her.

I leaned down to kiss her neck, her jaw, her lips. "Come back to me, sweet genius. Please."

"It'll take a few hours," Darius told me. "And we have a much bigger problem right now."

I glowered at him, disagreeing entirely with that statement. Nothing could matter more than Calina. "I can't feel her," I said through my teeth.

He considered me for a moment. "Your connection is fresh. You don't know how to find her yet. But her body will heal."

"It feels like… like…"

"Like your soul just died?" he offered.

"*Yes.*" And I bloody hated it.

"Dulling the connection via unconsciousness or temporary death can be alarming at first. It's unsettling. But it's also normal to experience temporary disassociation," he returned.

Then he flicked his gaze to the left, drawing my attention to the now silent room.

Well, shit.

Something snapped into place within my brain as his words registered. *Temporary disassociation.*

Not being able to feel her is normal.

She'll revive herself soon.

Because she's immortal and it's only a broken neck.

All things I already knew. It'd been the sudden lack of a connection that I hadn't known how to handle. It'd left me vulnerable and lost and so utterly broken.

Then Lajos had reached for her with the intent to bite and…

Fuck.

I'd lost it.

I blinked and shook my head, clearing it for the first time in what felt like hours but was more realistically only minutes, maybe even seconds.

It had been a momentary slip of sanity brought on by the most unexpected of causes.

I slowly took in the scene, and the full force of what I'd just done forced my return to the present.

Everyone was watching us.

Including Jasmine.

And they looked absolutely horrified.

My mind finally began to work again as I processed my actions from beginning to end.

Lajos had killed Calina.

I'd killed Lajos.

Several important members of his constituency had observed the exchange.

Now they were all waiting for whatever came next.

Because this was unprecedented. Royals didn't just kill other royals. The bloodlines were too precious. There were rules. There were procedures. I'd just disregarded all of them because of my emotions winning out over reason.

Shit.

Darius had called it a justified killing, which would have been true a hundred and eighteen years ago.

But not under Lilith's reign.

Except she was dead, too.

I quickly processed our options before meeting Darius's gaze once more. "Call Lilith. It's time to report a murder."

"Are you sure?" he asked, a double meaning underlining his words.

"It's time."

He considered me carefully, probably assessing my sanity. Then he slowly nodded and echoed, "It's time."

CHAPTER THIRTY-FIVE

JACE

Jasmine stood ten feet away from our table, her tan skin abnormally pale.

She knew she possessed no chance here in a fight. She was a third-generation vampire. Just like Lajos. That made me not only older but also stronger. Something I'd clearly proved when I'd beheaded the royal on the floor. He hadn't been able to fight, let alone voice a protest. I'd moved too quickly for him to even process what was happening until death had snagged his soul.

Good riddance, I thought as I carefully laid Calina longways along the bench-like seat. Her spine needed to be adequately aligned for her neck to properly heal.

I brushed my fingers through her hair, thankful that Lajos hadn't ripped her head clean off. He could easily have done so in his position, and then she would have truly died.

Because there was no coming back from a severed neck.

However, in his arrogance, he probably hadn't wanted to waste any additional energy on what he'd considered to be trivial. So a simple snap had sufficed. Because he hadn't known about her immortal links.

Beheading was the only way to guarantee death.

Hence the reason I'd sawed through his neck.

Unfortunately, Lajos's true death appeared to be causing some confusion in the room. As the royal who had killed him, it would only make sense for me to inherit this region.

Except I fucking hated Hawaii and its penchant for hot sunshine. Hell would be more comfortable.

The constituents would also likely wonder how Lilith would punish me for it—and it probably seemed unlikely to them that she would give me Lajos Region as a gift.

That explained some of the more calculative gleams in the room—the older vampires wondering if they stood a chance of profiting from this massacre.

I would provide one.

Just not in the form they anticipated.

Leaving Calina to heal on the bench, I finally stood and glanced at the frozen human on the table. She hadn't moved an inch from when she'd originally placed herself there as food.

I admired that obedient demonstration but also pitied it.

She appeared to have forgotten how to live, having already accepted her pending death. Many of the other mortals held a similar look to them throughout the room.

It was a sickening display of morbidity that made my stomach churn.

I frowned. "I want all the living mortals up on this platform. Now."

Several vampires glanced at each other in confusion.

"Did I stutter?" Stark superiority underlined my tone, daring them not to comply with the master among them. Oh, they might think Lilith intended to punish me. But she wasn't here to stop me from doing more damage.

And none of them stood a chance against me.

Even if ten of them banded together, I'd slaughter them all.

I was faster and stronger, something I demonstrated now by phasing to the edge of the platform. It happened in less than a blink, my ability one only ancients possessed. I rarely used it, as I seldom had cause to demonstrate my power. However, I would now. Even if it meant removing a few more heads.

Fortunately, intelligent life began to stir below as a few vampires gathered the breathing humans and brought them to me like some sort of sick offering of fresh meat.

I observed them, watching those who treated the mortals with more care than the others.

Those were potential allies.

The others were sadists that lived in this region for a reason.

Of course, I could have deciphered that based on who had played on the stages and who had only observed from the shadows. I suspected some of those had only been here to see me, or maybe Jasmine, not the show.

Word would have spread of our visit, and it wasn't uncommon for a vampire to request an audience to discuss a potential relocation. The best way to do that would be to catch the attention of the royal in a club or at dinner and hope the royal waved them over for a quick chat.

A few of these vampires might just get their wish.

Most of the humans remained absolutely still, even the ones who were thrown haphazardly over the rope into the VIP area around me.

"Only fourteen," I said, sighing. "What a waste."

"Indeed," Darius agreed. He'd sent a message off to "Lilith" a few minutes ago. We were waiting for a callback, which everyone in this club knew.

A few had made some texts of their own, likely to spread word that I'd just killed Lajos.

I wasn't concerned.

If anyone wanted to seek revenge, I welcomed it. Calina's still-silent state left me in a lethal mood. I could use a little outlet for the violence brewing inside me.

Instead, I focused on the mortals by pulling a few up off the floor and leading them to the other leather benches in this area. It was Lajos's private area, reserved only for special guests such as other royals. The platform's size rivaled Lajos's ego, making it large enough to accommodate all the mortals and then some.

After situating the last of the humans from the floor, I ventured over to the female on our table and carefully lifted her into my arms.

Her head lolled backward, lifeless.

Yet she hadn't been bled.

This was what happened when a human psyche broke—they stopped caring or feeling. Having to carry the instruments to her own death had probably been the final nail in her coffin.

I brushed the tangled strands from her face as I carefully laid her on an empty bench. "You're safe," I whispered to her.

She wasn't.

Not yet.

But she would be.

Her lack of awareness stung as I left her there in a cloud of her own misery. There was only so much I could do in a world consumed by prestige and violence. But what so many failed to see was that humans weren't the only ones suffering.

Some of the vampires lurking at the edges of the room worked here.

It was their job to prepare the meals, while all they could eat were the scraps. And they probably lived in this godforsaken establishment, too.

Because this whole society was built around honoring and worshipping royals. Young vampires were left to starve. Those of inconsequential lines were given menial jobs to earn their keep.

This wasn't a utopia, even for those who lived forever.

It was a fucking dictatorship.

With Lilith as queen. And some unknown entity that she considered to be her *king*.

I glanced at Darius, then at the room as everyone remained still and silent, watching, waiting, and willing me to make my next move.

But I couldn't.

Not yet.

Soon.

I phased back to Calina, the demonstration of power purposeful and one meant to keep the masses focused on me. Then I bent to kiss my *Erosita's* head once more. I still couldn't feel her, which concerned me greatly. But I also knew barely any time had passed since Lajos had snapped her neck.

Maybe ten minutes at most.

It just felt like time was moving slowly because of how quickly

I processed everything and our next steps.

However, I'd been planning for this moment for what felt like an eternity. It wasn't how I wanted it to happen. Fuck, it wasn't even close to how I'd anticipated moving the pieces along the board.

But Lajos had forced me into checkmate by taking down my queen.

There had been only one play left for me as king.

So I'd made my move, finally coming out of the shadows, to proclaim myself as the rightful ruler of this game.

There was just one more aspect to resolve, and the buzzing on my wrist told me it was finally time.

I selected a button that put Lilith's voice on speakerphone.

"Yes?" she asked, the AI Damien had created a perfect replica of her bored tone.

"Lilith, darling. I need to report a murder."

A slight pause followed. Then the AI said, "Oh?"

"Yes. I just killed Lajos." The words came easily and without care. Even if I'd been speaking to the real Lilith, I still wouldn't give a fuck. The bastard had touched my mate. He'd deserved his fate.

Silence fell, both over the phone and in the room, as everyone waited for their "Goddess" to speak.

"Perhaps it's time we go on video chat?" I suggested.

"Hmm." The voice on the other side came from a mind as old as my own. He would easily translate what I intended here. And he proved that by saying, "All right," in Lilith's voice. "Ready when you are, *King*."

My lips twitched, and I glanced at Darius with an arched brow. "There has to be a screen somewhere around here."

"I can help with that, My Prince," a voice called from the corner of the club. A vampire with spiky brown hair stepped into the dull lighting, his head slightly bowed in reverence. "There's an auditorium system that Lajos uses to, uh, broadcast."

I could only imagine what *broadcast* meant. It was likely related to Lajos's renowned proclivities for tormenting his harem in front of an audience—something he'd obviously wanted to do with Calina.

Then he'd killed her instead.

Just to prove a point.

Well, that worked out well for you, didn't it? I thought as I stepped over his body on the floor to head down the stairs toward the unnamed vampire.

His identity came to me as I moved closer, his boyish features memorable because of the slight scar above his right green eye.

He'd won the Immortal Cup a decade or so ago.

Given his ratty clothes and unkempt hair, I suspected he was one of the vampires who worked and lived in this establishment.

"What name did you choose?" I asked him as I approached. He would have been born a number without an identity. But one of the few gifts given to those who gained immortality was an identity, however meek it might be.

"Mouse," he replied.

I arched a brow. "You chose the name *Mouse*?"

He shuffled his feet a little. "Uh, well…"

"Lajos named you Mouse."

He nodded, his eyes falling to the floor.

Yet more proof of what was wrong with this world. "We'll fix that," I promised him. "Now, how do I hook this up to the screen so we can all see Lilith?"

Mouse requested my phone, which I pulled from my pocket and handed to him. He did a little maneuvering in the system menu, then Ryder's face populated a massive curtain against the back of the stage.

"Ah, there you are," I said, amused to find him leaning against the wall of what appeared to be an elevator. "That's a lovely makeover."

"Says the king," Ryder replied in Lilith's voice. He cringed at the sound and started fussing with something on his end while muttering, "Fucking AI bullshit. How do I turn this shit off?"

"Am I, though?" I asked, ignoring his little tangent.

"Are you what?" he asked, his regular voice finally coming through. "Much better."

"King."

"Well, you did volunteer."

"Hmm. Not quite how I remember it," I admitted, recalling the meeting in Silvano Region shortly after Ryder had taken Lilith's head. "Where's Lilith?"

"I'm on my way up to her now."

That explained the elevator.

While Ryder traveled, I addressed the room of confused faces. "I can sense your misunderstanding. I promise this will all make sense just as soon as Lilith appears."

Several of the vampires looked at each other, and Ryder peered down at us. "Show me the room."

I frowned and glanced at Mouse. "How do I do that?" I understood how my phone and watch worked, but not this giant-ass screen.

The young vampire did a few things behind a curtain, followed by Ryder saying, "Oh, that is quite an audience. Where's Lajos?"

"Behind Jasmine," I answered, glancing up at the VIP area. It was just one step above the room, giving it a superior ring on a platform outlined by velvet rope.

Ryder peered down at us again, then his fingers appeared as he did something on his end. "Telecommunication bullshit," he muttered to himself, his eyes squinting. Then his eyebrows popped up. "Ah, there. Yes. Zoom. Nice. Hmm."

"We can all hear you."

"As though I care," he drawled, cocking his head to the side as a ding sounded.

He stepped out of the elevator but paused to evaluate whatever detail he'd pull up. Then his fingers appeared again, in front of him this time, suggesting he'd made the image of the room surround him.

A useful trick on certain devices. I could have done that with mine, but I needed the larger screen.

"Clean cut," he finally said. "And not a speck of blood on you. I daresay I'm impressed. But what happened to the doctor?"

"Lajos snapped her neck."

His eyebrows flew upward again, probably at the growl in my tone. "And so you killed him?"

"I did."

"That's not very diplomatic of you."

"Ryder."

"What? You're supposed to be king now, preach diplomacy and all that shit, yeah? Or have you rethought your approach to leadership?"

"Stop stalling."

"Oh, I'm not stalling. I'm genuinely curious as to how calm and cool King Jace lost his head. Wait, no, allow me to rephrase. I'm genuinely curious as to what caused calm and cool King Jace to lop off a head. Yes. That's what I meant."

I rolled my eyes. "Always so chatty."

"Now who's stalling?"

"Lajos snapped my *Erosita's* neck. I returned the favor by severing his."

True shock registered on Ryder's features, followed by understanding. "Well. That's an intriguing development." His fingers appeared again and disappeared after another moment. "Nicely done. I approve. Want to compare it to my handiwork?"

Finally. "Please."

The entire room appeared to be stuck in a state of confused surprise, no one daring to move. Not even Jasmine. Although, she did appear a bit green.

"You all might want to record this," I called. "I'll be asking you to share Lilith's verdict shortly." Since it was about to be leaked regardless.

Ryder didn't comment, just started whistling as he walked down the familiar hallway of the penthouse in his inherited tower.

Then he made a show of opening Damien's door.

And continued through the room while whistling a tune I now recognized as an old rock song. *Another one bites the dust*, I hummed along in my head, smirking at his sick humor.

He did a little shuffle as he approached the door securing the walk-in fridge and bobbed his head along to the beat.

Leave it to Ryder to be a showman.

I just shook my head and let him have his moment. He whistled a few more beats, then flipped the camera toward his hand as he gripped the handle to open the door.

"Lilith, darling, we have company," he said, panning upward to display her holding her head in her lap. Benita was next to her, partially frozen but still alive. Damien hadn't finished punishing her for what she'd done to his little mouse.

Yet another reason to change the name of the man beside me.

"Smile," Ryder cooed. "I know how much you love being on

film."

"Oh. My. God." Jasmine's voice echoed off the walls.

"I believe she preferred *Goddess,*" Ryder replied casually. Then he walked over to bend down near her head and nodded. "Yes. She still does. Of course, she's a very dead Goddess. Personally, I think it's a much better look on her."

"I agree," Darius called out.

Murmurs erupted in the room as the reality of the situation began to settle into their minds.

The initial shock had rendered them all speechless.

Now it seemed they were taking my comment to heart and snapping photos and videos.

"How's my angle?" Ryder asked, tilting his device back to flash a grin next to Lilith's head. It was a morbid-as-fuck selfie but certainly conveyed the point. "I want to make sure I'm displaying my best features here."

"You look amazing," I deadpanned.

"Excellent. Am I done yet?"

"I think the point has been communicated. Unless you want to reprimand me for killing Lajos?"

"Hmm, no. I can't say I'll miss him much."

"Brilliant," I replied. "Thanks for joining the party."

"Sorry I couldn't be there in person."

"It's a lot less bloody as a result."

"Says the man who just lopped off another royal's head," he drawled. "Definitely an effective way to announce your new role as king."

"King?" Jasmine repeated, her voice holding a shrill note to it. "You *killed* Lilith."

I lifted my gaze to where she stood, her cheeks no longer green but a bit flushed.

"Technically, Ryder killed Lilith," I replied. "She tried to torture him with a device that abuses the *Erosita* link, and he retaliated."

"Willow helped," Ryder added.

Jasmine sputtered in response, her gaze wild. "*You cannot be serious.*"

"Deadly," I replied. "Would you like to join Lajos or remain alive long enough to attend the council meeting next week? I mean, assuming it's not moved up." I looked at the screen, trying to find the camera that Ryder could see through and giving up after a wasted second. Because it didn't matter if he could see me or not; he could hear me. "I suppose you should go ahead and send an alert via Lilith's phone."

Ryder grinned. "I'm starting to see why Damien likes you." He hung up without another word.

A scream came from the platform as Jasmine lost her ever-loving shit. She sounded like a damn banshee.

Darius picked up a knife from the table and sent it into the back of the woman's skull, then rubbed his temples as she fell to the floor. "What a fucking headache."

Chaos erupted in the next second with several vampires running for the building's only exit, but I phased to the doorway to stop them. "Back up and sit the fuck down. *Now*."

Several of them jumped backward upon not only hearing me but also seeing me appear in front of them.

One fell at my feet.

The others froze.

Then they promptly reacted by doing exactly what I'd demanded.

There were only seventeen of them in the room. The most powerful one had already been killed. The other had a knife in the back of her skull.

Which left me and Darius with a group of lesser vampires.

Most of them didn't actually sit; they knelt with their heads bowed, recognizing me as their elder and leader.

Only two stared at me straight on.

I tasted their age on the air, noting their less-than-a-thousand years.

Then I phased behind them to snap their necks.

The vampires nearby shuddered in fear, aware that I could rip their heads off if I so desired. But they'd shown me a semblance of respect. Therefore, I'd let them live for now.

"All right. This is what we're going to do," I started, pacing in front of the vampires and ignoring the human remains littering the nightclub. "I want you to send copies of those videos and pictures to everyone you know, ensuring the world learns that Lilith is dead."

It wasn't the way I'd originally intended for this information to be distributed, but Lajos had changed all that when he'd killed Calina.

I paused to search for her mind again, then swallowed when I still couldn't reach her.

Focus, I told myself, taking a deep breath. *Almost done*.

Actually, no, I was nowhere near done.

I walked over to the stage to lean back against it and considered the kneeling vampires before me.

"We all were humans once," I said softly. "Some of us more recently than others. Can you look upon the stage behind me and say this is okay? That the way we treat humans is fair and just? We're superior in all ways, but with that superiority comes a sense of responsibility to protect the weak. Instead, we weaken mortals even more and enslave them."

My focus shifted to the platform once more, to the humans who were listening to my every word and refusing to risk a look.

"I remember a time where I had to seduce my prey. Where I had to work for my blood. Where humans presented the potential to be a conquest. Now they just bend over and take it. And frankly, I'm bored as fuck by it."

A few of the vampires stirred at that, their gazes flicking sideways to meet those of their allies and friends.

"There was once a vampire who believed we could coexist with humans in a very different manner than what has been done. Many of you know his name despite Lilith outlawing our ability to mention it. *Cam*. The oldest of my generation. The oldest among us."

I pushed off the stage to resume pacing.

"Lilith tells everyone he's dead. He's not. He's hidden in a bunker somewhere, perhaps even here in Lajos Region." I paused to evaluate the vampires once more, searching for any hint of a reaction to my words. "We've already found several of her secret research facilities. We're aware that Bunker 37 is in Lajos Region. But we're not sure which island."

I waited, allowing the bait to settle. We already had a pretty sound idea of where the bunker was located based on intelligence from Lajos's former Vigils, but I hoped someone here might want to prove their worth via helpful means.

It took a few more seconds before a female with dark hair cleared her throat and a pair of almond-shaped eyes lifted to mine. "I don't know where the bunker is, Your Highness. But I think I can help you find it."

"How?" I asked, noting her torn wardrobe. She likely worked here with Mouse.

"His office, My Prince. He has one here in this building, as it's his preferred club."

I nodded. "That's helpful. Anyone else?" I took in the group. "I'm offering you all an opportunity here. You might not agree with reform. You might prefer the status quo of this bloodbath. But you're in for a rude awakening when you realize the blood shortage of our world. We've grown gluttonous, and there's not enough blood to sustain us all at the rate of our consumption. Very few regions have enough to maintain."

I pointed at Jasmine's still form.

"If you don't believe me, evaluate Jasmine Region. She wanted to meet with me today to propose a trade—blood for tech. And there's a reason she was desperate enough to call me for support. She's not the first. She won't be the last. Because unlike many of my brethren, I appropriately regulate blood in my territory."

No one spoke.

I blew out a breath and ran a hand over my face.

"Look, change is upon us. It's your decision. Either you're tired of this bullshit and want to see what I'm proposing, or you prefer the status quo. Send your videos and messages, then toss your phones and devices onto the stage. If you want to learn more about my plans, stay. If you prefer our current world of chaos, leave. I won't stop you. Because I'm not Lilith and I don't believe in ruling through fear."

And I was too fucking tired of all this to say anything else to make them stay.

I needed to find Cam.

Then we would address the council.

Assuming everyone met next week.

Who the hell even knew now? All that planning, all my acting and persuading… gone. Ruined. Destroyed for a female.

I nearly laughed at the insanity of it all.

But then I felt a little inkling of life stir in my chest. A tug on the bond. Calina's spirit latching onto my immortality to begin the process of rebirth.

And I knew it'd all been worth it.

Such a bizarre, unexpected shift of thought and feeling.

Yet I accepted it. My soul told me it was right, and I was never one to shy away from my instincts.

This wasn't what I'd planned. However, that made our union so much more exquisite.

With a nod, I addressed the crowd with a final remark. "Send your correspondence. Make your choices. And fuck the Blood Alliance."

CHAPTER THIRTY-SIX

LILITH

Now that you've reviewed the ally and resistance files, it's time to discuss the takeover protocols.

First, you will need to alert our allies of your risen state. They are anticipating your arrival and will be most welcoming of the news.

Second, I suggest arranging—

Please stand by for an important message from your virtual assistant.

Message to commence in three, two…

My liege, I have urgent news from our allies. Royal Lajos was just murdered by Royal Jace. The reasons are still forthcoming, but it appears he has taken an Erosita. *His allegiance has always been questioned due to his ties to old methodologies. He's seen on video mentioning Bunker 37, thereby suggesting he is working with the resistance and is part of our recent breach. How would you like to proceed?*

To continue surveillance, click—

Surveillance continued.

I suggest you consider reviewing the wake-up protocols next, my liege. They contain the necessary details on how to rouse ancients from their rest, which, due to recent events, might be necessary to secure your leadership.

Especially with your familial ties to certain key resistance members, such as your brother.

If you would like—

I'm sorry, the system does not recognize that command.

Please choose from the following—

I'm sorry, the system does not recognize that command.

Please choose from the following prompts: For more information on the wake-up protocols, select Wake Up. For more information on surveillance protocols, select Surveillance. To return to your current log, select Return.

I'm sorry, the system does not—

I'm sorry, the system does not—

Stand by for live assistance.

Beep.

Beep.

Beep.

Beep.

Bee—

Silence command accepted.

CHAPTER THIRTY-SEVEN

CALINA

Ugh, I thought, my body vibrating with pain. *Lilith must have killed me again.*

And like every other time, I couldn't remember the details yet. They would come to me soon in the form of a nightmarish image. Another haunting memory for my dreams.

I sighed and waited for the inevitable while reveling in the in-between state where I was alive yet not awake.

Agony splintered down my spine, followed by a soothing warmth.

That's… different.

The stroke came again, this time accompanied by a featherlight touch to my throat.

Mmm, an alluring scent followed, reminding me of the wilderness. *Trees. Woods. Sunshine on leaves. Salt.*

How did I recognize those aromas? I'd never been to the woods or witnessed the…

Wait.

An image of a man graced my thoughts.

Handsome. Strong cheekbones. Square jaw. Seductive silver-blue irises.

Arrogant twist of full lips.

I reached for him, his presence a hypnotic lure that drew me from the recesses of my mind into a world of intelligence and stark reality.

Except, I wasn't awake.

But I could see *him*. His mind. His wicked thoughts. His anger…

Lajos.

I flinched at the memory of the royal vampire grabbing my neck and *twisting*.

Ow!

Although, I couldn't feel it. Not quite. I was seeing it through someone else's eyes.

Jace.

Warmth touched my heart as I thought of the name. Then another of those sensual strokes traveled down my spine, a sense of amusement following.

I can hear you, little genius. Let me see those pretty eyes. I want to see what color they are today.

I frowned, not understanding the intrusion of the masculine voice.

Until suddenly I did. Not because the voice explained it, but because his psyche reminded me of our link.

He was my mate.

I'd died. His immortality had brought me back. Or had it been my own? That remained to be seen.

Oh, but he had a beautiful mind! So full of wonder and knowledge, his experience ageless. And the power… this being… *my Jace*… possessed an incredible amount of strength and skill.

He could phase—*teleport*—a mile at a time.

I'd had no idea he was so fast. So strong. So… *otherworldly.*

My soul swooned a little at being linked to such an impressive male.

However, his mental prowess seduced me most.

Intricate.

Layered.

Strategic.

Brilliant.

I fondled his mental strands and sighed in contentment as I swam from one thought to the next. He felt me inside his mind, his amusement at my exploration evident in the exterior section of his psyche.

He encouraged me to dig deeper, to see him in a way no one else ever had. Because he suspected I might just be the only person who could truly understand.

He was right.

Our minds were absolutely compatible, something we would never have confirmed without our connection.

I sensed how much he cherished the uniqueness of our mating. Neither of us planned for this, but it made sense in every rational review of our situation.

He wanted to keep me forever.

He felt unworthy because of what had happened with Lajos.

But he also vowed never to make that mistake again—something both our minds agreed was better than any apology he could voice.

I considered his perspective on our mating, the practical manner in which he decided we should pursue it long-term.

We strengthened each other. I provided him with a mental playground to bounce ideas around on, and he gifted me immortality and protection.

A pragmatic relationship.

But there was an aspect I disliked.

Monogamy.

Jace… wasn't monogamous.

Yet I could sense from his memories of Lajos that sharing me would never be an option. Which meant he intended for me to be faithful.

But what about him? Would Jace be faithful to me?

He heard me ponder those questions, his mind stirring up an array of responses that left me uneasy inside. Mostly because he didn't seem to know.

I opened my eyes, the world dark and sensual as I found myself in bed beside Jace.

He didn't speak, his gaze studying mine as he balanced on his elbow beside me.

I wanted to tell him that the notion of sharing him bothered me. Except I couldn't define why.

Yes, he was my mate. Our minds were married as well as our souls. But what about our hearts?

Did either of us want a romantic connection? A love match? Was that even possible for someone like me or him?

He cupped my cheek, his lips curling into a soft smile. "Blue."

My forehead crinkled. "Blue?" It came out a little rusty, sort of like a croak.

He reached around me to retrieve a glass of water from the nightstand and brought it to my mouth. "Drink."

I didn't question him. I parted my lips and allowed the cool liquid to drizzle down my sore throat. It provided an almost instant relief, reviving me in a manner I hadn't expected.

"Your eyes," he said as I took another sip. "They're blue."

I contemplated that for a moment and nearly nodded. Because that made sense. My lycan side tended to be more prevalent in situations involving death or pain.

Jace listened as I puzzled over that fact a little more, thinking back to the other times my eyes had been blue. Such as when I'd felt threatened.

"Or aroused," he added. "They're blue during sex, too."

"They are?" That might explain the animalistic urges I'd felt in the bedroom with him.

"Are you going to call those natural now?" he asked, eavesdropping on my thoughts. "Similar to how you only reacted to my vampiric sensuality because it was a *natural* inclination?" He phrased it as a taunt, his question clearly rhetorical.

"You've provided sufficient scientific proof to the contrary," I told him, conceding that I'd been very wrong in my original theory.

"I'd suggest providing even more, but we don't have time to play right now." He returned the water to the nightstand, which caused him to reach over me again. Only, this time, he stayed there and pressed his lips to mine.

I returned his kiss and searched his thoughts to learn more about our supposed time limit.

The answer appeared quickly.

Bunker 37.

He had the coordinates from Lajos's former Vigils, and he'd confirmed them after reviewing some of Lajos's files.

I listened as he detailed the office he'd explored while I recovered from my injury. He told me everything of use that he'd found inside Lajos's private space, which wasn't much but enough to confirm he'd known about Lilith's projects. At least the ones in his territory.

Which had led Jace to wonder how Luka hadn't known about the bunker on the Majestic Clan lands.

But he'd disregarded that curiosity as he read through several correspondence messages between Lajos and Lilith.

Jace's tongue stroked mine, his kiss an intoxicating blend of desire and intellectual stimulation.

I moaned, disliking our timeline yet also looking forward to the prospect of answers.

Definitely not just your vampiric gifts, I thought at him.

He chuckled, his palm slipping up to cup my breast. *I'll hold you to that later.*

I shivered at the promise in his words and at the realization that I was naked.

His mind whispered the reason why—*mine.*

He didn't like that Lajos had not only seen me in that gown, but he'd touched me as well.

How the situation had ended had only stirred more guilt and anger.

So he'd stripped me, as well as himself, and held me for the last two hours while I finished healing.

His kiss deepened, his touch turning molten as I deciphered and translated this revelation. It was proprietary and thoughtful and so different from my other death experiences, where I'd woken up cold and alone.

Jace protected me.

Because he *cared.*

I marveled at the concept as our embrace turned into something more intimate than sexual. His touch shifted from my breast to my neck, his tongue whispering foreign benedictions into my mouth.

I stopped analyzing and just allowed it to happen.

Same as him.

Our bodies talking instead of our minds.

It was a stunning moment of passion and promise, interrupted only by the rumbling sensation beneath the bed.

We're on the plane, I realized, not having noticed much beyond Jace until now.

Yes. Bunker 37 is on a different island. He pushed the coordinates to my mind, telling me we'd only taken off thirty minutes ago. He'd waited until he'd felt my essence thriving in our bond because he hadn't wanted to enter the bunker without me.

Two minds are better than one, he added, explaining his decision.

What he didn't mention was the lingering reason in his mind, the one that finalized his choice—he understood the importance of my going with him. He didn't want me to miss the opportunity to find the files regarding my creation.

Thank you, I whispered as our kiss slowed to a natural pause. I opened my eyes to meet his alluring gaze, his features ones that redefined the meaning of beauty. He truly was remarkable, all even lines and a perfectly symmetrical nose.

The title of *king* absolutely suited him.

"Does that make you my queen?" he teased softly as the jet shifted around us to announce our descent.

I wasn't given a chance to respond—not that I had a reply to give—because a deep voice began speaking.

"Did it ever occur to you to inform others of your intentions before acting?" a cultured voice asked. "Oh, who am I kidding? Of course it did. It's you, the master chess player. So should I be insulted by not at least receiving a text as a warning?"

"Kylan." Jace stilled above me, his gaze going to the speaker on the nightstand. "Did Darius patch you through?"

Kylan. Vampire Royal. Ally. My brain quickly tossed out those details upon hearing the familiar name.

"Don't tell me the lack of an announcement or warning bothered you, Jace. It's not like you didn't just do that to me in the form of Ryder blasting the alliance with a photo of him grinning like a loon while holding up Lilith's severed head."

My brow furrowed. *Why would Ryder send such a message?* Jace had said they needed more allies on their side before announcing her death.

What did I miss while unconscious?

It hadn't occurred to me to ask *how* Jace had gained access to Lajos's office. I'd been too distracted by the details and our next destination to dig deeper.

But now I understood because now I could *see* the details I'd missed before.

You killed Lajos, I breathed, watching the memory unfold. With it came a wave of despair and fury, Jace's reaction to my death. He'd worried it was permanent.

He'd been worried about *me*.

My lips tried to form a response to that, but I couldn't even think of one, let alone voice it.

Not that I had a chance to because Jace was already replying to Kylan.

"If given the opportunity, would you kill Robyn?" he asked, the question a departure from what Kylan had said, but my link to Jace's mind told me why he'd chosen that inquiry. He saw the situation as somewhat related to his decision regarding Lajos.

Robyn had hurt Kylan's property as some sort of sick and twisted game. She'd insulted his superiority in the process, similar to how Lajos had disrespected Jace by snapping my neck.

But it went deeper than that.

Jace didn't consider me his *property* so much as his *mate*, something I heard whispers of in the back of his thoughts. Despite being human and far less experienced, he saw me as his equal, at least mentally. All because of how similarly our minds worked.

I considered that as Kylan said, "I'm not sure how that's related, but death would be suitable for her, yes. Are you offering me the opportunity?"

"That's not for me to offer," Jace replied. "And it's related because Lajos killed my *Erosita*. Thankfully, it was temporary. But it didn't feel temporary at the time, and I reacted."

More silence fell over the line while Jace recounted the incident and his instinctual reaction. He'd thrown away over a century of planning… for… for *me*.

I marveled at the revelation, hearing how he'd processed the decision and how he didn't regret it. Not even now. Not even after having me alive beneath him.

Lajos deserved his fate. Those words revolved through his mind, not necessarily for me to hear, just a statement of fact that he continued to repeat.

It wasn't the way he'd intended for any of this to happen.

And there wasn't anything he could do to change it.

He'd already begun concentrating on the future and the next steps, which primarily focused on finding Cam as soon as possible.

"I'm not sure what shocks me more," Kylan said slowly. "The fact that the master strategist deviated so severely from his course or that he did it for a woman. An *Erosita*. You, of all vampires, were the last I ever saw taking a permanent mate."

"I could say the same to you," Jace replied, his lips against my neck. I listened as he contemplated Kylan's term *permanent mate*, his mind calculating the veracity of the wording and finding it appropriate. "How is your Raelyn?"

"She's currently talking to Willow about a baby lycan," Kylan said slowly. "Another detail I'm rather confused by."

"Hmm, well, Ryder will have to catch you up on that one, as we're about to land and I need to find Calina some clothes." He rolled off of me with the words, then went to the closet while mentally telling me to stay on the bed. The jet's decline made the floor unsteady, and he didn't want to risk me falling in my recovering state.

I was fine. But I didn't mind admiring the view of him walking around naked.

I heard that, little genius.

It's an instinctual reaction to your supernatural physique," I told him.

"Ah, and the *Erosita* has a name," Kylan said, interrupting our mental flirtation. "Where did you find her?"

"In the same place as the lycan pup Raelyn is learning about now," Jace replied.

"The labs."

"Yes. And we're on our way to a third one that supposedly has information on Calina's creation. We're hoping to find Cam, too."

"The elusive saint meant to save us all. I wonder how he'll feel about this deviation from the plan."

"He'll be too busy focusing on future strategy to be concerned about my life choices." Jace's tone held a note of censure.

But Kylan merely chuckled in response. "I suppose we'll see. Anything I can do to help?"

Jace returned to the bed with a pair of jeans and a white sleeveless shirt. "Put these on."

"Put what on?" Kylan asked.

"I'm talking to Calina."

"Rude," Kylan drawled. "I'm on the phone."

"Yes, a call I don't remember accepting."

"Life is full of surprises, mate."

"Isn't that why you called—to express your dislike of surprises?" Jace's tone reflected a note of irritation, but a hint of a smile caressed his lips, suggesting he was teasing Kylan more than chastising him.

"I never claimed to dislike it, just expressed my displeasure over being left out of the fun."

"So you called to pout," Jace replied, amusement edging out the annoyance in his voice.

There was a long history between these two very old vampires, one shrouded in a deep friendship that had fractured due to their similar interests. I caressed the memories, learning more about their past and their shared outlooks.

By the time I finished reviewing the thoughts, the call was done and Jace stood before me in a pair of jeans and a black T-shirt. "Are you going to keep poking around in my past or put on clothes?"

I considered that for a moment, my mind still very much connected to his. "You don't want me to put on clothes," I said, picking up on that opinion in his thoughts.

"Yes, I would prefer you wander around naked every day, all day, but only for me. Not others. And we won't be alone on this mission. Hence, clothing is required." He gestured to the pants and tank top on the bed.

I noted the lack of underwear and heard him reply mentally that it was deliberate. It seemed the thin white fabric was intentional, too.

His silver gaze glittered with wicked intent after I dressed, his focus immediately falling to my chest. "Perfect." Then he handed me a thick vest. "This is for protection."

"For me or for everyone else?" I asked him, catching the double use of the word in his thoughts.

"Both. Protects you from any potential gunfire. And it protects everyone else from me killing them for seeing you in that top."

I slid on the vest as requested as I said, "You chose my outfit."

"Yes. For me, not them."

I just shook my head and accepted the socks and shoes he handed me next.

Jace gripped my shoulders to hold me steady as the jet touched the ground, his strength and stability a masterpiece of experience and age and power.

I marveled at it as I finished lacing up my tennis shoes, the black color the same as his own.

Upon finishing, he pulled my hair up into a ponytail, then gave me a once-over and a nod. "Good as new."

"I won't feel that way until after a shower," I admitted, the stiffness of rebirth a leftover sensation that crawled along my skin.

Jace paused, considering the option, then said, "We'll do that after we're done."

I nodded in agreement, the labs taking priority in my mind.

I may finally find out who I am. What I am. Who I'm linked to. How I was made.

And all of that was far more important than a shower.

"I'm ready," I told him.

He bent to press his lips to mine, his mind holding a whole myriad of emotions and thoughts that seemed to fire at once. But they were all there and gone faster than I could decipher them, his practical side quickly taking over. "All right. Let's go, little genius."

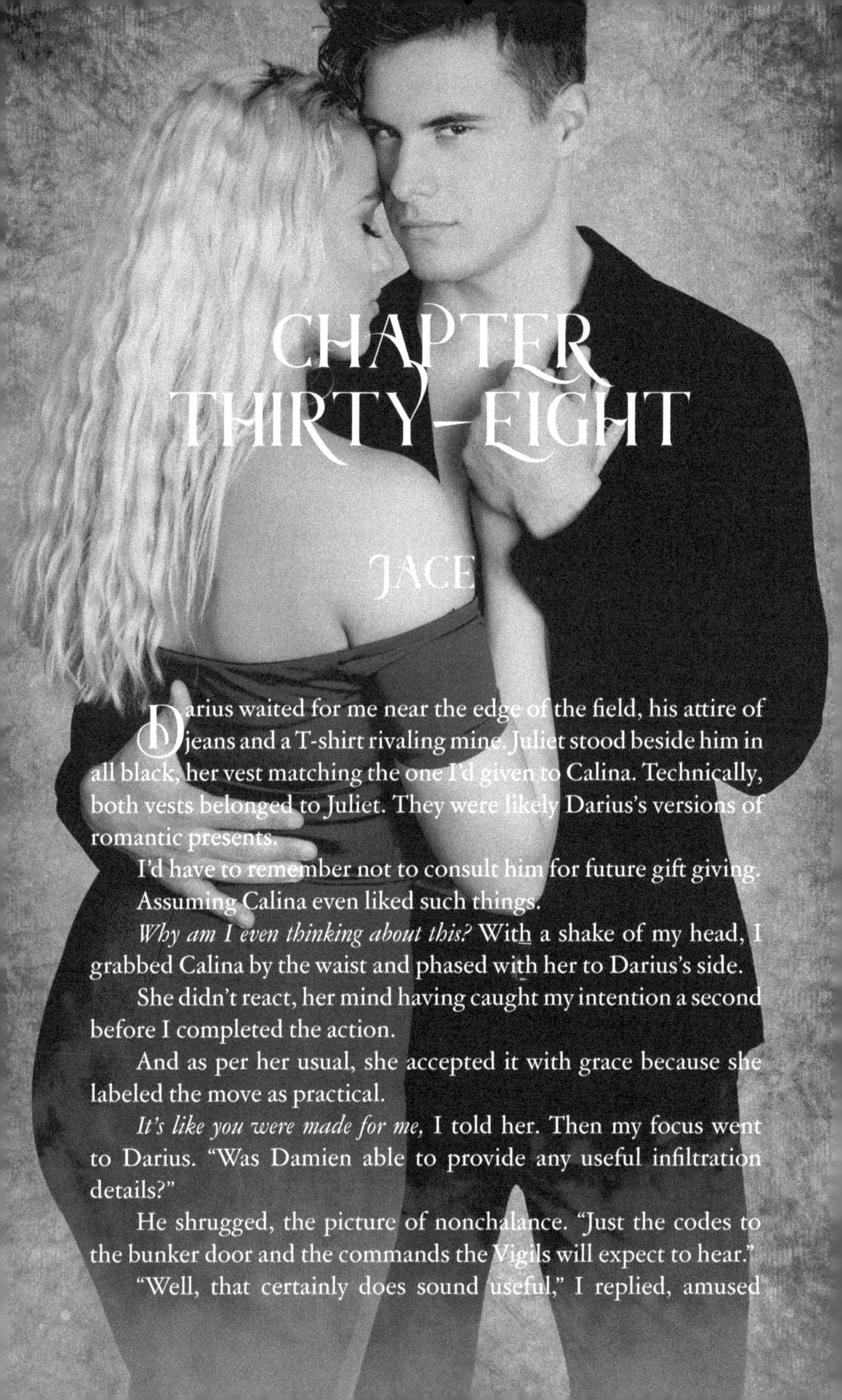

CHAPTER THIRTY-EIGHT

JACE

Darius waited for me near the edge of the field, his attire of jeans and a T-shirt rivaling mine. Juliet stood beside him in all black, her vest matching the one I'd given to Calina. Technically, both vests belonged to Juliet. They were likely Darius's versions of romantic presents.

I'd have to remember not to consult him for future gift giving.

Assuming Calina even liked such things.

Why am I even thinking about this? With a shake of my head, I grabbed Calina by the waist and phased with her to Darius's side.

She didn't react, her mind having caught my intention a second before I completed the action.

And as per her usual, she accepted it with grace because she labeled the move as practical.

It's like you were made for me, I told her. Then my focus went to Darius. "Was Damien able to provide any useful infiltration details?"

He shrugged, the picture of nonchalance. "Just the codes to the bunker door and the commands the Vigils will expect to hear."

"Well, that certainly does sound useful," I replied, amused

by his deadpan delivery. "You sound disappointed, Darius. Is it because we won't be drawing blood upon entry?"

"I think I've seen enough bloodshed to last me a few days," he returned, referring to Lajos's nightclub we'd attended and all the dead humans we'd found while searching the premises for anything useful.

We hadn't discovered much other than a few key documents in Lajos's office that confirmed his ties to Lilith. Afterward, I'd called for one of my planes to come pick up the remaining vampires—only two had left after my speech—and the humans from the club.

It'd taken time and energy to organize, my mind more focused on Calina's recovery than the actual task of helping others, but we'd managed to wrap it all up in under eight hours. Ivan had agreed to help handle their temporary accommodations in my tower—something I'd given him written jurisdiction to do.

I'd sort the rest out later. Including finding permanent accommodations and appropriate jobs within my region for the vampire refugees.

I'd also face Jasmine at some point. I'd left her on the floor of the club with the two broken-necked vampires. They would all be awake by now. Probably pissed, too.

Leaving them to wake in their twisted states hadn't been the best form on my part, but I had an ancient vampire to find. And locating Cam took priority over politics at this point.

"Shall we?" I gestured to the bunker ahead.

No one had come out to greet us, suggesting they didn't have external surveillance. That didn't surprise me, given that the other two bunkers had also seemed to be lacking in exterior cameras.

The primary purpose of the bunker security is to keep the occupants inside, Calina said. *At least that was the case at Bunker 47.*

From what Damien said, it was the same at Bunker 27, I informed her.

Darius started walking by way of answering, his stride confident as Juliet followed at his side.

Calina and I trailed behind them, her arm casually brushing mine along the way.

"I'll let you lead since Damien gave you all the details," I said to Darius.

"It's like you're grooming me for leadership."

"Well, Hawaii is available. I know how much you adore the sun." I fought the urge to glance upward at the beacon in question. *So fucking bright.*

Do you need blood? Calina asked, her tone serious.

I smiled at the offer. *Mmm, tempting, but you've fed me well this week. I may need a bite after we're done here, though.*

Her resulting shiver seemed to touch my own skin, her anticipation hot and wild in our bond.

I really could become addicted to feeling you so intimately, I murmured. *Actually, I already might be.*

"Give it to Trevor," Darius said, drawing me back to our conversation about Hawaii. The fact that it took him a beat to respond told me he'd actually considered the offer all the way through.

"Trevor as a royal?" I nearly laughed. "No." He thought too much with his cock to be of any use in politics. Which was why I'd left him to entertain my harem.

And interestingly, I didn't mind at all that he and Ivan were actively playing with my consorts.

Yet the mere notion of them touching Calina had me wanting to growl.

She was absolutely off-limits to everyone but me.

"Make him a sovereign, then," Darius suggested.

I shook my head. "He's too young."

"Then give it to Ivan. Trevor will follow."

"You wouldn't miss your progeny?" I asked, genuinely curious. Darius had sired Ivan a few centuries ago. And Ivan had sired Trevor soon after. It marked them as somewhat close to the royal line, as fourth-generation and fifth-generation vampires in Cam's line.

"They need more responsibility." Darius paused a few feet from the hut sitting atop the bunker. "Aside from fucking your harem, I mean."

My lips twitched. "It's one hell of a responsibility."

An odd little note of annoyance trickled from Calina's mind to mine, causing me to glance at her. She didn't outwardly show anything, but I sensed her trying to focus a little too hard on the bunker door.

"Ivan certainly has a knack for politics," I said, still watching her. "He's also proven to be an expert at the game. I suppose I could reward him with the territory, assuming that's how all this plays out. For now, I'll let him continue on with his current task." Something I might need him to do indefinitely, as it seemed the thought of me having a harem irked my *Erosita*.

Would it bother you if I had a harem? she countered, still not looking at me.

Yes, I answered immediately.

She didn't reply, her point made with the feelings her question had evoked.

Because if I felt that way about her, then she likely felt the same way about me.

I frowned, considering that for a moment while Darius keyed a code into the exterior door.

A click sounded, confirming our entry.

Then the door whispered open to reveal an entrance that reminded me of the one at Bunker 47, only with functioning lights and clean floors.

Darius stepped through first, his posture telling me he was relying on vampiric ability alone despite the pistol holstered at his waist. I had a similar one strapped to mine, as did Juliet and Calina.

However, I argued that Calina possessed a far superior weapon at her disposal.

Experience.

She studied the corridor, noting the similar pattern and features to Bunker 47. Her mind told me the elevator's position before we found it, the structure of the building clearly identical to the one she had lived in for decades. This didn't surprise her since she'd never really noticed any differences when leaving her experimental captivity for her new role.

She took it all in with a note of calmness and understanding, her logical side focusing on the practical uses of her history, not the emotional impact some of those lab tests had on her psyche.

Such as the one with the lycan on her thirtieth birthday.

I could feel those memories lurking outside her thoughts, her psyche blocking them with pragmatic barriers that forced her to concentrate on the here and now. It was fascinating to observe.

Most humans would have broken beneath the weight of her previous experiences in Lilith's "care."

But not Calina.

She was strong. Intelligent. A fighter. She didn't dwell in the past, just used her background to bolster her future.

I admired her more with each passing minute, this link between us granting me so much more depth and exposure to her than anyone else in my existence. Which was fascinating. I felt as though I knew her better than I knew Darius, better than even my father or Cam.

Her blue eyes met mine, the green color still nonexistent. She understood my fascination, her mind telling me that she'd never known someone so deeply.

It cemented our connection that much more.

Breaking it would dismantle something so utterly beautiful. So unique. So *precious*.

Did you bring a watch? she asked me, her gaze lowering to my wrist.

I slipped my hand into my pocket to reveal the device I'd taken off one of the Vigils at the server farm. Darius and I had anticipated needing one after learning about their importance at Bunker 47. *Darius has one in his pocket, too.*

She nodded. *You'll need that to call the elevator.*

Calina started forward, then frowned over her shoulder.

We also need to close the exterior door, she added. *The surveillance will have shut off upon entering the code outside, and the Vigils would have been made aware of the incoming visitor. Same with whoever is in charge here. Shutting the door and entering the elevator code will prompt the system to reset, with the surveillance coming back online by the time we reach the main level.*

It was on the tip of my tongue to ask her why the surveillance would shut off, when I picked up the answer from her mind.

The floors were all numbered in an untraditional order, making it impossible for the occupants to determine which level was closest to the surface.

Temporarily turning off the surveillance ensured that no one would be able to discover the entry protocol, thereby making escape impossible because all the doors on each level looked exactly the same.

Some of the rooms had surveillance inside, but not all. Which was how the vampires and lycans had narrowed down which levels and doors to check during their attempted breakout.

Fascinating, I said after reviewing all the details in her mind.

The lack of entry and exit surveillance is why it took so long for the lycans and vampires to find an exit in Bunker 47, she added. *Your arrival is likely the only reason we were able to escape.*

And you were monitoring the surveillance feeds while they all tried to find a way out, waiting for them to figure it out for you. A cruel yet intelligent method for finding the exit.

It'd also kept her alive since all the supernaturals in her bunker had wanted her dead.

Although, if the Vigils from this bunker were sent to the server farm, then at least some of them knew how to leave this place, I mused, thinking through the protocols. *Does that mean surveillance works differently here?*

Potentially. Or Lajos never intended for them to return. They were supposed to go to Bunker 27 first, thus allowing them access to a wealth of information, something Lilith would genuinely have frowned upon.

I ran through that possibility and nodded. *He likely intended for them to return to Lajos Region, where he would've apprehended the research details and then destroyed the Vigils.*

Except they sent the data ahead, she reminded me. *So they never really had a reason to return.*

True, I agreed, thinking it through. *He may have intended for them to be terminated—*

The door slammed, causing us all to turn in surprise.

Then a buzzing against my thigh had me meeting Darius's gaze.

We'd discussed the potential for something like this to happen. It had taken us almost fourteen hours to reach this bunker due to all the events on the main island. Which meant Lilith's allies would have had plenty of notice regarding our intentions.

Not to mention the red flag thrown onto the play when the Vigils never returned.

This scenario had been entirely expected as a result.

Except we'd anticipated someone attacking almost right away. Yet my senses told me there was no one else on this floor apart from us.

I turned toward the elevator, listening intently for movement inside and hearing none.

Nothing else happened.

No lights flickered.

No alarms.

But I picked up on the change in the air, as did Calina.

Pulling out the watch, I read the numbers on the screen and cursed as they started counting down.

"Another doomsday protocol," Calina whispered, her eyes wide. "And if it went to that watch, then it's the one signaling for the Vigils to kill everyone in the lab."

"Then we had better get moving because we only have eight hours to search this bunker before it explodes." I was already heading toward the elevator, but Calina's concerned thoughts stopped me.

A horde of supernaturals had worked on the exit door in her bunker for hours with no success.

The only reason it had opened was because of Damien's explosion from the *outside*.

I pulled out my phone to check my signal and found it blocked.

Darius followed suit, his expression telling me his phone reflected the same issue.

"Well, shit." I quickly calculated our options, my focus going to Calina once more. "We need to get you to a computer so you can send a message to Damien." I slipped the pistol from my hip and glanced at Darius. "Looks like you're going to get that bloodbath after all."

"Brilliant," he deadpanned, mimicking my pose. "I hope we have enough bullets."

CHAPTER THIRTY-NINE

CALINA

"If the signal went out on the watches worn by the Vigils unit at the server farm, then Damien already knows," I said, halting Jace midstep again. "Unless that signal was meant specifically for us, triangulated somehow to this specific location or something."

I glanced around, noting that none of this felt right.

"A protocol wouldn't be set for the watch of a dead man," I continued out loud. "And Lilith would have intended for that unit to die before returning here, something she would have conveyed to Lajos in the protocols. Which means that this might not be a trap at all, but a fail-safe engaged as a result of using the watches marked for destruction."

She would have thought of every potential outcome, including the notion of Lajos betraying her and deciding to keep the Vigils alive—something I felt certain she would have been against. Allowing anyone to know too much would have been considered a weakness to her legacy and her operation.

Jace stared at me while I continued puzzling through all the procedures in my mind, searching for the path Lilith would have chosen.

She'd triggered the doomsday sequence at Bunker 47 upon her death. Yet she hadn't destroyed any of the others, at least none that we'd found. Which meant she'd considered something there too valuable for anyone else to find.

But when the files hadn't been sent as expected, a team of Vigils from this location had been sent to the server farm to retrieve them. They'd sent a copy to this location but were supposed to rendezvous at Bunker 27.

"Did Damien ever find out why they were supposed to go to Bunker 27?" I asked, my focus on Jace because he would understand my question since he was actively in tune with my mind.

He studied me as he replied, "I don't think he ever gave them a chance to find out. He went in with guns blazing and cleared out the lab."

"I wonder if they were sent there to die." It would make sense. They'd already sent the files here, and they'd never mentioned a return mission, just that they were supposed to stop in Bunker 27.

Of course, the return mission had been implied.

But Lilith would never have intended for them to actually see it through.

She would have had another protocol waiting for them at Bunker 27, one where they would've been taken care of and the information would've been officially confirmed.

Except they had shown up with Damien.

And the security procedure had never been triggered.

"You have a mole," I said, straightening my spine. "Who all knew that Damien was with the transport?"

"A mole?" Darius repeated.

Jace held up a hand, his gaze intent as he jumped through the logic in my mind. "Someone canceled the protocol."

I nodded. "To lull us into a state of comfort."

"So we would end up here," he concluded, his attention falling to the watch. "Do you think it's a fake timer?"

"I don't think we can trust anything at this point," I admitted. "It could even be a bluff. The security protocols at Bunker 47 sent the Vigils to each floor to wipe out all the occupants. But you haven't heard the elevator move yet. That doesn't add up."

"You're right." He looked at Darius. "I don't hear anyone except for us."

"Are you thinking the bunker was evacuated?" Darius asked.

"I'm not sure," he replied. "If this was a trap to kill us, the lab would have already exploded. And based on what we saw of Bunker 47, we would absolutely be dead."

"So what's the game here?"

"Checkmate," Jace murmured, puzzling it through. "Lilith adored a good show. This is ours. Either we indulge her or we try to leave."

"Or we outmaneuver her," I interjected, realizing the key to all of this. "I'm supposed to be dead. There's no way she accounted for me to be here."

"But if I have a mole, as you suggested, then whoever is in charge now knows you're here, too," he pointed out.

"Yes. That's true. But whatever this is, I'm the wild card." Because I was supposed to die at Bunker 47. My files were the ones she'd wanted to have sent here. Something inside me was key to all this.

The question became, did the person in charge know my importance in Lilith's life? Because I was willing to bet they didn't know every detail. Lilith had never been the type to share. It was why she'd always visited by herself.

"You were her best-kept secret," Jace translated, responding to my thoughts.

"Or maybe it's not me at all, but something in my head. Which could actually be what all this is about—whoever is in charge either needs something from me or has no idea what detail I possess."

I just needed to figure out what I knew that was so important.

"We need to find a computer room or a lab with server access." The answer would be in the files somewhere.

"Hold on, I'm trying to understand the plan here. You want to search for files and try to determine the purpose of this game, just to what? Be killed for our trouble at the end?" Darius didn't sound impressed. And when phrased that way, I agreed.

"I don't think the end goal is our death," Jace replied. "Lilith didn't kill Cam. She didn't attempt to kill Ryder either. I've always wondered why, particularly regarding Cam as he so obviously opposed her. But maybe whoever this *liege* is told her to keep them alive. I imagine the same rule applies here."

"That's a dangerous guess."

"It's a practical estimation based on previous behavior," Jace corrected. "It's possible the one in charge just wants to gloat or that Lilith has set all this up as some sort of morbid endgame finale. But I really don't think our death is the goal here. We represent two ancient bloodlines. And as Damien said to me recently, there's power in blood. They won't want to waste it."

"No. They'll want to harvest it." Darius sounded even less impressed than before. "I much prefer the bloodbath option."

"Well, we'll keep it in mind as we discover our true purpose here." Jace grabbed his shoulder. "If this is the true endgame, then Cam may be down there somewhere."

Darius sighed. "I hate vampire politics."

Jace smiled. "And yet you're so skilled at playing the game. Let's win this one, yes?"

Yes, I agreed despite the question being for Darius. He conceded as well, and the two of them began discussing options on how to proceed.

"I don't think the elevator goes down," Juliet said softly, causing both men to look at her. "I think it goes into the mountain."

She pointed down the hallway in the opposite direction from the door we'd entered.

"That's an interesting theory," Jace said. "Why do you think that?"

"The tour book I read on the way here notes that Kauai has many caves. They were popular attractions in the old world. If I were building a bunker here, I would take advantage of a natural structure."

Jace blinked, then looked at Darius. "You gave her a Kauai guidebook?"

The other vampire shrugged. "She enjoys reading."

"He enjoys giving me books," Juliet corrected. "He gave me several on Hawaii while we were in Jace City."

Jace gaped at Darius. "Where the hell did you find them?"

"Humans died. Libraries didn't," Darius deadpanned. "I've kept all my books. And I sent Trevor on an errand to grab some things while arranging our travel."

"Of course you did."

"I think she's right," I interjected, uninterested in how Juliet had made her guess. Time was precious, and we had a puzzle to solve.

Ignoring them, I started toward the door at the end of the corridor. It looked exactly like the one we'd entered, only it was on the opposite side.

The keypad resembled the ones I'd used at Bunker 47.

Jace appeared with the watch, and I took it, curious to test my theory regarding the terminated use of the device.

I scanned it and wasn't surprised when it said "Access denied."

Darius tried the watch against the pad by the elevator, eliciting a similar response that echoed down the pristine white hallway.

I considered our options, then typed in a master code that would have worked to open a door at Bunker 47.

"Access denied."

Biting my lip, I thought, *What would Lilith do?*

It'd often taken thirty minutes to an hour for her elevator to arrive at Bunker 47. It was possible that she'd merely sent a signal ahead to announce her impending appearance. However, I'd always suspected that she'd entered the building and then occupied herself for a period of time while she kept us waiting. Sometimes I'd even sworn she was watching us stand in our requisite positions in the lobby, just to make sure we were obedient little pets.

She'd enjoyed keeping everyone in limbo because it had provoked fear.

However, she would've been pragmatic about it.

Which meant there was likely some sort of computer room on this level. Somewhere she could've passed the time, spied on her employees, and caught up on the research before demanding a verbal update.

It had always been a test with her. She'd wanted to ensure I gave every detail in accordance with what she already knew.

When I'd passed, she'd rewarded me by killing me.

A measure of control.

One I'd understood too well for it to be as effective as she'd desired, which had only angered her more.

So where would you go? I wondered, glancing around the corridor, scanning each door. *If there are computers, you need them to be cool. Away from the elevator or train behind that wall.*

There were only two doors on the opposite side.

Both had keypads.

With the watch not working, I'd need an override code. *So what would you pick?*

It'd be personal to her. Something few others would know about because she'd trusted no one. Nothing obvious. Nothing pertaining to her alliance life, but perhaps to secrets in other labs.

Like Bunker 47.

What is it you wanted to protect and hide? I mused, moving toward the first door to study the keypad and handle. Then I wandered to the other to compare them, attempting to note which was better used.

Hmm, but your code would have been known by Lajos, I thought, frowning. The Vigils had said he'd delivered the server farm order personally to them, which meant he'd frequented the bunker. And like Lilith, he'd probably spent time here before venturing inside.

So what would you trust him to know? I wondered, thinking through what little I knew about him. Jace's mind helped fill in some of the blanks, but I knew this would be more personal. Something between Lajos and Lilith.

Did you know about me? I asked, the question for Lajos, not Jace. There'd been a hint of familiarity upon our meeting, a note that had left me uneasy beside him. Like he'd been playing some sort of twisted game rather than truly displaying interest in me.

It'd been written in his touch.

And his comments.

I recalled what he'd said about my name and his familiarity with the origin.

"A variant from Selene."

His comment had sent a chill down my spine, something about it unsettling me at the time. Because Lilith had said that to me once as well. It was why she'd chosen my name. *Selene* had meant something to her.

Selene was the goddess of the moon in Greek and Roman religion, Jace said, his mind otherwise quiet as he observed my thoughts. But he also relayed an important piece regarding Nyx's origin as the goddess of night.

The two went together in name and ideology.

Deciding to take a chance, I typed *Selene* into the keypad, curious to see what it would do.

A click sounded, but the door didn't open.

It needs a follow-up phrase, I realized, trying *Nyx* next.

Another click.

All right. I was about to key in *Lilith* when Jace's whisper of a thought gave me pause.

Vesperus, he breathed.

What?

It's Vesperus, he replied, his voice certain. *Nyx's consort.*

That wasn't a name I knew, but I heard the history of it through his mind. The gift Nyx had bestowed upon the Blessed Ones came from her love for Vesperus, a vampire-like god who required blood sacrifices to live.

Our feeding supposedly keeps him alive, Jace whispered.

It certainly fit the other two names in context. But I wasn't sure how Selene entered into the equation. Regardless, I tried *Vesperus*.

A third click sounded, this one causing the door to open of its own accord.

Why Selene? I asked Jace as I pulled it the rest of the way open.

"Selene was the mother of the first lycan," Jace replied out loud.

My brow furrowed. "Nyx created her?"

"Sort of." He stepped forward to peer into the room as the lights came on. "Selene was an *Erosita* created by one of the vampires of my generation. But they weren't in love. He did it so a Blessed One could keep her forever. It didn't work out as expected."

I followed him into the room, noting its rectangular shape and alternate door. It seemed the entry point didn't matter. This entire side of the hallway was one large server area, and definitely where Lilith would've gone.

"I'm familiar with that name," Juliet said as she joined us inside the room. "Selene, I mean. She's written in your books about the *Erosita* bond." The last sentence appeared to be directed at Darius.

"Yes. It's said that she's the reason *Erositas* must remain faithful to their vampire mate," he explained as I wandered over to what I guessed was the main computer.

"The *Erosita* connection is meant to be cherished, and Selene defied that gift by sleeping with the Blessed One," Jace added from right behind me, his focus on me while he spoke.

"Which Blessed One?" Juliet asked.

"Fen," Darius murmured. "Not only did Nyx take away her immortality, but she also cursed their child by turning her into the first lycan. She's immortal, like the Blessed Ones, but all of her kind eventually die. Which is why vampires often see lycans as lesser—they don't live forever."

The computer flared to life as I sat down in front of it, the screen asking for another password.

"And they're cursed," Jace said, referring to why vampires felt lycans were beneath them. "Lilith always saw the alliance as a gift because we agreed to divide the territories evenly."

"But the preference always weighed in our favor," Darius murmured.

"True," Jace agreed. "Any guesses on the password?"

I had several, so I merely nodded and started typing. I doubted Lilith would've used the same words as the door codes.

So I went through other details known about her.

Cane.

"Access denied."

Michael.

"Access denied."

Calina.

"Access denied."

I stared at the screen, then keyed in a password I knew from Bunker 47 again.

"Access denied."

Drumming my fingers over the desk, I evaluated my options. All systems had an administrator password associated with them. It was how I'd circumvented the lockdown procedures in my own lab.

Using my knowledge of computers and backdoor protocols, I went to work on cracking through her outer layer of security by first going through the forgotten password area and switching the profiles within the system.

Jace watched, his admiration shining through our bond.

Meanwhile, Juliet and Darius continued discussing the origin of lycans and vampires, which led to her discussing worship protocols at the Conventus.

I paused as she recited the prayer they'd made her repeat several times a day. "An anagram," I whispered, hearing it as she spoke.

To her eternal,
Give our devotion,
Defer every second,
Savor more of our night,
Worship in loving light,
Revel in sensual euphoria,
And glorify all immortal nights.

I typed in the words as they formed in my mind. *The goddess will rise again.*

"Access denied."

Hmm. I tried another combination. *TGWRA.*

"Access accepted."

Jace's shock rippled through me as Darius said, "That bullshit prayer actually has meaning?"

"Apparently," Jace replied. "I think it means Lilith was insane."

"Obviously. Nyx has never been seen, and for all we know, she's very much alive. Fuck, she may not even exist at all." Darius's tone held a note of disbelief that I ignored in favor of the files populating the system.

Everything in Bunker 37 had just been revealed before my eyes.

Starting with surveillance of the underground labs.

A chill prickled my spine at the familiarity of it all, particularly the room I'd spent far too much time in. Someone new occupied it now. A male with tangled dark hair and hunched shoulders.

"Cam," Jace breathed. "That's Cam."

CHAPTER FORTY

JACE

Calina clicked the video on the screen, enlarging it.

I cursed and looked at Darius. "We need to figure out how to move that elevator. Now."

"On it," he replied, already moving.

"Is there some sort of control on this system?" I demanded, my heart racing in my chest. *Cam's here. He's in this fucking bunker. He's—*

"Something isn't right," Calina said, interrupting my thoughts.

"Nothing about any of this is *right*," I countered.

"No, I mean with the footage." She blew it up even larger, her focus on the wall. "It's… " She tilted her head, looking at some detail I seemed to be missing.

Then a memory of her clawing at the walls slammed into my mind, her nails bleeding as she tried to pull herself upright after one of the harsher experiments.

There were grooves in the cement.

Grooves that were missing from the room now.

I listened as she reasoned through her memories and the image before her, trying to pick out subtle details only she would notice.

Subtle things that told her what she was watching wasn't

actually here, but somewhere else.

She started shifting between screens, pulling up a variety of feeds at once, her gaze scanning, her mind working, as she tried to puzzle through what she was actually seeing and comparing it to her memories.

I calmed as I listened to her, my rational mind helping to sort through desire from reality.

A false lead, she kept saying to herself. *A video they want us to see.*

Because whoever put it there knew it would send Darius and me into a frenzy.

This whole fucking situation was just one giant game of chase with Lilith leading the way by leaving breadcrumbs for us to follow.

Calina was tired of trailing after her.

She took charge now by pulling up all the files she could find, the items hidden in plain sight. All things we would have missed had we jumped onto the elevator to find Cam.

The dates were all wrong.

The footage of Cam in that cell was from weeks ago, not now.

I saw it as Calina pulled up each frame and then did some back-end trick to review the time stamp.

"These are not from Bunker 37," she finally said. "But someone put them here knowing we'd find them." She started looking around the room, as did I, and we both spotted the camera at the same time. "Someone definitely knows we're here."

"Can you track the location?" I asked, narrowing my gaze at the surveillance equipment in the corner.

"I can try," she replied, already moving items around on the screen. "I want to know where this other lab is, too. The setup is exactly the same as Bunker 37. But the walls aren't right."

Darius and Juliet had already joined us again, Darius likely having heard our conversation from the hallway. They both studied the screen while I stared directly at the camera, daring whoever was watching us to make a move.

Someone was on the other end of that feed.

Someone wanted us to waltz into a trap.

Someone was about to pay.

Who are you? I wondered. *The infamous liege? Another ally? Some royal with a vendetta? A lycan, perhaps?*

No, I doubted it was the latter. A lycan would never approve of the research happening in these labs.

Perhaps it was a Blessed One, but I couldn't imagine who would approve of this behavior from Lilith. One reason many of them slept was to retain their ties to humanity. Perhaps one had awoken without others knowing and lost his or her mind in the process.

"Go back," Juliet said suddenly, causing Calina to pause and flip the screen again.

"To this one?"

"Yes." Juliet leaned over her shoulder, studying the image of a female human with her head bowed. "I think that's my matron."

"Matron?" Calina repeated.

"A trainer of sorts from the Conventus," I explained, sharing a look with Darius as Calina pulled up the video Juliet had flagged and hit Play.

The human stumbled forward, her right leg appearing to be lame and incapable of graceful movement.

Someone growled over the speakers.

But the female didn't stop, her movements clearly coerced as she continued toward the cell. My eyes widened at the familiar man behind the bars. "Holy shit."

"Well, that complicates matters," Darius muttered, his hand going to the back of his neck. "I thought he was asleep."

"As did I," I replied, flinching as the white-haired vampire grabbed the female and sank his fangs into her neck.

Juliet's hand flew up to cover her mouth. I didn't need a verbal confirmation to know that was definitely her matron. It was written in the depths of her brown eyes.

However, seeing it all unfold unlocked a potential path in my mind, one I followed with ease as I drew an obvious conclusion.

"A recently awakened ancient and a matron," I said, meeting Darius's gaze. "That can only be one place."

Italy had always been neutral territory in this new era because it housed the chosen resting place for the ancients. However, the lands were notoriously under Lilith's rule because of the Conventus's location in Rome.

More specifically, the Vatican.

Both above and below ground.

She owned all of it as the leader of the alliance, making it an easy territory to hide secrets in.

Such as an ancient vampire controlled by a supernatural-mind-manipulating weapon.

What better place to hide him than in an area surrounded by sleeping immortals?

No one to hear him scream or beg.

It was a fucking crypt.

Darius's expression told me he already understood, but I voiced it out loud anyway.

"Cam is under the Vatican." I was sure of it. "How did we not see that?"

"Because it's a sacred resting place that we could never have imagined being defiled," Darius replied, sounding frustrated. "Fuck. If we can prove this, there's not a chance in hell anyone would blame us for taking Lilith down."

"Unless an ancient is the liege." I glanced at the camera again. "The question is, which one?"

Darius and I started going through the possibilities, the names ones we hadn't discussed in a very long time. Over half of them were ruled out right away based on their known desires to preserve human life—they were the source of our essence. And for those who believed the origin stories, they saw their blood as revered sacrifices meant to keep our legacies alive.

Calina kept searching the logs for any mention of the liege or the Blessed Ones and first-generation vampires while we spoke. She interjected a few times with findings. Most of them were interesting details about technology, including the specs to the various weapons Lilith had manufactured over the last century.

We skimmed the details on the mental-manipulation gadget she'd used on Ryder, then scanned another log about a memory-refining tool.

But none of the files revealed the answers we truly needed.

An undetermined amount of time passed. Hours, maybe. We discussed and reviewed several other items on the computer, all the while remaining otherwise undisturbed by whoever surveilled us from above.

Whoever it was wanted us to discover these files.

Or maybe we weren't being watched at all.

We gave up caring, going through the files again, the logs, the surveillance, and then returning to our discussion of the infamous liege and who it might be.

As we started discussing some of the crueler ancients, such as Icarus and Nephthys, it became clear there could be a few potential culprits here. Even Fen was on the list because if anyone had cause to be angry, it was him and his lycan offspring.

However, one thing remained unclear to me.

"How did she wake them up?" There were ancient ceremonies required to rouse an old one from slumber. And it would have required willingness and agreement from multiple royal lines, including my own. "I'm positive my father would never give his blood or his permission for a ritual. And I sure as fuck didn't."

Darius appeared uneasy, his gaze shuttering. "No. But if Cam did, your line wouldn't be needed."

"He'd never do that."

"He might do it for Ismerelda," Darius pointed out softly, his gaze flicking to Juliet. His expression said, *Something I would understand.* Because he would do it for Juliet.

And from Ryder's recounting of his conversation with Lilith, she knew about Izzy's location.

Which meant she could have used that to threaten Cam.

"Shit." I ran a hand over my face and jaw, considering that outcome. Cronus was the older brother, thereby marking him as slightly more powerful than my father. In theory, his bloodline could supersede my own.

I glanced at Calina, wondering if I would make a similar sacrifice for her. Only, her intense focus on the screen distracted me from my thoughts, mostly because hers were suddenly all I could hear.

She'd found the records regarding her birth.

While searching for information about Selene, I realized upon hearing the surprise in her thoughts.

Calina Selene, born March 17th, she read, the year twenty-two years prior to the revolution that had created our new world. *Subject named by her mother.*

Calina clicked the file pertaining to her mother, and my jaw nearly hit the floor.

Mira.

I gaped at Darius as he reacted to the face on the screen. "That's not fucking possible," he breathed.

However, as Calina continued to review the files, it became very clear that it wasn't just possible, but true. There were videos, voice files, signatures, and ample other details that demonstrated not only Mira's involvement but also her willingness to help.

And as Calina began to dig into Mira's files, it became evident as to *why* Mira had helped.

Just as Calina's name suddenly took on a whole new meaning.

"Mira is Selene's daughter," I whispered, awed by the revelation.

"How is that possible?" Darius asked. "Wouldn't we have known? We didn't meet Mira until, when, shortly before the revolution? Surely someone would know her or recognize her from before."

I slowly shook my head. "It's rumored that she chose eternal sleep instead of a life of solitude. Anyone she turned would be long dead by now, making her identity impossible to determine."

"And she would have been asleep in the catacombs," Darius said, leading us right back to our theory of Cam's location.

"Precisely." I palmed the back of my neck, blowing out a breath as I added, "She met Luka about two decades before the revolution. Shortly after Calina's creation. She's been part of this from the beginning."

"But why?" Darius pressed. "Why would she do this?"

"To create immortal lycans," Calina whispered, her focus still on the screen as she reviewed some sort of report. "I was the first successful test, which is why she gave me a name. However, it's because of the immortal links I have to my father." She opened a new report, displaying another familiar photo. "Lilith's *Erosita*. Michael."

All thoughts of the camera overhead and Cam's location fled as Calina continued reading through all the files about her creation and her immortality.

The purpose had been to create an immortal lycan.

They'd achieved it by using the *Erosita* link and Mira's genetics, then encasing the fetus in the womb of a rare blood type. Which, we found through reading, was part of what made Mira so unique.

Her mother hadn't just been an *Erosita*, but a human of a unique essence similar to the golden blood running through Calina's veins.

The blood virgins, like Juliet, were all related to that rare blood type as well. They weren't golden bloods, but a variant, which explained why Lilith had chosen to keep them housed over the catacombs.

They were being used for experimentation as well, something the files revealed as Calina continued to dig through the various reports.

Everything was linked.

Vampires. Lycans. Blood virgins. *Erositas*.

Calina was created by genetically manipulating the part of the brain where the *Erosita* connections resided in immortal beings, infusing her essence with her mother's bloodline, and then wrapping it all up in an irresistible blood type that made her even more appealing.

Lilith's goal had been to create immortal humans who could be fucked and bled to death, only to rejuvenate themselves to do it all over again.

But Mira's goal had been to find a way to prolong lycan life.

Somehow, the two had agreed to work together. Which explained how Mira had been able to circumvent Lilith's technology, even in her own territory.

Because Lilith had allowed it.

Just as she'd allowed Majestic Clan to operate as a safe haven for humans.

"Mira told her everything," I realized, skimming the logs with Calina. "And now someone has allowed us to find out." I glanced up at the camera again. "Is it you, Mira? Are you the liege?" It seemed impossible. But she was older than Lilith. Potentially even more powerful.

"It says here that Lilith woke Mira up after the first lycan was discovered by humans," Calina said, interrupting my staring contest with the camera.

Who are you? I wondered at it. *Why are you letting us in on your secrets now?*

We were still in the heart of a game. The distraction had been avoided, but we hadn't been punished yet for finding all these details.

Which meant whoever was in charge wanted us to know these things.

"That's why they created the lab," Calina continued. "Mira wanted to strengthen lycan kind to ensure it never happened again."

"Is that what it says?" I asked, finally looking at the screen again.

"No. But it's what makes sense." She pulled up a log entry entered by Mira displaying her trials and errors. All of them predated the revolution and when she met Luka. The final was exactly two years after Calina's birth, with Mira leaving instructions for future researchers to continue her work.

"She trusted Lilith to keep her updated," I realized out loud, reviewing the ending of her log. "She might have no idea that you're even still alive."

"Unless she's watching us now." Calina glanced up at the camera. "But I think the liege is Michael."

I shook my head. "Michael's dead."

"No." She clicked on the screen to bring up another log dated around the time of her birth. "He's a vampire."

My brow furrowed. "That doesn't make any sense." But as I read the words on the screen, they began to paint a very disturbing picture.

He'd been attacked by humans.

Nearly died.

Until someone of royal descent had given him blood to bring him back to life.

The name on the screen had me blinking. "That's impossible. He would have told me." I focused on Darius. "Did he tell you about this?"

He wore a similar expression of dismay. "No. Cam never mentioned saving Michael."

"It has to be a lie," I said, wondering just how much of any of this was actually true. "This… all of this… it's too…" I couldn't find the words. Mostly because *unbelievable* seemed like an understatement.

And yet the proof of it all stared up at us on the screen.

"Cam would—"

The ground beneath my feet shook as an explosion rippled down the hallway outside the doors. My gun dropped into my hand as I phased to the doorway to find rubble all over the floor.

And a smirking Kylan standing near the blown entryway. "See, now, *this* is why you invite me out to play. I'm helpful when I want to be."

CHAPTER FORTY-ONE

JACE

"What the fuck are you doing here?" I asked, both shocked and thankful for Kylan's unexpected arrival.

"Well, I was talking to Ryder, like you suggested. And he was going on and on about some human pets he's had to adopt to please Willow. I guess he issued an edict stating a lab pup named Petri and his biological parents are officially under his protection?"

"Gretchen and James," I translated, somewhat amused to learn of this development. Louis would be most disappointed. But only someone courting suicide would risk Ryder's wrath, and if he'd chosen to protect them for Willow's benefit, then they were fortunate indeed. "They were two of Calina's lab assistants in Bunker 47."

"Hmm, I see." Kylan considered that for a moment. "Well, anyway, in the midst of Ryder's bitchfest, Damien called him about some sort of watch alarm. Then he mentioned not being able to reach you. And long story short, I was the closest and I have the fastest jet."

I narrowed my gaze at the subtle jab. We were both collectors. And he did, indeed, have the fastest jet out of all of us. Because he'd outbid me at an auction. "For now," I said through my teeth, responding to his claim.

He shrugged and crossed one ankle over the other. "We'll see." He arched a dark brow, his matching hair sweeping over his forehead in a fashionable *I just blew some shit up* kind of way. "So. Did you find Cam?"

"Yes and no," I admitted, glancing down at the watch I'd forgotten all about while reviewing the files. We were down to nearly an hour left. "We think he's in the catacombs under the Conventus in Italy."

Kylan arched a brow. "With the ancients?"

"Yeah."

Kylan snorted. "It would be just like Lilith to disturb the peace. The whole Goddess bit really did go to her head, didn't it?"

I would have agreed with him, but a note of alarm in Calina's thoughts had me returning immediately to her side. It was a video of her tied to a table, screaming, as a lycan—

Fury licked through my being, followed promptly by acute terror as Calina's emotions overwhelmed our bond.

I reached around her to close the window, then I grabbed her chin and forced her to meet my gaze.

No words were spoken.

Just an intense moment of silence underlined in my silent vow never to let anything like that ever happen to her again.

She swallowed, some of her fear abating. But the unease remained, her stomach churning at having stumbled upon that particular file.

Darius said something to Kylan in the hallway, confirming he and Juliet had left to give us some much-needed privacy. Because he'd likely seen all the details, just as I had.

I-I was just clicking through the reports, a-and it—

"You don't need to explain anything to me," I told her, releasing her chin to cup her cheek as I knelt before her. "You've wanted answers. You've found them."

She swallowed again. "Th-that wasn't an answer I wanted."

"I know." I drew my thumb along her cheekbone, noting her still-blue eyes. "But some of them were ones you needed. Although, it still doesn't explain our connection."

"I think it does," she whispered, her mind providing me with a glimpse into the analysis she'd already performed on the subject.

With the ties to the *Erosita* bonds inside her mind, she was strongly predisposed to become a vampire's mate. And I was the first one to exchange blood with her, my essence the only vampire blood she'd ever swallowed.

She'd also never been fucked by a vampire.

Until me.

Making me her technical first, despite the lycan link.

Maybe it's not about being a virgin so much as being untouched by other vampires, she whispered into my mind. *Or I'm just unique.*

Or it's both, I told her, marveling once again at how her mind worked so similarly to mine. These were heart-wrenching reveals that would have brought most women to tears, but not Calina.

The video frightened her, but she didn't cry. She just cataloged the memory as accurate while shivering in revulsion and immediately returned to her pragmatic consideration of what to do with the information.

"We need to go to Italy," I said, our path clear.

"I think you should review Mira's phone records and communications first," she countered, causing my eyebrow to arch. "Because I don't think it's just Cam in Italy. I think we'll find the liege there, too. But she should be able to confirm what we need to know."

"Or we could grab her and demand she answer our questions," Darius suggested from the doorway. "Of course, we'll need Luka's assistance with that. And he may not be keen on interrogating his mate."

"He will be when he learns of her betrayal," I said, my focus turning to the computer. "We need to download as many of these files as possible. And we're running out of time to do it."

I waited to see if Calina had any qualms about the potential of kidnapping and torturing her mother for information, but she didn't display even a speck of emotion on the topic. As far as she was concerned, it was the right path.

Darius agreed as well and left to gather the equipment we needed from the jet.

Meanwhile, Calina went to work with gathering all the files

into a central location for export.

I stood behind her and kept glancing at the camera, certain we were being observed. *Why aren't you doing anything?* I wondered at the person behind the surveillance. *What web have you created to ensnare us now?*

Because letting us leave with all these details felt counterproductive to the end goal.

Unless Lilith had always intended for her research to be known.

I contemplated the potential of that revelation as Calina worked. Darius joined us again, saying something about Rae and Juliet returning to the jets to maintain a safe distance. I merely nodded, my mind working through Lilith's plan and trying to decipher exactly what she'd intended here.

We'd been operating under the assumption that Lilith's research would upset the alliance, thereby making it something we should share.

But what would she gain by us showing it to the lycans and vampires of the world?

Chaos, I heard Calina whisper to me.

Frowning, I considered that.

The lycans would be furious to learn what Lilith had been doing to their kind. Then to find out that Mira, the first lycan in existence, had helped… would just worsen everything entirely.

Unless Mira didn't actually know. She'd trusted Lilith to continue her research, except they'd shared separate goals.

Can you run a search for our names? I asked Calina, curious if Darius or I was ever mentioned in any log.

I already did. There's nothing about you in there. Not even in the files I found on Cam.

"You found files on Cam?" I was so surprised I spoke the words out loud.

"Yes. And the device Lilith used to incapacitate him." She pulled up the logs to show me a video of him on his knees, screaming while Lilith spoke casually to him about what she intended to do to Izzy.

My blood burned at her taunts, my mind automatically replacing Izzy's name with Calina's.

And I realized Darius was right. If Lilith had threatened Izzy to force Cam's compliance, he would have agreed. Because I'd do the same.

I marveled at that realization while Calina showed me a few more items in Cam's file. Most of it seemed repetitive with Lilith using the device to torture him, keeping him locked in a room and curled in the fetal position while she taunted him on repeat.

"What's the most recent file on him?" I asked, checking my watch and noting we were down to ten minutes.

"The last sentence in his file says, *Refresh Protocol*," she said, glancing at me as she read the date out loud.

"That's when Lilith died."

"I know," she replied.

My jaw clenched. *What the fuck is a refresh protocol?*

The answer eluded me as Calina finished loading the final files. With a quick glance at my watch, I noted we had two minutes to escape and met her gaze. "Reminds me of our first date."

"I'm not sure I would call that experience a first date."

I grinned. "You ended up naked afterward."

"Not by choice."

"Ah, yes. I forgot. It's all about my vampire prowess." I grabbed her by the hips and lifted her into the air. "Legs around my waist."

She obeyed, her irises glowing with sensual intent. "If you want to strip me after this date, I approve."

"I do owe you a shower," I murmured, wrapping my arms around her lower back. "And we have a long flight ahead of us."

I had to make a few calls first, but those would be quick.

Or I'd have Darius make them.

I started to phase while my mind negated the task of deferring to Darius. Luka needed to hear the news from me directly.

In person, I thought as the night air surrounded us. *He needs to see the files to believe them.*

Calina didn't reply, just encircled my neck with her arms and held on while I ran toward the jets. They'd moved to a beach about two miles away from their original landing site.

When we finally arrived, Calina froze, her gaze on the moon hovering over the water.

It was like the sun all over again, only this time I was privy to her thoughts.

So innocent and young and beautiful.

She'd never seen the beach before, let alone the ocean. And she was captivated by the sight.

I gave her the moment to admire the view, wincing only slightly when I felt the ground quake beneath us. Part of me hadn't thought the labs would detonate, that whoever led this game was bluffing.

Maybe we weren't being watched at all.

But my instincts told me someone had been observing us the entire time.

And soon, we would find out *who*.

I set Calina down on the beach, aware that she wanted to touch the sand and the water. She handed me the bag she'd slipped over her shoulder—the one holding all the devices Darius had brought to us before disappearing with Kylan—and wandered over to where the waves rolled over the edge of the beach. She knelt, her thoughts joyful and filled with awe.

I admired the view and the sweet excitement in her mind.

It made me want to ensure I was there for all her firsts, that I made every dream and curiosity she owned come true.

A soft giggle filled her mind as the water brushed her fingertips, her lips curling into a smile I wanted to engrave into my memory and never let go.

This female was firmly inside my soul. Her face the only one I wanted to see. Her heart the only one I needed to own. Her body the only one I desired to possess.

At some point during our time together, I'd fallen off a cliff of lust into something much deeper.

Perhaps it was our link.

Perhaps it was fate.

Maybe even some combination of both.

But this female had begun to mean something to me that defied reason and understanding.

She made me want to drop the bag of devices, rush over to her, and carry her out into the ocean. Strip out of our clothes. And make love among the waves.

It was such a vivid yearning, one that encompassed all my thoughts and vision, so much so that I didn't realize Kylan had joined me until he cleared his throat.

"Hmm, so it is love, then," he mused, his hands in the pockets of his black slacks, the sleeves of his dark dress shirt rolled to his elbows, and the collar unbuttoned at his neck. "You wear it well, old friend. Congratulations on finding your heart."

I nearly corrected him, my old habit of nonchalance desiring an outlet.

But I couldn't voice the words.

Because I didn't want to lie. I didn't want to degrade what Calina and I had. I wasn't sure if it was love. That seemed too light a term for the marriage between our minds. She felt like my other half, making a life without her impossible to fathom.

She'd died, and I'd been so lost that I'd killed a royal and ruined over a century's worth of plans. Yet I knew if it happened again, I would do the same damn thing.

Because she was mine to protect.

I would never apologize for avenging her.

Kylan cleared his throat. "Darius just spoke to Damien. It turns out he already suspected Mira because one of the lab techs recognized her from afar. He didn't say anything because he wanted more proof, but he's keeping tabs on her."

I nodded. "Then it sounds like we're heading to Majestic Clan."

"Indeed we are. Ryder is making arrangements with Edon, Silas, and Luna to meet us all there."

"Another meeting," I said, my gaze still on Calina. "And almost in time for the original one Lilith had planned."

"Funny how that works," Kylan drawled, his hand clapping against my shoulder once before he started to tug the bag away from me. "Darius and Juliet will fly with me so you can properly play with your new pet."

Normally, I would argue with such a statement and remind him of my superior position.

But he was older.

And I really didn't want to debate the gift he'd just given me.

So I merely nodded my gratitude and continued watching my mate play in the water. She'd taken off her shoes and rolled her pants to the calves to truly experience the waves. It was such a youthful thing to do, but she deserved this moment. It helped her relax and forget the memories brought up in those files. It helped her escape from the truth of her heritage. And it made her smile.

That last part was all I needed to know that this moment mattered to her.

A new experience for her mind.

I sat on the beach while she continued to splash around, her gaze only lifting once as Kylan's jet took off. He would have to stop for fuel along the way, while we were fully stocked from the Lajos City airfield.

So even if I gave Calina another thirty minutes here, we'd still beat them to Majestic Clan.

Knowing that, I leaned back on my elbows and watched my little nymph dance in the moonlight, her blonde hair sparkling as she spun around with a laugh.

"You might as well strip, little enchantress," I called to her. "I'd enjoy the show, and I'm going to make you undress before we get on the jet anyway." Her clothes were soaking through from the water.

She stopped spinning and glanced at me.

Then, ever so slowly, she pulled the bulletproof jacket off to reveal her tight white tank top beneath.

I bit my lip, the sight of her in the moonlight striking. It outlined her breasts perfectly, including her hardening nipples.

A wave tumbled into her, the liquid splashing around her waist and dampening the fabric near her flat abdomen.

She responded by pulling the fabric up over her head and giving me a full view of her perfect tits.

Mmm, now there's an alluring sight. Enchant me more, darling. Make me so hard that I can't even walk.

Her eyes glittered with yellow rings in the dark, her lycan side evident in her gaze.

That only turned me on more.

I'd always fancied the animal nature of lycan kind. And my female clearly had a beast inside her that rivaled my own.

I stretched my legs out and crossed them at the ankles, admiring the view from my elbows as Calina unzipped her jeans and started hopping around to remove them.

It was humorously erotic, the fabric clinging to her legs as she fought to rid them from her thighs.

She lost her balance in the waves, causing me to sit up.

But she stood again in the next breath, her blonde ponytail

soaked and her lips pulled into the biggest of smiles.

She finished kicking off her jeans, leaving her naked and beautiful as she rolled into the waves again.

Do you even know how to swim? I wondered, suddenly concerned when she didn't resurface. *Calina?*

She didn't reply.

"Shit." The Pacific Ocean had a serious undertow, making swimming at a beach like this rather dangerous for an inexperienced swimmer.

I didn't bother disrobing, just phased to the water where she'd last been and nearly fell over as she jumped out of the waves at me. I caught her by the waist, my heart skipping a beat in surprise.

And she laughed.

I blinked.

"Did you just…?" I couldn't even phrase the question. She'd played a trick on me. Something I would have realized had I taken a minute to read her mind, but my instinct to save her had come first. "That's a dangerous move, Calina."

She giggled again, drunk on life. Or maybe just drunk on salt water. "You're welcome to punish me, Your Highness."

I arched a brow. "Is that what you want?"

She considered it for a moment, her pretty eyes reflecting the pale moon. "I want you." She leaned in, her lips brushing mine. "You wanted me naked, right? Willingly? Here I am. And now I want you."

A growl tickled my chest, the need to take her up on that nearly derailing all my thoughts.

But I didn't have enough time to ravage her properly.

On the jet, however, I would.

And I'd already promised her a shower.

"Mmm," I murmured, phasing back to the jet and up the steps without care for Calina's clothes on the beach. "We can go now," I said to Sal as I passed her. "Calina and I will be in the back if you need me."

"Yes, My Prince," she replied dutifully. Although, I didn't miss the note of amusement in her tone. It seemed my newfound infatuation entertained everyone.

Given my history, I supposed I deserved that.

But it felt right.

Like this was exactly where I should be.

Calina made me stronger. Happier. More strategic. *Complete*.

"I'm starting to wonder who I was before you," I admitted as I carried her into the bedroom and directly to the en-suite bathroom. "You've changed me irrevocably, Calina. I'm not sure I'll ever be the same."

"Is that bad?" she asked, her smile having disappeared into a more serious expression.

"I never knew I needed to change," I told her. "But now that I know who I can be with you, I wonder how I was ever satisfied before."

I set her on the bench and finished removing my clothes while she watched from beneath a hooded gaze. A dozen ideas scrolled through her mind, all of them centered around my cock and each of them more appealing than the last.

But none of them were what I intended to do to her.

"Stand up, little genius," I said, reaching over to turn on the water. "There's a part of you I haven't claimed yet. And I intend to make every inch of you mine."

CHAPTER FORTY-TWO

CALINA

I shivered at the promise in Jace's voice.

What part? I wanted to ask, but the dark intent in his gaze had me complying with his command instead. I also heard murmurs of it in my mind, his intention one I would never have considered.

His hands found my hips as he pulled me under the falling water, the shower larger than any I'd ever seen. Except for the one at his home in Jace City—the bathtub alone had been made for five or more people to enjoy at a time.

Something I didn't want to think about because it only brought up whispers of Jace's past.

He caught my chin, forcing me to look at him. "I won't apologize for my past, Calina."

"I never asked you to." Nor would I ever ask him to. It was just a part of him that I had to accept. Besides, it was the future that concerned me more.

He canted his head, his grip on my chin and hip tightening as the jet began to move around us.

The water continued to pour around us, the warmth washing away some of the ice forming inside me at the thought of what our future held.

Our bond was undefined. I might be able to sleep with others. I might not.

But Jace absolutely could.

And I strongly disliked that notion.

I wanted to call him mine, just as he'd said moments ago about me. Yet I felt as though I couldn't stake a similar claim because he really wasn't mine at all.

The *Erosita* link was unfair in that regard, giving the vampire all the control and leaving the mortal reliant on the connection to survive.

Jace continued to study me, the air between us charged with unspoken words and a myriad of thoughts. He could hear each of mine, including my hesitancy regarding our future together.

His previous experiences had created the male before me. I'd never begrudge him for that. But I wondered how it would impact our relationship long-term.

He didn't believe in monogamy.

Meanwhile, monogamy was the only choice for me unless I wanted to risk my immortality.

But that inspired an interesting question. *Do I want to live for an eternity tied to an unfaithful mate?*

"You've not once asked if I want to be faithful," Jace said after a beat, the water continuing to rain down around us as my ears popped from the jet's increased altitude. "You just assume I won't be."

"You've not given me a reason to believe otherwise," I pointed out. "And I can hear your mind, Jace. I know what you want."

"You know what I'm questioning," he corrected. "That I'm trying to determine my desires just as much as you are."

I nodded. "You're afforded the opportunity of choice. I am not."

He released my chin, his fingers tracing my jaw up to my hair, where he removed my ponytail with a swift tug. My neck arched a little in response, causing his gaze to drop to my exposed throat before slowly returning upward to my eyes. "Do you want me to turn you? To make us equals?"

"No," I answered immediately. "My blood sustains you. If you turn me, you'll lose that."

I also didn't want to be a vampire. I preferred my current state of being. My solitary concern was about our future, not the present.

It was just a habit of my mind to always plan, to understand where we were heading so I could make the appropriate adjustments to my mental process to accept the inevitable.

Which, in this case, seemed to be Jace straying.

And for whatever reason, I found myself having a hard time accepting that eventuality.

"You don't trust me to remain faithful," he said, his gaze searching as he listened to me reason through our bond and the potentials that lay ahead.

"I'm not sure you'll want to be faithful," I corrected him. "And I don't like the idea of forcing you to be someone you're not." It wouldn't suit either of us. He would end up hating me for it, just like I would despise him if he ever forced me into a permanent submissive role. That wasn't me at all, similar to how him being in a relationship didn't fit his preferences.

"You're failing to understand something important, Calina," he said softly, his fingers combing through my wet hair as his opposite palm went to my lower back to pull me closer to him. "You've already changed me."

His lips whispered across mine, his fingers knotting in my damp strands as he held me to him.

"I'm not sure how it happened, or really when, but you're inside me now," he murmured against my mouth. "I don't want to lose that or you. I don't want to share you, either. The very thought of it makes me murderous."

He allowed me to see that inside his mind, the fury he'd felt when Lajos had touched me, and his later vow never to let another do it again.

"So I understand your desire not to share me, too. But if I'm honest, I'm not sure anyone else will ever intrigue me again. I haven't looked away from you once, Calina. I haven't even considered the possibility. You're all I can see." He cupped my cheek as he pulled back to stare into my eyes. "This is all very new to me. And it's not that I don't fancy monogamy, darling. No one has ever given me reason to consider it. Until you."

He kissed me again, this time with more intent, his emotions warming through our bond and enchanting my very soul.

Because I felt the truth of his words like an arrow through my heart.

Neither of us knew what the future held for us, but we were tied together forever now. We would tackle the obstacles as they presented themselves to us.

However, there was one certainty inside Jace that made me weak in the knees.

He wanted me long-term. Not short-term. Not right now. But forever.

And he would do whatever he needed to do to ensure I always remembered that.

This wasn't about his former proclivities but about his new desires—his desire for *me*. His *Erosita*. His mate. His mental equal.

He saw me as the part of his soul that he never knew he'd been missing, and there was no way he intended to lose me now.

With his mouth, he whispered promises of forever. And with his mind, he proved that he was already mine.

No one knew him better than I did because he'd never connected to anyone on this intimate level. He gave me free access to every thought and memory, holding nothing back. He even showed me how easy it would be to shut me out, to block me from his mind entirely.

Yet he'd not once even considered doing that to me. Not even when he'd thought it might be best for my protection.

No. He'd embraced me more with each passing second, his mind marrying mine in a manner few others ever experienced.

I belonged to him and he belonged to me.

Nothing else mattered beyond that knowledge.

If I wanted monogamy, he would give it to me because my desires rivaled his own. He showed me that in his mind, the openness to spending eternity with me and me alone.

You're all I want, he whispered into my thoughts. *You're the one I never knew I needed. All the others were passing amusements on my path to finding you, my true equal, my intended mate. None of this should even be possible, but fate ensured we would find each other. And now I'll do everything to make sure I'm worthy of you, Calina. We'll figure this out as a team. Just you and me. Because that's who we are together.*

My heart threatened to explode, the sensation new and a little unnerving. But I welcomed the heat that followed, the warmth stroking every inch of me as he deepened our kiss.

His earlier notion of claiming every part of me melted into a new kind of need, one founded in mutual affection and the promise linking our spirits.

Goose bumps pebbled down my arms, my body reacting to the onslaught of emotions and thoughts coming from him, all of them grounded in his intentions for us, his vows to keep me safe, and his desire to deepen our connection even more.

He wanted a future.

He wanted to explore all the opportunities that existed between us.

And most importantly, he needed me.

It was all so new, so young, yet ancient in our minds. Like we'd already known each other for an eternity but had just found each other again.

I never want to lose you, he said, his hands returning to my hips as he lifted me into the air.

My legs automatically circled his waist as he pressed my back up against the wall. The cool tile sent a shiver down my spine that his groin soon counteracted as he pressed himself into the apex between my thighs. It left me hot and cold. Aroused and aware. Ready and on the edge of begging for more.

You're mine, Calina, he vowed. *Just as much as I'm yours. The bond may only require one of us to remain faithful to the other, but the connection is founded on the need to create an immortal soul mate. I have no desire to ever belittle that gift, love. No desire to ruin anything between us. I've always adored sex, not necessarily the art of being playful with others.*

He angled his hips and slid inside me without warning, his cock filling me to completion and drawing a gasp from my lips.

It's fucking that I enjoy, he informed me, his voice a sensual hiss to my senses. "More specifically," he continued out loud. "It's *you* that I enjoy fucking, Calina. Only you." He drove his point home with a harsh thrust, stealing the air from my lungs and swallowing my resulting cry of passion with his mouth.

Every shift of his hips was accompanied by a new thought. A

promise. A sensation. An emotion. A benediction.

He told me how he would never tire of being inside me. Not just sexually, but mentally, too.

He told me how he wanted to keep me.

He told me how he wanted me to keep him.

He told me we were destined for each other.

He told me our spirits had been engaged for eternity and we just didn't know it until we'd finally met.

He thanked me for existing. He thanked fate for giving him a perfect mate. He worshipped me with his mind and body, his lips caressing mine before traveling to my neck to lick and suck at my pulse without breaking the skin.

He was addicted to my essence.

He called me an enchantress.

He called me *his*.

His hands stayed on my hips, angling me to receive him deeper, his body telling me to obey him. To come. To shatter around him. To squeeze his shaft hard and claim him as mine.

I obeyed, my thighs clenching as an orgasm rippled through my limbs, leaving me trembling and shaking against him.

Tears tracked down my face, not just from the pleasure of our union but also from the words he'd echoed into my thoughts and the emotions that went with them.

We kissed again, our tongues speaking for us now as he continued to fuck me against the wall. He wanted me to climax again, to prove to him with my body that I was exactly where I should be.

I panted, the exertion of his power and strength a brand to my being, forcing me to comply and meet him move for move.

That sensual part of me—the one he'd awakened—woke up and stretched.

My inner animal.

The wolf I would never be allowed to see.

She only existed inside my spirit, but she recognized this male as her equal. Her mate. Her other half.

She urged me to bite him.

To sink my teeth into his neck and mark him for everyone to see.

Do it, he encouraged, catching the need inside my mind. *Bite me, Calina. And I'll return the favor.*

My insides burned at the prospect, not just from the thought of tasting him but also from the knowledge of how his bite made me feel.

I stopped thinking. I acted. My tongue traced the masculine line of his throat to his muscular shoulder. Then I bit down as hard as I could, my soul rejoicing at the bold claim.

My male.

Yours, he agreed, his fingers suddenly in my hair as he held me to him. His pace had slowed, his torso tense against me as though he was fighting his impending pleasure.

I wanted to drive him over the edge like he always did to me.

But I sensed his need to wait. His desire to make me come again before he exploded. And his intention to flip me and fuck me from behind soon after.

There would be soap first.

A quick rinse.

Then an animalistic fucking as he let his beast free and mounted me the way he desired.

I quivered at the prospect, the thought alone tightening my abdominal muscles and making my insides clench around him. His fingers remained in my hair as his opposite hand left my hip to venture to the sweet spot between my thighs.

All it took was one thrum of a finger against my clit to send me sky-high into an oblivion littered with blinking stars.

He drew the pleasure out of me, playing my body with a skill only he possessed, lengthening my bliss until he joined me in the exquisite agony of orgasmic rapture.

I shook, screamed, and cried, the sensations too much with his enchanting blood on my tongue, his thickness penetrating me deeply, his seed claiming me from the inside.

My vision began to blacken.

But his teeth in my neck yanked me back to the present as I tumbled into yet another spiral of intensity that destroyed my ability to think.

He remained inside me as he soaped us up.

He kept us connected intimately while he washed my hair.

He held me against the wall, using the shower sprayer to find the right angles and motions.

I watched him work, my eyelids heavy, my body useless.

But ripples of pleasure continued to warm me inside, my being already revitalizing and preparing for more.

He was still hard.

His silvery eyes were still darkened with wicked intent.

And his touch continued to evoke quivers of longing.

He was an addiction that I would never quit. An experiment with no end. The perfect partner for me to explore for eternity.

His mind echoed the same thoughts, his lips curling at my lust-drunk reaction.

"I'm going to keep you in this state for our entire flight," he decided on a low murmur. "You're going to be so sore and used when I'm done that you probably won't be able to walk. But that's all right. I'll carry you. Then I'll fuck you again because the thought of you delirious and limp from my attentions will just make me want to repeat every exquisite moment."

I shuddered, his idea one I accepted without much consideration.

"And that's why I'm never going to tire of you," he added. "I'm just as addicted to you as you are to me, perhaps even more so. You've slain me, Calina. I never expected it. But I'll also never fight it. We're too good together, love. In every way."

He kissed me again, his tongue whispering more of those delicious promises into my mouth.

I barely felt his prodding fingers at my backside.

It was just right.

He was right.

He wanted to claim me completely, take every hole, own me entirely.

I accepted because I was already his. And he was already mine.

"Yes," I told him, answering a dozen unasked questions. "Yes, Jace."

His lips captured mine once more, the pressure behind me building as he used water and something slippery to prepare me for his entry. It was a beastly need inside him, growing with each passing second. He needed to be there, inside me, taking me in this final manner.

Then he had thousands of other ways he intended to fuck me.

Every idea spilled through my thoughts, each one more sordid than the last.

And all they did was make me burn that much more for him.

He finally slipped out from between my thighs, the emptiness immediately making my heart ache. But then he was shifting my hips again, moving me higher, still facing him, as he angled himself against my other entrance.

This was undeniably intimate, the intensity only deepening as he met and held my gaze.

He didn't thrust.

He slid in slowly, his mind walking me through the reactions, telling me to relax, to accept him, to allow him this final claim.

A tremble worked through me, the fullness entirely different from the front. But he quickly fixed that by sliding two fingers into my channel and stroking the place deep inside me.

"Jace," I breathed, his name a prayer and a curse as he began to move.

"How do you feel?" he asked, his eyes still holding mine. "Tell me how you feel, Calina."

"Full," I whispered, arching into him.

His thumb found my clit, his fingers still deep inside, as his opposite hand grasped my hip to keep me in place.

"I feel *owned*," I added on a groan as he pushed all the way forward and stretched me wide. I wasn't sure if I wanted to cry or beg for more, the sensation unlike anything I'd ever anticipated.

He didn't move apart from his fingers gently stroking that spot inside me. A quake stirred in my abdomen, spilling out through my limbs and rendering me useless.

"Perfect," Jace murmured. "You're so beautiful, Calina. And so damn perfect." His eyes glittered with the truth of his words, then he kissed me and started to move.

There was nothing soft or gentle about it.

He was too powerful to go easy. He took me with a need driven by the predator inside him, and my inner beast responded in kind, welcoming his possession by clamping down around him and urging him to fight harder. Push more. Plunge deeper.

My nipples ached, the taut points rubbing against his chest as he devoured my mouth and claimed my body.

He set me on fire.

He branded my soul.

He stamped a promise into my mind that went straight to my heart.

We were in this together. Forever. For eternity. Our bond went so much deeper than love or frivolous conventions. I didn't need those words from him, because I understood his intentions from his mind.

This was us.

We existed as one.

For always.

His forehead met mine, his breath hot against my lips as he held my gaze once more. Everything I felt for him reflected back at me in those icy orbs.

Adoration.

Respect.

Desire.

Intelligence.

Partnership.

It was all right there. Hot. Intense. Passion. I sighed, my body breaking beneath the ferocity of his attentions and the vows of his heart.

My legs trembled.

My stomach clenched.

His teeth sank into my neck.

And his name escaped my mouth on a breath as I fell into a whirlpool of intense sensation. It burned through my veins, drawing tears from my eyes as I drowned in a rapturous wave of insanity.

He'd broken me.

I was too lost to the sensations to care.

Darkness. Happiness. Ripples of energy. Strength. A virile groan. Hot seed inside me. Muscles spasming, masculine perfection, the woodsy scent of the forest.

Love.

All of it surrounded me at once.

Followed by the plush comfort of warm cotton.

A strong male body holding me in the sheets.

His cock inside me again.

Driving me forward. Keeping me in this state of blissful unawareness.

I cried. I screamed. I lost my voice.

I drank his blood.

He drank mine.

Mates drowning in passion and shared essences.

So much fucking.

So much pleasure.

So much intensity.

He licked away my tears. He traced every path of my body with his tongue. He guided my mouth to his cock. He filled me with his essence. Forced me to swallow. Then returned the favor by going down on me, too.

I was lost to it all, living in a cloud of oblivion that I never wanted to escape.

Until my body couldn't take it anymore.

And darkness finally came, pulling me into a dream.

A dream where he stayed between my legs. Licking, sucking, and drawing out more pleasure, even while I slept.

Waking me with orgasms.

Lulling me back to sleep.

Just to repeat it again.

At some point, I lost my mind entirely. Gave it to him for safekeeping. And trusted him to be my guide in this passionate embrace.

"I love you, Calina," he whispered against my ear. "You might not need the words, but I want you to hear them. To know that I've never said that phrase to anyone else. Only you. Only ever you."

He pressed his lips to mine, my body too exhausted to allow a response.

Then he gave me a little more of his blood.

Which lulled me into a final state of rest.

Dream of me, little genius. Dream of us.

CHAPTER FORTY-THREE

JACE

I nibbled on Calina's clit, drawing her back into our reality with an orgasm that had her back bowing off the bed. She looked so beautiful in her flushed, well-fucked state. It was a shame that we would be landing soon.

"Ohh," she moaned, her legs quivering on either side of me as she came down from her climax.

I grinned as her mind begged me to stop yet to keep going at the same time. I obliged the latter request by shifting down to her femoral artery and indulging in her sweet essence.

"Jace," she hissed as she tumbled into oblivion once more.

I chuckled, amused by how easy it was to coax pleasure from her. Then I licked her slick folds, soothing her with my tongue as she came down from her high.

She shook so hard the bed practically trembled.

My poor Calina.

She had no idea what I could do to her. Because this was only the beginning and we had eternity to test each and every one of her limits.

"You're going to fuck me to death," she accused, her voice

hoarse.

"Good thing you'll just come right back," I teased, crawling up her beautifully pleasured form and purposely settling between her thighs.

She jumped as the head of my cock touched her swollen bud, her lips immediately parting on a groan of pleasure-pain.

I kissed her gently, acknowledging her body's need to recover, and bit my tongue before slipping it inside her mouth. She sucked greedily in response, her desire for my blood overtaking her ability to think. But after two swallows, she relaxed beneath me, her body well on the way to recovery already.

Calina sighed and drew her nails up my back to my nape, holding me to her as we lazed together for a few more tender minutes.

Our embrace remained soft and fluid, our minds entirely open to the other.

You said you loved me, she marveled.

I nuzzled her nose and grinned against her mouth. "Yes, I did." I nipped her lower lip, not harshly, just adoringly. "I meant it, too."

Her eyes—which were still blue with no signs of green—captured and held mine. "You do," she replied. "I can feel it."

"Mmm." I pressed myself against the dampness between her thighs. "That's just my cock, sweetheart." I pulled back to look at her. "No, wait, that's just my *vampire prowess*."

She rolled her eyes and laughed. "*Jace prowess* is more accurate."

"Hmm," I hummed. "I like the sound of that."

"Of course you do. You're just arrogant enough to claim full responsibility for all this." She gestured between us, her eyebrow raised in a taunt.

I gave her an affronted look. "You know I take that kind of sass as a challenge, right?"

"I do."

"Well, I'm going to require ample testing scenarios now," I pressed.

She pretended to consider. "I accept."

"Of course you do," I said, purposely repeating her words. "You're just the kind of researcher who would desire a myriad of test rounds in the lab." I sighed dramatically. "My cock is going to be exhausted when you're done."

"Seems only fair after what you just put me through today," she pointed out.

"Oh, that was just me proving my devotion," I told her. "And testing your ability to keep up with my hunger."

"How did I do?"

"Beautifully," I admitted, smiling. "But I'll need more evidence to fully confirm your stamina."

She nodded, her expression taking on a serious gleam. "It's wise to test a theory more than once. One time might be a fluke."

"Doubtful, but I'll enjoy achieving the same results over and over again." I nearly started on that challenge; however, a change in pressure told me we were on our final descent.

So I just kissed her instead.

Holding her all the way until we landed.

Then I ensured her wounds were all healed and helped her dress. It was a shame to cover all those curves, but I didn't want anyone else to admire her apart from me. Hence the long-sleeved black shirt and jeans. I adorned a similar attire, only with dress pants instead of jeans.

I sensed Damien waiting in the lounge area of the jet before we exited the bedroom, his leather and spice scent familiar.

He stood as we entered, his expression telling me I wasn't going to like whatever he had to say.

Which meant it could only be one thing.

"Mira," I said.

"Yeah, I need to show you something." He gestured to the laptop he'd already set up on the table.

I stepped forward, my gaze on his screen. "It must be important if you couldn't wait until we disembarked."

"I thought you might want a moment to review what I've found before Luka arrives. Which will be any minute now," he replied as he returned to his seat. "I hacked into Mira's phone. I've been translating her encrypted messages for the last hour. You need to see these."

Calina and I stepped up behind him, our interest mutually piqued.

"She's definitely not who we thought she was," Damien said,

his screen displaying evidence of such. "But she's not in charge."

He brought up a message that just said, *Report your status.*

"This is from someone at Bunker 7, which I've gathered is code for their home base." He glanced at me. "Seems Lilith was a fan of the number seven."

I'd already determined that after hearing all the bunker names. "Did she reply?"

"Not until five minutes ago. I'm still decrypting it. But that's not what I wanted you to see." He started rearranging the windows on his screen, displaying a message from the day Lilith died.

"Who sent that?" I asked, reading the note about Lilith's death.

"Mira did," he replied, his voice holding a note of irritation. "It's what activated the protocols. And this one"—he clicked on another message—"includes instructions on how to frame another pack member as the mole in Majestic Clan."

I read the evidence on the screen, my jaw clenching. "I hope Luka hasn't doled out punishment yet."

Damien's expression hardened. "Mira volunteered to do it."

"Of course she did." Which meant the poor male was likely very dead. "Is Luka bringing Mira here to meet us? That's something he would typically do."

"I don't know," Damien admitted. "I've been too busy trying to—"

His computer beeped, distracting him.

"She just sent another message," he said, his mouse dragging the gibberish into some sort of application.

Decryption app, Calina told me. *Really quite fascinating, as he created it himself.*

Do I need to worry about just how fascinating you find that? I asked, arching a brow at her.

Her blue eyes twinkled back at me. *Just keep me high on your Jace prowess, and we'll be fine.*

Noted, I replied, amused by her teasing.

But the growl from Damien had me immediately focusing on the screen and the message unraveling before us.

My heart stopped.

Oh, fuck…

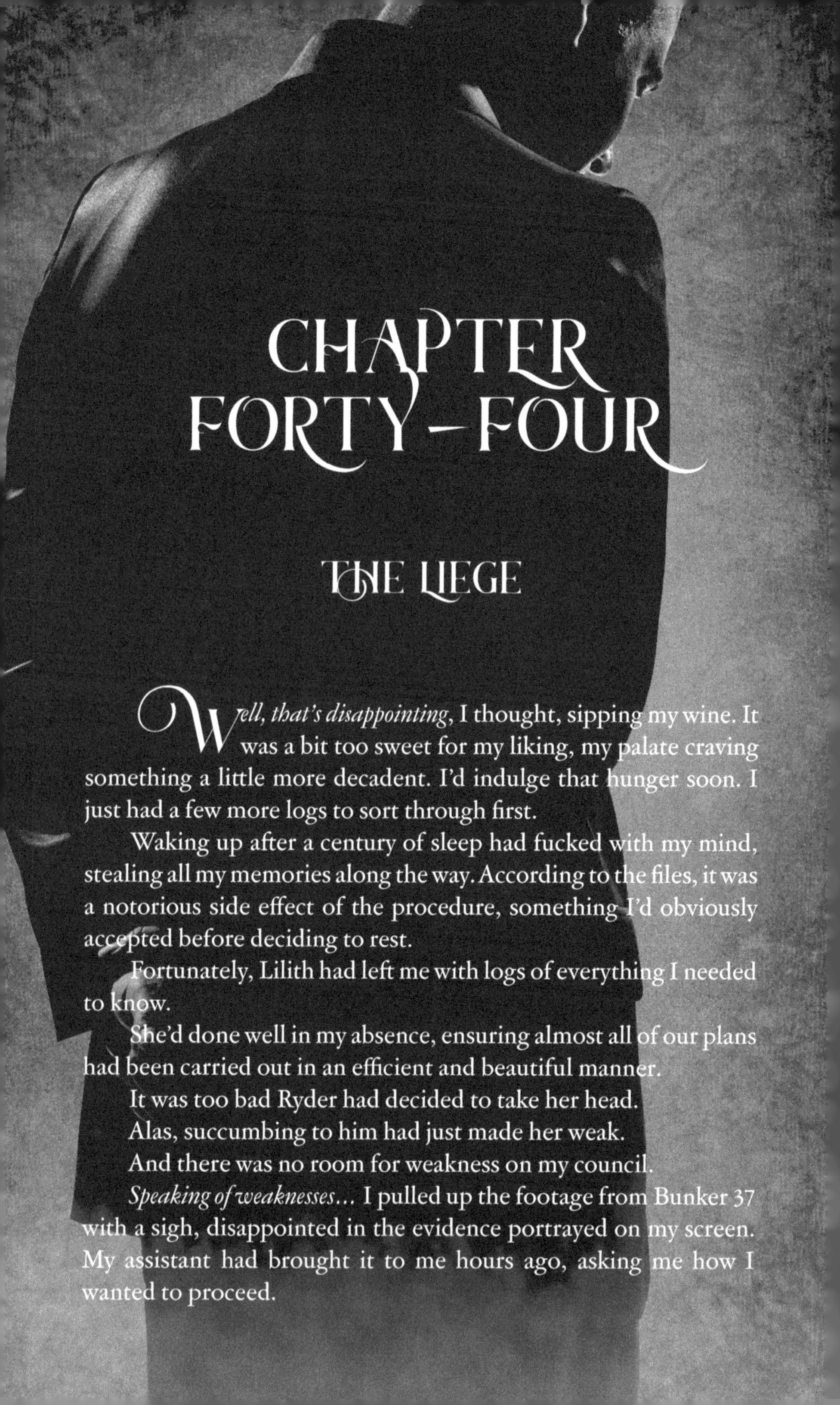

CHAPTER FORTY-FOUR

THE LIEGE

Well, that's disappointing, I thought, sipping my wine. It was a bit too sweet for my liking, my palate craving something a little more decadent. I'd indulge that hunger soon. I just had a few more logs to sort through first.

Waking up after a century of sleep had fucked with my mind, stealing all my memories along the way. According to the files, it was a notorious side effect of the procedure, something I'd obviously accepted before deciding to rest.

Fortunately, Lilith had left me with logs of everything I needed to know.

She'd done well in my absence, ensuring almost all of our plans had been carried out in an efficient and beautiful manner.

It was too bad Ryder had decided to take her head.

Alas, succumbing to him had just made her weak.

And there was no room for weakness on my council.

Speaking of weaknesses… I pulled up the footage from Bunker 37 with a sigh, disappointed in the evidence portrayed on my screen. My assistant had brought it to me hours ago, asking me how I wanted to proceed.

I sighed—a sound I'd made far too many times today.

It seemed my brother had impacted Darius's and Jace's mental capacities. My assistant had suggested a destruction protocol that would destroy the problem, but I'd told him that ancient blood was just too precious to waste.

Besides, with Lajos's and Lilith's recent deaths, we couldn't afford to spill any more blood.

So I would let Darius and Jace learn more about the operations. Then I'd handle them personally when the time came. Maybe they would come to their senses along the way.

A knock sounded at the door, drawing me from my musings. I'd sent my assistant off on an errand to find the files on my brother several hours ago. Hopefully, he'd found them. "Enter," I called to him from my desk.

He entered with a fully executed bow, his long blond hair touching the ground before he finally straightened. "I've finally heard from our asset."

"Oh?" That news certainly interested me. Of course, finding the lost files would, too. But we'd address that momentarily. "And?" I prompted, arching a brow at the young vampire.

Apparently, I'd saved his life once. He'd been serving me ever since, even while I'd slept. And, according to Lilith's logs, he was quite useful, too.

He started through the center of my room, bypassing the two couches and the coffee table before reaching the chairs on the other side of my desk. Rather than sit in one, he continued forward and set a tablet on the table for me.

A message scrolled across the screen.

My position here has officially been compromised. I'm on my way, my liege. And I'm bringing your Erosita *with me.*

I read it twice, then sighed. "I suppose it was only a matter of time before the resistance realized Mira's true loyalty." I'd reviewed her files when refamiliarizing myself with my allies. She was the original lycan, immortal, and devoted to improving this world by strengthening our superiority over humankind.

To prove that, she'd been in charge of watching my *Erosita* for me while I'd slept.

Apparently, Ismerelda had a penchant for disobedience. I

couldn't remember a damn thing about her, which told me she'd never meant much to me.

But I suspected the blood I craved was hers, something I would soon confirm.

Well, that news did appease me greatly.

"When do they arrive?" I asked.

"In ten hours or so, my liege."

"Excellent," I replied, drawing my hand down my tie before glancing at the surveillance on my computer again. It was several hours old, but I kept watching it. There was just something about the way Jace had looked at the camera, like he could *see* me. "I suppose that means the resistance is aware of my awakening, yes?"

"It's likely that they are, yes," my assistant replied.

I nodded, considering what to do with that information. Most of the logs had been reviewed, leaving me certain of the path forward.

The question became, could I convince the rebels to join me? Or would I be forced to fight them?

I drummed my fingers on my desk, considering my options.

Well, if they already know, then what choice do I really have? I mused, grinning as I met my assistant's bright green eyes. "I need you to find me a phone, Michael."

CHAPTER FORTY-FIVE

JACE

My position here has officially been compromised. I'm on my way, my liege. And I'm bringing your Erosita *with me.*

I read the message three times, my mind refusing to accept what it said.

This couldn't be about Izzy.

It couldn't be a message for Cam.

He wouldn't do that. He would never partner with Lilith. He… he *valued* humanity and human life.

"This has to be wrong," I said even while my mind began to puzzle together all the pieces, the game finally revealing itself inside my head.

I'm bringing your Erosita *with me.*

Mira had been working for Lilith. Guarding Izzy. *Why?*

For Cam.

Except he would never be a willing participant in any of this. Unless Lilith had somehow coerced him.

Or…

My eyes widened as a new path formed, a potential outcome that had me sick to my stomach.

Shit. The logs. The fucking protocols.

"Do you have the logs?" I asked Damien, my mind racing. "Can you find the most recent one Lilith recorded? I need to hear it again."

However, Calina was already thinking about a different log, the one that had initiated them all.

If you're watching this, then something has gone terribly wrong and the necessary fail-safes were engaged. Including the one you're experiencing now.

Her memory was better than mine, the visual clear in her mind. Mostly because that log had resonated with her as her own doomsday protocol had somewhat correlated to that one.

Calina started thinking about all the research she'd reviewed, the mental-manipulation weapons meant to subdue immortals, and the potential applications of those.

What if she…? Calina paused, still sorting through the notion as I followed her path through all the potential outcomes. She started considering what Lilith would do, what fail-safes she'd put in motion to ensure the continuation of her projects.

Cam was her biggest threat to that success.

He was the unequivocal figurehead for the entire resistance operation.

Or he could be her greatest weapon.

If only she could mold his mind, Calina thought. Then her eyes widened as we gaped at each other.

By wiping it, we thought at the same time, both of us recalling the memory refining tool mentioned in the research files at Bunker 37.

The necessary fail-safes were engaged. Including the one you're experiencing now, Calina repeated the log again. *Jace… What if that was her way of explaining the memory loss to him?*

Bloody hell, I breathed, realizing she might be right.

All of this… they're the protocols Lilith engaged upon her death, the ones Mira's initial communication enabled, Calina whispered. *In addition to the doomsday protocol. So while you've been busy trying to find him…*

Her videos have been brainwashing him, I finished for her.

Because no way was he the real Liege.

But that didn't mean he knew that.

Lilith had erased his memory, then spoke to him in those

logs as if all this was his idea. As though she were a servant to *his* madness. And without any background or history in his mind, he would have had no way to fight it.

"*Fuck.*" I ran my fingers through my hair, hoping like hell we were wrong yet feeling inside that we were absolutely right.

Cam's been stuck in a cave somewhere, watching those logs, and thinking he's the one responsible for this change. It almost felt unbelievable. And yet, it was just like Lilith to leave us with one final mindfuck in the form of a brainwashed Cam.

One of the logs began to play in the background as Damien watched. But I didn't look. Instead, I picked up on the subtle cadence and intentional uses of the term *you*, *my liege*, and *my king.*

She sounded so damn reverent.

Like she was worshipping the deity she spoke to and praising him for all this madness.

It wasn't a partner at all. It wasn't Michael. It was fucking Cam.

"That conniving cun—"

My phone began to vibrate, cutting off my curse.

One glance was all I needed to know who it was.

He'd let us live in the labs because his strategic mind would have told him that spilling our blood would be a waste. Cam would want to convince us to join him. He'd see it as a challenge.

For the wrong fucking side.

I swallowed, then stole a deep breath and accepted the call. "Hello, Cam," I greeted as soon as his image appeared.

He grinned. "Jace. It's been a while."

"Indeed," I replied, trying to keep my voice from reflecting any emotion. Attempting to tell Cam that he'd been brainwashed wouldn't work without sufficient proof, and I couldn't do that over the phone.

Of course, if he was actually watching the surveillance footage from Bunker 37, he might be able to enlarge the video we'd seen of his torment. But I doubted I could convince him to try.

The Cam I knew was stubborn.

And if Lilith's videos had convinced him that he was the Liege, it would take a lot for me to undo that mindfuck.

I needed time and a plan.

I also needed to see what we were working with here.

"How was your nap?" I asked, playing into the charade.

He shrugged. "I don't remember much, but I feel rested enough. Not too pleased with some of the things I've learned since waking up, though."

"Oh?" I arched a brow. "Such as?"

His lips curled. "You truly are a master at politics."

"I learned from the best," I admitted, referring to him.

"A compliment." He sounded impressed. "Does that mean we can discuss all this tomfoolery you've been up to lately with trying to undermine my life's work?"

My jaw threatened to tick at those words, Lilith's final act serving as a punch to my gut.

How she would've loved to have heard Cam say those words.

Thankfully, the bitch was very dead.

"I'm not sure what you mean," I said, my attention divided between my conversation and hearing Calina in my mind.

Keep him talking, she was saying. *Damien is doing a trace.*

I didn't reply or acknowledge her, just held Cam's gaze. His dark hair appeared to be recently trimmed, as did the stubble along his chin. The Cam I knew liked his beard. It seemed this new version preferred the five o'clock shadow look.

Someone is there with him, I thought, my instincts firing. *And it's not Mira*.

Which meant we still had an unaccounted-for party.

"Come now, Jace. Are we really going to play this game?"

"As I recall, it's a game we both thoroughly enjoy," I returned.

He gave me a pitying look as he shook his head softly. "My brother really did a number on you, didn't he?"

"Cane?" Was that what the logs had told him, that Cane had been the one to organize the resistance? "Maybe you should wake him up. Find out more." If Cam was in the catacombs like we suspected, then he was near Cane. Rousing him from his five-hundred-year sleep would be an eye-opening experience and would debunk whatever Cam knew.

"I'll consider that after I review his files," he replied, a note of irritation in his tone as he looked off-screen.

"I'm still looking for them, my liege," a soft voice said.

My brow nearly furrowed. Instead, I pasted an inquisitive

expression on my face and asked, "Who's that with you, Cam?"

"No one of consequence," Cam muttered, his annoyance palpable. "Find it now."

"Yes, my liege," the male voice promised. But it was too faint and submissive for me to recognize it.

Was it just some human?

Or another ally of Lilith's?

"One would think my assistants would be more useful," Cam said conversationally, his blue eyes meeting mine again. "Especially considering I saved his life prior to the revolution."

The information swirled in my mind, piecing together in sequence with everything we'd learned from Bunker 37.

Calina's father.

Michael.

Cam saved his life.

Michael became a vampire.

He's the assistant.

It took significant effort to maintain my bored expression because inside I was shouting at Cam to see reason. But I knew it was too soon to fix this.

We needed to approach this strategically. Slowly. With information and proof easily at our fingertips.

And even then, it might not be enough.

The air changed in the jet, the presence one I recognized, but I didn't look at him. Instead, I said, "So when do you intend to announce your awakening, Cam?"

Darius stilled at the doorway. I couldn't see him, but I felt him.

"Soon," Cam replied. "I have a few more tasks that need to be completed first, including a meeting with my *Erosita*. Apparently, she's grown a little too independent during my sleep."

The way he said it sent a chill down my spine and had Damien freezing in front of me.

Cam wouldn't be able to see him with how I'd angled my camera. Just me. And maybe a few loose strands of Calina's hair.

But he didn't pay her any mind.

Because Lilith had essentially told him that *Erositas* and humans didn't matter. They would hold no worth to him whatsoever.

Will he hurt Izzy? Calina asked.

I swallowed, the truth whispering through my mind. *I don't know.*

"I'm sure you'll be able to bring her to heel," I said out loud, testing the boundaries.

He merely shrugged. "We'll see, I suppose." He stretched his arms over his head and rolled his neck. "Well, I'll let you return to your little rebellion. Send my regards to Darius, too. And I'll be seeing you both very soon."

Cam cut the call before I could speak. Not that I knew what to say. Instead, I met Darius's gaze and said, "Cam's alive. And he thinks he's the Liege."

Darius's expression rivaled my own shock and dismay.

"Well. That presents a problem," Kylan said as he stepped onto the jet. He must have been waiting in the doorway, listening. "Isn't he our savior?"

I just stared at him. Sarcasm would not fix this situation.

He smirked anyway, walking all the way inside with Rae behind him. "Well. It's not all lost yet," he continued, his arm encircling Rae's waist. "We still have Izzy."

I shook my head. "No. Mira is taking her to him right now."

"Yes. I heard that part. Which means our weapon is about to enter enemy grounds. That's brilliant."

"How?" I demanded. "He clearly doesn't remember her, or anything. He might kill her."

Kylan snorted. "You underestimate the value of an *Erosita* bond." He glanced at Calina. "Sorry, sweetheart. Give him time. He'll understand."

A growl worked up my throat at him calling her *sweetheart*. But then his words began to register, as did the understanding in Calina's mind.

She was thinking about what she would do to fix me if my memories were all destroyed.

I'd make you remember, she said flatly.

I'd fight you, I admitted, putting myself in Cam's shoes.

And I'd fight back, she returned without missing a beat. *I'd win, too.*

She sounded so confident that I looked at her. *Would you?*

Absolutely. I felt her mind kissing mine, reaffirming our link through the unique marriage of our thoughts. *You're mine, remember?*

I held her gaze, the realization that she was right settling inside my heart. *Yes. Just as you're mine.*

See? She sounded so proud. *I'd win.*

She was right.

Which meant Kylan was right.

We'd just sent a weapon behind enemy lines.

I could send Cam as much evidence and proof as I wanted, but it might never be enough.

Izzy, however, had a thousand years of shared memories with Cam. If anyone could reawaken his humanity, it was her.

"This is in Izzy's hands now," I realized out loud, meeting Kylan's gaze before looking at Darius. "She's the only one who can fix him now."

"It's a good thing she's just as stubborn as him," Darius said, sounding defeated.

"Oh, she'll give him hell," Damien promised.

"She will," I agreed, glancing at the space where Cam had just been hovering in the air. Then I looked at Calina. *You'd give me hell, too.*

I absolutely would, she agreed. *I'd bring you back.*

Yes. She'll bring him back, too. Because the alternative was too bleak to consider.

Everything we'd done had been at Cam's behest.

To find him, just to lose him again...

No.

That wasn't going to happen here.

Cam would be king. *Our* king. And Izzy would be the queen to make it happen.

They were the primary players on the board now.

All right, Izzy, I thought. *Your move. Make it count.*

I turned toward my queen, my hand finding hers.

We might not be engaged in this next round of chess, but we still had our own game to play. The one I'd started when I'd removed Lajos's head. The one Ryder had initiated by killing Lilith.

That wasn't over.

We had a rebellion to finalize.

And hopefully, when the time came, our king would be ready

to join us.

If not, then I'd play the role.

With Calina at my side.

Because fuck the alliance.

It was time to welcome the new future.

It's time to fight.

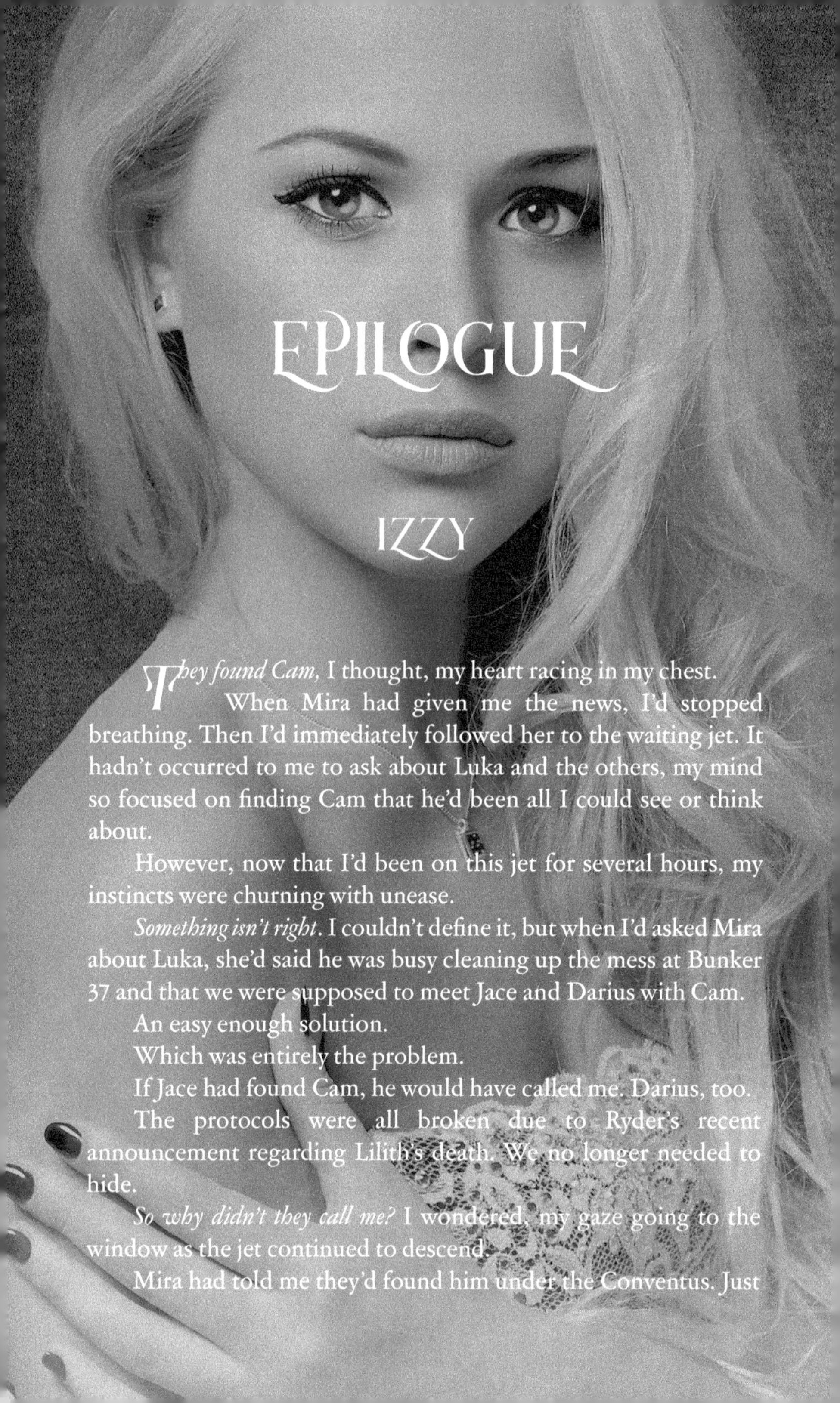

EPILOGUE

IZZY

They found Cam, I thought, my heart racing in my chest.

When Mira had given me the news, I'd stopped breathing. Then I'd immediately followed her to the waiting jet. It hadn't occurred to me to ask about Luka and the others, my mind so focused on finding Cam that he'd been all I could see or think about.

However, now that I'd been on this jet for several hours, my instincts were churning with unease.

Something isn't right. I couldn't define it, but when I'd asked Mira about Luka, she'd said he was busy cleaning up the mess at Bunker 37 and that we were supposed to meet Jace and Darius with Cam.

An easy enough solution.

Which was entirely the problem.

If Jace had found Cam, he would have called me. Darius, too.

The protocols were all broken due to Ryder's recent announcement regarding Lilith's death. We no longer needed to hide.

So why didn't they call me? I wondered, my gaze going to the window as the jet continued to descend.

Mira had told me they'd found him under the Conventus. Just

thinking about the catacombs beneath Rome gave me chills. All those cold, sleeping immortals. Crypts. Skulls. Former ritual sites.

I'd not lived through the creation of that tomb.

But Cam had.

And I'd seen the memories of it in his mind.

There were age-old rituals that kept the ancients from rising before they were ready. However, their spirits were very much alive down there. Cam had once called it a protective measure meant to deter humans. I'd told him it worked because just visiting the Vatican had made me feel cold.

Why can't I feel you? I wondered, thinking at Cam. *Why are you still blocking me?*

I knew he'd done it originally to protect me. But if he was with Jace and Darius now, then that meant he was okay and should be willing to talk to me.

Yet I couldn't sense him at all.

It was as though he'd erected a barricade between our minds, cutting me off from the other half of my soul.

"You're sure he's okay?" I asked Mira for the hundredth time.

"Positive," she replied, her focus on the tablet in her hands.

I tapped my fingers against my armrest, the sense of unease remaining. Maybe it was because I hadn't seen or heard from Cam in over a hundred years.

The agony of being cut off had dulled over the last century, but my heart continued to ache. I'd dreamt of this moment so many times, of finding Cam and reigniting our bond.

Nothing about this felt right.

Because I can't sense you, I decided.

Maybe we needed to touch each other again to rekindle the link?

I frowned. *That can't be right. I should be able to feel our connection, but I can't. Why?*

My pulse continued to race, something I hoped Mira took as excitement. For some reason, my instincts told me not to confide in her. Which was also strange. I'd known her since before the revolution. But something about her demeanor now struck me as off.

Or this was all just in my head.

Maybe I'm nervous, I thought. Considering how I'd felt about Cam in the beginning, nervousness would be an appropriate response. He'd been this enigma of a male with his long, dark hair and striking blue eyes.

I'd thought he was a god.

And he sort of was, with his ancient history and vampiric abilities.

Butterflies ignited in my belly as I recalled our first meeting. It'd been in the dark, but his eyes had practically glowed beneath the moonlight. And he'd escorted me home, saying the streets were too dangerous for a young girl like me to be wandering alone.

He hadn't been wrong.

He'd been a predator lurking in the night, looking for a drink. And he hadn't been alone, either.

Goose bumps pebbled down my arms at the recollection of how captivated I'd been by his charm and beauty. He hadn't bitten me. Hadn't even touched me. Just protected me, something he'd continued to do for weeks before making a move.

His kiss had set my blood on fire.

His touch, too.

And I'd never strayed from him ever since.

Over a thousand years of love and adoration.

He'd promised me forever and I'd accepted.

Then the revolution had happened.

One hundred and seventeen years of torment. One hundred and seventeen years of perpetual loneliness. One hundred and seventeen years of missing him.

But he's alive. That, I could feel. I just couldn't sense *him*.

My heart remained lodged in my throat as the jet finally touched the ground. The feeling didn't abate as Mira stood, her stiletto heels digging into the carpet as she smoothed out her pencil skirt. I'd worn jeans and a sweater, preferring comfort over fashion. But now I wondered if I should have dressed for the occasion.

This is Cam, I reminded myself. *He doesn't need to be impressed. He just needs me.*

I glanced out the window, wondering if I could see him. But the airfield was vacant on my side.

Mira walked to the door, her steps certain.

I tried to copy her, but I couldn't shake the sense of wrongness inside me. It grew with every movement, the sense of dread a weight in my mind that refused to wane.

The early morning air didn't help when we exited.

Neither did the figures looming in the shadows in the distance.

Why isn't Cam right here waiting for me? I wondered, still following Mira.

All the reunions in my head did not measure up to this moment. I'd expected tears. Hugs. Kisses. *Love.*

None of that happened.

My steps began to slow, confusion holding my breath captive.

Then one of the figures moved forward, stepping directly beneath the light above.

And my heart stopped.

Cam.

I started forward again, picking up speed, my mind rejoicing at the sight of my mate. Too long I'd been without his strength. Too long I'd been without his touch. Too long I'd been without his bite.

"Cam," I breathed, running now.

But he didn't open his arms for me.

He didn't even smile.

Just stared at me through cold blue eyes, the color reminding me of hard sapphires. They glittered in the early light. His cheekbones appeared carved from stone. His dark hair had been cut shorter. Stubble replaced his usual beard.

However, it was his stance that confirmed something was truly wrong here.

His legs were braced, his hands tucked behind his back, his shoulders holding an arrogant line.

There was nothing friendly about him. Nothing familiar. Nothing… *right.*

I slowed as I reached him, searching his expression for answers. While all he did was stare back at me with mild annoyance lurking in his gaze. "Is she always this disrespectful?" he demanded.

My brow furrowed. "What?"

"Yes," Mira replied, having joined us. "But you have to remember that she's from a time when humans had rights. Those are hard habits to break."

I frowned at her. "What are you talking about?"

"See?" she prompted.

"Yes. Unfortunately, I do." He sounded disgusted, his cultured tones flatter than I'd ever heard them.

"Cam," I whispered, not understanding any of this. Not understanding him. It was definitely my Cam, but it wasn't at the same time. I couldn't hear him. I couldn't feel him. And I'd never had him look at me in a such a way, as though he couldn't stand the thought of touching me.

"Why do I keep her?" he asked, again talking to Mira and not to me.

"You like the way she tastes," Mira replied. "And you enjoy the challenge."

He grunted. "Sometimes I question my own sanity."

"What the hell is going on?" I demanded, looking between him and Mira, then noting the men behind Cam. "What's wrong with you?"

"How do I shut her up?" Cam asked.

"Typically with your teeth." Even Mira sounded wrong, like she didn't have a care in the world. Which wasn't the female I knew at all.

Have I fallen into another universe? A different realm? Is this just a bad dream?

"Hmm, all right," Cam hummed, his palm snagging my nape. "I am hungry."

"Cam!" I cried out, trying to free myself from his hold.

"Quiet," he snapped back.

My lips parted on a sound that turned into a scream as his fangs sank into my throat.

There was nothing gentle about this.

Just a vampire indulging his inner beast.

No endorphins. Only pain.

I clawed at his shoulders, trying to force him to see reason while shrieking at him through our bond. *What are you doing? Why are you doing this? Cam! Stop!*

He didn't reply.

Because he couldn't hear me.

I was blocked from his mind.

When I tried to speak out loud, he used his free hand to cover my mouth as his feeding turned violent. There was no care or finesse. No sweet words. No soothing touch. Just a savage mouth taking far too much from my veins.

You're… you're… you're killing me… I told him, stunned. *Why, Cam? What's happening? Talk to me!*

Tears streaked down my cheeks, my sight blinking in and out between strange dots of black and white.

I… I'd never died before.

I knew our link would bring me back.

But I didn't understand.

He'd never bitten me like this. Had never before withheld the endorphins.

This was some sort of wicked punishment, one I couldn't define.

"Wh-why?" I mumbled behind his hand, my voice barely existent.

"Because that's your purpose," Mira told me, her words underlined with a darkness I didn't recognize.

And I didn't have the energy to question her again. Or really to think.

My world was fading.

My consciousness blinking in and out while Cam continued to feed.

Please, I begged. *Please… let this be… a nightmare.*

But deep down, I knew this was real.

I could feel it in the way Cam held me.

The way he continued to drink even as my vision went black.

Something had gone very wrong.

My Cam would never…

I shivered, my body chilling to impossible depths.

I barely felt his fangs now.

But my mind remembered.

My last breath… burned… my mind… fading… all because of… my lover's… cruel… *bite.*

The Blood Alliance Series Continues with Cruelly Bitten

Cruelly Bitten

Once upon a time, humankind ruled the world while lycans and vampires lived in secret.
This is no longer that time.

Ismerelda
The male I'm forever bonded to is now a monster. A cruel beast. A vampire without remorse or any memories of our previous existence together.

He has no idea who I am. What I mean to him. Who we used to be together. But I'm not giving up.

He will remember me. I vow it.

Cam
I'm a vampire king. A superior being to all the rest.

Except *her*. The female who refuses to bow.

I'm going to break her. Destroy her. *Reform* her. And when she's finally learned her place at my side, I'm going to end her.

Because I have no need for a disobedient pet. I'm meant to rule this alliance, and that's exactly what I'll do.

Welcome to the new reign.
It's filled with blood, overflowing with broken alliances, and littered with death.
My kingdom. My rules. My future.

Author's Note: *Cruelly Bitten* contains dark content. Please read the warning note inside. Also, while this story can be read as a standalone romance, this series is best enjoyed in order.

MUSIC PLAYLIST

Kingly Bitten

Another One Bites The Dust - Queen
Can't Help Falling In Love - Tommee Profitt
The Curse - Agnes Obel
Enemy - Tommee Profitt
Game of Survival - Ruelle
In the End - Tommee Profitt
Legends Never Die - League of Legends
Lovers Death - Ursine Vulpine & Annaca
Monsters - Tommee Profitt
Nihilist Blues - Bring Me The Horizon
Parasite Eve - Bring Me The Horizon
Saints - Echos
Sick Like Me - In This Moment
Smells Like Teen Spirit - Malia J
Til the Light Goes Out - Lindsey Stirling
Vendetta - Unsecret
Without You - Ursine Vulpine & Annaca

ABOUT THE AUTHOR

USA Today Bestselling Author Lexi C. Foss loves to play in dark worlds, especially the ones that bite. She lives in North Carolina with her husband and their furry children. When not writing, she's busy crossing items off her travel bucket list or chasing eclipses around the globe. She's quirky, consumes way too much coffee, and loves to swim.

Want access to the most up-to-date information for all of Lexi's books? Sign up for her newsletter here.

Lexi also likes to hang out with readers on Facebook in her exclusive readers' group — Join Here.

Where To Find Lexi:
www.LexiCFoss.com

Lightning Source UK Ltd.
Milton Keynes UK
UKHW010021070223
416578UK00001B/70

9 781685 300388